James Patterson's previous [...] include ALONG CAME A [...] [...], JACK AND JILL, CAT A[...] [...], WHEN THE WIND BLOWS, POP GOES THE WEASEL, CRADLE AND ALL, ROSES ARE RED, 1ST TO DIE, SUZANNE'S DIARY FOR NICHOLAS, VIOLETS ARE BLUE, MIRACLE ON THE 17TH GREEN (with Peter de Jonge), 2ND CHANCE (with Andrew Gross), THE BEACH HOUSE (with Peter de Jonge), FOUR BLIND MICE, THE JESTER (with Andrew Gross), THE LAKE HOUSE, THE BIG BAD WOLF, 3RD DEGREE (with Andrew Gross), SAM'S LETTERS TO JENNIFER, LONDON BRIDGES, and most recently SANTAKID. He resides in Florida.

Praise for James Patterson's bestselling novels:

'Makes Kay Scarpetta's lot look positively fairytale' *Mirror*

'A master of the suspense genre' *Sunday Telegraph*

'Unputdownable' *The Times*

When The Wind Blows

and

The Lake House

James Patterson

headline

WHEN THE WIND BLOWS first published in Great Britain in 1998
by HEADLINE BOOK PUBLISHING

THE LAKE HOUSE first published in Great Britain in 2003
by HEADLINE BOOK PUBLISHING

First published in this omnibus edition in 2005
by HEADLINE BOOK PUBLISHING

A HEADLINE paperback

10 9 8 7 6 5 4 3 2 1

ISBN 0 7553 2663 6

Typeset in Times

Printed and bound in Great Britain by
Clays Ltd, St Ives plc

Headline's policy is to use papers that are natural, renewable and
recyclable products and made from wood grown in sustainable
forests. The logging and manufacturing processes are expected to
conform to the environmental regulations of the country of origin.

HEADLINE BOOK PUBLISHING
A division of Hodder Headline
338 Euston Road
London NW1 3BH

www.headline.co.uk
www.hodderheadline.com

When The
Wind Blows

AUTHOR'S NOTE

When I began this book, I had absolutely no idea how close to reality the story would actually be. Over thirty medical doctors and research scientists helped at the conceptual stages, and then again when the manuscript was nearing completion. As one transgenic technologist from the University of California told me, 'Two to three years in the future I wouldn't have any trouble suspending my beliefs about the events described in *When The Wind Blows*. Much of this will come to pass.' A medical doctor and Ph.D. at the National Institute of Health said, 'The book is on a par with *Jurassic Park*. Both stories have elements that are absolutely true. Most people are not going to believe the breakthroughs that are coming in the future. *When The Wind Blows* is definitely in the realm of ideological possibility.' These doctors and researchers went into considerable detail, but I don't want to spoil any of the surprises or suspense in the story you are about to read. I don't think you will ever forget reading *When The Wind Blows*, but don't think of this story as a fable. It is tomorrow's headlines.

Above all, I would like to thank Maxine Paetro, who was deeply involved with the book almost from the beginning, and who was important through the arduous research, writing and editing process.

PROLOGUE

FIRST FLIGHT

ONE

'**S**omebody please help me! Can anybody hear me? Somebody please!'

Max's screams pierced the clear, mountain air. Her throat and lungs were beginning to hurt, to burn. The eleven-year-old girl was running as fast as she could from the hateful, despicable School. She was strong, but she was beginning to tire. As she ran, her long blonde hair flared behind her like a beautiful silk scarf. She was pretty, even though there were dark, plum-colored circles under her eyes.

She knew the men were coming to kill her. She could hear them hurrying through the woods behind her.

She glanced over her right shoulder, painfully twisting her neck. She flashed a mental picture of her little brother, Matthew. Where was he? The two of them had separated just outside the School, both running and screaming.

She was afraid Matthew was already dead. Uncle

Thomas probably got him. Thomas had betrayed them and that hurt so much she couldn't stand to think about it.

Tears rolled down her cheeks. The hunters were closing in. She could feel their heavy footsteps thumping hard and fast against the crust of the earth.

A throbbing, orange-and-red ball of sun was sinking below the horizon. Soon it would be pitch-black and cold out here in the Front Range of the Rockies. All she wore was a simple tube of white cotton, sleeveless, loosely drawn together at the neckline and waist. Her feet were wrapped in thin-soled ballet slippers.

Move. She urged her aching, tired body on. She could go faster than this. She knew she could.

The twisting path narrowed, then wound around a great, mossy-green shoulder of rock. She clawed and struggled forward through more thick tangles of branches and brush.

The girl suddenly stopped. She could go no further.

A huge, high fence loomed above the bushes. It was easily ten feet. Triple rows of razor-sharp concertina wire were tangled and coiled across the top.

A metal sign warned: *Extreme danger! Electrified fence. Extreme danger!*

Max bent over and cupped her hands over her bare knees. She was blowing out air, wheezing hard, trying to keep from weeping.

The hunters were almost there. She could hear, smell, sense their awful presence.

She knew what she had to do now, but she was

petrified to try it. It was forbidden; it was unthinkable.

'Somebody please help me!'

But there was no one around to help her – nobody except Max herself.

TWO

Kit Harrison was headed to Denver from Boston. He was good-looking enough to draw looks on the airplane: trim, six foot two, sandy-blond hair. He was a graduate of N.Y.U. Law School. And yet he felt like such a loser, such a sorry chump.

He was perspiring badly in the crammed and claustro-phobic middle-aisle airplane seat of an American Airlines 747. He was so obviously pathetic that the pleasant and accommodating flight attendant stopped and asked if he was feeling all right. Was he ill?

Kit told her that he was just fine, but it was another lie, the mother of all lies. His condition was called post-traumatic stress disorder and sometimes featured nasty anxiety attacks that left him feeling he could die *right there*. He'd been suffering from the disorder for close to four years.

So yeah, I am ill, Madam Flight Attendant. Only it's a little worse than that.

See, I'm not supposed to be going to Colorado. I'm supposed to be on vacation in Nantucket. Actually, I'm supposed to be taking some time off, getting my head screwed on straight, getting used to maybe being fired from my job of twelve years.

Getting used to not being an FBI agent anymore, not being on the fast track at the Bureau, not being much of anything.

The name computer-printed on his plane ticket read Kit Harrison, but it wasn't his real name. His name was Thomas Anthony Brennan. He had been senior FBI Agent Brennan, a shooting star at one time. He was thirty-eight, and lately, he felt he was feeling his age for the first time in his life.

From this moment on, he would forget the old name. Forget his old job, too.

I'm Kit Harrison. I'm going to Colorado to hunt and fish in the Rockies. I'll keep to that simple story. That simple lie.

Kit, Tom, whoever the hell he was, hadn't been up in an airplane in nearly four years. Not since August 9, 1994. He didn't want to think about that now.

So Kit pretended he was asleep as the sweat continued to trickle down his face and neck, as the fear inside him built way past the danger level. He couldn't get his mind to rest, even for just a few minutes. He *had* to be on this plane.

He *had* to travel to Colorado.

It was all connected to August 9, wasn't it? Sure it was. That was when the stress disorder had begun. This was for Kim and for Tommy and for Michael – little Mike the Tyke.

7

And oh yeah, it also happened to be hugely beneficial for just about everybody else on the planet. Very strange – but that last outrageous bit was absolutely true, scarily true. In his opinion, nothing in history was more important than what he'd come here to investigate.

Unless he *was* crazy.

Which was a distinct possibility.

THREE

Five armed men ran quietly and easily through the ageless boulders and towering aspens and ponderosa pines that were characteristic of this part of the Rockies. They didn't see her yet, but they knew it wouldn't be long before they caught up with the girl. She was on foot after all.

They were jogging rapidly, but every so often the man in front picked up the pace a significant notch or two. All of them were competent trackers, good at this, but he was the best, a natural leader. He was more focused, more controlled, the best hunter.

The men appeared calm on the outside, but inside it was a different story. This was a critical time. The girl had to be captured, and brought back. She shouldn't have gotten out here in the first place. Discretion was critical; it always had been, but never more than right now.

The girl was only eleven, but she had 'gifts,' and that could present a formidable problem outdoors. Her senses were acute; she was incredibly strong for her size, her age, her gender; and of course, there was the possibility that she might try to fly.

Suddenly, they could see her up ahead: she was clearly visible against the deep blue background of the sky.

'Tinkerbell. Northwest, fifty degrees,' the group leader called out.

She was called Tinkerbell, but he knew she hated the name. The only name she answered to was Max, which wasn't short for Maxine, or Maximilian, but for Maximum. Maybe because she always gave her all. She always went for it. Just as she was doing right now.

There she was, in all her glory! She was running at full speed, and she was very close to the perimeter fence. She had no way of knowing that. She'd never been this far from home before.

Every eye was on her. None of them could look away, not for an instant. Her long hair streamed behind her, and she seemed to flow up the steep, rocky hillside. She was in great shape; she could really move for such a young girl. She was a force to reckon with out here in the open.

The man running in front suddenly pulled up. Harding Thomas stopped short. He threw up his arm to halt the others. They didn't understand at first, because they thought they had her now.

Then, almost as if he'd known she would – she took off. She flew. She was going over the concertina wire of the ten-foot-high perimeter fence.

The men watched in complete silence and awe. Their eyes widened. Blood rushed to their brains and made a pounding sound in their ears. They couldn't believe their eyes.

With a sudden flourish, she had unfurled her wings. They were white and silver-tipped and appeared to have been unhinged. The wings sailed to a point above her head, seemingly of their own accord. Their span was nine feet. The sun glinted off the full array of her plumage.

She opened to a full wingspan and the movement seemed effortless. She was a beautiful, natural flyer. She flapped her white and silver wings up and down, up and down. The air actually seemed to carry her along, like a leaf on the wind.

'I knew she'd try to go over.' Thomas turned to the others and spat out the words. 'Too bad.'

He lifted his rifle to his shoulder. The girl was about to disappear over the nearest edge of the canyon wall. Another second or two and she'd be gone from sight.

He pulled the trigger.

BOOK 1

GENESIS 13:7

CHAPTER ONE

The day started to go a little crazy when Keith Duffy and his young daughter brought that poor crushed doe to the 'Inn-Patient,' as I call my small animal hospital in Bear Bluff, Colorado, about fifty minutes northwest of Boulder along the 'Peak-to-Peak' highway.

Sheryl Crow was singing ever so raucously on the tape deck. I flipped saucy Sheryl off when I saw Duffy walk inside carrying that poor doe, standing like a dolt in front of *Abstraction, White Rose II*, my current favorite Georgia O'Keeffe poster.

I could see the badly injured doe was pregnant. She was wild-eyed and thrashing when Duffy hefted her onto the table. Half-thrashing, in truth, because I suspected her spine was broken at midpoint, where she'd been clipped by the Chevy 4×4 that Duffy drives.

The little girl was sobbing and her father looked miserable. I thought he was going to break down, too.

'Money's no object,' he said.

And money *was* no object because I knew nothing was going to save the doe. The fawn, however, was a maybe. If the mother was close to term. If it hadn't been mashed too badly by the four-thousand-pound truck. And a few more ifs besides.

'I can't save the doe,' I said to the girl's father. 'I'm sorry.'

Duffy nodded. He was a local builder, and also one of the local hunters. A real knucklehead, in my humble opinion. *Thoughtless* probably described him best, and maybe that was his best quality. I could only imagine how he must be feeling now, this man who usually bragged on his kill, with his little girl begging to save the animal's life. Among his other bad habits, Duffy occasionally stopped by and brazenly hit on me. A sticker on his 4×4 bumper read: *Support Wildlife. Throw a Party*.

'The fawn?' he asked.

'Maybe,' I said. 'Help me get her gassed down and we'll see.'

I gently slid the mask over the doe's face. I kicked at the pedal and the halothane hissed through the tube. The doe's brown eyes showed terror, but also unimaginable sadness. She *knew*.

The little girl grabbed the doe around the belly and she started crying her heart out. I liked the girl a lot. Her eyes showed spunk and character. Duffy had done at least one good thing in his life.

'Damn, damn,' the father said. 'I never saw her until she was on the hood. Do your best, Frannie,' he said to me.

I gently peeled the little girl off the deer. I held on to her shoulders and made her face me. 'What's your name, sweetie?'

'Angie,' she sobbed out.

'Angie, now listen to me, sweetheart. The doe doesn't feel anything now, understand? It's painless for her. I promise you.'

Angie pushed her face into my body and held me with all of her little-girl strength. I rubbed her back and told her that I would have to euthanatize the doe, but if its baby could be saved, there would be a lot of work to do.

'Please, please, please,' said Angie.

'You're going to need a goat. For milk,' I said to Duffy. 'Maybe two or three of them.'

'Not a problem,' he said. He would have acquired nursing elephants if I'd told him to. He just wanted his little girl to smile again.

I then asked both of them to please get out of the exam room and let me work. What I was about to do was a bloody, difficult, and ugly operation.

CHAPTER TWO

It was seven in the evening when the Duffys came to the Inn-Patient, and maybe twelve minutes had already gone by. The poor doe was out cold and I felt so bad for her. *Frannie the Sap* – that's what my sister, Carole, calls me. It was my husband David's favorite nickname for me, too.

A little less than a year and a half ago, David was shot and killed in the physicians' parking lot at Boulder Community Hospital. I still hadn't recovered from that, hadn't grieved enough. It would have helped if the police had caught David's murderer, but they hadn't.

I cut along the abdominal line with my scalpel. I exteriorized the uterus, flipping it out intact onto the doe's open belly. I cut again, this time through the uterine wall. I pulled out the fawn, praying I wasn't going to have to put it down.

The fawn was about four months, nearly to term, and as best as I could tell, uninjured. I gently cleaned the babe's air passages with my fingers and fitted a tiny mask over its muzzle.

Then I cranked on the oxygen. The fawn's chest shuddered. It started to breathe.

Then it bawled. God, what a glorious sound. New life. Jeez, Louise, the whole magical thing still makes my heart go pitter-patter. Frannie the Sap.

Blood had spattered on my face during the surgery, and I wiped it off with my sleeve. The fawn was crying into the oxygen mask and I let the little orphan snuggle up against its mother for a few moments, just in case deer have souls, just in case . . . *let mother say good-bye to her child.*

Then I clamped off the cord, filled a syringe, and euthanatized the doe. It was fast. She never knew the moment she passed from life into death.

There was one can of goat's milk in the fridge. I filled a bottle and popped it into the microwave for a few seconds to warm.

I removed the oxygen mask and slipped the nipple into the baby deer's mouth, and it began to suck. The fawn was really beautiful, with the gentlest brown eyes. God, I love what I do sometimes.

Father and daughter were huddled close together on my antique daybed when I came out into the waiting room.

I handed the fawn to Angie.

'Congratulations,' I said. 'It's a girl.'

I walked the family of three out to their creased and dented 4×4. I gave them the can of goat's milk, my phone number, and waved good-bye. I briefly considered the irony that the fawn was riding home in the same vehicle that had killed its mother.

Then I was thinking of a steaming, hot bath, a cool glass of Chardonnay, maybe a baked potato with Wisconsin Cheddar – life's little rewards. I was feeling kind of proud of myself. I hadn't felt that way for a long time, not since David's death changed just about everything in my life.

I was about to go inside when I realized that there was a car in the lot, a shiny black Jeep Cherokee.

The door opened and a man slowly got out. Headlights hit him from behind and for a moment he was haloed in light.

He was tall, slender, but muscular, with lots of blond hair. His eyes quickly took in the place. The big porch deck festooned with hummingbird feeders and a couple of wind socks. My trusty-dusty mountain bike. Wildflowers everywhere – mountain lupine, daisies, Indian paintbrush.

Now this part is more than a little weird. I'd never seen him before. But my limbic brain, a dumb little organ so primitive it bypasses logical thought, locked on to his image and stayed there. I stared at him, and I felt a rush of something akin to recognition. And my heart, which has been stone-dead for the past few months, sputtered, caught, and jumped into life for at least a couple of seconds. That kind of ticked me off, actually.

I figured that whoever he was, the mystery man was lost.

'We're closed for the night,' I said.

He stared at me, unapologetic about the intrusion into my front yard.

Then he called me by name.

'Dr O'Neill?'

'Does she owe you money?' I said. It was an old Comedy Store line, but I liked it. Besides, I needed a passable joke after the euthanasia of the doe.

He smiled, and his light blue eyes brightened, and I found that I couldn't look away from them. 'Are you Frances O'Neill?'

'Yeah. It's Frannie, though.'

I took in a face that was cool, yet had a touch of warmth. The directness of his eyes sort of nailed me to the spot. He had a fine nose, a strong chin. His features held together too damned well. A dash of Tom Cruise, maybe even a little Harrison Ford. Something like that, or so it seemed that night in the bloom of the Jeep's headlights.

He brushed off his slouchy hat, and a lot of sandy-blond hair shifted and gleamed. Then he was standing in front of me, all six two of him, like a glossy photo from an L.L. Bean catalog, or maybe Eddie Bauer's. Very serious-looking, though.

'I've come from Hollander and Cowell.'

'You're a real estate broker?' I croaked.

'Did I catch you at a bad time?' he asked. 'Sorry.' At least he was polite.

'What makes you think that?' I asked. I was all too aware that my jeans were soaked in blood. My sweatshirt looked like a Jackson Pollock painting.

'I'd hate to see the guy who lost the fight,' he said, surveying my appearance. 'Or do you dabble in witch-craft?'

'Some people call it veterinary medicine,' I said. 'So, what's this about? Why did Hollander and Cowell send you at this time of night?'

He hooked a thumb toward Bear Bluff's center, where the real estate office is.

'I'm your new tenant. I signed the papers this after-noon. They said you left everything in their capable hands.'

I'd almost forgotten I'd put the cabin on the block. It's a quarter of a mile back in the woods behind the clinic, and it used to be a hunting shack until David and I moved in. After David died, I started sleeping in a small room at the clinic. A whole lot of things changed for me back then, none of them good.

'So? Can I see the place?' L.L. Bean said.

'Just follow the footpath behind the clinic,' I told him. 'It's a four- or five-minute walk. It's worth it. Door's not locked.'

'I don't get the guided tour?' he asked.

'Much as I'd love to, I've still got a couple of chickens to kill and some spells to cast before I sleep. I'll get you a flashlight—'

'I've got one in the car,' he said.

I lingered in the doorway as he crunched back to his Jeep. He had a nice way of walking. Confident, not too cocky.

'Hey,' I called out to him. 'What's *your* name?'
He looked back – hesitated for a half-second.
'Kit,' he finally said. 'I'm Kit Harrison.'

CHAPTER THREE

I will never forget what happened next. It was such a shock for me, a hard kick in the stomach, or maybe even the side of my head.

Kit Harrison reached into the Jeep – and he did the unspeakable – he pulled a hunting rifle off a silver-metallic gun rack. That son of a bitch.

I couldn't believe what I was seeing. My flesh crept.

I yelled at him, loudly, which is so unlike me. 'Wait! Hey! You! Wait right there, mister! Hold up!'

He turned to face me. The look on his face was serene, cool as it had been. 'What?' he said. Was he challenging me? Did he dare?

'Listen.' I let the big screen door bang shut behind me and marched fast and hard across the gravel beachhead. No way was I going to have somebody with a hunting rifle on my land. No way! Not in his or my lifetime.

'I've changed my mind. This is no good. It's not going to work. You can't stay here. No hunters. No how, no way!'

His gaze returned to the Jeep's interior. He snapped the glove compartment shut. Locked it. He didn't seem to be listening to me at all.

'Sorry,' he said without looking at me. 'We made a deal.'

'The deal's off! Didn't you just hear me?'

'Nope. A deal's a deal,' he said.

He grabbed a torch lamp from inside the car door, a reddish duffel bag, then he took up the hideous rifle in his other hand. I was apoplectic, kept sputtering, 'Look here.' But he ignored me, didn't seem to hear a word.

He kicked the Jeep door shut, flicked on his Durabeam flashlight, and casually headed down the path into the woods. The woods sucked up the light and the sound of his retreating footsteps.

My blood was knocking hard and fast against my eardrums.

A goddamn hunter was staying in my house.

CHAPTER FOUR

It was nearly dark and the hunters still hadn't found the girl's body. They were bitterly cold and hungry and frustrated as hell, and they were also scared. There would be unfortunate consequences if they failed.

They had to find the girl.

And the boy as well – Matthew.

The five of them walked through the thickly wooded area where they believed the girl had fallen. She should be right there! They had to locate the specimen called Tinkerbell and destroy her, if she wasn't already dead from her fall and the gunshot.

Put Tinkerbell to sleep, Harding Thomas was thinking as he led the search team. It was a euphemism he used to make moments like this easier: *Put somebody to sleep. The way they do with animals. Not death, not murder – just peaceful sleep.*

He thought he knew the precise area where the girl had dropped like a shot from the sky, but there wasn't any dead body flattened on the ground, or hung up in the towering fir trees.

They certainly couldn't leave her out here, couldn't risk hikers or campers finding the body. What a titanic disaster that would be.

'Tinkerbell, can you hear me? Are you hurt, honey? We just want to take you home. That's all,' Thomas called in the gentlest voice he could manage. It wasn't so hard: he had always liked Max and Matthew well enough.

Tinkerbell was a code name, and it was what he'd always called her. *Peter Pan* was young Matthew's code. He was *Uncle Tommy.*

'Tinkerbell, where are you? Come out, come out. We're not going to hurt you, sweetheart. I'm not even angry at you. This is Uncle Tommy. You can trust me. If you can't trust me, who can you trust?

'Can you hear me? C'mon, kiddo. I know you're there. Trust Uncle Thomas. There's no one else who can help you.'

CHAPTER FIVE

S he was alive. Amazing, amazing, amazing!

But Max was hurt, shot, and she didn't know how bad the wound was. Probably not too bad, since she hadn't passed out yet, and there didn't seem to be much blood.

She'd been hanging on to the top of a tree for hours, hidden in thick branches. At least she *hoped* she was hidden. She tried to be still. Silent. Invisible.

Max was shivering, and the whole thing was crashing out of control.

She really, really wished Matthew was with her. They would give each other strength and hope and words of wisdom. It had always been that way with the two of them. They were inseparable at the School. Mrs Beattie, the only truly nice one there, called them 'inseparable at birth,' and the 'Bobbsey Twins' – whoever the heck they were. When Mrs Beattie died, everything had gone bad. Real bad. *This* bad.

The woods were crawling with men. Bad ones – the worst creatures imaginable. There were at least a half-dozen of them. *Hunters – killers.* They were frantically searching for her, and also for Matthew. They had rifles and flashlights.

Uncle Thomas was one of them, and he was the worst. He had pretended to be their friend . . . but he was the one who would *put you to sleep.* He had been a teacher, a scientist, and now he was just a killer.

'We're not going to hurt you, sweetheart.' She mimicked his voice, his phony, insincere manner.

The one good part was that she didn't need to *see* them walking in the woods. Her hearing was incredibly acute. It was capable of separating sounds as close together as a thousandth of a second. It was one of her very coolest gifts. She could hear the tiny hum of distant mosquitoes, and the angry twitter of a wren. She heard aspen leaves rustling a half-mile away. She wondered if Matthew was anywhere nearby. Was he listening, too?

'Tinkerbell, can you hear me?'

Yes, she could hear the pathetic sickos as they hunted for her. She had heard them when they were far away. She heard every footstep, every little cough and sniffle, every hot, smelly breath they took, wishing it would be their last.

One of them spoke, and she recognized a particularly insensitive guard from the School. 'We shoulda brought dogs with us.'

'Shoulda, coulda, woulda.' One of the others ranked on him and laughed. 'She's a kid. They both are. If we can't find a little kid we better pack it in.'

Dogs! Max bit down on a cry. Dogs would find her. Dogs were better at this than men. Dogs had special powers, too. Humans were the weakest species. Maybe that was why they could be the meanest animals.

The wind came up again, angry and howling, and she was reminded of how cold it got out here. She gripped the tree hard, listening intently, until she couldn't hear the hunters at all. For the moment, they were gone.

Slowly, painfully, she shimmied down the pine tree and stepped cautiously out into the woods.

Then she ran. She had to find cover. She had to find Matthew before it was too late.

CHAPTER SIX

His three-year-old boy, little Mike, used to like to say that he was 'sore afraid of the dark.' Kit had just loved that expression.

He would roar and hug Mike the Tyke against his chest whenever he said it. He could still feel those sweet baby hugs. The thought of it all left him sick and empty as if he'd been hollowed out and the core of his being tossed away.

Of course, he was feeling all kinds of things right now. He was investigating what he believed was the most important case of his career – and he wasn't supposed to be here. He had been taken off the damn thing. He wasn't even sure if the case was active at the moment.

So yeah, he was 'sore afraid.'

He put away his mountain gear and clothes in the cabin, but only so that everything would look normal if he was being watched, or if someone happened to search the room. It was possible, even likely, that Frannie O'Neill or someone else would be watching him.

The cabin was modest, not overly decorated, but surprisingly homey and warm. There was a Rumford fireplace built with local granite. Hammered tin lanterns covered most of the mantle. A cozy sheepskin was thrown on the bed.

He pulled down the shades and quickly undressed. Then he turned off the lights and climbed into bed. Slid the rifle underneath. The gun was part of his cover story as a hunter, but he didn't mind having it around as extra protection. It couldn't hurt.

I'm supposed to be in Nantucket on vacation. Cooling my jets; getting my head on straight. Maybe I should have gone there. But I didn't, did I? Second time I screwed up on that.

August 9, 1994, was the first screwup.

He closed his eyes, but he didn't sleep. He waited.

With his eyes shut tight, he remembered a private talk he'd had with the assistant director of the FBI. He'd gone over the head of his superior to get the meeting.

He remembered the highlights, as if it had happened yesterday.

The assistant director had a *look* on his face, as if he were incredibly superior, and he couldn't believe his time was being wasted by a field agent.

'I'm going to talk, you're going to listen, Agent Brennan.'

'That would seem to defeat the purpose of the meeting,' Tom had said.

'Only because you don't understand the purpose of the meeting.'

'No sir, I guess I don't.'

'We are trying to cut you some slack because of a tragedy in your personal life. You are making it hard for us, damn near impossible. Hear this, and hear it well. Let your wild-goose chase go. Let the witch-hunt end today. Let the case with the missing doctors go, or we will let *you* go. Understood?'

Kit lay in the dark, and he remembered the meaning, if not the exact words of the assistant director. And yes, he understood.

So here he was in Colorado. He'd obviously made a choice. He'd gone with conscience over his career.

He was a goner.

CHAPTER SEVEN

I t was quarter past eleven that night when he threw off
the sheepskin cover and climbed out of bed.

He hurriedly dressed in the dark. A black T-shirt and
black warm-up pants pulled over his hundred and eighty-
pound frame. A black ball cap. High-topped Converse –
Larry Bird's brand. *His own* brand since he'd been ten
years old and running the roads and playground hardtop
of South Boston.

There was a full moon shining outside. He scanned the
tall pine trees, looking from left to right through the
bedroom window. He repeated the procedure until he was
sure that no one was out there – watching, waiting for
him to appear.

He opened the cabin door and slipped outside into the
crispy, cool night air. He felt a little like Mulder in *The
X-Files*. No, actually he felt a lot like Mulder – and Mulder
was a fricking nutjob and a half.

Kit Harrison made his way back down the winding

forest trail toward the animal hospital. He knew that
Frances O'Neill had a room there, and that she'd lived in
the clinic since the death of her husband, David. He knew
about Dr David Mekin, too. Actually, he knew more about
David than about his wife. David Mekin had studied
embryology at M.I.T. in the 80s. Then he'd worked in San
Francisco. Kit had a dozen pages thick with notes on Dr
Mekin.

He did know a few things about Frannie. He'd done
some homework. She had a veterinary degree (D.V.M.)
from the Colorado State Teaching Hospital at Fort Collins.
C.S.U. was also the national center for wildlife biology,
and she had done a minor in wildlife. The school had a
good reputation, especially for surgery. She was the
founder of a local 'pet loss support group.' She'd had a
thriving veterinary practice until her husband's death.
She'd been the family breadwinner. Lately, she'd let the
business end of her practice slide.

It took him less than three minutes to get back to the
main house. 'The Inn-Patient,' as she called it. This was
where it would really start for him.

There was a bright light burning on the front porch, and
a shimmering, yellowish light in a window on one side of
the house. A Manx cat sat guard at one of the other
windows, eyeballing him suspiciously, not moving a
whisker.

He stopped to catch his breath, or maybe just to stop
his heart from racing so much. He checked to see if
anybody else was out there with him.

He needed to forage around inside the animal hospital

– but probably not tonight. He passed close behind a matching pair of tall pines. He was less than ten feet from one of the brightly lit windows.

He jumped back suddenly.

Jesus! She had scared the hell out of him.

Frannie O'Neill was standing right there in the window, framed in soft light. She was naked as the day she was born. He sucked in a quick breath. It was the last thing he'd expected to see. Like being poked in the eye.

She didn't see him, thank God. She was busy drying her long brown hair with a fluffy white towel. Pretty hair. Pretty everything, in fact.

She was a whole lot more attractive than she made herself out to be. Very pretty, very alive eyes. Slender, and in good shape. Seriously good shape, actually. Her skin had a healthy glow. She was thirty-three, he remembered from his notes. Her husband, Dr David Mekin, had been thirty-eight when he died. When he was murdered.

Kit turned away. She was still up, so there was no way he could check out the house tonight. He didn't want to spy on a naked Dr O'Neill from outside her bedroom window. It made him feel like a creepy little shit. No matter what else he might be, he wasn't a Peeping Tom.

He made his way back to the cabin – with the image of Frannie O'Neill still on his mind. Actually, she was *burned* into his optic nerve. Her eyes had a special glint that hinted at a sense of humor he hadn't experienced during their initial meeting. She was definitely prettier than he'd expected her to be. And she might be a murderer.

CHAPTER EIGHT

Tuesday morning was finally here.

Annie Hutton had been waiting on pins and needles, but right now she felt fine, strangely relaxed and ready.

Actually, Annie Hutton had a high level of comfort and well-being whenever she visited the in vitro clinic at Boulder Community Hospital. The staff at the clinic seemed to have thought of everything and its potential negative or positive effect on mothers-to-be. They were just super and she was fortunate to be working with them.

The toney waiting room had warm yellow walls with bright white trim. There always seemed to be freshly cut flowers. And an array of all the right magazines, current issues, too: *Mirabella*, *AD*, *Town & Country*, *Parents*, *Child*.

Best of all was the 'up,' positive, well-trained staff, and especially her doctor, John Brownhill. Dr B. was talking to her now, asking all the requisite questions during her eight-month checkup. He seemed so *interested* in how she was feeling. Was she experiencing Braxton Hicks contractions, anything unusual?

'No, everything is fine, knock on wood,' Annie said. She smiled positively, mirrored the confidence she felt from him and the rest of the staff.

Dr B. smiled back. Not too much, not condescending or anything like that, just right. 'That's great. Let's run a few tests and get you out of here in time for the "Rosie" show.'

Annie knew that in spite of how relatively chipper she felt, she was still a high-risk patient. Dr Brownhill told her she had insufficient placenta. On this visit, Dr Brownhill and his nurse, Jilly, were going to use a fetal heart monitor to check the level of stress to the fetus during contractions. The idea of the FHM test made her a little nervous, but she tried to be as upbeat as her doctor and nurse.

Jilly squeezed electro-conductor jelly onto Annie's stomach. Annie noticed that the jelly had been pre-warmed for her comfort. They thought of *everything* here. Jilly then placed two wide plastic strips around her abdomen. *Very* gently.

'Comfortable? Anything else we can do?' Dr Brownhill asked.

'I'm fine, good. Jelly's just the right temp.'

It happened so suddenly, almost as if it were a bad dream. 'Baby's heart rate is dropping,' Dr Brownhill said. His voice cracked. 'One hundred, ninety-seven, ninety-five.' He turned to Jilly. 'We have to crash her, stat. Hold on, Annie. Hold on tight.'

Everything moved so quickly after that, and efficiently,

under the tense, crisis circumstances. Everything was a blur for Annie. Then she went out.

Less than forty minutes later, much sooner than expected, Dr John Brownhill personally brought the new-born to the premie nursery. According to the Apgar scores from the delivery room, the boy was in excellent health, but every precaution was being taken, anyway.

A clean tube was inserted into the infant's windpipe, a pressurized hood was fitted around the tiny head. This ensured that a continuous supply of low-pressure oxygen would be directed into the sacs of the slightly immature lungs.

A blood analysis was done from a plastic tube inserted into the umbilicus.

An electronic thermometer was taped to the infant's skin.

A nasogastric feeding tube was inserted into the nose. Breast milk was fed through it, just in case the infant boy wasn't quite ready to suck.

A neonatal intensive-care specialist hovered over Annie Hutton's precious little boy, checking everything, making sure he was okay.

'He's doing fine. A-okay. The boy's in good shape, John,' one of the specialists told Dr Brownhill. 'Head's forty-one centimeters, by the way. Big head about himself.'

'As well he should.'

John Brownhill finally left the premie nursery and climbed the two floors to where Annie Hutton was recovering from her C-section.

The twenty-four-year-old mother didn't look nearly as

well as her infant son. Her ash-blonde hair was wet with perspiration plastered in tight curls. Her eyes were vacant and lost. She definitely looked like someone who had recently undergone an unexpected C-section.

Dr Brownhill came right up to her bed. He leaned in close and spoke in his usual soft, reassuring tone. He even took her hand.

'Annie, I'm so sorry. We couldn't save him,' he whispered. 'We lost your baby boy.'

CHAPTER NINE

The Hutton baby arrived at the School within hours of its delivery in the Boulder clinic. A team outfitted in what looked like space suits rushed out to meet the Boulder Community Ambulance. They hurried the infant inside. There was a high degree of excitement in the air, exultation, almost glee.

The head doctor at the School was on premises for the exam and watched closely, supervising, lecturing at times.

Heart rate, respiration, skin color, muscle tone, reflex responses were checked. Baby Hutton scored a perfect ten.

The boy's length and weight were checked. Tests were performed to check for cardiac murmur, heart engorgement, subconjunctival hemorrhage, jaundice, asexuality, hip displacea, clavicle fractures, skin mottling.

There was a nevus, a tiny birthmark on the right hip. It was noted as an 'imperfection.'

Most of the testing involved the boy's gross and fine

motor coordination, and also his ability to manipulate the environment. The head doctor remained in the lab for every test, commenting on each as it was completed.

'The head circumference is forty-one centimeters. That would be normal for about a four-month-old. That's why the C-section was necessary, of course. The heart is larger as well, and more efficient. His heartbeat is under a hundred. That's simply wonderful. What a little champ.

'But watch Baby Hutton. That's the key. That's where the real drama lies. He's listening to us, and he's *paying attention*. See that? Look at his eyes. Newborns don't fix and follow – never. He's actually tracking us from one to the other. Do you understand what that means?

'Infants never remember objects after they disappear. He does. He's definitely watching us. Look at his little eyes. He already has memory. He's just a *super* baby!'

CHAPTER TEN

I woke up trying to catch my breath, crying softly over a horrible, crushing dream about my husband, David. It was the way I awoke almost every single morning these days.

I missed David so much and that hadn't changed since the night a year and a half ago, when a crackhead shot him in a lonely parking lot in Boulder.

David and I had been inseparable before his death. We skied all over Colorado and the rest of the West. Spent Sundays at a health clinic for migrants in Pueblo. Read so many books that both our small houses could have doubled as lending libraries. We had more friends than we knew what to do with sometimes. We loved and lived a full life just about every minute of the day.

I had a thriving big- and small-animal practice. Early each morning, I went off to farms and ranches where I took care of horses and other large animals. People from all over the county brought their smaller pets to me at the

Inn-Patient. For what it was worth, I was named 'Veterinarian for the 90s' by the *Denver Post*.

Now, everything was changed, the arc of my life was dipping in the wrong direction, and it didn't seem reversible. I thought about David's murder all the time. I bothered the police in Boulder until they asked me to stay away. I rarely went on house calls anymore, although cases still came to me.

I flung myself out of bed. I threw on my old faithful blue plaid robe and stuck my feet into slippers I'd been given for Christmas by a couple of cute kids whose coyote-mauled puppy I'd stitched up.

The slippers were made to look like cocker spaniel heads. Dopey eyes staring up, pink tongues lolling, floppy ears, the works.

I turned on the tape deck – Fiona Apple's unmistakable, throaty moan; eighteen years old and full of piss and vinegar and creative craziness. I liked that in a diva.

I opened the door from the 'master suite' and entered the lab. I was greeted by my favorite poster for this month: *Fox hunting is the unspeakable in full pursuit of the uneatable – Oscar Wilde*.

First things first. I filled the coffeepot with hazelnut vanilla. Once the java started to perk, I began to look in on my patients.

Frannie O'Neill, this is your life.

Ward One is a twelve-by-twelve room with a sink, a single window, two tiers of neat, clean cages. The bottom tier held three boarders: two dogs and the roommate of one of them, a common leghorn chicken.

One of the dogs, a standard poodle, had ripped his catheter out again, despite the e-collar I had on him. I chewed him out in all of the sixteen words I know in French so he'd understand me. Then I reinserted the tube in place. I ruffled his topknot and forgave him. *'Je t'aime,'* I said.

Ward Two is a slightly smaller replica of Ward One, but without any windows on the world. Some of my 'exotics' were caged in this room: a bunny with pneumonia, not going to make it; a hamster that I received by way of UPS with no accompanying note.

And there was a swan named Frank that my sister, Carole, rescued from a pond out by the racetrack. Carole thinks she's St Theresa of the wilds. At the moment, my sister was off camping in one of the state parks with her daughters. I almost went with her.

My coffee was ready. I poured myself a steaming cup, added whole milk and sugar. *Mmm, mmm good.*

Pip was at my heels. Pip's a Jack Russell terrier, a funny little boy who'd been turned in as a stray but had probably been abandoned. He did a little up-on-hind-legs dance that he knows I like. I kissed him, poured out a bowl of kibble, added in the last of some Rice Chex.

'You like?'

'Wuff.'

'Glad to hear it.'

I strolled back out to the front of the house. That's when I saw the triple-black, macho Jeep. L.L. Bean man. Kit Whatever. The hunter was back in my yard again. He was standing beside the Jeep, rifle slung over his shoulder.

Then I got a glimpse of a slack form lying over the hood.

Oh, God, no! He's already shot something! He's murdered an animal on my land. That bastard! That shit!

I had seen plenty of carcasses and dead animals up in these woods, but this was my land, my private property, and I thought of it as a sanctuary away from the world's madness.

'Hey, you,' I shouted. 'Hey. Hey, there!'

I was halfway across the front porch, in a full, huffing rage, when he stepped away and opened the Jeep door. I realized that what I thought was a body was the wrong color to be an animal.

It was maroon. More like a duffel bag.

He turned to face me at the sound of my voice. He half waved, smiled that nearly irresistible smile of his, which I answered with a seething look that ought to have set him on fire on the spot, burnt him right to the ground.

'Morning,' he called. 'God, it's beautiful up here. This is heaven, isn't it?'

Clutching my robe closed, I bent down, and grabbed up the 'mourning' paper, as I call the *Post*, since it's always so full of bad news.

Then I turned heel in my cocker spaniels and stomped inside.

CHAPTER ELEVEN

D iscretion was critical.

It was a very warm and sticky afternoon in Boulder, but not under the tall and stately fir trees that lined the spacious and orderly backyard of Dr Francis McDonough's house. And certainly not in the sparkling blue twenty-five-yard pool, which was around seventy-two degrees, as it almost always was.

The pool was surrounded by white wrought iron, curlicued leaf furniture, big comfortable ottomans, a settee covered in floral Sunbrella fabric. Urns of seasonal flowers were spotted around the pool as well as canvas-topped market umbrellas.

Frank McDonough was doing laps, and it astonished him that almost twenty years after he'd been a Pac-10 swimmer at California-Berkeley, he still loved to swim against the pace clock.

Dr McDonough enjoyed his life in the Boulder area tremendously. His sprawling ranch-style house had an indelible view of the city as well as the plains to the east. He loved the bite and crispness of the air, the exquisite blueness of the sky. He had even gone to the National Center for Atmospheric Research to try and find out why it was so, why the sky out here was blue? He had moved from San Francisco six years ago, and he never wanted to go back.

Especially on a day like today, with the Flatiron Mountains towering in the near distance, and his wife, Barbara, due home from work in less than an hour.

He and Barbara would probably barbecue black bass on the patio, open a bottle of Zinfandel, maybe even call the Solies over. Or see if Frannie O'Neill could be pried away from her animals out in Bear Bluff. Frannie had been a college swimmer, too, and Frank McDonough always enjoyed her company. He also worried about her since David's tragic death.

Frank McDonough stopped swimming in midstroke. He halted just as he was about to reach the south end of the pool and make his ninety-first flip turn of the afternoon. He'd seen a flash of hurried movement on the patio. Near the Weber grill.

Someone was out there with him.

No, more than one person was on his patio. There were several people, in fact. He felt a twinge of fear. What the hell was going on?

Frank McDonough raised his head out of the water and flipped off his dripping Speedo goggles. Four men in casual dress – jeans, khakis, polo shirts – were hurrying toward him.

'Can I help you guys?' he called out. It was his natural instinct to be nice, to think the best of people, to be polite and courteous.

The men didn't answer. *Odd as hell. A little irritating.* Instead, they continued walking across the deck toward him. Then they started to run!

A table went over on the deck. Votive candles broke, newspapers and magazines flopped on the deck.

'Hey! *Hey!*' He looked at them in total disbelief.

All four of them had jumped into the pool's shallow end with Frank McDonough.

'What the hell is this?' McDonough started to seriously yell at the intruding men. He was confused about what was happening, frightened too.

They were on him like a pack of dogs. They grabbed his arms and legs, pinned them, twisted hard. He heard a sickening *crack* and thought his left wrist had been broken. The fast, powerful movement hurt like hell. He could tell how powerful they were because he was strong, and they put him down as if he were a ninety-pound weakling.

'Hey! Hey!' he yelled again, choking on a noseful of water. They had his head pushed back so that he was looking straight up into the infinite blueness of the sky.

Then they were forcing his head under. He tried to catch a quick breath, but got a mouthful of water and chlorine, and gagged.

They held him under the surface, wouldn't let him up. His legs and arms were caught in a powerful vise. He was being drowned. Oh, God, it didn't make a shred of sense to him.

He tried to thrash.

Tried to break free.

Tried to calm himself.

Frank McDonough heard his neck snap. He *couldn't* fight them. He felt his life force ebbing, flowing out of him.

He could see the figures in their soaking-wet clothes wavering before him in the sparkling, clear blue water. His eyes were pinned wide open. So was his mouth. Water flooded his throat and entered his lungs in a terrifying rush. His chest felt as if it would implode, which he actually wanted to happen. He just wanted the awful internal pressure and pain to end.

In an instant, Dr Frank McDonough understood. He saw the truth as clearly as he could see his own approaching death.

This was about Tinkerbell and Peter Pan.

They had escaped on his watch.

CHAPTER TWELVE

It is about a forty-minute drive from Bear Bluff to Boulder, if you keep the pedal to the metal, if you really fly.

I tried my best to make the drive in a semisane and controlled manner, but I failed miserably. Everything about the drive and the night was a ghostly blur.

I couldn't stop seeing Frank McDonough as I had known him for the past six years – smiling, and incredibly full of life. I hadn't been leaving the Bluff much lately. Not for the last four hundred ninety-three days, anyway. Now, I *had* to go to Boulder.

Frank McDonough was dead. His wife, Barb, had called me in tears. I couldn't make myself believe it. I couldn't bear the painful, terrifying, awful thought.

First David, and now Frank. It didn't seem possible.

I tried to call my best friend Gillian at Boulder Community Hospital. I got her answering machine and left a message that I hoped was coherent.

I tried to call my sister, Carole, but Carole didn't pick up at the camping site where she was staying with her two girls. Damn, I needed her now.

I heard awful, wailing police sirens before I actually arrived at Frank and Barb McDonough's ranch house in Boulder. They live close to Boulder Community Hospital, which makes sense, since they both work there. Barb is a surgical nurse and Frank is the top pediatrician.

Frank *was* a pediatrician. Oh, dear God, Frank was dead now. My friend, David's friend. How could it have happened?

The Boulder police sirens were blaring at an ear-piercing level, and they seemed so eerie, so personal, as if they were meant for me.

Just hearing the police sirens brought back so many powerfully bad memories. I had spent months bothering the Boulder police about solving David's murder. I'd tried to solve it myself for God's sake. I had questioned parking lot attendants, doctors who used the lot late at night.

Now everything, all the bad memories about David's murder, came flooding back to me. I couldn't bear it.

CHAPTER THIRTEEN

'I'm Dr O'Neill,' I said, and I pushed my way past a tall, burly Boulder policeman stationed on the familiar, whitewashed porch. 'I'm Barb and Frank's friend. She called me.'

'Yes, ma'am. She's inside. You can go right in,' he said, doffing his visored cap.

I barely noticed the sprawling ranch house or Frank's beloved Xeriscaped landscaping. Instead of lush green lawns, hundreds of small, colorful plants dotted the yard. Frank had planned everything with water conservation in mind. That's the way he was. Always thinking about other people, thinking ahead.

I was numb, and at least partly in denial. The McDonoughs were the couple that David and I were closest to when he worked at the hospital. They had rushed to our house the night David was shot. Barb and Carole and another friend, Gillian Puris, stayed the night with me. Now here I was in Boulder under similar circumstances.

A woman burst from the front screen door of the house as I was hurrying up the stairs. It wasn't Barb McDonough.

'Oh, God, Gillian,' I whispered. Gillian is my best friend in the world. The two of us hugged on the porch. We were both crying, holding on to each other, trying to understand this tragedy. I was so glad she was here.

'How could he drown?' I muttered.

'Oh, God, Frannie, I don't know how it happened. Frank's neck was broken. He must have tried a shallow dive. Are you okay? No, of course you're not. Neither is poor Barb. This is so bad, so awful.'

I cried on my friend's shoulder. She cried on mine.

Gillian is a research doctor at Boulder Community and she's a crackerjack. She's so good she can afford to be a rebel 'with a cause,' always up against the hospital bureaucrats, the admin jackals and jackasses. She's a widow, too, with a small child, Michael, whom I absolutely adore.

She wore hospital scrubs and a lab coat with her ID badge still pinned to the lapel. She'd come straight from work. What a long, terrible day for her. For all of us.

'I have to see Barb,' I said to Gillian. 'Where is she, Gil?'

'Come on. I'll show the way. Hold on to me. I'll hold you.'

Gillian and I entered the familiar house, now uncharacteristically dark and quiet and somber. We found Barb in the kitchen with another close friend, Gilda Haranzo. Gilda is a pediatric nurse at the hospital. She's part of our group.

'Oh, Barb, I'm sorry. I'm sorry,' I whispered. Words never seem to work at times like these.

The two of us fell hard into each other's arms. 'I didn't understand about David. Oh, Frannie, I didn't understand,' Barb sobbed hard against my chest. 'I should have been better for you back then.'

'You were great. I love you. I love you so much.' It was the truth, and it was why this terrible moment hurt so badly. I could feel Barb's loss as if it were my own.

Then all four of us were hugging and consoling one another as best we could. It seemed only yesterday that we all had husbands and would get together for barbecues, swimming games, charity gigs, or just to talk for hours.

Barb finally pulled away and yanked open a cabinet door over the sink. She took out a bottle of Crown Royal. She cracked the label and poured four large glasses of whiskey.

I looked out the kitchen window and saw a few people from Boulder Community standing in the backyard, out near the pool. Rich Pollett, Boulder's chief counsel, was present. He'd been a good friend of Frank's, a fly-fishing partner.

Then I saw Henrich Kroner, president of the hospital, *Rick* to his friends. Henrich was an elitist snob who thought his narrow focus in life made him special, and didn't realize it made him very ordinary. It struck me as odd that Henrich of all people would be here, other than that the McDonough house was so close to the hospital. But then again, everybody loved Frank.

I had a sudden and painful flash of memory that cut like a knife into my heart. A few years back, David and I had gone white-water rafting with Frank and Barbara. Afterward, we'd gone swimming in calmer waters. Frank was as much at home in the water as an otter. I could still see his powerful freestyle stroke.

How could he have died in his pool?

How could Frank and David both be dead?

As I sipped the bracing whiskey I couldn't come up with a single answer. I felt like a top that wouldn't stop spinning. I had another drink and another after that until I was finally numb.

Gillian almost seemed as concerned about me as she was for Barbara. That's the way she's been since David's death, especially since I wouldn't let the murder be. It's as though I'm her adopted child. She reminds me of how I could imagine Emma Thompson might be – smart, but sensitive, thoughtful, funny, too.

'Come home with me tonight. Please, Frannie,' she said and made a needy face. 'I'll build a fire. We'll talk till we drop.'

'Which would be pretty soon. Gil, I can't,' I said and shook my head. 'A hurt collie's coming in the morning. The Inn-Patient is already full.'

Gillian rolled her eyes, but then she smiled. 'This weekend then. No excuses. You'll come.'

'I'll be there. I promise.'

I helped put Barbara to bed; I kissed Gillian and Gilda good-bye; and then I headed home.

CHAPTER FOURTEEN

The familiar, welcoming sign loomed in swirling mists of bluish-gray fog: *Bear Bluff Next Exit*. I signaled for a right turn, cruised down the off-ramp and felt the usual *two* lumps in the road.

Then, I zagged onto Fourth of July Mine & Run Road, a narrow two-laner that cuts through five and a half unmarked miles of woods until it reaches Bear Bluff. The Bluff is basically a drive-through town. It has a gas station, a Quik Stop, a video store, and me. We all close by dark. There's a local saying – *Happiness is seeing Bear Bluff in your rearview mirror, but you better look damn quick*.

I couldn't wait to get home. I wanted to escape into blessed sleep. I felt distant, unreal. I'd also had too much to drink.

The unlit road looped around rocky outcroppings through the forest. Dense tree growth made reluctant way for the narrow, concrete thoroughfare, and for the dancing headlights of my Suburban.

I slowed the car, and concentrated on getting home in one piece.

Deer were bound to dash out at me, and I wasn't in any shape for sudden-death decisions.

I saw something strange, a streaking white flash in the woods to my right.

I gently applied the brake. Slowed down some more. Peered hard into the shifting shadows of the woods.

I hoped I was wrong, but the white flash looked like a young girl running. A little girl had no business out here in the middle of the night.

I braked to a full stop. If the young girl was lost, I could certainly give her a ride to her home. I felt something was wrong, though. Maybe she was being chased by someone? Or she might be lost?

I left the engine running and got out of the Suburban. The ground fog lifted some, so I walked a few yards into the woodland. My skin was prickling with apprehension.

Stop.

Look.

Listen.

'Hello,' I called in a soft, tentative voice. 'Who's out there? I'm Frannie O'Neill. Dr O'Neill. The vet from town?'

Then I saw the white streak again, this time darting from behind a tall, blue-green spruce. I scrutinized, looked closely, concentrated, squinted fiercely.

It was a young girl, yes!

She looked to be about eleven or twelve, with long blonde hair and a loose-fitting dress. The dress was ripped and stained. Was she all right? She didn't look it from where I stood.

She'd heard me, seen me, she must have. The girl started to run away. She seemed afraid, in some kind of trouble. I couldn't see her very well. The fog had returned in ragged shreds.

'Wait!' I called out. 'You shouldn't be out here by yourself. What are you doing? Please, wait.'

She didn't wait. She actually sped up, tripped over a log, went down on one knee. She shouted something that I couldn't make out from where I was standing.

My heart started to beat faster. Something wasn't right about this. I began to run toward her. I thought she might be hurt. Or maybe she was high on something? That made some sense to me. Maybe she was older than she looked from a distance. It was hard to tell through the scarves of fog.

There was only the dimmest light from a thin slice of moon, so it was hard to tell, but it looked to me that her proportions were a little odd. Her arms were sheathed with something—

I stopped running. Hard! My heart started to thunder. I could hear it.

It couldn't be.

Of course, it couldn't be.

I almost screamed. I gasped for breath, steadied myself against a tall spruce.

The little girl appeared to have white and silver wings.

CHAPTER FIFTEEN

hat I saw was way beyond my abilities to imagine, beyond my comprehension, my system of belief, and maybe beyond my ability to communicate it right now. The little girl's arms were folded back in a peculiar way, but when she lifted them – feathers fanned out.

It wasn't humanly possible, but there she was – *a girl with wings!*

Spots jumped in front of my eyes. Colors, coruscating reds and yellows, danced. I was definitely a little high from the Crown Royal, but I wasn't drunk. Or was I very drunk? Was I so freaked out by Frank McDonough's death that I was hallucinating?

Close your eyes, Frannie.

Now open them again, slowly . . .

She was still there! No more than twenty yards away. The girl was watching me, too.

Don't faint, Frannie. DON'T YOU DARE, I told myself.

Go slow. Go really slow here. Don't make any sudden noise or movement to scare her off.

I watched as the girl awkwardly found her feet. One wing was folded neatly behind her. The other wing dragged a little. Was she hurt?

'Hey,' I called again, softly. 'It's all right.'

The young blonde girl turned toward me. I guess she was close to five feet tall. She gave me a fierce look with her large, wide-spaced eyes. I stood in the ferny glade in the milky moonlight. Everything around me was shifting shadows. I watched, dizzy and panting, not knowing who was more frightened, her or me.

She shot me a grim look of horror and ran away again, into the night, farther into the woods surrounding Fourth of July Road until she was just a blur.

I followed until it was too dark to see in the dense woods. I finally leaned against a tree and tried to review the last few minutes. I couldn't do it. My head was spinning too fast.

Somehow I managed to get back to the Suburban. I climbed inside and sat there in the dark.

'I did not just see a young girl with wings,' I whispered out loud.

I couldn't have.

But I was sure that I had.

When I could manage to drive, I went to the police station in nearby Clayton, a burg of about three thousand. Actually, the station is an outpost for the main office in Nederland. I stopped the Suburban on Miller Street, less than a block from the station house.

I desperately wanted to continue down the peaceful village street, but I couldn't do it, couldn't make myself.

I *had* been drinking . . . and driving. It was already past two in the morning, way past the witching hour in Clayton.

Now that I wasn't actually *looking* at the girl . . . I wasn't completely sure what I had seen. I just couldn't tell my story to the local cops. Not that night, anyway. Maybe tomorrow.

I went home to sleep on it – or more likely, to sleep it off.

CHAPTER SIXTEEN

Kit was sweating, just like he had on the American
Airlines flight from Boston. Damn it, he still
couldn't fly very well. But he had to.

The pilot of the Bell helicopter shot a look across the
cockpit at him. He didn't bother to conceal a smirk. 'You
okay? Never been up in one of these eggbeaters, huh? You
don't look so good, Mr Harrison. Maybe we should head
back?'

Kit almost lost his cool with the guy. The pilot was an
asshole of the first order. Actually, he'd flown in plenty of
helicopters before, flown in snow-blind blizzards, bad
rainstorms, and on dangerous raids. There had never been
a problem until August of '94.

He'd been a good agent until then, one of the best.
Resourceful, bright, hardworking, tough enough. It was a
matter of record in his personnel file. So what the hell had
happened to him?

'The natural color of my gills is green. I'm just fine. I'm

all right.' He tried a little self-deprecating humor.

'Whatever you say, Kermit. It's your dime.'

Yes, it sure was his dime, and he didn't have a lot of them to blow on costly surveillance junkets like this. But he felt he needed an overview; he had to see the big picture; take in the lay of the land. And the *real* big picture here had to do with subjects as lofty and important as the survival of the human race. He believed that, or he wouldn't be out here on his own.

Kit tried looking down at the treetops again. Acres of ponderosa pines with aspen groves nestled in. Occasional 'blowouts' – stacks of trees blown down in winter. And of course, the snowy peaks of the Continental Divide.

There was a lab out here somewhere near the Divide. Kit knew that much. Where the hell could it be?

The helicopter passed over Gross Reservoir. Then he could see the Eldora ski area, and the small town of Nederland. Then another picturesque reservoir – probably Barker, if he was reading the maps correctly. Off in the distance, he spotted Flagstaff Mountain. Closer in was Magnolia Road, Sunshine Canyon.

He knew what he was looking for . . . the end of civilization as we know it. A brave new world. That's all. It was out here somewhere.

He thought about Dr Frank McDonough again. Dr McDonough had been on his list. McDonough, and also David Mekin and his wife. He had wanted to meet with Dr McDonough – a pediatrician with a background in embryology.

Unfortunately, he'd been a day late getting here. Blame

his boss, Peter Stricker, for that. No, hell, blame himself.

Dr McDonough was victim number four. Four doctors had been murdered that he knew of. Four doctors with suspicious pasts, dubious presents, and now, no futures at all.

He watched a couple of paragliders off in the distance. They almost seemed to be flying. They looked so free.

'Okay, let's go down,' he finally said to the rent-a-chopper pilot. He had his overview, anyway; he had the lay of the land. It was the right first step for the investigation.

The pilot grinned and gave Kit a thumbs-down signal. What a jerk. 'Hang on to your insides . . . Kermit.'

F-you, Sky King, Kit thought. He didn't say anything, didn't want to start a scene up here. Especially not up here.

The helicopter swooped and went into a steep dive. He knew it was a physical impossibility, but his stomach seemed to drop before the rest of the chopper and its contents.

He was feeling unsatisfied and uptight as he left the tiny High Pines Airport at around ten thirty in the morning. He needed help, but knew he couldn't ask for it from the Bureau. He was on his own, and that really sucked.

CHAPTER SEVENTEEN

Have faith and pursue the unknown end. Oliver Wendell Holmes said it and Kit had always believed it. He still did, so here he was in the Rocky Mountains. Pursuing the unknown end, and trying like hell to keep the faith.

He needed answers, or maybe he just wanted to hear a familiar voice. He called Peter Stricker's office in Washington. This was going to be tricky, but he thought he could pull it off. He might just be able to get a little help from the Bureau.

Peter Stricker was in charge of the Northeast sector of the FBI. They were still pretty good friends. Up until two and a half years ago, Peter had actually worked for him.

Then Kit's world turned upside down, and he wound up working for Peter. And last week, Peter had threatened to can him if he didn't make his job priorities the same as the ones the Bureau had for him. And Peter had put the warning *on paper*.

Even before the official threat there had been signs. He'd been passed over for promotion after the accident in '94 – though God only knows if that was the reason. More likely, it was his stubbornness and insubordination that had stalled-out his career in the FBI. Also, his obsessiveness with cases that fascinated or scared the living shit out of him. Like this case that had brought him out to Colorado. He could see potential leads, looming problems, possible solutions, where others didn't.

He had always been an 'unusual' FBI agent. Hell, that was why they *said* they had recruited him out of N.Y.U. Law. During his interviews he'd been told that the Bureau wanted him *because* they were too straitlaced and traditional, and therefore too predictable. He was supposed to represent a new, evolved kind of agent. And he sure had! For a while, anyway.

They had sold hard on the idea of breaking out of the envelope, working outside the box; but once he was inside the organization, he discovered that the FBI really didn't want to change very much. Actually, the Bureau had tried to change him. And when he wouldn't budge, they resented the hell out of it. One of his superiors said, 'We didn't join you, Tom. You joined us. So why don't you cut the prima donna horseshit and get with the program like the rest of us?'

Because he was different. He was *supposed* to be different. That was the deal – and a deal was a deal.

Except that the Bureau wasn't keeping their end.

They resented the corduroy sports jackets, un-logoed ball caps, the jeans, the dock shoes he insisted on wearing to work, and not just on Fridays. And that he read 'serious' novels like *Underworld* and *Mason & Dixon* and anything Toni Morrison wrote. And that some days he rode his Cannondale racing bike to and from the office in Boston.

They were bugged by his longish hair and his every-other-day shaving habits and his slight swagger, which didn't represent cockiness, just the fact that he liked to walk around with music playing in his head.

Most of all, though, the Bureau was incensed by his casual approach to discipline. Right from the start, he was called a loose cannon.

Worse, he probably *was* a loose cannon. He'd been one as a gritty middleweight in the Boston Golden Gloves, and as an outspoken, and pretty unconventional under-graduate at Holy Cross, and even at N.Y.U. Law. Hell, he was a bus-driver's son, one of five sons. He had no business being at N.Y.U. Law, or maybe even at Cross. Why shouldn't he speak his mind?

He'd gotten away with it in school, but not at the Federal Bureau. No loose cannons were permitted in the FBI. Not even ones who had solved at least two 'unsolv-able' murder cases during the past five years.

Awhh, stop the horseshit, he finally told himself. He was in trouble because he'd been pursuing the 'human experiments' case for the past year and a half. Against orders. He had repeatedly disobeyed orders that went high up the chain of command. He was *still* disobeying orders, and much worse than that.

'This is Tom Brennan for Agent Stricker,' he said when Stricker's overly pleasant, overly efficient assistant came on the line. 'How are you, Cindy? Is Peter there for me?'

'Oh, it's so nice to hear from you, Tom. One moment please.' Cindy was overly polite as ever. 'I have to check and see if he's at his desk. Be right back to you.'

Surprisingly, Stricker picked up immediately. He spoke in a whisper – *always*. Made you pay attention. The trademark Stricker sibilance.

'Tom. Terrific. How is paradise? How is Nantucket? You're supposed to be sailing, riding the surf. Hanging out at the beach. Get the hell off the telephone.'

'I'm calling from the beach.' Kit manufactured a high-spirited, buddy-to-buddy laugh. 'Actually, I'm being pretty good for me. I'm on my way to becoming a world-class beach bum up here. There's just one little thing.'

'There always is, Tom. Always just one thing, always a hitch in your swing. You're supposed to be getting used to not worrying about the little things,' Stricker told him in the usual soft tones. 'Wasn't that our deal?'

'I know, I know. It was. And I appreciate the few weeks up here. It's just that – I was on the Web this morning. I happened to see that a Dr Frank McDonough was drowned in Colorado yesterday. It really weirded me out. Did you see it, Peter?'

Stricker couldn't mask his annoyance for a second longer. His whisper rose a notch. 'Tom, please let this phantom case go. Stay *off* the Web for a while. Christ, man. It's already started to wreck a pretty terrific career.'

'Not really. But anyway, there was a Dr McDonough in the original Berkeley think-tank group. I'm sure about that. Would you mind having somebody follow through with it? Maybe Michael Fescoe? Or Manny Patino? Just for my peace of mind? Check and see if it's the same Frank McDonough.'

He could tell that Stricker wasn't at all happy with the way the call was going. 'Okay, Tom. I can do that for you. I'll check up on the deceased. It's Dr Frank McDonough, right? You work on the personal demons. Work on your tan. Find some nice Nantucket chick to hang out with. Make love, not war.'

'If he's the same McDonough, he's number four, Peter. Doctors Kim, Heekin, Mekin, McDonough.'

'Right, I know all the particulars of the case, Tom. I know you think there's a missing link, even though the folks in Quantico don't see it that way. I'll take it from here. You take care of the sun and sea.'

'Thanks for the help, Peter. You're the best. I'll check in about McDonough, though. Maybe tomorrow?'

He could hear Stricker's sigh. If it was possible, his voice got even lower. 'Give me your number on the island. I'll call you there.'

'No, it's okay. I'll check in. It's really no problem. I'll call you tomorrow. Well, the sun and sea beckon. I even met somebody who I kind of like. I like her looks, anyway. Thanks again for the help, Peter.'

He had to strain to hear Stricker's response.

'No problem. Try to relax, though. Promise me, Tom. This isn't something you have to worry about anymore. No loose cannon shit. That was our deal. I'll get the info you need on Dr McDonough. I'm doing it because of our friendship.'

Kit hung up the pay phone, and he let out a deep breath. Man, he hated to lie to Peter – and now it was what he did for a living. His whole life had suddenly become a lie.

CHAPTER EIGHTEEN

Stop it, Matthew! Don't play with my head right now. I'm not in the mood for it.

Max had just thought of another of Matthew's dumb lines: Why do kamikaze pilots wear helmets? She could actually hear the sound of Matthew's dumb laugh at his own dumb jokes. Hardee-har-har! He always did that. Annoying little twit that he was.

She still hadn't found her little brother and she didn't know where else to look. Maybe at this slick, modern-looking house up ahead in the woods? Or maybe she could at least get a little food there. Some water?

F-o-o-d was on her mind. No, f-o-o-d was her mind.

Uh-oh, Spaghettios! She remembered a favorite line from TV. She knew just about everything that had ever been on the tube. Every show, every dumb and dumber commercial, every character in every show. The TV had been her baby-sitter, her mom and her dad, her hundred closest friends at the School.

Max stopped walking, stopped thinking idle thoughts. She cautiously eyed the house standing up ahead. *Careful now. Be ever so careful.*

The house looked dark and quiet and it made her wary and afraid in some deep place inside. A brier thicket grew around it. *Oh, please don't throw me in the brier patch.*

She picked her way along the edge of the thicket and up a steep slope toward the modern construction of thick plate glass and rough timber.

Nobody home, nobody home! Please let there be nobody home. Please, please.

Let there be F-O-O-D here.

Her heart thudding, she tiptoed up a wooden flight of stairs and onto the back porch. She peered through sliding glass doors that needed a washing with Spic & Span real bad. She noticed things like that. The genius was in the details, right?

Forbidden, forbidden, forbidden, she was thinking. *Nobody was supposed to see her. Ever. If they did, then they would die, too.*

Max put her fingers to the sealed lips of the glass sliders and pulled. Her dula/thumb had been modified into a hand. Her fingers worked fine. She had been made that way.

The doors gave, opened. She was in!

Trap! she thought, but it was already too late.

CHAPTER NINETEEN

I t wasn't a trap, after all. There was nobody waiting inside the house. The owners were obviously stupid, or really sloppy people, because they left their back door unlocked and unprotected. But no one was there to capture, or maybe even kill her.

The house was sloppy and disorganized inside. A family definitely lived here, though. She could tell by the mess of kids' stuff. Bikes, rollerblades, video games.

'Matthew,' she whispered. She was hoping against hope that he might have found the same house. Maybe he was hiding in here somewhere. 'Where are you, bro? It's me. Max!'

She tiptoed into the kitchen. A refrigerator hummed noisily. A fridge – oh, God, yes. She pulled open the refrigerator door. She basked in the cool air and the frosty light of the bulb. Her eyes hungrily searched the shelves.

She grabbed a can of soda pop. *Sprite. Obey your thirst! Okay, I think I will.*

She had a brief guilt trip that stealing food and soda pop was wrong. And that it just wasn't a nice thing to do.

Oh, screw that. I've been shot. I'm being hunted. I need to eat and get some fluids in my body. End of story.

Max drank, then she began to gorge herself. Flying *really* made you hungry. It took incredible energy.

She peeled clingy plastic wrap off a glass bowl. *Uh-oh, Spaghettios!* She pushed cold spaghetti into her mouth. She didn't care if the spaghetti was cold, just so long as it was food. Not good food, not great food, just food – food.

Got milk? Yippee! There was milk, too. She sniffed – it was okay. Barely. She gulped it down right from the carton.

She found a knife in a pie dish and she used it to hack off a large, sticky chunk of apple pie.

It was the best pie she'd ever eaten. No contest. No pie-eating contest, she thought. She grinned. She loved wordplay, any kind of play. Pie play, whatever. She was smart – really smart. That was the way they had made her, right?

Max looked in the freezer for more goodies.

Ooohh! Ooohh! Look what's in the freezer! Klondike ice cream bars – a full box! What would you do for a Klondike bar?

She ate *two* Klondike bars, one for each hand. She craved sugar.

Suddenly, little fingers of apprehension started to walk up the back of her neck. Pin feathers rose at her nape. She hunched her shoulders and listened.

Were the hunters out there? Was Uncle Thomas nearby,

ready to pounce on her? Maybe he'd take her back – or maybe just put her to sleep.

She was dying to take a look around the house, though. *Curiosity killed the cat*, she thought. *But not the girl.*

She crept silently down the hall. She couldn't resist this – a real house. Nobody home. What a treat!

'Creepycat. Kittytoes,' she whispered. It was a saying from the School – from when she was little, when she thought little kid thoughts. It probably came from Mrs Beattie, who had been her nanny, then her teacher. Everything good in her life came before Mrs Beattie died.

A bathroom was revealed behind a slatted door at the end of the hallway. Gross! Everything was black inside. Black toilet, black tub, black sink, even black soap. She looked longingly at the shower stall, black and glistening behind a clear curtain. She was sticky and dirty everywhere. Disgusting! Almost more than sleep she wanted to be clean. She wanted to feel hot water flow onto her body and her hurt wing, just above the second joint. Obviously, the wing wasn't hurt too bad, though. Probably just clipped.

Max wound her long blonde hair back and around her ears and listened hard for any sound in the house.

There was none. She was sure of it. Her fingers found the light switch. Caressed it. Pressed it!

Light blazed in the black bathroom. Eerie.

She tensed to run – but that seemed kind of stupid. She was alone here. So she stepped all the way into the bathroom and closed the door. Locked it.

Then she saw herself in the mirror.

Four foot ten of her, with the most beautiful wings of anyone who had ever lived. Ever, ever, ever.

She touched her hair. Tilted her face slightly forward.

'I'm beautiful,' she whispered. 'I really am, aren't I? I'm a good girl, and I'm pretty. So why are they trying to kill me?'

CHAPTER TWENTY

Gillian was on the phone first thing in the morning. 'I *hate* it that you're up in the mountains all alone. Are you all right, Frannie?'

'I'm fine. What time is it? Where are you?'

'The hospital, where else. It's eight o'clock. So you slept all right?'

'Like a baby, Gil.'

'Liar.'

'You know me so well,' I said and laughed. I was almost awake now. It was beautiful outside my window.

'And isn't that nice,' Gillian said. 'For both of us.'

I let her get back to work, and then I had a thought – a bad one. It was this completely irrational but powerful fear that something might happen to Gillian, that maybe all my friends were in some kind of danger.

I knew it didn't make rational sense. But still, I *felt* it.

I spent part of the morning driving back to where I'd

stopped my car the night before. Where I had, or hadn't, seen – *what*?

I was feeling hyper, maybe a bit hungover, and even a little spiritual. It was the hungover part that gave me pause for the most thought, and doubts. Had I been drunk the night before?

Had Frank McDonough's death affected my already bruised psyche?

The only trouble was that the more I tried to convince myself that I hadn't seen her, the more convinced I was that I had.

Two speeding trains of thought came to mind.

Congenital birth defects.

And the brave new world of biotechnology.

I had some knowledge of both fields, so I let my mind play as I drove around in my dusty blue Suburban looking for my winged girlfriend from the night before. I thought to myself, let's take a little mind trip down the road of genetic abnormalities, defects, disorders, aberrant syndromes. Actually, as I thought about it, I remembered spending an afternoon with David on the very subject. We had even contacted the prestigious Mutter Museum, which is part of the Philadelphia College of Physicians.

Mutter was happy to supply examples of deformities they'd come across in recent years. They ranged from boys in Mexico with apelike hair all over their bodies to children with duplication of body parts, pituitary abnormalities such as dwarfs and giants, skin diseases that made some people resemble lizards more than human beings.

I don't remember exactly what got David and me on the subject, but we did spend a couple of weekends on it. He also pulled out a book on the subject from his vast collection in storage: *Anomalies and Curiosities of Medicine*. I thought *Anomalies* was still around the house somewhere, but I couldn't locate it that morning. Maybe it was back in the cabin along with the modern-day Neanderthal, Kit Harrison.

As I drove around the Bluff and nearby Clayton, I tried to let my mind run free. I didn't rule out anything yet. I even considered the possibility of *extraterrestrial visitors*. I finally rejected it, the idea of another E.T., but maybe I shouldn't have.

I have a pretty strong memory. I'd been number one in my high school class, and the files in my head were filled with more information than I had expected. I had actually examined a hermaphrodite, a child having both male and female reproductive organs. I'd also come across humans and animals with missing body parts, and several with duplicate parts. I'd seen two ears on one side of a little girl's skull. A boy with six toes. A girl with four breasts. In vet school I'd also witnessed what toxins and pesticides can do to alter livestock. Not a pretty sight, and not one you ever forget.

As far as pictures go, I'd seen images of 'formed fingers', that is, horns, on a human head. A parasitic horse body growing from an otherwise perfect one. A second head growing on the head of a calf. From somewhere in the back of my brain came a tidbit from ancient Babylon: *An infant born with the face of a lion means the King shall not have a rival.* I had once seen a child with the ears of a lion.

But never a very pretty, otherwise normal-looking girl with a pair of beautiful white and silver wings! Maybe she *was* an extraterrestrial.

Of course, there was also biotechnology and genetic engineering as a serious area of exploration and mystery. David's chosen field, I reminded myself.

My memory files in David's specialty area were a little less comprehensive than I would have thought. David and I had been good at sharing most things, but he never liked to talk much about his work.

Strange, as I thought about it now. David rarely brought work home with him. I, on the other hand, was always ready to chat about the Inn-Patient, or the beautiful colt I had delivered at four the previous morning on somebody's horse farm.

So what did I already know about biotechnology? From the broadest overview, biotech involved harnessing natural biological processes of microbes and of animals and plant cells. Cross-species research and experiments would be in the field of molecular biology, too. David had been a molecular biologist, and a good one, though he never made much money as a researcher.

I remembered a couple of things he'd talked about that might relate to a little girl with – say it, Frannie – beautiful silver and white wings. When the film version of *Jurassic Park* came to Boulder, David told me that the idea of cross-species genetic work was actually a whole lot less far-fetched than the wonderful movie dinosaurs. He said cross-species experiments were being done now in a number of independent labs. The experiments were sometimes illegal.

Biotech was definitely the new frontier in science. It can, and undoubtedly will, push evolution farther and faster than anything has in history. The question, though, is whether we're ready, emotionally and morally, for what we will be able to create in the very near future. I remembered that David said that *most* serious work was still being accomplished with fruit flies, and I found that profoundly reassuring.

David had also told me something interesting in light of what had happened to me the night before. He said that in the area of genetic manipulation, 'Things always go awry. It happens all the time, Frannie. Goes with the territory.'

Things always go awry.

CHAPTER TWENTY-ONE

I t had been a busy and productive day for Kit. He'd been a functioning FBI field agent again. It felt good, excellent. He was working alone, but at least he was off the Bureau's long, restrictive leash.

He had taken a chance by interviewing the widow of Frank McDonough. Barbara McDonough didn't seem to know anything beyond the obvious, but the more they talked, the more certain he was that Dr McDonough had been murdered. McDonough had been an excellent swimmer for one thing, a former college star. For another, he'd supposedly broken his neck making a shallow dive, but his wife claimed he never dived into the pool.

He had talked to three other associates of McDonough at Boulder Community Hospital. He'd also called in a favor from a good buddy at Quantico. McDonough's name was being run against every doctor working in the area around Boulder. He was looking for solid connections, which was about all he could realistically do on his first day in town.

Kit had just gotten back from Boulder, when he spotted Frannie O'Neill hiking in the woods behind the cottage where he was staying. It was almost five in the afternoon.

Frannie looked nervous and distracted. Of course, he didn't know her very well, but that was the impression he had. *Now where the heck was she going?*

She was moving quickly: a woman on a mission. What mission, though? He thought it might be worth checking, and he had nothing better to do for another hour or two.

She was wearing khaki shorts and a red-plaid flannel shirt, and he couldn't help remembering how she'd looked the night before. That image was still burned into his mind. A pretty picture, so maybe he didn't want to let it go too easily.

He followed Dr Frannie through the woods at a safe distance. She never looked back, but she did appear to be looking for something. Actually, she was moving so fast he finally lost sight of her.

Damn it.

He lifted a pair of Rangemaster binoculars to his eyes. He searched everywhere for Frannie O'Neill. Images jumped, giving him extreme close-ups of pine bark, the shapes of leaves, a patch of blue sky.

He finally spotted the red-plaid shirt again. She was still trekking at a fast pace through the woods, a bright blue knapsack on her back, an intent look on her face. She was preoccupied, oblivious to his own tiptoe through the woodlands. Or was she?

What the hell was she doing out here? Did it have anything to do with her husband's work? Or possibly with his death? Or Dr McDonough's?

She took a sharp right fork around a bend. *Don't go that way, Frannie. Shit! Shit!* She'd disappeared into the pines, aspens, and scrub oaks again. Fifteen minutes following her over hill and dale had already taught him not to give up the high ground. He continued *upward*, hoping she would appear below him.

Seconds later, he saw Frannie O'Neill come into view again. Late-afternoon sunlight spilled onto her face. She was definitely pretty; a real midwestern beauty, and he liked that. Her blue-green eyes sparkled in the light, and continued to search for something.

The narrow path she'd been sticking to widened, then it branched onto a wider dirt road. A dirt road to where? Was something important out here? Another building? Maybe a lab hidden in the woods? Did Frannie O'Neill work there?

She trekked on, even picked up the pace. She really moved through the woods, didn't she? She knew her way?

Kit thought he could hear traffic now. He was almost sure of it.

'What the hell? Traffic up here?' he mumbled under his breath.

The dirt path opened out to the back of a macadam parking lot! The lot was a dark rectangle behind a small town market. It appeared that she'd taken a shortcut through the woods to Clayton. She was in the next town over. What was she doing?

Kit watched in mild disbelief as she stopped near a flat rock at the edge of the woods. She unhitched her blue knapsack and flipped it open. She started taking out small boxes, cans, paper items, and setting them on the ground.

'What in hell is she doing?' He didn't get this at all. It made no sense.

He refined the focus on the binoculars. He looked closely at the contents of the knapsack. He could even hear Frannie's voice drifting up to him. He liked the melodic sound of it, even under the mysterious circumstances.

'Party!' she called.

Party? Party for whom? Party for what? This was no time for a party!

'Come on, kiddies.'

Kiddies?

Children?

As he watched, she emptied cans of food onto paper plates.

Suddenly, an incredible number of cats appeared. They began to materialize from under cars, from behind packing crates at the rear of the supermarket, from the tall grass. Tails up, they came scampering, talking back to her.

'Party time. Good kitties,' she said. Not kiddies – *kitties*, Kit realized.

He held the binoculars to his eyes, transfixed by a large herd of feral felines: coal black ones, orange ones, spotted ones, striped ones, one three-legged, and one trailing kitten collected at Frannie's soup kitchen. She was good with them. She seemed kind of sweet and nice, actually. She *acted* exactly the way she looked: like a decent enough person.

'C'mon, Momma Cat,' he heard her call. She was beaming – a big, generous, good-hearted smile. 'Whitey. Big Boy. Freakazoid. Howza Susie Q?'

Yes, this Frannie O'Neill was one to watch, all right. She was the key to everything, no doubt.

CHAPTER TWENTY-TWO

K it finally started to laugh, and it was probably the first time he had since coming to Colorado. He had always been pretty good at laughing at his own expense. For a moment, he sat watching the rubbing, chatting, chowing down. Just watching 'the party.'

No, he was watching Frannie O'Neill. He was admiring her sweet way with animals, listening to the music of her voice, remembering her perfect-enough-for-him body. Jesus – he had a little schoolboy crush on her, didn't he? No doubt about it. Perfectly harmless, but this wasn't the time or place for it.

He purposely turned away and hurried back through the woods. It was an ideal time to check out her house, to check her out. He was thinking and acting like a field agent again. And violating her trust was also a good way to break away from the danger of a schoolboy crush on her.

She didn't lock her doors, of course. So he looked

through her room at the Inn-Patient, and he was good at it. She'd never know anyone had been in here. Still, he felt guilty about intruding in her house. Maybe she hadn't known a thing about what her husband had been involved in. But maybe she had. And maybe she was involved, too. He didn't know enough about Frannie O'Neill to rule her out. She might surprise him and be extremely dangerous.

He made a few notes along the way. He was going strictly by the book, even though he no longer had to.

Simple clothes and needs. Jeans, cowboy boots, pocket T-shirts. No evidence of much money spent on herself.

Nice taste, though. Simple, attractive, classic – about what he would have expected.

A small collection of birdhouses. Why birdhouses? Wedding photos, one of her and David kissing under a blue umbrella. A Mac Performa 575. An old model, and not expensive.

Here and there an extravagant touch: a formal black silk chiffon dress; a diamond and sapphire cocktail ring; a half-ounce of Eau d'Hermès.

He thought that he'd kind of like to see her in the black chiffon dress, and smell her perfume.

No papers – scientific or otherwise. Nothing of David's work. That was a little odd. Where were David's papers? She wouldn't throw them out? Would she?

Books – a few of them spread open around the bedroom: *If Wishes Were Horses: The Education of a Veterinarian; Veterinary Epidemiology; Into Thin Air; In Search of Human Beginnings; Midnight in the Garden of Good and Evil.*

Nothing incriminating there, quite the opposite.

A touching keepsake. A model boat her husband had constructed, signed, and dated. 'David's ship – March 22, 1969.'

A child's drawing of a girl and a happy dog stuck up on the fridge: 'To Dr Frannie. We love you. Your friends, Emily and Buster.'

He finally stuck his notebook into his back pocket, took one last look around, then got out of there before Frannie O'Neill returned. In a way, the search had turned out badly for him. He didn't believe she was involved.

Anyway, he felt he was getting closer to something. He knew it in his gut and had from the beginning.

Why hadn't anyone believed him?

CHAPTER TWENTY-THREE

I t was a little past ten and the woods and mountains appeared to be closed for the night, but I knew better. I was thinking about the winged girl again.

For the umpteenth time, I seriously considered calling the sheriff in Clayton, or even the Colorado State Police, but how could I? What would I say to them? 'Hi. Lately I live alone up in Bear Bluff. I'm mostly of sound mind and body. But here's the thing, I'm pretty sure I saw a little girl with wings. I was drinking a bit that night, upset over the death of a friend. C'mon up here and see for yourself. Better bring a nice big net – *for me*!'

I was up working late at the Inn-Patient, thinking through what I ought to do – all the possible options. I'd already talked on my cell phone to both Barb McDonough and Gillian. I had just knocked down a wild kittycat I'd brought home from one of my mercy missions in Clayton.

I was carefully shaving the wild cat's belly before spaying her. I was concentrating on the electric clippers when I heard someone behind me say, '*Hello? Hi in there?*'

I jumped about ten feet in the air. I was feeling extra spooky, anyway. Birds in my belfry and that sort of thing.

'Hello? Dr O'Neill?'

I turned toward the screen door and saw none other than Kit Harrison standing there. I gave him a look to kill, or at least badly wound and maim. 'See what you made me do? Please leave now.'

He came in. He walked closer, peered down at my patient. 'No, what?' he asked.

'You made me shave her nipple off.'

He winced and said he was really sorry, which was better, halfway considerate. I almost believed that he meant it because of those damn blue eyes of his. He quickly explained that the door was open, that he'd called out and I hadn't answered.

'How serious is it?' he asked, peering at the cat.

'Well,' I said, not looking at him, 'her career as a topless dancer is pretty much over.'

In fact, the injury was minor. She wasn't going to be needing nipples anymore, anyway. I tightened Kitty's restraints, vigorously swabbed her with Betadine. Then I covered her midsection with a sterile drape with a slit for where the action was going to be happening.

'Swing that light over here,' I said to him. 'Please.' Surprisingly, he did what he was told. Maybe he thought he was going to get laid. He looked like the type that often got what he wanted.

I opened the cat's lineum alba with my scalpel, then sliced into the pelvic cavity. I took a sideways glance to see how Mr Kit Harrison was taking the operation. He seemed okay, which disappointed me. I had *hoped* he would faint.

His blond hair was damp, as if it had had a recent wash, and he smelled like what a good, old-fashioned all-American hunk smells like – Ivory soap. No Hermès Equipage for this boy.

'So, what is it?' I asked him as I worked. 'Got enough towels? Hot water? Room service okay?'

'The cabin's fine,' he said. 'I like it very much. I give it four stars, five diamonds, the highest rating.'

Pity.

He continued. 'I heard there's a good place to eat over in Clayton. Two stars at the very least.'

'Yes, there is. Probably about half the houses, if you're ever invited for supper, which is unlikely. People around here don't much trust city folks. And then there's Danny's Grill. And Villa Vittoria for pretty good pizza and pasta.'

'Come have a bite to eat with me when you're finished here. Or I'll bet we could even get an invite at one of those houses,' he said.

'No, thanks,' I said, wielding my scalpel, jiggling it between thumb and forefinger. 'You want to do something really nice, something I'd *appreciate* – you can just pack up your gun and yourself, and move on.'

He cleared his throat before speaking. 'It seems I've gotten off to a bad start with you, Dr O'Neill. And you know . . . you actually don't know a thing about me,' he said from behind my back. 'You really don't know who I am.'

I went back into the cat, treated the uterine ligament, then began stitching. Kitty was purring now, which meant she was coming to. But she would be scared and hissing up a storm.

I was a little scared myself, and I didn't like being that way. Unbidden, a chill came over me. I had left my door open. There was a man sitting behind me, and as he had said, I didn't know a thing about him.

I turned to face him, but the stool behind me was empty.

He'd left as silently as he'd come.

CHAPTER TWENTY-FOUR

Max had slept really well inside the house, whoever's house it was, the messy, careless family's amazing, wonderful, stocked-with-goodies house. She was out on the porch at daybreak and the sky was a whole bunch of different shades of pink and red bleeding into a swatch of blue.

'Good morning, forest! Good morning, beautiful sky! Good morning, sunshine! I feel like flying high into the Rockies. Who wouldn't? Maybe I'll find Matthew today.'

She stood perfectly balanced on the wooden railing of the deck of the house where she was hiding. She was still wearing the sleeveless white cotton tube she had escaped in, and the same ballet slippers. She was edgy with excitement. It was such a perfect day for flying.

Matthew? Matthew? Where the heck are you? Come fly with me? Come on down, Matthew. Please don't be dead.

The wind was blowing noisily against the steep hill

behind the house and she could feel the cool updraft frisking her legs.

She raised her wings, just a little. *Testing, one, two, three, four.*

She wanted to check to see how much pain there was, whether or not she could tolerate it; but she already knew she was feeling pretty good. She wasn't hurt too bad. She'd live, at least for the moment.

Air buffeted against her feathers, making a soft drumming sound, the gentlest tympani. Her heartbeat accelerated in anticipation.

Max took a deep, sweet breath of the mountain air, of wildflowers, of pine needles, and before she could chicken out, she pushed off!

She was more prepared for the vertigo this time and for the sensation of her stomach actually rising up in her chest. Instinct took over. She beat her wings hard against the air. *Flapping counters gravity*, she told herself. She had learned all about flying from Mrs Beattie at the School. She just wasn't allowed to fly. Flying was forbidden.

As her upper arms swung out, her shoulder bones rotated easily and naturally in their sockets. The elbow joints automatically opened, her wrists extended, and her feathers spread.

She found herself rising without having to do another thing! It was unbelievably quiet up here. She was riding on the air, and it was a hundred times easier than swimming. It was easier than walking.

Max rose in a thermal vortex. The air seemed alive, *pushing* her upward from below. She knew a little about thermal vortexes. She'd read everything she could at the School, and she retained most of what she read. In School terms, she was supposed to be a genius. So was Matthew, of course. So where the heck was he?

She could hear birds chirping, but didn't see many of them yet. She circled effortlessly as she continued to climb. Flying was the best thing. Definitely. No wonder it had been forbidden for her and Matthew.

Other people would have to be on drugs to experience anything even close to this. Each one of her feathers was wired directly into her nervous system so that her brain knew the exact alignment.

When she was so high that she could blot out the house with a fingertip, she encountered another small miracle.

The hill behind the house was connected to other hills, making a ridge that stretched to the ends of her sight-line. The wind blowing into the ridge had nowhere to go but up, so it formed a standing wave of air along the entire hilly crest.

Max embraced the air with her open wings, and she caught the wave. The breeze whipped her long blonde hair behind her. Her hair was a stream in the wind.

Then the earth was sliding along silently beneath her. Except for the whisper of air through her feathers, it was completely quiet up here. She soared as if exempt from the laws of gravity. And she saw others taking advantage of the same airflow.

A red-tailed hawk, a pair of vultures, and smaller crows floated as effortlessly as she did. The hawk circled her, watched her. She stared back at its dark, hard eyes.

'Chill out,' she said to the bird.

She skimmed the treetops, then dropped beneath them, and finally dipped into the dark green shadows of the woods. She lightly brushed the edges of the trees with her wingtips.

She whipped tight figure eights through the trees.

What a ride! She felt incredibly connected to the natural world, to the rest of the universe.

She was made for this!

Suddenly she slowed herself. The ground was rushing at her. She landed too fast, too hard. Pain mainlined through her body and into the hurt shoulder. She stared straight ahead and couldn't believe what she saw.

It was that woman again.

She was a few yards up ahead.

CHAPTER TWENTY-FIVE

'**D**amn you, whoever did this. Damn you to hell!' I cursed loudly, and my voice resounded with the echo.

I reached down and hauled a horrifying leghold trap out from under a mat of wet and muddy leaves in the gully. Fortunately, it hadn't been tripped by some poor animal.

Suddenly, I heard something big moving in the woods. The noise was *close*. Definitely a large animal. Or maybe the pitiful trapper himself?

I froze with the trap dangling from my hands. I turned slowly.

'OhmygoodGod,' I whispered under my breath. The bird-girl was twenty paces away. It was the same young girl. She was looking at me, staring hard. What I was seeing wasn't possible. But there she was. And she definitely had wings.

Her face, and probably the longish blonde hair,

reminded me of Jessica Dubroff, the seven-year-old pilot who had crashed her plane and died tragically a few years back. The young girl standing before me brimmed with the same kind of spirit and spunk. It was in her eyes. She seemed a normal enough girl – except for the plumage, the beautiful wings.

I was shaking badly. My legs were as wobbly as the ones on my old kitchen table. *This isn't happening. It can't be happening. Get control of yourself right now. Take a deep breath.*

The girl stopped walking through the woods. Her white dress, a smock really, was torn and badly soiled. Her blonde hair was tangled and snarled.

She was very still, watching me. Like a hawk, so to speak. Had I found her, or was it the other way around? Was she tracking me?

I was dead sober this time. It was broad daylight.

This was real. She was as real as I was – sort of. And she was less than thirty yards away from me.

For a long, silent moment we stared at each other. The clearest green eyes looked out at me from her face. The green of her eyes was edged with yellow. Her eyes showed no fear, but her body language was cautious.

'Hi,' I said softly. 'Don't go. Please.'

I saw her eyes lower a notch to my hands.

I still gripped the animal trap. Ugly metal teeth and jaws attached to a rusty chain. The apparatus looked nasty, meant to maim.

Suddenly the girl looked frightened, very afraid. She

turned, and began to move away in a hurry.

She must have thought the trap belonged to me! No wonder she looked so horrified.

'It's not mine,' I called after her. 'Wait. Please.'

I dropped the wretched trap and scrambled up a steep gully after her. She was moving fast. I saw a flash of white far ahead of me.

Where in the name of God had she come from? Some kind of mind-boggling birth defect up here in the mountains? An experiment of some kind? *Things always go awry.*

The ground seemed to be fighting me as I climbed. Shale slid off underfoot and clattered down into the gully. I told myself not to run. She would think I was in pursuit. But I ran, anyway. I couldn't lose her.

'I won't hurt you,' I shouted. 'I'm a vet, a doctor.'

To my surprise, the young girl sped up. Why? Because I'd told her I was a doctor? I followed as quickly as I could through the deep, thick woods, but I soon realized that I'd lost her.

I felt sick, totally defeated. I'd had two great chances to make contact. What if I never saw her again? Had anyone else seen her around here?

Then I heard the sharp sound of cracking wood.

It came from straight above me.

I looked up.

The girl was poised on a sturdy branch of a tall oak. I was certain that she was no more than eleven or twelve. She was watching me again. Had she picked me out for some reason? And then, why me? I kept thinking of David and I didn't know why. What could possibly connect David to this young girl?

'Please. Don't run away. I won't hurt you. That animal trap wasn't mine – I was clearing it away. I hate it, too. My name is Frannie. What's your name?'

She didn't answer and I wondered if she *could* speak, or *how* she spoke. Instead, she spread her magnificent wings; they were like eagle wings or, perhaps, angel wings.

Suddenly, she leaped from the high branch. It was incredible. She looked like a high diver, the best I'd ever seen, or ever would see.

Then right before my eyes, she flew.

She actually flew like a bird. No, she flew as a young girl might fly, or a woman or a man, if people were meant to fly. She soared through the air.

And that changed the course of my life forever.

CHAPTER TWENTY-SIX

Nine-year-old Matthew couldn't stop himself from quivering like a damn Slinky toy on a steep flight of cold, stone stairs, headed down to a dungeon. He hadn't been able to stop shivering since he and Max left the School and they had separated for safety's sake.

Max, go right.

Matthew, go left.

It's our best chance. Go, go!

We'll meet again someday.

He wondered if he would ever see his big sister again, though. He couldn't imagine not seeing Max, and he almost couldn't bear that he hadn't seen her in two whole days.

They had never been apart for more than a few hours before. Being separated was how they were punished at the School, and it was the absolute hairy armpits for both of them. Uncle Thomas knew that, the cunning traitor. He had pretended to be their friend, but he was the one out here looking for them now. He was the one who would *put them to sleep.*

Matthew had to get his mind somewhere else for the moment. He couldn't lie here in this dark, slimy hiding place and think about missing Max. The trouble was, the worst thing, there was nothing else in his past that he missed. Oh, maybe the rec room TV, but not too much. Maybe the bad food at the School, but that was only because he was freaking starving now. Maybe Mrs Beattie, but she was dead. Probably murdered.

He tried to tell himself a joke, a dumb riddle: *How did a fool and his money get together in the first place?* He didn't laugh, not today, not out here in the dark cold with his face pressed down in the crummy old dirt.

He and Max had promised they would meet somehow, somewhere, and that was what kept him going. Man, he missed Max's smile. He even missed her little motor-mouth that never stopped flapping.

Matthew cocked his head and listened closely. He heard a noise nearby, down close to the ground. Rustling leaves? Footfall?

Just the wind whistling in the trees. Nothing else. He breathed a sigh of relief. And then—

'Matthew the Great? Come on out, kiddo. Come out of there. I know you're close. I've got footprints. I've got a bead on you, son. Is your lovely sister with you?'

It was Uncle Thomas, and now Matthew really began to shake. He felt sick to his stomach and he couldn't breathe very well and he thought he might die of a heart attack at nine years old.

'You've always been a good boy. We both know that, kiddo. Come out by yourself and I'll go easy on you. Pinkie swear, I will.'

He *had* always been good, obedient. Matthew did know that. He hated that Uncle Prick Thomas said 'pinkie swear.' That was something between Max and him, nobody else. They would join pinkies and make a promise to each other, 'pinkie swear' on it. Just Max and him.

He was busted now, though. No way out. The boy rose up on his wobbly legs. Man, he was shivering all over: legs, arms, the muscles of his face, even his butt. He was filthy, too, smelled awful, and it embarrassed him.

He peeked out of the hiding place.

There was Uncle Thomas. Several of his henchmen were with him. Man, he wanted to trust them. He even kind of wanted to go home.

'Ah, there you are, Matthew. There you are,' Uncle Thomas said. He sounded nice enough, sounded like a friend.

Uncle Thomas watched the stunning blond boy walk slowly forward. Matthew was good-looking, just like his sister. His wings were off-white, with silver and navy blue markings. An extraordinary specimen.

Matthew loved to tell jokes, and he told one now. He told jokes when he was nervous or scared. 'If you shoot a mime,' he said, 'should you use a silencer? Hardee-har-har.'

Uncle Thomas fired once. No silencer was necessary. Matthew, the good boy, flopped down hard on the forest floor.

BOOK 2

TINKERBELL LIVES

CHAPTER
TWENTY-SEVEN

Harding Thomas sat on the ground beside nine-year-old Matthew. He spoke softly, even tenderly. 'I'm sorry I had to use a stun gun on you. You know that I love you and Max.'

Matthew's eyes were red-rimmed and still tearing. It was hard not to feel pity for the small boy, but Thomas knew this wasn't the time for sentimentality. He had a job to do.

'I don't believe what you say anymore,' Matthew whispered.

'You used to believe me, Matthew. We were friends. I'm here now because I'm your friend. There was talk of putting you to sleep. I disagreed. I couldn't do that to you, son. Now I want you to help me find Max. You have to help me save her.'

Matthew spoke so softly it was difficult to hear him. 'What do I do? How can I save my sister?'

Thomas nodded approval and he finally smiled at the

boy. 'I want you to fly, and then call out for Max. You're the only one who can save Max.'

He showed something – it looked like a length of fishing line, a large spool.

'Listen to me closely,' he said, 'this clear line is imposs- ible to break. They use it to catch thousand-pound tuna in the Pacific. I'm giving you a hundred yards of line to run with. You follow me?'

'Yes, Uncle Thomas.'

'You are a good boy, and you're helping me save Max. Only you can save her now. Don't forget that.'

Uncle Thomas attached the tether to a khaki vest around Matthew's chest and waist. The other end was strung around a thick oak that sat high on the side of the mountain. This was as good as it was going to get. The trap for Max was set.

Thomas checked the tether to make sure it was secure. He had grown up on farms and ranches. He knew about animals and birds, how to treat them.

'Go ahead and fly. You have my permission. You also have my permission to call out for your sister. Now, fly! Go and fly, Matthew.'

Matthew did as he was told. He couldn't wait to get off the ground. With a sudden flourish he unfurled his wings. He ran as fast as he could away from the big oak until he figured he had enough speed for liftoff.

He flapped his wings hard and they appeared to unhinge. Then Matthew was airborne. He banked in a slow circle, drifting down a lazy vortex toward the rising sun.

He felt so free that for a few breathtaking seconds he almost forgot what he was doing, why he was up here.

But then he heard Uncle Thomas from his hiding place below. He hadn't believed a word that had come out of Thomas's mouth. He and the other guards were down there with rifles. They were a firing squad. They were killers, and they were going to shoot Max down as soon as she appeared.

'You call for her! I don't hear you yet, Matthew!'

Matthew flew out as far away as he could from Thomas and his taunting voice and the sturdy tree he was bound to.

He was thinking: *Can you see me, Max? Are you watching me fly? Are you nearby?*

Matthew finally began to yell at the top of his lungs. 'Max! Max! Max! Can you hear me?' he called. 'Can you?'

And then Matthew raised the volume. He knew what he had to do to save Max. He began to screech even louder.

'Stay away. Stay far away from me. Max! It's a trap! It's Uncle Thomas and the others. Get away from here, Max! They have guns.'

CHAPTER TWENTY-EIGHT

Max was nowhere near the place where her little brother was shouting his warnings. Another morning had broken. She'd made it through the night without being caught or torn into bite-sized pieces and eaten by a bear or a mountain cat.

She had a big breakfast and then played the CD-ROM game Tomb Raider II. She *loved* Lara Croft, the game's heroine. She wanted to be Lara Croft.

She left the safe house where she was hiding at around seven thirty in the morning. She wanted to explore.

Max peered through the interlaced branches and leaves of a bush covered with plump, ripe blueberries. She saw something that interested and terrified her at the same time. Her eyes blinked fast and hard a couple of times. Her pulse was racing just about off the charts.

She stared through the berry bushes at two little kids. They seemed a lot like her. Like her and Matthew, actually. The kids were obviously out on an early morning walkabout in the woods, too. Had they already spotted her?

The girl was dressed in blue-jean overalls, a Red Dirt T-shirt, high-top sneakers. It was a pretty cool outfit. Her red hair was half caught in a purple scrungie; the rest of it curled around her face. She was picking berries that matched the color of her funky nail polish.

The boy was probably four or five and reminded her of Matthew when he was that little. He was banging a rhythmic beat on an aluminum pail with a stick, singing a song Max had never heard before.

A-rumpty-rump-dump.

A-rumpty-rump-dump.

Max's skin rippled. Her inner voice urged her to fly away, but she was stuck. She had to stay there. Anyway, she wanted to talk up a storm to the kids. She desperately, desperately needed help, and she had secrets to share. God, did she have *huge* secrets to tell. What would Lara Croft do at a time like this?

A-rumpty-rump-dump.

She was definitely scared, but what was she afraid of, she wondered. She was bigger than either of them. She was a whole lot stronger. No contest there. She had special gifts, and she was probably smarter, too. No big deal, but she was.

The little boy looked up from his pail drum and spotted her green eyes staring into his bright blue ones. He stumbled backward, shouting, 'Hey! I see you! *Hey!* Who are you? Hey!'

Max was so unnerved, she screamed, and the two children began screaming, too.

The girl recovered first. She grabbed her brother's hand and gave it a good, strong jerk.

'Stop it, Bailey,' she commanded. She kept her distance but didn't back away farther. Her eyes were wide with fear. 'Who are you? This is *our* family's property. It's private property. Posted everywhere on the trees. You must have seen signs!'

The girl was probably around eight. She was huffing, puffing, and her face was beet-red, but she was putting up a brave big-sister front.

Max was impressed. God, she ached to talk to these kids, to play some games with them. She just wanted to *talk* to somebody.

'Who *are* you?' the girl asked again.

That, Max thought, was a very good question. As she considered it, the girl continued to talk at her. Nervous pitter-patter, which was okay with Max.

'I'm Elizabeth Ellers, all right. This is my little brother, Bailey. He's five. I'm nine. Now, what are you doing out here? Speak your piece.'

Little Bailey stared Max up and down, then he pulled away from Elizabeth and walked closer. He made a wide circle around Max.

Amused, she turned as he turned, trying to keep him from getting too good a look at her wings.

'What's wrong with your arms?' He blubbered a few words.

Max hesitated. What would these little kids think of her wings? Did she dare? She wanted to. She really wanted to.

She shrugged her shoulders, locked her elbows into position. Then Max slowly extended her forearms and the joints unfolded. Her feathers realigned with an enticing, whispering sound.

Bailey's and Elizabeth's blueberry-stained mouths dropped open – wide. Bailey *oohhed*, and popped his purple fingers into his mouth.

Max knew that her wings were quite beautiful. The primary feathers were arranged in tiers of snowy-white shafts; the barbs of each shaft nestled tightly against the next, forming an airtight seal. The undersides of the wings were lined with smaller secondary feathers, and her skin glowed through them. It was rosy-pink from freshly oxygenated blood.

Ooohh!

CHAPTER TWENTY-NINE

'Jeez caramba!' Bailey exclaimed. Whatever was that supposed to mean? *Jeez caramba? Cheese caramba?* Was that the way kids talked around here in the Colorado boonies? Guess so. *Jeez caramba? Okay, fine then.*

Max extended her index fingers, forcing her wings out to their fullest length. Her wingspan was nearly half again as wide as she was tall.

'*Oohh!*'

Bailey shrank back toward his sister. His blue eyes were bigger than ever. He was actually a little cutie, though.

'Are they real?' Elizabeth Ellers finally got up the nerve to speak again. 'They look like it.'

Max grinned. She knew she was trying to get the other kids to like her. 'Of course they're real.'

'Do it,' Bailey whispered. '*Please* do it. Fly for us.'

Elizabeth held Max's eyes. She whispered, too, as if this

were an outdoor church or something. 'We won't tell anybody. We promise.'

The small boy nodded solemnly. Up and down, up and down, and then sideways. He made a hurried sign of the cross where his heart was. 'Cross my heart and hope to die. Cross both our hearts. Please. Do it. Just do it.'

'If I do, you can't tell. It's just between us,' Max said. 'And *never* cross your heart and hope to die. It could happen.'

'We won't tell,' the boy said.

'If you do, I'll come get you.'

'Are you a vampire or something?' Bailey asked. He looked nervous and afraid again. His eyes crossed.

'Yeah, I'm a vampire. *No*, I'm not a vampire. Are you a little midget Martian? Are you from *Mars*?'

Elizabeth finally laughed out loud and Max could have hugged her. 'You got that right. He's definitely from Mars. What's your name?'

'Oh . . . *Tinkerbell*.'

They all shared a pretty good laugh. She wanted to show off, but she also wanted to share something about herself. She loved to share, actually. She had always been a good girl, thoughtful, kind to others. She believed that sharing was essential to a good life. There was one absolutely true thing she'd learned at the School: what goes around, comes around.

Max saw that the path ahead of her was flat and free of rocks and roots. She started to run.

It only took four or five steps before the air seemed to split around the thick leading edges of her wings. The air currents lifted her, raised her aloft.

'Jeez caramba!' she yelled, wondering if the kids got the humor.

She flew straight up – then dived at Bailey and Elizabeth. Instinctively they ducked, and Max laughed hysterically. She loved to play with other kids. Loved it more than anything.

And she desperately, desperately wanted to tell them the secrets. Except if she did, they would be in danger, too. Cross their hearts and hope to die.

Max beat her wings up and down, up and down. She was free-floating now! She circled overhead, tracing the outline of a cloud. Softly banked left, then right.

Down below, Elizabeth and Bailey Ellers watched in stunned silence. They held both hands out over their eyes, staring up intently without blinking.

Soon the kids were very small below her, but she could see their upturned faces, their O-shaped mouths perfectly. Max knew they couldn't help. They were too little; they were helpless themselves – helpless and clueless. Besides, she couldn't bear it if they got hurt because of her and what she knew.

She waved her hand 'bye-bye.' Bailey and Elizabeth waved back.

'We won't tell!' Bailey hollered. 'Cross our – *nothing*.'

'Come back,' Elizabeth Ellers called. 'We can be friends.'

Max missed them terribly, almost before they were out of sight. Bailey and Elizabeth. Nice kids. Good people. Maybe they could have been friends if she could have hung around for a while.

And she missed Matthew, of course. She missed her own little brother so much. It tore a huge, ragged hole in the center of her chest.

As she soared high across the brightly golden meadowland that adjoined the woods, she felt achy and alone. Inside somewhere, she knew she wasn't meant to be alone.

She was just a little kid herself.

A-rumpty-rump-dump.

A-rumpty-rump-dump.

CHAPTER THIRTY

David's arms were thrown limply over my shoulders, and I was dragging him through a desolate, bone-white desert that seemed familiar. The sun was a big clock in the sky and the second hand was ticking off the seconds between life and death. I'd been here before.

'Hurry, Frannie. Please,' David panted. He whispered hoarsely against my cheek. 'I'm sorry, sweetheart, but you have to hurry. We don't have much time.'

I was tired, so tired from dragging David's limp form, and yet I couldn't put him down. 'Hold on,' I said to David. 'Please.' I felt his warm sticky blood at the back of my neck and my hair bristled. Tears flowed down my cheeks.

'I'm here,' he said. 'I'll always be here for you.'

His feet dragged in the sand. He was so heavy. I adjusted my grip, but didn't stop moving forward. My arm muscles were incredibly sore and weary. I could feel his heartbeat against my back, but it was faint, almost gone.

As he always did, David began to tell me stories about our marriage. Joyful, happy stories that only reminded me about how full our life had been. Two successful practices; serious talk about having a child, maybe two or three kids if we were lucky.

'We should have had kids, Frannie. We shouldn't have waited.'

'Don't,' I said. 'Please don't, David. I don't want to hear this.'

But he wouldn't stop. 'Remember our fifth anniversary? We stayed at that perfect little inn in Vermont, you know the one. Made love all day, Frannie. Had breakfast, lunch and dinner in bed,' he said.

'Of course I remember, David. I'll never forget Vermont.'

He started to hum. It was the lovely, haunting theme from *A Man and a Woman*. He'd adored that movie. I had, too. We'd seen it five or six times. I stopped walking suddenly.

'Are we there?' David asked.

I looked into the distance. I saw only the glare and shimmering heat of the endless desert.

'Yes,' I said. 'We're here.'

I let David down from my back and tenderly laid him out under the sun. I stretched his strong arms straight out to the sides. His hands and feet were bleeding; so was the gaping bullet wound near his heart.

'I'm sorry for what I did,' David said. 'I'm so sorry, Frannie.' I didn't understand what he was saying, why he was sorry, but I nodded as if I did.

I took off all of my clothes and made the softest

possible pillow of them. I tucked the pillow of clothes gently under his head. It was the single most heartbreaking thing I have ever done.

'Thank you,' said David. He looked at me with clear, loving eyes. 'I knew you wouldn't let me die.'

Then David died again – just the way he always did, every single morning.

The alarm on my windowsill went off. I awoke from the disturbing dream. It seemed so real, but of course David had died in a parking lot in Boulder, not in some mysterious desert.

I opened my eyes in my tiny bedroom at the animal hospital. My bare arms were stretched back and holding on to the headboard above me. My eyes were teary, my cheeks wet. My chest ached, as if I'd been struck with a hammer. I remembered that not so long ago I'd had a good life. There had been someone I loved, and who loved me.

I kicked off the jumble of blankets. An image came to me and shocked me a little. The dream, the nightmare fantasy, was starting to break up, and though I was losing the pictures, I felt steeped in shame.

I saw a man with blond hair in a denim shirt. He was wearing a smile as bright as the sun. I saw myself turning toward him.

I got up quickly from the mess of covers that was my bed. Why should I feel so ashamed?

I blinked away the unbidden image of Kit Harrison, and walked to the window that faced back into the woods. I threw it open and breathed deeply. I could almost taste the pines and grass.

A faint morning breeze brushed across my damp skin. I began to feel better. I had started to turn away from the window when I heard it. A horrifying sound that chilled me to the bone.

CHAPTER THIRTY-ONE

The long, wailing screech that I heard coming from the nearby woods was ghastly. It took me only a minute to throw on jeans, workboots, the same T-shirt I'd worn the day before.

I stopped in the minilab long enough to fill a syringe with Ketamine hydrochloride, and I put the anesthetic in my knapsack. Pip was barking loudly for breakfast, but he would have to wait. I couldn't take the time.

'I'll be back,' I shouted as I bolted for the door and burst outside.

The continuing sound of shrill screaming pierced my eardrums. The dew soaked my shoes and I slipped a couple of times but I kept on running as fast as I could.

I followed the pitiful sound, almost certain that I knew where it was coming from and what had happened.

The woods behind my clinic slope down toward a deep stream, almost a small river. Winter runoff had cut deep gullies into the woods. In summer the gullies are dry and partially filled with woodland debris. Choice places for predators to hunt for rodents.

Choice, too, for trappers to set illegal traps.

The high-pitched yipping got louder and then stopped abruptly as the animal panted for breath. When it started up again, the sound nearly broke my heart.

I made my way across the top of a gully and finally saw the fox. The beautiful, reddish-brown animal was dangling down in the gorge by one foreleg, scrabbling futilely with the other. It was a terrible, wrenching sight.

I saw what had happened.

A trap had slammed shut on the fox. It tried to pull itself free and had backed up over the edge of the chasm. The leg was gripped by the teeth and chain of the trap, and the fox's body banged and scraped against the gully's wall.

My stomach balled up. This was such needless, gruesome torture. For what? Somebody's expensive coat in Aspen or Denver? The female was in agony; she was going mad, and why shouldn't she?

'Hang on,' I said to the fox, in a low, unthreatening voice. 'I'm coming.'

Oh, God, I'm not going to hurt you, little foxie.

The trap chain was double-looped and locked around the tree. I rattled the lock hard, but it wouldn't release.

'Damn it!'

I thought of trying to haul the fox up by the chain, but she'd bite me. Besides, I forgot to take my gloves and she might be rabid.

I hurriedly looked for a place to climb down. The gorge

wall was lined with loose shale. I found what I thought was a good safe spot and decided to chance it. No good. The shale gave way and I made the ten-foot descent on my butt.

My noisy approach sent the fox into increased fear and frenzy. She was terrified, snapping her jaws and drooling from the mouth. I saw that the leg was completely engloved. The trap's teeth were gripping bare bone.

'It's okay, girl.'

I stood below the fox and looked for some way to inject her with the Ketamine. There was a nearby ledge on a level with my shoulders, but it was obviously too thin and too narrow. I didn't trust myself to hang on to it and get the needle into her leg at the same time.

The fox's continual high-pitched whine was driving me crazy. Soon she'd go into shock, and very soon after that she'd die.

I knew I couldn't save her by myself.

CHAPTER THIRTY-TWO

K it was slugging a long, arcing home run high over the famed 'Green Monster' wall in Boston's Fenway Park. His two boys were watching from seats along the first-base line. Suddenly he was torn from his baseball heroics, the remnants of sleep.

There was a loud, insistent banging at the cabin door. He placed his hand on the rifle he kept under the bed, slid it along the floorboards.

'Yeah? Who is it?' he called. He pushed himself to a sitting position so that he could see through the window.

He parted the curtain and saw Frannie O'Neill with the serious frown she usually wore for his benefit. She always managed to look good to him.

What now? What did she want?

He stepped into his jeans, zipped his fly, buttoned up. More impatient banging on the door. *Where was a clean shirt? To hell with a shirt.*

'I'm coming.'

He opened the door, but before he could ask what crime he'd committed Frannie started to speak a blue streak of fast, barely intelligible words.

'I need your help,' she said. 'Please. I *really* need you to help, Mr Harrison.'

Mr Harrison? 'Sure. No problem. Shoes,' he said, and ducked inside to grab his sneakers.

He followed her, bare-chested, as she sprinted ahead of him to a rocky gorge a few hundred yards back into the woods. He could hardly keep up with her. She could really move on those long legs of hers. *Mr Harrison was it now?*

'What the—' He stopped in midsentence.

It took him only a second or two to recognize what it was that was hanging from nasty metal jaws and jangling chains.

'Oh, Jesus, Frannie.'

The fox was a sickening sight, and he finally understood why she hated hunters so much, why she had been so mad at him since he arrived – with a gun.

The poor animal's reddish-brown coat was soaked and spattered with fresh blood. The fur and flesh on its foreleg had been stripped forward from elbow to paw by the teeth of the leghold trap. Its breath was coming hard. Its intermittent barking was hoarse and weak.

'I can't reach her,' Frannie panted. She was out of breath. 'I tried it by myself. No use.'

She looked as if she were going to break down, and Kit felt choked up with the same emotion. What had happened to the young fox was cruel and heartbreaking, and it made him angry, too. How could anybody do this to an animal?

'What do you want me to do? How can I help?'

She held a syringe clasped tightly in her hand. 'I have to get this into her leg.'

'Okay. I got you.'

Kit skittered down the steep, muddy slope. He surveyed the gorge from top to bottom. Then he climbed back up.

He squatted above the fox that was suspended about three feet below the edge. He measured and weighed the animal with his eyes. Then he quickly scanned the underbrush for a fallen branch.

'This could work,' he called to Frannie.

It was about three feet long and only a couple of inches in diameter.

She looked perplexed. 'What are you doing? What could work?'

It was easier to demonstrate than to explain. Kit lowered himself until his face and shoulders were hanging over the lip of the gully.

'Please be careful,' he heard her say.

He brought the stick close to the fox's mouth. She was spraying foam with every exhaled breath and her eyes were dulling over. Kit wondered if she could even see him.

He touched the wood to the fox's lips.

She snapped wildly, clamped her teeth hard around the branch, tried to break it in two.

Would the damn branch hold? Kit slowly, slowly, eased

the fox up, up ... and finally over the edge of the embankment.

'Stick her, now,' he gasped.

Frannie was right there. She jabbed the needle into the animal's hind leg. Pushed the plunger. The fox kicked, then collapsed as the drug took effect.

Kit caught the animal as it dropped like a furry, stuffed toy into his arms.

'Well done,' said Frannie. 'God, we did it.'

She took the fox from him and gently laid it down on the ground. Kit yanked open the trap's trigger mechanism and Frannie carefully released the animal's leg.

'Very well done. Wow. Thank you. Thank you. You're a great paramedic partner.'

'You're welcome. It was nice working with you. What a team. Glad we could help Foxie Lady.'

And wonder of wonders – Frannie O'Neill finally gave him a smile.

It was almost worth the wait.

CHAPTER THIRTY-THREE

'Yahoo, Mountain Dew!'

Max was flying again. She couldn't resist the fluffy clouds, the high-pitched whistle of the wind, the perfect, deep blue skies over the Rockies. *Who could?* She drifted calmly, effortlessly, as she surveyed a lake below, the wooded slopes of surrounding ridges.

The slate-black surface of the lake drew her closer. She could see thermal inversions rising off the water. Her teacher, her friend, Mrs Beattie, had told her about wind currents, and how hot and cold affected flight. Max still retained all the information; that was one of her gifts.

Her wingspan cast an elongated shadow on the dark treetops below. Max watched the shadow, raced with it. She reached out, then ahead, then back, as if she were rowing. She flew faster and faster over the curved rim of the earth.

Mrs Beattie, she thought. *The School, her old home.*

She could remember it vividly, only mostly she didn't want to. She couldn't help remembering, though – especially the worst things, and there were so many of them to choose from.

Early one morning, Mrs Beattie had come to the small dormitory where she and Matthew slept. Mrs Beattie had been their teacher for three years. Before Mrs Beattie, there had been nannies, and other tutors; but they had changed all the time. None of them had showed very much love or caring. It wasn't allowed at the School. Just science, work, discipline, testing, testing, testing.

'Max . . . Matthew,' Mrs Beattie had whispered. Max was awake instantly, even before her teacher was at her bedside.

'We're awake,' Matthew squawked. 'We heard you coming.'

'Of course you did, dear. Now listen to me. Don't speak until I've finished.'

It was something bad – Max could tell it was. Neither she nor Matthew said a word.

'Sometimes bad things happen to good people,' Mrs Beattie whispered. Besides being a teacher, she was a doctor. She administered exams, especially the ones to test intelligence – Stanford-Binet, WPPSI-R, WISC III, the Beery Tests, Act III, all the rest.

'They're going to put us to sleep, kill us, right? We've been expecting it.' Matthew couldn't keep quiet for too long.

'No, dear. You're both very special. You're miracle children. You don't have to worry. But darlings, little Adam was put to sleep last night. I'm so sorry to have to tell you.'

'Oh, no, not Adam! Not Adam!' Matthew moaned.

He and Max hugged Mrs Beattie tightly and they couldn't stop weeping, couldn't stop shivering. Adam was only a little baby. He had the most beautiful blue eyes, and he was so smart.

'I have to leave now, dear. I didn't want you to hear this from Mr Thomas. I love you, Max. Love you, Matthew.' She hugged them close to her. 'Don't think badly of me.'

Soon after that, Mrs Beattie was gone, too. One day, she just never came back to the School. They never saw or heard from her again. Max was sure she had been put to sleep.

Max suddenly realized that she was flying too fast and without looking where she was going. The memory of the School had upset her.

She changed direction and went into a steep climb toward the sun. Its brilliance shattered her vision, a blizzard of multicolored shades. Blinded, Max kept climbing, drawing in air that grew cooler and thinner in her lungs.

Finally, when she couldn't stand it for a second more, she looped the loop. Then she went into a nose dive.

She fell straight toward the shimmering blue water of the lake.

Her wings felt glued to her sides. The air roared in her

ears. Her lungs burned. She hit the water at a perfect angle.

Splashdown!

Unbelievable!

God, how she loved to fly.

CHAPTER THIRTY-FOUR

Harding Thomas stopped for coffee and a sugar hit at the Quik Stop in Bear Bluff. 'Coffee, black as my heart,' he said to the counter clerk.

That was when he overheard the big-eyed, red-headed kids babbling to their mother near the freezer full of Ben & Jerry's ice cream.

Thomas wasn't really listening to the kids as he was handed his coffee, not until he heard, 'She was like a big, beautiful bird, Mommy. Like a Power Ranger, 'cept she was a real girl.'

Harding Thomas jerked to full attention when he heard that little mouthful of news. He almost dropped his coffee. Spilled some steaming java on his hiking boots.

The kids' mother was wandering toward the checkout counter, mesmerized by the latest issue of *People* magazine. Her floppy thongs slapped the worn-out tan-and-brown linoleum floor. She was about thirty-five, fat folds rolling over the top of baggy Champion shorts.

The kids were cute, though, and they sure were animated.

Thomas snatched a Snickers off a snack rack on the counter. He walked toward the checkout line, too. He stood behind the mother and her kids.

Mama had apparently communicated to the kids to shut up in the public place. Good advice, but a little too late.

'I overheard your kids. A flying girl from outer space,' he said with a pleasant chuckle and smile. 'Just like you read about in that crazy rag, the *Star.*' He hooked his thumb toward one of the tabloid newspapers displayed near the counter.

'We *did* see a flying girl,' the boy insisted, blew his cover immediately. 'Didn't we, Elizabeth?'

His sister shot him a warning look, but the boy didn't care. Thomas looked skeptical, which was no problem. He was hoping to draw them out some more, and he was unusually good with kids.

Two mountain bikers entered the minimart just then. They were plastered in mud, carrying helmets, wearing bike shoes. Thomas hoped they wouldn't hear anything. Fortunately, they continued to the rear of the store.

'Bailey, Bailey,' the mother said. 'What am I going to do with you?'

She turned to Thomas, smoothing her henna-colored hair with her hand, self-conscious under his gaze. 'They watched *Hook* on video the other night. Now what does he see? Tinkerbell flying about in the woods, right. So he says. I suppose it's a good thing.' She smiled. 'He has a truckload of imagination and they say it leads to creativity later on.'

The boy's voice cracked with hurt and indignation. 'I'm not making this up! We saw the girl in the woods near the blueberry bog. She *said* her name was Tinkerbell and she flew real high over the trees. Cross my heart.'

Harding Thomas thought he knew the place they were talking about. He'd been through the bog a couple of times with his search team, but they hadn't seen any trace of Max. He tossed two singles onto the counter, then said 'So long,' in the general direction of the woman and her children.

CHAPTER THIRTY-FIVE

Thomas followed the woman and her kids in his off-white Range Rover. The family had an old, dented, and weather-beaten Isuzu pickup. The mother wasn't in any big hurry to get home from the Quik Stop and following them couldn't have been easier.

As Thomas tailed the pickup, he thought about his life. Once upon a time, he'd taught science at the Air Force Academy. He'd been a captain. Dr Peyser had contacted and recruited him for a job. He had explained his dream, and Harding Thomas understood and believed the first time he heard it. He wasn't the only one. And he believed that the dream, the vision of the future, was worth protecting. So he followed the Ellers family from the Quik Stop.

When the pickup pulled into a deep-rutted, weed-infested driveway, Thomas understood why the family wasn't hurrying home. The house was a disaster.

The off-white paint was blistering and peeling on every surface. The front porch sagged and almost looked dangerous to walk on. The grass near the house was at least a foot and a half high. The name Ellers was nearly faded off the mailbox.

The mother and her kids were just getting out of the truck. Thomas accelerated, and pulled in behind the Isuzu. The woman looked up alarmed. So did the two kids.

Harding Thomas hopped out of the Range Rover, threw his hands in the air, produced a big, friendly grin. He played Uncle Thomas for them. He could appear to be everybody's friend when he needed to.

'Hey. Hi, kids, remember me? No need for alarm. Smile, you're on *Candid Camera*! I just had a thought about what the kids might have seen in the woods. Thought it might be important to you.'

'I didn't say I saw anything,' the older girl protested, 'because I didn't. Neither did my extraterrestrial brother. He's a big fat storyteller, that's all.'

'Mister, I don't think—' The woman started to say something.

'They saw an eleven-year-old *girl with wings*.' Harding Thomas stopped her in midsentence. 'I believe what the boy said. The truth is, I've seen the girl myself. I'd like to tell you what I know and you can do the same for me.

'May I come in for a few minutes? I promise, this is vitally important. Your children are telling the truth, strange as it sounds.'

Harding Thomas produced his wallet, and a card that identified him as a lawyer with the Justice Department.

Thomas wasn't with Justice, but the business card worked like a charm.

The Ellers family had to be questioned, and then, unfortunately, they had to disappear.

They had seen Tinkerbell.

They went inside and Harding Thomas tried to make the question and answer period as nonthreatening as possible.

'I know this is weird, and a little scary, kids,' he told them. 'I'm a little shook up myself.'

'Would you like coffee, sir?' the woman asked him. He wasn't sure how well the fake ID had worked with the kids, but it had certainly gone over with her.

'It's Thomas,' he said, 'and coffee would be great. I just had a cup, but I could sure use another under the circumstances.'

The mother went off to make coffee – probably instant, but at least she was out of the way for the moment.

'You can call me Uncle Tommy,' he said to the two wide-eyed kids.

'We didn't see anything,' the girl continued to insist. 'My brother belongs in a loony bin.'

'We saw the girl with wings. We saw her fly!' the boy thrust out his chin and proclaimed.

'No, we didn't.' His sister stared him down.

Harding Thomas brought his first down hard on the living-room coffee table.

'Yeah, you did! You saw the girl, and you saw her fly. Now tell me everything else – or I'm going to hurt you and your mama. You look in my eyes, and know what I'm saying is the truth.'

The two children looked – and they knew, and they told what they knew about the girl with wings.

CHAPTER THIRTY-SIX

Kit made the forty-mile drive from Bear Bluff to Boulder. He was *definitely* starting to feel like an agent again, to feel like the Tom Brennan of old.

He parked the black Jeep on a congested side street a few blocks from Boulder Community Hospital. As he walked there he saw evidence of the city's celebrated mix of '60s hippies, 'granolas' from the '80s, Gen-Xers, and plenty of relatively normal-looking, Rocky Mountain High natives, too.

Mostly, though, he was looking over his shoulder, afraid that he might be followed, that someone had already spotted him.

He needed to talk to a Dr John Brownhill at the hospital's in vitro clinic. Dr Brownhill had past associations with two of the murdered doctors in San Francisco and Cambridge, Massachusetts. It was all recorded in Kit's earlier reports at the FBI.

As he sat in the waiting room, he couldn't help noticing

how user-friendly the clinic was. The walls were painted a soft yellow and there were fresh-cut flowers on the magazine tables. That was good for the mothers-to-be, and it was good for him, too. He needed to relax some if he could.

'The doctor will see you, Mr Harrison,' said a tall black receptionist who was sunny and pleasant. Everyone he saw at the clinic seemed that way, soothing and helpful.

'The doctor's office is just down the hall, first door on the right. You can't miss it.'

He walked purposefully down a plush beige-carpeted hallway to Dr Brownhill's office. He took a quick, deep breath before he turned inside. *Here we go.*

Dr Brownhill was impressive to meet. Silver streaks were beginning to show in his long, reddish-brown hair. His complexion was ruddy. He looked to be in excellent physical shape. He had a toothy, Andy Hardy smile that was disarming. It seemed to Kit that he'd have a wonderfully reassuring bedside manner.

'I'm a little curious, Mr Harrison. You're here alone. Is this visit about your wife? Or perhaps a girlfriend?'

Kit still wasn't quite sure how he should play the tricky interview. There were a lot of ways to go.

'I'm a senior agent with the FBI,' he said in a self-important tone he rarely used in the field. 'I'm in Colorado as part of a murder investigation.'

It was a subtle thing, lasting only an instant, but he caught a slight tic under John Brownhill's right eye. 'I don't understand,' the doctor said. 'A murder investigation?'

Kit's face betrayed nothing. 'You came here from San

Francisco? You were at University Hospital there. Another in vitro clinic.'

Brownhill nodded. 'Five years ago, and I've never regretted the move. I can't imagine why the FBI would want to talk to me, though. Murder investigation? I help couples have babies they otherwise wouldn't be able to have.'

Kit peered into the doctor's eyes, measuring him. 'Did you know Dr James Kim while you were working in San Francisco?'

'Yes, I knew James Kim. Not very well, I'm afraid. We were both in California around the same time. Please tell me what this is about. I have pregnant women waiting out there to see me.'

Kit nodded sympathetically. 'I interviewed Dr Kim in May. He was involved with illegal experiments in the Bay area. He told me that a doctor by the name of Anthony Peyser was hiding out here in Colorado. He said that both he and you had worked with Dr Peyser.'

Dr Brownhill shook his head. 'Now wait a minute. That's simply not true. Yes, Dr Peyser was accused of unethical practices in the lab he supervised at Berkeley. But I had nothing to do with the lab or with the experiments. I've never been accused of any wrongdoing, and I'm certainly not in hiding.'

Kit lowered his voice. 'Do you know that James Kim is dead? He was murdered a week ago in California. That's part of the reason I'm here.'

John Brownhill seemed genuinely surprised. 'I didn't know. I'm sorry to hear about Dr Kim. I still don't see how

I can help you, though. I have no idea what happened to Dr Peyser.'

Dr Brownhill tried to get up and leave. Kit held up a hand. 'I have one other subject. It's important, doctor. Would you tell me about Dr David Mekin? You worked with Dr Mekin here as well as in San Francisco. I understand that the two of you were friends. David Mekin was *murdered*. Is that a coincidence, too?'

Dr Brownhill rose from the chair at his desk. 'You'll have to excuse me now. I have patients to see. David Mekin was a friend and I don't care to revisit his death again.'

Kit took his time getting to his feet. He left the in vitro clinic. He thought that he'd accomplished what he needed to do.

He had gotten a doctor there uncomfortable, gotten him to hedge and probably lie. He had rattled some cages, and that was a good start.

CHAPTER THIRTY-SEVEN

N ight had fallen across the foothills east of the Rockies. The sky was a dense midnight blue and covered with gleaming stars. The security team crouched at the edge of the clearing near the summer house.

They wore night goggles and looked like a police or army strike force about to move into serious action.

They had the girl. They'd spotted her not too far from the blueberry bog.

The house was a perfectly yuppified weekend place, a modern A-frame with enormous windows looking out on the mountains. Nouveau riche folks from southern California owned it and only stayed there on weekends.

Harding Thomas took in all the details. It was just after ten and the place was mostly dark. Except for the grayish-blue light in one downstairs room. Then a brighter, almost white light.

A television set was on, and she *loved* TV. She called the TV at the School her 'mom and pop,' 'the baby-sitter,' and her 'pal.'

'Let's get her now,' Thomas whispered to the others. 'She's eleven, but she's strong,' he warned. 'She's stronger than most men. She has a *designer* chest and shoulders.'

'What is she, supergirl?' one of the others asked.

'That's about right,' Harding Thomas told the man. 'You'll see if you screw up. Just don't think of her as an eleven-year-old girl.'

The steps to the first level of the deck were tight and practically new and they squeaked. Harding Thomas stepped around pots of geraniums stacked on the landing. There were three pairs of discarded in-line skates, Roces Barcelonas.

The hunters adjusted their night goggles. They climbed the next flight of stairs in a hurry, making more squeaking noises. They brushed past metal deck furniture, moving even faster now. It was the same team that had taken out Dr Frank McDonough in his swimming pool.

Light through the picture window continued to glow and flicker. It was definitely light from a TV. Thomas peered inside, saw a family room laid out before him.

Halogen lamps, all of them off. A telescope on a tripod. A DUB video player. Custom armchairs upholstered in burlap coffee bean bags that read 'Product of Guatemala, 50-lbs' and 'Product of Yemen, 50-lbs.'

An overstuffed sofa sat right under the window. Max

was lying on it. She was asleep, curled up in her own wings.

'Thank God,' Harding Thomas whispered under his breath.

CHAPTER THIRTY-EIGHT

Max heard the *squeak, squeak, squeak*. The noise was coming from outside on the deck. She pictured everything that was supposed to be out there.

She kept her eyes closed, but she was awake and alert and knew something very wrong was going on outside the house. She'd been dozing under a musty old Indian blanket. Now she felt a cold shadow fall between herself and the moon.

She slipped open her eyes, tilted up, and there he was – Uncle Thomas had found her. That traitor, that terrible liar.

He was standing outside the picture window. He'd brought along his sidekicks. Three or four other men. Trackers! Hunters! Killers!

Max's mind and her body screamed, FLY.

FLY, FLY, FLY AWAY FROM HERE!

She couldn't fly, though. Not in the living room with its low ceilings and the clutter of heavy furniture.

You're strong. Incredibly strong.
Be strong now!

So Max rolled real fast off the sofa. A table toppled over. Magazines went flying – *Los Angeles, Variety, Hollywood Reporter, Details.*

A metal chair came crashing through the window! Reflexively, she threw her arms over her face. Shards and splinters of glass showered everywhere around her and cut her, but not too badly.

'NO!' she screamed at the top of her voice. 'Get away from me! Get away!'

The long hallway between the living room and the bedroom stretched out before her, beckoned.

Be strong! Be gone!

Moonlight white as bone streamed through the bedroom door that was half open at the end of the hall. A Jacuzzi encased in lime-green terrazzo was visible off the bedroom. Max flung herself toward the bedroom with full speed and full strength.

Don't look back! Just go, go, go! You're a lot faster than they think you are. And maybe, just maybe, they don't want you dead after all.

The bedroom window was open – her escape hatch. She'd left it that way – just in case she needed one. And boy, did she ever need one.

She took off halfway down the hall. She was flying real fast *inside the house* and this was beyond tricky, beyond smart, beyond sane.

She didn't know if she could pull it off, though. Would this work? Could it?

But then she found herself shooting through the open window like a missile leaving its halo, only the halo was almost too small for the missile. Her wing clipped the frame. Wood splintered! Pain stabbed her bad shoulder! 'Ouch,' she cried out.

But Max was flying again – and for the second time, somebody was shooting at her. Trying to kill her? Or just wing and capture her?

'Screw you, Uncle Thomas!' she yelled at the top of her voice, not even bothering to look back. 'Go to hell.'

He yelled at her. 'I've got Matthew! I've got your brother, all right. You come back. I've got Peter Pan.'

CHAPTER THIRTY-NINE

Max was shivering badly as she hid in the crown of the tallest, fullest fir tree she could find. If she couldn't see them, then she figured that the hunters couldn't see her. Was that true? Was that the way it worked? She prayed that it was so.

What was it that Uncle Thomas had yelled? His exact words? *I got Matthew?* . . . *Or, I've got Matthew?*

Were they out here trying to kill her? Or just get her back to the School?

She knew this much: 'Visitors' had come to the School . . . to see her and Matthew. To examine them carefully and talk about them . . . and then what?

Max couldn't stop the shaking, couldn't make her teeth stop chattering, hitting together until they hurt. She began to cry. She couldn't stop crying. She was sobbing like a baby.

Little baby! she mocked herself. *Cry baby! Cry baby! Cry, cry, cry your baby eyes out.*

She was lying on her belly and legs. Her arms were wrapped for dear life around a stout, knobby branch. Soon exhaustion overcame her and her eyes simply closed. Just like that, all systems were down.

Max slept. At least she hadn't been put to sleep. She hadn't been caught. Not yet, anyway.

Her mind was in a terrible turmoil when she opened her eyes again. She couldn't believe that she'd let herself fall asleep. How much time had passed? Minutes? Hours? Where was Uncle Thomas and the other security guards? His little band of killers?

It was still night, and she was still hugging the big, gnarly branch as if it were her best and only friend in the world. About a mile away, the house she'd been staying in was silhouetted against the moonlit sky. All the lights were off now.

She couldn't make out movement or sounds anywhere in the woods. No hunters. No Uncle Thomas.

Only when she was sure the immediate danger had passed did Max feel the terrible, aching pain of loss. The house was no longer safe for her. She was homeless again. She wished Matthew were here and just the thought of him brought tears to her eyes.

I got Matthew!

Or – I've got Matthew!

She had to think, to remember the precise sound of the words.

Which was it? Was her little brother alive, or had they put him to sleep? Was poor Matthew dead?

A strange, high-pitched humming sound broke into her

thoughts. It increased steadily in volume. *Hummmmmm.* That was the sound.

She looked up and Max saw tiny lights tacking across the sky. The lights came closer, and the noise got even louder.

It's a bird, it's a plane, it's . . . a *plane!*

She'd seen airplanes fly over the School now and again. American Airlines, America West, United, smaller jets and prop-planes. Whenever she saw an airplane, she wanted to fly. But it had been forbidden. *You fly – you die!* That was the School motto. Catchy, huh?

Stars blinked and twinkled everywhere, and the full moon had a kindly look on its face. It was as if the man in the moon himself were looking down on her. He seemed like an okay guy, but right now Max didn't trust *anybody*.

She had an idea. A crazy one, maybe. Take it to the Max, she thought. That was her motto, and she was definitely living by those words now.

She stood up on the wide, sturdy tree branch, bounced a little on the balls of her feet. She still had her trusty ballet slippers, though they were wearing a little thin.

She spread her wings, let them rise above her head. Max took a slow, deep breath. Let it out. Took in another one, just like the first.

'You fly – you die,' she whispered.

Then she pushed off and flew.

CHAPTER FORTY

U nbelievable!
The night air was cool and damp and thick as
she cut through it as fast as a missile. The air
stung her cheeks, numbed her nose, made tears slip out of
her eyes.

God, it was so cool, so wonderful, so magnificent to fly.
She couldn't have even imagined how it would feel. No
one could, unless you did it yourself, and who could do it
but her? The pleasure of free flight overrode all thought,
all other bodily sensations. She just let it happen. She
stretched her wings and the air seemed to suck her
upward as if it had a will all its own.

The thumbs of her hand, the dulas, or bastard wings,
knew what to do automatically. Reflexively, she spread
them outward, and immediately they acted as slats would,
bleeding air through the slots, re-establishing airflow over
the top of her wings, giving them lift.

She continued up, and up, higher than she had ever

been before. Everything was so distant and tiny down below. She was nearly on a level with the approaching, groaning plane.

The air around the plane's propellers churned up the entire night sky. She understood the man-made machine's incredible power for the first time. As hard as she beat her wings, Max found that she was suddenly flying in place.

Then, for a split second, she was outside the brightly lit cockpit. Maybe twenty or thirty yards away. She could see inside.

The pilot turned in her direction. She thought that he saw her – just for an instant. Probably not enough time for him to be sure of what he was seeing.

She winked at him. Made a face. She loved to play, and she just couldn't resist.

Then Max closed her wings and did a fancy loop that propelled her away from the plane and any danger of a collision.

See that, mister big-shot pilot? I don't need a man-made plane to fly. I just need a little sky space.

I was made for this.

CHAPTER FORTY-ONE

I knocked on the cabin door, the cabin that I *own*, the little house where David and I had lived once upon a time. This was right up there with the weirdest things I've done in a while, and I occasionally do talk to geese and chipmunks.

But since Kit Harrison had gone out on a limb for me, literally, and since he was handsome as sin, I felt it was only right to accept his invitation to dinner that night. He had even promised to cook.

I'd put on a weathered, chambray shirt and clean jeans. Clean, semipressed clothes – imagine that. Even a few drops of Hermès perfume I'd bought once upon a time in Aspen. I also had a bottle of decent Pinot Noir in the crook of my arm.

Very, very weird. Bringing a bottle of wine as a gift to my own house.

When Kit Harrison pulled open the door I noticed three things immediately: the clean shave, the fresh haircut, the smell of good old-fashioned Ivory soap.

'Where'd you get the haircut?' I asked.

'You don't like it?' he said, and looked a little hurt.

I was surprised he was so sensitive about it, or anything else. He hadn't seemed the type. Actually, he was surprising me in a lot of ways. I had been too tough on him in the beginning, and he'd even taken that well.

'Bob's Hair Joint. In town,' he said. 'Do I look really bad?'

'No, I like it. It's very nice. You look great, actually. Bob Hatfield did a *great* job.'

'Thanks,' he said, and showed his modified Tom Cruise smile. The way Cruise did in *Jerry McGuire*, cocky and yet vulnerable at the same time. He took the bottle of wine from me, opened it with a flourish, poured two glasses.

'You look pretty great yourself,' he said. 'Honestly, you do.'

'Thanks.' Suddenly I was the shy and vulnerable one. In my own house.

Kit handed me one of my wineglasses, originally purchased at Marshall Fields' in Chicago, if I remembered correctly. I sipped some, then went to the refrigerator and put ice in the glass.

'Water that vino down,' he said, and grinned again. 'We don't want this dinner to get out of hand.'

'It's not that. I always drink wine coolers.' I told a little white lie. Time was when David and I partied a bit – in Boulder, here in Bear Bluff, in Denver. Life had been good to us. For a while, anyway.

Actually, this was the first time in a year and a half that

I'd stood in this room, in the presence of a man, and David's image and taste were everywhere; overflowing bookshelves, familiar couch, the muted watercolors of northern Wisconsin on the walls. I had spent so many hours obsessing about David's senseless murder. I felt scared, but I couldn't tell Kit why. I felt a little guilty, too, though there was no reason to be. Was there?

I made funny, polite chatter about the fox and how she was doing and then I asked if I could help out with dinner.

'I think I've got it all under control. Thanks, anyway,' he said. He was doing better than controlling it; he was mastering the chicken breasts, the garlicked green beans, the grilled, red potatoes, a miso salad. The smell of it made my tongue get up on its hind legs and beg.

Kit had his back turned to me, which was a good thing. I let out a big, deep breath. I couldn't believe how nervous I was, how excited, how completely over the top my emotions were.

I accidentally brushed his butt as I got silverware out of the drawer. Firm, sculpted, very pleasant to brush against. That caused me to inhale sharply again. 'Where'd you learn to cook?' I asked.

'My wife taught me what my mother hadn't. My mother strictly specialized in Italian. Once I learned to expand my culinary art, we took turns every other night. Kind of cool, fun.'

That caught me off guard. I hadn't thought about him that way, married, or any way, really. An Italian mother? *You don't know a thing about me*, he'd said.

'My wife died,' Kit told me then.

'I'm sorry.' I really was. He'd already touched me with the idea of alternating nights cooking with her. David would never have done that.

'Yeah. It was almost four years ago.' I could see the pain etched on his face. He had loved her. It was obvious.

'What happened, Kit? You mind if we talk about it?'

'No. I'm fine now,' he said and forced a smile. 'Occasionally, I even like to play the martyr.'

'Ouch. You're tough on yourself, huh?'

'I guess. It was a small plane crash.' His voice was so low I could barely hear him. It was as if he were talking to himself. 'My wife. My two little boys.' He let out a sigh, and as I watched in stunned silence, he almost lost it.

The cabin was so silent that the sputtering chicken and the stiff breeze against brittle windowpanes sounded explosive. I wanted to hug him, to make some kind of human contact, to make the terrible hurt and sadness leave his blue eyes.

'I was supposed to drive everybody to Nantucket. A family vacation, long overdue, much deserved by them. Then I had to work. I was deeply involved in my, uh, career. They took a plane up there without me.' His face sagged. 'The plane went down between Rhode Island and Nantucket. It was the ninth of August in ninety-four.'

'I'm so sorry,' I said.

Now I felt so guilty about everything, right from the first time I'd ever seen him. I had been all wrong about Kit Harrison and it made me feel bad.

CHAPTER FORTY-TWO

K it refused to dwell much in the past; and for one
night at least, so did I. We had some good, honest
laughs, and talked easily for the next hour and a
half. I liked his company, the breadth of things he knew
about: *Cosi fan tutte*, rockabilly, raising children, professional hockey, fiction, nonfiction, antiquities, and so on
and so forth.

His personal history was pretty interesting, too. He told
me just enough to whet my appetite. His father was Irish
and had been a bus driver in Boston; his mom was Italian,
a former nurse at Children's Hospital. Mike and Maria
were still alive and well, living in Vero Beach, Florida,
these days. He had four brothers, 'all of them smarter and
better-looking than me.' He had attended Holy Cross
College in Worcester, Massachusetts, on an academic
scholarship. Then Dartmouth Law 'on a prayer.' Then
N.Y.U. Then came the FBI. Kit was an FBI agent, on
vacation in Colorado.

I did get the sense, though, that he was holding back a few things, but maybe I was wrong, and besides, why should Kit feel obliged to tell me everything about himself just because we were suddenly on speaking terms.

'Let's go for a moonlit ride,' I said after we had finished our dinner, which was as good as at many a pricey restaurant in Denver. Truth was, I didn't feel like going *home* quite yet. 'You mentioned having a drink over in Clayton. Let's go there tonight. I'm buying.'

He thought it was a good idea, so we took Kit's Jeep over to Villa Vittoria. It's a pretty good Italian place with a cozy bar, where jaded locals and even more jaded tourists seem to get along in relative harmony.

That particular weeknight, one of the older waiters was playing the piano and singing, if you could call it that. I knew Angelo and he was a sweet man, a very good headwaiter, but he was an embarrassingly bad singer. He was an uncle of the owner, which sort of explained why they let him sing on slow weeknights.

Kit and I sat at the bar, as far away from Angelo as possible. We tried to talk over the excruciating crooning, but he was miked, so it was impossible. We finally began to laugh, careful that Angelo didn't know his singing had given us giggling fits.

'He's dying up there,' I whispered. 'I feel so sorry for him.'

'He's sure clearing out the bar fast. I've never seen live entertainment have quite this effect before,' Kit said. Then he stood up from his barstool. 'Hold the fort. I'll be right back.'

I watched with building curiosity as Kit walked over and talked to Angelo. They both started to laugh conspiratorially, then the men looked my way.

Now what? I didn't like this too much. What were Kit and Angelo up to?

'We have a request from the audience to hear "Nel Blu Dipinto Di Blu," also known as "Volare,"' Angelo announced. I thought of his butchering the beautiful old song and I cringed. 'And to help me with the vocals, straight from the New England Conservatory of Music, Mr Kit Harrison.'

Straight from the New England Conservatory of Music?

Angelo played a little intro to the old Domenico Modugno song, and I noticed that his pianowork wasn't actually so bad. Now how about Kit's vocals? And their duet together?

Kit leaned into the mike, and he actually looked as if he knew what he was doing. He looked pretty sure of himself. 'This is for Dr Frannie O'Neill. She's a wonderful doctor of veterinary medicine, a real lifesaver. I hope this rendition is worthy of her in some small way.'

I modestly nodded my head, and smiled nervously. Honestly, I didn't know what to say or think. About Kit Harrison. And especially about being serenaded by Kit and Angelo in the local hangout.

Kit began singing 'Volare.' And he wasn't just worthy of me, he was very good. He had a beautiful tenor voice, and he was in control of it all the way through the song.

New England Conservatory? Was that a cute joke, or was it the truth? Who was this man? Everybody in the restaurant and bar had stopped to listen and watch. Kit could really sell a song, and everybody was buying, even the local rednecks and their dates.

When he and Angelo finished, just about everybody was clapping, cheering them on. Kit and Angelo took a few comical bows, then Kit came back to me at the bar.

'The lovely signora approve?' Kit asked. 'It was okay?'

I couldn't even be flip. 'Thank you. You were terrific, *magnifico*. I'm very touched. New England Conservatory?'

'Actually a bar *near* the conservatory. "Sparks." I played and sang my way through college and law school. I also worked summers on the Cape.'

Flashback time. Kit and I were working side by side, saving the fox. He was asking me to dinner in Clayton. Little generous acts that left me feeling both cared about and maybe too vulnerable, too fast. My throat ached from the sudden tenderness I was feeling. I was also conscious that I could easily be hurt right now.

'You're quiet again,' he said. 'Don't be. Please. I didn't mean to have that effect.'

'I'm just thinking,' I said. But I couldn't tell him that I was thinking about him and the effect he *was* having on me. So I told him something else. *Trust me*, he'd said, when he helped rescue the fox. For some reason, I did trust Kit now.

'I saw something the other day in the woods,' I said as we sat at the bar. 'Something that's going to sound unbelievably crazy to you. I almost can't believe I'm saying this. To you, or anybody else.'

I stopped myself from going on. Kit looked a little

alarmed, but I definitely had his attention.

'What did you see, Frannie? Finish what you were about to say.'

I stared into Kit's deep blue eyes.

God help me.

I bit my lip.

What if I was making a mistake?

You don't know a thing about me, he'd said.

'I saw a little girl . . . I think she was about eleven or twelve. A wild girl. And this is the really crazy part, Kit. She had wings – this girl has wings like a bird's.'

His expression froze and his mouth dropped open a little.

I wished I could take back my words, but I couldn't. It was too late for that.

'I know,' I said. 'Sounds unbelievable. But Kit, she was as real as I am sitting here. I saw a little girl with wings. And I saw her fly.'

CHAPTER FORTY-THREE

K it felt that the top of his head had just blown off. He was trying not to show it. He had to remind himself that he was a professional, an agent with the FBI, a smart, pretty sane person.

So, he had been right that something was going on out here. He'd been right to follow the case to Colorado, and anywhere else it would take him now. Why in hell had the Bureau pulled him off this case? It made no sense. Jesus, Jesus! Frannie O'Neill had seen a little girl with wings. And she'd just told him about it. That was important, too. It meant she couldn't be part of it. Didn't it?

'When did this happen?' he asked. He didn't want to interrogate Frannie, but he had to know what she had seen. A little girl with wings? Experiments on humans? What kind of experiments? What was happening out here?

'You believe me?' Frannie said, and did a doubletake.

She looked surprised, and then pleased.

He thought that when she looked at him like that he could probably believe the earth was flat, the moon was made of blue cheese, that there was such a thing as unconditional love at first sight, and happy endings, and little girls who could fly.

'I do believe you, Frannie,' he said.

'Good, because I saw the girl *twice*.'

Frannie looked like a young girl herself as she recounted both sightings in the most vivid detail, with great enthusiasm and obvious emotion. Her arms actually flapped when she described the girl and recounted how she had flown. Her eyes were huge as saucers, and she was talking even faster than she usually did. She didn't frown at him once.

In fact her innocence and exuberance made Kit want to tell her everything he knew, things he shouldn't tell anyone about the case, but especially not a woman whose husband might have been involved. *I shouldn't lie to Frannie, though. Not ever again. Lying to Frannie is a really bad thing to do,* he told himself.

'Listen, first thing tomorrow morning,' he finally said, 'we'll go and look for the girl. We'll look together. We'll find her.'

'So you really do believe me?' Frannie asked. She continued to look incredulous, and maybe even a little needy.

'I really do,' Kit said. He gave her a big wink. 'And I'm trained to know whether or not somebody is lying.'

Then Kit reached out for Frannie, took her into his

arms, and he gently, gently kissed her in their quiet corner of the bar.

And Frannie O'Neill finally did surprise him – she kissed him back.

BOOK 3

FOUR AND TWENTY BLACKBIRDS, BAKED IN A PIE

CHAPTER FORTY-FOUR

The sound of shattering glass interrupted the quiet of the house in the upscale suburb of Denver. The sudden noise jolted Dr Richard Andreossi from his peaceful slumber.

Baby Sam was asleep across his chest, both of them having dozed off for a mid-afternoon nap. Sweet dreams of the best kind, visions of sugar plums dancing in their heads.

More glass rained and clattered to the hardwood floor. *Jesus, the sound was coming from the study.*

Dr Andreossi carefully lifted Sam off his chest, so that he didn't wake. He laid the infant boy in a nest of couch cushions.

'Be right back, Sam the Man,' he whispered. 'You just sleep. Hush, baby, hush.'

Richard Andreossi had been meaning to cut down a branch that was banging at the window of the study. He'd been too busy, too tired out by the newborn, and his responsibilities as a father. *Forty-seven-year-old softies aren't built for this*, he knew, but Megwin had desperately wanted a baby and now there was no looking back.

He hoisted his blue-plaid Gap boxers up around his ample waist. Stepped into his scuffed-up, off-white sneakers. He heard another crash. Sounded like a lamp going over! What the hell?

Had an animal gotten inside? Squirrel? A small bird? He quickly shuffled his sneakered feet down the hall, looked into the room.

It took him a couple of confused seconds to comprehend what he saw, and even then he didn't completely understand.

A tall, well-muscled man dressed in a hooded, gray running suit and Nikes was methodically dropping things onto the floor, making a huge mess in the study. The mess seemed calculated. The man was doing this on purpose. Dr Andreossi recognized him.

'What the hell are you doing in here?' Andreossi finally asked. 'Why are you here? What do you want?'

The intruder had knocked half the heavy books and loose papers off the antique rolltop desk. Dr Andreossi could feel sweat rolling down the back of his neck, his sides.

He gauged the distance to the intruder. He was worried about his own safety, but even more about little Sam's.

'It won't work,' the man said. 'You can't move that fast.' Suddenly, he drew a pistol, like some kind of Western gunslinger. He pointed it at the doctor's face.

'What do you want from me?' Dr Richard Andreossi's

mind flashed through the full grid of logical possibilities. He was a bright man and his brain was operating at full capacity.

'Nothing. Not a thing,' said the man with the gun, a Smith & Wesson semiautomatic. 'There's nothing you can do now. Two of the children have escaped from the School. You let us down at the worst possible time, doctor.'

Suddenly, Dr Andreossi confronted the possibility that he was about to die. His body went cold. His head became light. His insides were screaming *Sam, Sam, Sam.*

'My baby?' he whispered. 'On the couch.'

'Don't worry. Megwin will be home soon,' said the cold-eyed gunman. 'Your baby will be fine. We wouldn't harm your baby. We aren't monsters.'

Then Harding Thomas pulled the trigger three times.

CHAPTER FORTY-FIVE

Max was seriously afraid, but she was determined not to let her fear stop her from doing the right thing. She had to act grown-up now. She had to return to the scene of the crimes; she was headed *home*. She needed to see if Matthew was being held there, and some other worrisome stuff, too. Important stuff, no way around it, no more dodging the bullet. *Home again, home again.*

Of course, flying at night, without the help of radar or autopilot, was superdangerous and maybe not the smartest thing she'd ever done in her life. It was cloudy and threatening to rain, and she sure wished the light was better.

Watch out! She nearly crashed skull-first into a hill as she banked out of a raggedy-assed patch of fog. She rolled quickly to the left, flapped her wings hard and strong. Then she rose up above the cool, smoky air. Close call. Too close.

She was thinking about the School now, couldn't help it. She knew from 'Uncle' Thomas that the model for the way it ran was military schools. She also knew that Thomas had been a soldier at one time, that he'd taught at the Air Force Academy, even that he had grown-up children of his own. She and Matthew lived in a small dormitory. Everything in their lives had been on a tight, no-nonsense schedule: breakfast, study, testing, exercise, lunch, work projects, study, more testing, dinner, study, then bed. Then do it all over again. Then do it again. Do it again.

It was always like that until Mrs Beattie came. She did schoolwork with them as well as all the irritating testing, but she also introduced them to an amazing concept: playtime. Mrs Beattie had *never* been in the military. They had loved her. Until Mrs Beattie was put to sleep.

Around the time Mrs Beattie came, there had been other improvements as well. A 'boxcar' from the Boxcar Children series was installed. So was a new Apple computer. And on the weekends they got to go to woodworking and an art studio. Max had the idea that 'art' was part of the constant testing, but she didn't care. If the tests were more fun, she wouldn't have minded them either.

The School used the latest technology – it was an AMP Smart House, for one thing, which was pretty neat, and convenient, and efficient, of course. All the lights, thermostats, and door locks were on a tight schedule, too. They were always watched by a video security system. Guards could call into their cell telephones to open doors, even to run a bath or shower.

Maybe that was why she loved her new freedom so much.

Suddenly, she could see the School down below. She was almost home again. She flew easily, her wings very stable now. Then she power-dived toward the cluster of familiar buildings. This was it – now-or-never time. Put up or shut up, Maximum.

Something was wrong – she could see it immediately. She pulled out of her dive, fluttered, almost stalled-out, and then set down quietly in the woods.

She could feel the skin on her neck and back prickling with fear. She gasped, choked, couldn't quite catch her breath. Oh God, oh God, this was her worst fear.

Max watched several men in dark, scary jumpsuits rushing in and out of the buildings. They were loading heavy boxes into big gray trucks that were almost as scary as they were. It looked as if they were closing down the place, moving out, shutting the School.

There were too many of the suckers walking around out there. No way could she get closer and definitely no way could she get inside the School buildings.

She even heard guards in the nearby woods, so Max moved farther away from the School. She had to – she couldn't bear to get caught now. She felt like crying, but she wouldn't let herself break down.

I can't get caught. I can't! I'm the only hope, she told herself. *I'm the only one who can tell.*

She made herself angry, and the anger gave her more strength. It always did, never failed.

She hurried back deeper into the woods.

Safe for now. She had no idea about the time, but it must be close to morning. There was just enough light to see, *and to be seen* by the creepy bums in the woods.

She heard the movement close behind her. Someone was there. And they were coming fast.

Max turned – and realized too late that she had it all wrong. It was much worse than she'd thought. This was the end for her. No way out of this.

The mountain lion was too close, less than ten feet away. It was gray and tawny brown, about five feet from head to tail, easily two hundred pounds. It had stopped moving when she turned around.

The two of them began to play a survival game of dare to stare; dare to move first; dare to do anything except be scared out of your mind, and *show* it in your eyes.

The cat started to growl, and she could see huge, powerful, stained yellowish-brown teeth. She couldn't tell if it was afraid of her, or if it had sensed something different about her, but the cat hadn't pounced and killed her yet.

She wondered if she could run, and then maybe she could get up off the ground? If airborne, she might be okay. She might live to tell about this.

The lion continued to growl under its breath. Its mouth was open a crack. Otherwise, they were both motionless, their eyes still locked together. She couldn't imagine how this stalemate could possibly end with a good result for her.

Max needed to take a breath. She was suffocating, which limited her choices. She really had to chance it.

She began to draw in a slow breath – when the cat pounced. It leaped at her with lightning speed. It *knew* exactly when to attack. Instinct!

Max yelled, but amazingly, the sound came from anger and fierceness, not fear.

She spun away – faster than she thought she could move, faster than she ever had before.

I'm fast – like this cat, she thought, hoped, prayed, then *knew*.

The large cat stopped and turned, seemingly with one fluid, powerful move. Its huge paws were like brakes in the dirt. It seemed a little surprised, though.

Max sent a powerful swipe to the side of the cat's head. The cat staggered sideways, but quickly came at her again.

Max showed a flash of wing, then pulled it away even faster. She swiped at the cat again, connecting solidly with jawbone. She couldn't believe how good it felt. The animal spun out of control.

This gave Max time to run a few steps, to take off into the air. In a rage at losing its kill the cat ran after her and jumped, took off as if it too had wings. The big jaws snapped fiercely, but got only an air sandwich.

Max continued to climb stairs of air until she felt safe. Then she turned and looked down at the frustrated mountain cat. She made a face. '*Meow*,' she mouthed, as she flew away.

CHAPTER FORTY-SIX

Kit and I searched the dense, hilly woods high above the Peak-to-Peak highway. The Peak-to-Peak, Colorado Route #119 runs along the top of the foothills and the beginnings of the *big* mountains to the west. It was pretty futile going. We were like bloodhounds who'd lost the scent.

I had never done this kind of thing before. It was weird for both of us, and even weirder that we were doing it together.

We looked pretty good, anyway. Kit had on a pair of green hiking shorts and not too much else. He'd already stripped away a Dartmouth Law T-shirt to beat the sticky heat. I'd picked khaki shorts, mountain boots, and my lucky workout top; but so far we hadn't been too lucky.

The girl had to be somewhere, but where? Where would I hide if I had to seek cover out here? How would an eleven- or twelve-year-old be thinking?

My curiosity about her was a living thing now. I had

grown up in 4-H, been a Westinghouse Science Award winner, honors biology major, could have gone to medical school to be a people doctor, if I'd chosen to. I wanted to know anything and everything there was to know about the girl with wings. Who wouldn't? Who could possibly resist?

The comfortable cool of the morning had given way to a typical, blistering-hot summer afternoon. My backpack was pretty full, and heavy, and I was eager to put it down for a while.

I heard Kit panting lightly beside me, and I was glad I wasn't looking into his blue eyes right now.

Last night, I'd kissed him with my heart full of senti-ment and the rest of me high on sixty-dollar brandy. There was something so different about him, a sensitivity I didn't see in most of the men I knew, and which I hadn't allowed myself to see at first.

Maybe what had happened to his wife and two children started it, but I kind of thought Kit had always been that way. On the other hand, as he'd said himself – *you don't know who I am.*

'What do you think?' he asked, when we reached an elevated point in the trail. 'Which way do we head? You have any idea?'

Sure, I was full of ideas. 'I vote for the southern slope of that hill,' I said. 'If I were a runaway, maybe I'd hide where I could get a good view of the valley.'

'*That* slope?' he asked and rolled his eyes.

'It's only two or three miles from here,' I told him.

He mouthed, 'Only two or three?'

Cute. Funny. He definitely was that, but he had a serious side that I liked even more. The night before he had told me that he wasn't a hunter, but I didn't know much about what he *was*, did I?

'We can be there in a couple of hours if we put some real energy into it,' I said. 'You'll be surprised.'

'Aye, aye, captain. Whatever you say.'

'That's the spirit, Kit Carson. That's how the West was won.'

After another two hours of slip-sliding and hoisting ourselves up and down rocky inclines, we finally arrived on the leeward side of the slope the town is named for: Bear Bluff.

'Let's take a short break,' I said to the perspiring man alongside me. Actually, Kit looked even better with a sheen of sweat covering his body. I think he knew it, too. He was that rare person who was mildly cocky without being obnoxious. He was confident in himself, but there was also a touch of humility that I liked.

'You don't have to coddle me,' he said and grinned. 'I'm in decent enough shape – for a city boy.'

I laughed at his humor. *Yes, you certainly are in fine shape,* I was thinking to myself. *City boy or not.*

I eased out of my backpack and looked at my watch. It was a little before five in the afternoon. I dug a couple of navel oranges out of my pack and tossed him one. It was a wild throw but he caught it, anyway.

'Good hands,' I said, grinning like the fem village idiot. I kind of liked being goofy with him, though. I realized that I already trusted him enough to be my goofy self.

While we devoured the sweet juicy oranges, I looked around. I saw nothing too unusual, though. Some flattened grass where deer had probably slept. A shallow cave, too small to shelter a human. Turkey vultures circling above us turkeys.

What was I expecting to find up here?

A downy little bird-girl nest with a four-poster bed and an extensive Barbie doll collection?

Kit came up behind me. I smelled oranges and sweat. 'Frannie,' he said softly. He really did have a nice voice. A smooth baritone. I could listen to him for hours, and I had just the night before.

'Yeah?'

He was pointing toward the steepest part of the slope. '*Look*. Up there. Isn't that something?'

I turned my head in the direction of Kit's pointing finger.

Just over a clump of fir trees and boulders halfway up the slope above us was a large flying thing.

Not a hawk. Not a turkey buzzard.

It was *something*, all right.

The girl with wings!

She was soaring high above us, like a majestic eagle, only better.

'Oh God,' Kit couldn't stop repeating as he watched her fly in slow, wide circles above us. 'She's for real.'

CHAPTER FORTY-SEVEN

Kit was already in shock, and flat-out awe, and maybe even in denial at what he had seen. He and Frannie started after *her* – a young girl, who looked normal in almost every way, except that she had wings and she could fly.

She was flying, and she was up about five hundred feet above them.

They *climbed* the hills after her.

They *crawled* up rocky inclines at times.

And they quickly found out that the shortest distance between any two points is – to *fly*.

Kit stared up at the sheer face of the cliff and wondered how Frannie was able to find usable toeholds when he saw nothing but slick rock and possible death, or at least major broken bones. He had put his T-shirt back on, as if that would protect him if he fell.

He was no Neanderthal. It didn't bother him when a woman did things better than he did, but this was getting a little ridiculous. Frannie wasn't just in good shape – she was in great shape. She was nearly Olympic-quality at this climbing hill-and-dale-and-mountain thing.

He appreciated that she wasn't rubbing it in too much. Actually, she was helpful and encouraging most of the time.

'Don't look down,' she said to him. 'Look at me.'

'I can do that,' he said. 'I like doing that. Thanks for the tip. That actually helps some. Look at Frannie. Do as Frannie does. See? Frannie isn't falling to her death. You shouldn't either.'

He pulled himself up the ledge toward where she stood above him. His hand found a thick root and he grabbed it. His toe found a narrow crack and wedged in. He was doing okay.

Then he slipped.

He slid down several feet toward a rocky chasm. *Oh no, Jesus no.*

He grabbed at a whip of a tree, bent the sucker almost double.

It held, thank God.

'C'mon, L.L. Bean, you can do this,' Frannie called to him from above. 'Just be careful. Don't lose your focus.'

Panting, afraid of becoming a bleeding pile of flesh and of shattered bones, he slowly inched his way back up again. That was the thing about Kit/Tom . . . he didn't give up easily. He heaved himself over the lip of the rocky ledge. Normally, he'd have managed a snappy comeback, but he didn't have enough wind left in him to answer her.

'What'd you just call me?' he gasped eventually.

'What do you mean?'

Kit achieved a crawling position, then stood up. He lurched over to where Frannie was sitting on a rock, massaging her toes. Nice toes, long and lean and very flexible.

'Why'd you call me "L.L. Bean"?'

She squinted up at him, shrugged her shoulders. 'Your clothes, I guess. They're brand-spanking-new, city boy. L.L. Bean-type.'

'You're hurting my feelings.'

That cracked Frannie up. She bent at the waist and hugged her sides and laughed hard. Tears were streaming down her cheeks. Kit looked at her and started laughing, which only compounded his wheezy, exhausted whoops into hysterics.

'It wasn't *that* funny,' said Frannie, when she could finally speak again.

'I know,' he managed to say. 'It wasn't half that funny. But it *is*. Look at the two of us.'

Which sent them both into hysterical laughter again.

It was Frannie who recovered first. She wiped her face with the back of her hand. Then she hunted around in her pack, pulled out a first-aid kit and tossed it to him.

'Your stomach. There's blood on your shirt. *Ooohh*. I can't stand the sight of blood,' she kidded.

He doused the abrasion on his belly with alcohol without wincing. Frannie watched him. A cool expression on her face. After he was finished with the alcohol, he said, '*Ouch*,' and grinned.

Kit looked around, searched the surrounding hills with

his eyes. 'Well, we sure didn't catch up to her. She's gone again.'

'I keep wondering who her parents are,' Frannie said. 'Where the heck did she come from? Where does she live?'

There was no comment from Kit. Only dead silence.

Frannie stared hard at him.

'Wait a minute. You already know something about her, don't you?'

Kit blew out air. 'I knew something was going on. I uh, I *am* an FBI agent, Frannie. I told you that last night. That's also why I'm here in Colorado. I've been working on this case for three years.'

Frannie turned pale and stumbled over her words. 'What? What *case* is that? Am I part of a *case* now?'

'Don't go crazy, stay calm. Listen to me. It started in Cambridge, Massachusetts, at least I think that's where it started. A doctor named Anthony Peyser was performing experiments, trying to speed up human development, or so we believe.'

'You mean he was trying to effect human evolution, Kit? Is that what you're trying to say?'

'Something on that order. We don't know for sure. *I* don't know for sure. Peyser and a team of students he handpicked were into something important. There was a breakthrough of some kind. Then they got in serious trouble in Boston. They were accused of experimenting on humans – vagrants, street people, occasionally a student who needed extra cash. The end justifies the means sort of thing. You've probably read about small labs, even university research centers, accused of the same thing recently. The Army has done some pretty bad things.'

'Yeah, I have heard about it. Who hasn't? So you knew about this outlaw group of doctors all along. That's why you believed me about the girl, isn't it?'

'I trust you – period. That's why I believed you. How about trusting me a little now?' he finally said. 'Deal?'

'We'll camp here for the night,' Frannie answered.

She was tough when she had to be. But he sort of liked it.

CHAPTER FORTY-EIGHT

I needed to think about it some more, but I already suspected I was all right with what Kit had told me so far. Basically, I *did* trust him. I liked what I saw in his eyes.

'I'm going to the grocery store,' I told him, as I started back into the woods near our camp. 'Want anything?'

'*Denver Post*, M&Ms with peanuts, Prozac,' he joked.

'You're in charge of the fire.'

Kit nodded, made a grunting caveman sound, then gave me another of his patented smiles. I continued to be a little amazed at how well we were getting along.

There was a stream less than a hundred yards from camp. I strung a line on the portable fishing rod I carry in my pack. The stream was bubbling and boiling down the rocks. It eddied into a little pool I knew from another time up here. Maybe a hike with David.

Worms were thick in the leaf mold near the stream. I hooked one, tossed the line out onto the dark water.

Waited for dinner to swim along.

It took only a few minutes for me to catch a good-sized rainbow trout. I cut and tied my line, left the fish in the water, then restrung the pole. The fish was only about fourteen inches, but a half-hour later I hadn't caught another, and it would be dark soon.

One medium-sized trout would have to do for dinner. I'd brought along a couple of tomatoes and potatoes, so it wouldn't be too bad.

I had an eerie sixth sense that the girl was close by. When she'd shown herself before, it almost seemed as if she were teasing us, maybe even leading us up here. Why? Did she want to be found? Or maybe show us something? What, though? Where she lived? How she lived? Some other secret she needed to share?

I took the trout out of the cold stream, killed it quickly with a rock, refilled the canteen and headed back.

I found Kit at the campsite. *The FBI agent.* Out here on a big case that he wouldn't talk very much about. Well, somebody could definitely hide a lab up here. Stoned-out hippies had been hiding in these hills for years.

'Nice fire,' I said. It was a beauty.

'No Match-light either.'

He'd taken the potatoes out of the pack and they were already baking in the coals. A domesticated man – what fun! I handed him the canteen of water and showed him the fish. He whistled his approval. A frontier woman – what fun!

I was gutting the fish on a flat rock with a Swiss Army knife and Kit was licking his handsome chops when I said, 'I might be willing to share my trout with you – on one condition.'

I had his attention. Also, his smile was turned on again. At least I amused him.

'You tell me, no crap, what's going on, and you get to eat.'

'Fine,' he said. 'You win, Dr O'Neill. But I want to see half of that fish on my plate before I talk.'

'Deal,' I said.

I put the trout fillet into a pan. Set the pan onto the red-hot coals. The aroma was incredible, mouthwatering.

I walked over to where Kit was sitting and hunkered down next to him so that I could see the view. As if on cue, the sun set. Great brushstrokes of salmon and plum and whiskey colored the sky.

'Damn,' he whispered. 'They don't make them like this anywhere around Boston.'

I felt as strangely pleased as if I'd painted the sunset myself. For the moment at least, this was a really great adventure, a truly amazing one. Everything about it was appealing.

The fish was done in no time. I took the potatoes out of the coals, and sliced the tomato. Kit put everything on plates.

He and I ate and watched the breathtaking scene from our dinner table in the sky, talking quietly, but pretty much nonstop. The fish bones were in the ashes and we were sipping hot coffee. Kit, as he had promised, began to tell me what he knew.

He kept it a little sketchy, which he said he had to do.

The current crisis emanated from an outlaw biology lab. It had started with M.I.T. students and a few professors in the late 1980s. It had definitely involved experiments with humans back then. The man who ran the radical group was named Anthony Peyser. I told Kit that I'd never heard of him; I'd have remembered the name. Besides that, I didn't think I knew anyone who fit the description Kit gave me.

'There were charges in Boston, but the police couldn't prove anything significant. The group moved to San Francisco, then to New Jersey, a short stint in England, maybe to get European financing. Then back to Boston again.

'The second time they came to Boston I nailed them, at least I thought I had. They were experimenting on homeless people with fatal diseases, or so they convinced them. They helped a couple of them die sooner than they would have. Somehow, everyone involved managed to get bail – and then they disappeared off the face of the earth.'

'Until now?'

'Somebody in the group contacted a couple of past associates. Maybe they'd been in contact all along. I think that whoever it was might have been having attacks of morality and ethics. I wonder *why*. Anyway, Dr James Kim in San Francisco and Dr Heekin in Cambridge, Massachusetts, were contacted, and then ended up dead. They *really* don't like witnesses, Frannie. They're thorough, too, as you might expect scientists to be.'

I didn't like the sound of that, but I sure got the point.

Kit stopped talking abruptly. He just stared out as the

sun finally slipped below the horizon. I knew there had to be more to his story.

It struck me as funny, peculiar, *strange*, but I knew it was all over for me. Just like that! I liked looking at his strong face, the hard-chiseled cheekbones and chin. I liked the softness I saw in his eyes, too. It had never happened to me like this before, not even with David. I could intellectualize about it all I wanted to, but I was falling for Kit Harrison. Falling, or flying, I wondered?

'And that's all you know?' I asked him. 'You swear it is?'

'That's what I know for sure, Frannie. It's what you get for *half* a trout dinner.'

'All right, I guess that's fair. How's that scrape on your stomach?' I asked.

'I used to play rugby at Holy Cross, then in the Boston and D.C. beer leagues. I think I'll pull through.'

I frowned a little at the tough guy posturing. 'Did you put antibacterial gunk on it?'

'It's not *that* bad, doc. It's a scratch, a scrape.'

Fireflies flashed intermittently in the gathering dark. Once upon a time I knew a lot about fireflies, but I couldn't remember any of it now. I was thinking about the tufts of gold hair on Bean's chest and the abrasion roughing up his perfect skin. I was remembering the softness of his lips, and his gentle touch.

I was turning myself on. *He* was turning me on. Oh boy!

There were no sick animals to distract me, nothing to clean or jump up and do. I wished for a cigarette, although I don't smoke. I could have used a drink.

'I think I ought to take a look at it,' I finally said. I don't know why, but I spoke in a whisper.

I didn't think he was going to answer me, he was so quiet. Then Kit cleared his throat.

'Would that be in a medical capacity?' he asked.

'No. It would be in a fellow traveler capacity,' I managed to croak.

'Okay,' he said. 'I'm in your able hands. Let me get this shirt off.'

'Oh goodie.'

His blue eyes twinkled again. 'Dr O'Neill? Did you just say "Oh goodie"?'

'You can call me Frannie. I told you that before. And yes, that's what I said. Oh goodie.'

CHAPTER FORTY-NINE

Max was watching the two of them from a safe distance, at least she hoped she was safe. Her mind was going about a million miles an hour.

Warm tears streamed down her face and she couldn't make them stop. That got her angry. She hated to show any weakness, and she almost never did, but so much had happened in such a short time. She was on the run. No, she was *in flight*.

Max knew it was stupid, but she just couldn't keep the tears from flowing. She couldn't shake a particular image out of her mind. She'd been shocked when she saw the rock come down on the head of the poor fish. The woman doctor had been so cold when she did it. Just the way they were at the School. Cold, cold, cold.

How could she kill that fish? *Put it to sleep?*

It had been a living thing.

It probably had babies and a nice place to live in that beautiful stream back there a ways.

Now it was dead because the doctor had put it to sleep.

Max sat on a branch, shivering and crying softly to herself. She was never going to be safe out here in the world, and she felt terribly alone and sad. She missed Matthew so much that she couldn't even bear to think about him. The world outside the School was as scary as Uncle Thomas had always told her it was. Only he'd never scared her half as much as she'd been in the last few days.

At least she had found a safe, high place where she could see the man and woman and their roaring, blazing campfire. She didn't like to admit it, but the cooking fish did smell awfully good. Her stomach rumbled, reminding her how long it had been since she'd put anything solid in it.

She wished she had someone to talk to.

The woman doctor and her friend were sitting on the edge of the hill watching the sunset. The sun, as it went down, was pretty, like orange marmalade and grape jelly mixed together. *F-O-O-D*, she thought. *J-E-L-L-Y*. Sitting here, watching the same sunset they were watching, made her feel she was with them. Was she getting them all wrong? If she went to them and asked politely, would they help her? She liked to think that life could work that way. But no. She knew better.

She spied on the man and woman as they sat and talked around the fire. She could tell they liked each other.

She was having conflicting thoughts about the woman doctor. She wanted so badly to trust her. That was her instinct. She just couldn't see how all the gooey, soothing, *don't worry I'm not going to hurt yous* in the world could be believed.

Then the couple were eating their dinner, and watching that made Max ravenously hungry. She listened as they talked and laughed, even caught a few words. '. . . Thorn in the side . . . over the hill . . . antibacterial gunk . . .'

She wished she could sit with them and eat a baked potato at least. Potatoes were living things, too, but she could handle that.

She scrunched forward to watch, to see them better. *What's going on now? What are they doing?*

As she watched from the tree limb, the doctor went and squatted next to the man. She began to take off his clothes, his shirt first. The man was bigger than the doctor and he overpowered her! *What was he doing to her?*

He lay down on top of the pretty doctor, but she didn't push him away, didn't fight him at all. They were laughing, smiling, and then they began to kiss.

'They're mating,' Max whispered.

CHAPTER FIFTY

I had a first-aid kit in hand as I knelt down beside Kit. I carefully opened the buttons of his shirt. When I got to the one closest to his waist, I had to pull the bunched-up shirt out of his pants. He winced from the friction of cloth against raw skin.

'Sorry,' I said. 'Sorry.'

'It's okay, Frannie. I live for pain.'

I stared at firelight playing over taut chest muscles and a mat of bright curls. I reached for the tube of ointment, fumbled, and almost dropped it. The lid spun off into the dirt.

I put some of the medicated goo on my fingers and carefully touched his body. Odd. My fingers were trembling a little. I could hear my own breathing, which was too loud in my ears, but I was certainly focused on the task at hand.

So much so that I was surprised when Kit lightly grabbed my wrist.

'Did I hurt you?' I asked.

He shook his head. 'No, but you're killing me, Frannie.'

Kit put his free arm around my waist, and in one smooth movement lifted me and set me down on my back in the grass and pine needles, half covered me with his body. He was obviously strong, probably a hundred-eighty pounds, but he was also gentle.

My arms were high and tight around his neck. He pulled me against him and I felt him, *all of him*, against my thigh. I didn't have any fears or doubts about this, none at all. That surprised me, shocked me, actually, but there it was out in the open.

I wanted his mouth, and suddenly it was mine, as sweet and fresh as I had imagined. I was starving for this, the salty taste of him, the touch of his hands, the roughness of his day-old beard against my skin. I wanted Kit so very much, more than I could have imagined.

Kit lightly ran his hands over my breasts but there was too much fabric between us. I heard soft moaning sounds coming from my throat, which I barely recognized as my own. I tried to help him undress me. I was pulling at my workout top. I was struggling with his shorts, too. I hadn't felt like this in so long.

He looked at me and his eyes were warm and sincere and, most of all, honest. I recognized the look, and suddenly I realized how much he liked me, and how much I cared about him already. A bolt of lightning had hit me, and I never, ever saw it coming. I never suspected, never would have guessed this could happen.

It was kind of scary, but also unbelievably exciting and wonderful.

Two years of grief and repression had combusted in a rare moment. I felt his hand at my belt, cinching it tighter so that the buckle's tongue would slip from its notch. I heard the zipper of my shorts give way under his fingers. I wanted this to happen. I was melting, and it was my choice.

Cool air rushed around my thighs as he slid my shorts down to my knees. I shivered, and I loved everything about the moment, our first time like this, the suddenness of it, the surprise.

I reached for his belt. The leather was stiff, unyielding. I was wrestling with the buckle when I heard him saying my name. I shivered at the sound of it and I wanted him inside me now.

'Frannie, Frannie. Wait. Stop.'

Wait? Stop?

I forced myself to look at Kit's face. It was as if someone had suddenly turned on powerful bright lights. I blinked at him. *Wait? Stop?*

'We're both out of our minds,' he panted. 'I don't know where I'll be next week.' He sighed deeply. 'I don't even know where I'll be *tomorrow.*'

I wanted to say, so what? Instead, I felt a wave of almost unbearable sadness. One small particle of brain matter *was* still rational. It told me that I wasn't going to make love to Kit and get over it easily. I wasn't going to forget this night in the mountains, or him.

I nodded. 'Okay,' I said.

'Okay?'

'Okay. You're right. I wasn't thinking. Let's stop before we make a big mistake.'

'I'm sorry,' he said into my hair. He sighed again. 'I really want to do this. I love being with you. It's just that—'

I put my forefinger across his lips. 'Don't,' I said. We held each other for a good long time, long enough for our heartbeats to slow, anyway. I had stopped melting – but not really.

We kissed again, this time a gentler, more civilized kiss. To show we could still be friends? Then I stood up and pulled on my shorts.

I found my sleeping bag in a heap where I'd left it a few hours before and dragged it to the far side of the fire. How could I have been feeling so good, and now suddenly feel so unbearably bad?

'Frannie,' Kit said.

'Yuh?' I whispered. My voice sounded thick. *Yuh?*

'Bring your sleeping bag over here next to me.'

I hesitated. Shook my head in silence. I think that maybe my pride demanded a little distance. *Stop? Wait?*

'Do it,' he said. Then more gently, 'Please. I'm the G-man, remember? You're the civilian. I've got the gun. You'll be safer where I can see you.'

Ah. He did have the gun.

To hell with my doctorate in veterinary medicine. Forget that I could outrun him, outclimb him, and that I'd slept in these mountains gunless and manless other times before. I picked up my sleeping bag and unrolled it next to him. I did what Kit asked me to do.

'I'm sorry,' he whispered before I fell asleep. 'I'm really sorry.'

Very noble of you, Kit.

CHAPTER FIFTY-ONE

K it couldn't believe his eyes. The children were flying. The two of them looked so fine and free, like a pair of angels.

They did a graceful loop together and he had the sudden, terrible feeling that they might fall from grace. They were hundreds of feet in the air, easily as high as some small planes fly.

He looked around for Frannie, but she wasn't there. He didn't know where she might have gone.

He began to yell, and only hoped that the children could hear him.

'Little Mike, Tom! Come down here. Please come down before you fall. This is Daddy. Daddy wants you to come down.'

They couldn't hear him from so high, so far away.

Then suddenly both of his boys began to fall, to plummet, to drop like stones.

Neither of them had wings. They were in free fall.

He wanted to rescue both his sons, but he could only catch one of them. He had to choose, but it was impossible. He had to choose one son.

He watched as Little Mike and Tom both crashed horribly to the ground. He hadn't been able to save either of them. Out of nowhere – there were EMS ambulances, Rhode Island police cars, the wreckage of a small plane.

He was there at the nightmarish crash scene. Inside the smoking plane, looking through the twisted, crumpled seats and the dead passengers.

He found his two little boys and his wife in the terrible wreckage. He gently touched them and couldn't believe that they were dead.

And then Kit woke. It was early morning, a hint of salmon pink tinted the blue of the sky. He was in Colorado. In the mountains.

Frannie O'Neill was bent over him. 'Shhhh,' she whispered. 'She's up there. I can see her.'

CHAPTER FIFTY-TWO

Max woke with a terrible start.

She didn't know how much time had passed, but she'd obviously fallen asleep. It was morning again. She was wet-cheeked and shivering from the cold that had swept across the mountain between sundown and sunrise.

She felt small and alone and utterly abandoned on the mountainside. She missed Matthew and she even missed the awful, despicable School a little bit.

No! I can't think like that. I mustn't start acting like a loser. Losers lose! she told herself. *I'm not a loser.*

Max lifted her hand to wipe her cheeks and, as she did, felt something like spiderwebs all over her. Ugh! She pushed at the irritating, clingy stuff and it shifted but didn't melt away from her face.

What was this? What was happening? She opened her eyes wide. *Oh God!*

She saw shapes bending over her. People! She couldn't tell how many!

They were standing between her and the sun, and it took a moment for her to understand what was happening to her. When she did, she filled her lungs with air and screamed.

She screamed bloody murder! That scared them. The shapes backed off, then crystallized as the woman doctor and the man. They'd snuck up on her in her sleep. Bastards! Creeps!

Max screamed again, louder than she'd ever screamed in her entire life. The inside of her head was white with fear. She couldn't think straight, could only flail wildly at the net. But pushing only made the string snag and catch on her fingers and wings, her legs, feet.

Ohgodohgod what was this? What could she do? She had to escape!

They had her in some kind of strong animal net. They had caught her! The creeps!

Max scootched back on the ground until she was up hard against the bark of a quaking aspen. The leaves clicked and clattered together as she tried to raise herself to her feet. She was crying and shrieking, beating her wings furiously, hurting herself, trying to hurt them somehow. She wasn't though. They were too crafty – too human.

The woman doctor was talking to her, but she couldn't, *wouldn't* listen to what she was saying.

She would not be put to sleep! She wouldn't give up now! She wasn't a loser!

The man reached out to her and she batted his hand away. She struck out hard at him, remembering how Uncle Thomas would grab her to get control, to get his way.

The man's hand reached toward her again. Feinting one way – then clutching. *Sneaky, crafty man!*

He was trying to grab her and *win*. She bit his hand, really hurting him, and heard him say a swear word.

She kicked out hard with her strong legs. Missed him. 'Take it easy,' he was saying. 'Just take it easy. Jesus, she's strong, Frannie.'

His hand came again, reaching near her face, reaching for her wings.

Uncle Thomas was in her mind. She could see his despicable face. Ugh! Ugh!

Max covered her head, bent over, made herself into a little ball, but she couldn't escape the terrifying net. It dripped over her in folds and there was no end to it.

Oh, I made a horrible mistake. I shouldn't have been watching them. I shouldn't have rested.

The doctor was talking to her. Trying to, anyway. Typical doctor crap. Always so soft, the whispers, the lies coming so gently, so easily. Just like with Uncle Thomas and the other creeps.

'Everything's going to be all right. Please trust us. Please, darling. We won't hurt you.'

Liars! You are hurting me. YOU ARE HURTING ME NOW!

Max screamed again, even louder this time. But no words – just screams!

Her voice came right back at her in the mountain air, the echo mocking her.

This was so unfair. So bad!

The doctor tried to get closer and closer. Max saw something clutched in her hand. It wasn't a gun but it was just as bad.

No, it was much worse.

She knew what it was.

It was a needle!

Max would not be put to sleep.

NO! NO! NO! GET AWAY FROM ME! I'LL BITE YOU! I'LL KILL YOU!

She glared at the woman doctor with all the hatred and fierceness she could muster. Then she swung her gaze back to the man who was coming around behind her, sneaking around. She didn't know who to look at anymore, which of them was more dangerous to her.

She looked back at the doctor! Then at the man again. It was getting harder and harder to keep up with their movements.

The doctor started yelling, 'Bring her down, Kit. *Do it now!*'

Max wanted to call for help, but she knew that no one would come. There was no one anywhere who would help her. Except maybe Matthew. Oh God, where was her brave little brother?

She sucked in more air and opened her mouth to scream again. The scream never got past her throat.

CHAPTER FIFTY-THREE

We had the girl in a 'mist-net,' actually a couple of them. The nets were used to trap large wild birds for banding.

The netting was light enough so that it wouldn't damage wings or crimp feathers much. It doesn't so much bind as *tangle*, preventing her from doing anything but thrash. And she was thrashing!

I felt as if I were about to have my third – or maybe it was my fourth – heart attack in the last couple of days.

I was close enough to the girl to touch her. Swiftly, I did it – I touched her. All right, she was for real. She existed. She was flesh and blood and my fingers had just touched her miraculous wing. Below the wings and attached somehow were her arms. She was *double-limbed* and it looked and worked just fine.

She wasn't tiring, but I sure was. She was still furiously fighting the net. Her beautiful white and silver-blue feathers were floating around us, and I was terrified that she was going to hurt herself. She was in a rage state.

'Everything's going to be okay,' I said. 'We won't hurt you. I'm a doctor. It's okay.'

Either she didn't understand me or she didn't believe me, because she opened her mouth impossibly wide and screamed again. Her screaming was the most awful sound I've ever heard, like an animal shrillness but with a human undertone that made me think of the cries of mother seals, or maybe mother whales when their families are in danger.

I wondered if she had a human larynx, an avian syrinx, or both. The syrinx has no cords, just a sac at the bottom of the windpipe. It contracts to force air out. And maybe I had just heard it at full blast.

It hurt my ears to listen to her. My eyes, however, couldn't get enough.

Just as I'd thought, almost everything about her was, well, human – but not in conventional proportions. Her eyes were round, and incredibly intense, and seemed intelligent, or at least very focused. Her hair was light-blonde, quite long, and hanging way below her shoulders. Some of her feathers were also blonde, which made some sense, since both feathers and hair are made of the same material, keratin.

As I gorged on the vision of her, the girl was punching out at Kit.

I got a real good look at her mysterious, absolutely marvelous appendages. They were muscled and jointed as human arms are, but the forearms were shorter. Her fingers were elongated and cloaked in feathers out to the last joints of the digits.

Because they were made to fly, Frannie!

Jesus, Jesus. She was a miracle. She couldn't be – and yet here she was. How could this have possibly happened? How could she be here? How could I?

Her beautiful wings were feathered in pure white and, in the early morning light, I saw glints of blue and silver shining through. A strange feeling came over me then – I think I almost envied her. She was so beautiful, and she had such an amazing gift.

She could do what nearly all of us wish we could do – this little girl could fly. How in the name of God had it happened? Was she a miracle? An angel? No. Angels can disappear, get out of a net.

I snapped myself out of my trance, my inner thoughts. This was the wrong time and wrong place for it.

The girl was in a panic. She could damage her wings, and she could just as easily go into shock. I'd seen animals die of fright before. Their hearts just seemed to burst.

When Kit had tried to touch her, she'd been obviously threatened by his hand coming toward her. When I tried, she panicked, but not as fiercely. That showed me something – what, though? Had she been mishandled by men? Where? Who?

'Hang on to the net,' I said to Kit. 'Hang on to her.'

Then I ran as fast as I could back to the camp. I was going to have to subdue the winged girl, but God only knew how I was going to get a needle into a vein. God only knew, because I sure didn't.

When I returned moments later, the situation was exactly as I had left it: terror, hysteria, the child's face was even brighter red. Her veins were bulging dangerously. I told Kit he was going to have to bring her down.

He said something about an 'end run' and I'd seen just enough Sunday afternoon football to get his drift. I started talking to the girl again. Actually, I was making word music, soothing sounds, the kind you make when you're trying to get close enough to a badly frightened, eye-rolling horse to grab its halter. I was the bird-whisperer, right.

Kit got behind the girl. Good, good. Now if only she kept looking at me.

I waited until the very last moment to take out my syringe.

The girl saw it and screamed again, flailed, and Kit made a quick, desperate dive for her. In a tackle that would have made one of the champion Green Bay Packers proud, he grabbed, then lifted her straight up off the ground. Then he rolled with the girl nestled in his arms, neatly cushioning her fall.

We had her! We had her!

Now what?

CHAPTER FIFTY-FOUR

It was as if I were watching a terrifying, and yet mesmerizing dream that I was a part of, but didn't quite believe. The girl fought Kit as a full-sized man would. She was incredibly powerful, brave, but also stubborn and committed to getting away. Maybe that was a stunning clue about her origins, too, or at least how she had gotten free.

Luckily, Kit was stronger than most men, and he was that one man in a hundred who seemed to know his own strength. He subdued the girl without hurting her. She *was* strong, but I wondered if she was also light – for flying. I wondered if she had hollow bones?

I jumped right in there and hit her with the needle. The drug dropped her like a lead weight. Her piercing shrieks were still bouncing off the mountainsides, hanging in the air, but they were getting weaker.

And then she was out.

I didn't know she'd bitten Kit until I saw him squatting

with his right hand tucked under his left armpit. That wasn't good; it could be very bad, in fact. I grabbed his hand and looked at the bite mark. She'd left a perfect impression of uppers and lowers – but she hadn't broken the skin, thank goodness. Had she held back from hurting him? If so, why?

'You don't look so good,' I told him.

'I'm okay, Frannie. Take care of her.'

I took a deep breath and began to work. We got most of the net off the little girl, and I took her pulse. It was a normal sixty-four beats a minute. She was sleeping soundly, but for how long?

I moved long, wet strands of hair off her face. There were dark blue circles under her eyes and her lips were dry and cracked. Again, I was visited with an eerie feeling that this child had been physically abused. It turned my stomach.

'How long will she be out?' Kit asked.

'I'm not sure, but if she metabolizes at the same rate, say, as a large dog, she'll be out for a couple of hours. Oh hell, *who knows*?'

He nodded and the two of us continued to watch the girl in silence. We couldn't help ourselves. I wondered what Kit was thinking about, what he *knew*. He was lost in thought, or maybe awe. I put my hand on his shoulder.

'Let's get her down off the mountain,' I said.

I was having a powerful Sunday-school fantasy: perhaps this little angel *was* a messenger from God. But if she was, what was the message? And who was it for?

CHAPTER FIFTY-FIVE

Harding Thomas was furious, absolutely enraged. He kicked hard at the mound of ashes heaped in the campfire. A gray cloud of soot rose from the ground.

The fire was cold, and there was no telling how long ago it had burned out, or who had been there.

Except that he'd found a long, white feather nearby on the ground. She had been right here, and not long ago.

He turned to Matthew, his bait, only that plan didn't seem to be working out so far. 'She's losing her precious feathers.'

'Like hell,' Matthew sneered, but there was fear in his eyes. He *knew*. 'She's smarter than you, times a hundred.'

'Maybe so, but we'll find her soon. She's not far from here.'

Thomas put the white feather in his cap band and removed a cell phone from its leather pouch on his hip. He didn't want to make this call, but it had to be done. It was his duty. He tapped out a few numbers and was connected.

The reception was as clear as the mountain air. He weighed and measured each word as he spoke to the person on the other end.

'She's still out here, not in plain sight, but we're very close. Unfortunately, she might be getting help. Someone may have found her in the woods, or maybe she found them. No, I don't know that for certain, and I don't know who the hell it is. Maybe campers, or backpackers. We'll soon find out. Unlucky sons of bitches, whoever they are.'

CHAPTER FIFTY-SIX

The dose of Ketamine had worn off and the girl was literally bouncing off the walls. My cabin was too far from anything for anyone to hear her violent pounding and loud thumping, but I could hear her. Kit could hear her. We weren't concerned about the noise. We were afraid she would hurt herself.

I sat beside the door to the spare room. I talked to her through the door, soothingly, I hoped.

Of course, I had no idea what to say, where to start, or even how to communicate with her. But I knew, I thought, this would probably be the most important conversation of my entire life.

'My name's Frannie,' I began, trying to sound as non-threatening as possible under the circumstances. 'I'd like to be your friend. I want to help you. I'm sorry about what happened up on the mountain.'

The pounding stopped for a second, then it resumed again, even louder, wilder, and angrier.

'I'm real sorry about what happened back there, sweetheart. You're safe here, even if it doesn't seem like it. We had to catch you in order to help you. I don't like holding you against your will.'

The kicking and pounding, and shrill, frustrated screams continued. I had no idea whether she understood a single word I'd said. It certainly didn't seem like it.

I kept talking, anyway.

Talking very slowly, calmly, I told her that I was a veterinarian, a doctor who cared for animals, who cared about animals. It happened to be the truth, however self-serving, and that seemed like a good place to start with her.

'I wish I knew something about you,' I said. 'Since I first saw you on the road that night, I've been worried about you. I'm pretty sure you're hungry. Am I right? I wonder if there are people who love you and are looking for you right now . . .'

She was quiet for a moment. I breathed a sigh of relief. Had she finally understood?

Then the noisy commotion began again. She started kicking the walls, and I was afraid the place would fall apart. If I thought she'd been wild and crazy before, now she was really wound up. She let out a high-pitched shriek that could have shattered plate glass. What a syrinx she had.

I lowered my voice. I didn't even know if she could hear me, but I started talking again. 'Are you hungry?' I asked. 'My friend is a very good cook and he's making lunch. Spaghetti with tomato sauce. Do you like spaghetti?'

I stopped talking – held my breath.

Then I heard the distinct sound of *sobbing*. It was no longer hysterical screaming. It was more an exhausted crying, pitiful, and the sound was heartbreaking to me.

Did she understand? Sometimes she seemed to, but then I couldn't tell. I really wanted to help her. Strange – I wanted her to like me, too.

I knew what I had to do next. I took a very deep breath, then I exhaled slowly. 'I'm going to open the door. I promise I won't hurt you. I promise, I promise . . . Don't hurt me, okay?'

I opened the door just a crack and peered in. The girl was hunched over in the bed against the wall. She looked wired, unbelievably tense, and maybe ready to spring at me. Oh Jesus! I had the thought that she was larger than some mountain cats.

Don't be afraid of her, at least don't show it.

I cautiously slipped inside the room. My legs were definitely a shaky and unreliable means of transportation. My mouth was dry.

Then I did the unthinkable – I closed the door behind me.

Frannie the Sap.

I squatted down so that I wasn't standing over her. Animals feel less threatened with me that way. So what if I was completely open and vulnerable to an attack. I didn't think she would go after me.

I saw tears sliding down both her cheeks. She looked just awful, incredibly sad, used up. She was sniffling and hiccuping and crying all at the same time. She seemed so human, and in so much pain. She was breaking my heart and I didn't know how to help her.

Just a little girl. All alone, obviously sad. What had happened to her?

'Aw, Jeez,' I said softly. 'I wish I knew what to do for you, sweetheart. I'm really, really not going to hurt you. Neither is Kit.'

The girl wiped her face on her arm. The gesture was familiar and reassuring, very human and childlike. She was still staring at me. Her bright green eyes were intensely beautiful, brimming with tears.

Then she opened her small mouth. She looked as if she was trying to communicate something. What was it?

'I'd like some spaghetti, please.'

CHAPTER FIFTY-SEVEN

I'*d like some spaghetti, please.*

The little girl could talk.

Kit had to see this. Right now. I wanted him to see and *hear* her. Good God Almighty! I wanted the entire civilized world to hear this.

Just then Kit called out, 'Frannie, soup's on.'

I have no idea on earth what my face must have looked like at that moment. But I was striving for composure when I said to the girl, 'Shall we go to the table? That's Kit. I think the spaghetti's ready.'

She whispered, 'I'd like to wash my hands.'

Wash her hands? We were actually carrying on a conversation. We were, weren't we? Oh God.

'Just a minute,' I called out to Kit. He had no idea! My voice was a muffled squawk, but I thought he'd heard me. I opened the door for the little girl and she walked out past me. I'd asked her to trust me; I had to show some trust, too. She took a few steps, then turned back.

She hesitated. Her eyes held a question.

'Oh yeah,' I said and smiled. 'Turn right.'

She smiled back at me. The girl *smiled* at me and I *melted*. She was absolutely beautiful, and also charming. She was a little girl, for God's sake. She couldn't be any older than eleven or twelve.

I gave her a fresh towel and washcloth. 'Thank you,' she said, and closed the door to the bathroom. I heard her using the facilities and it seemed so unreal. The tap water ran, then shut off. Kit wasn't going to believe this. Hell, I almost didn't believe it myself.

A few moments later, the bathroom doorknob turned slowly and the girl opened the door. She emerged slowly, first just peeking cautiously around the doorjamb. God, she was something else! Her eyes were intelligent, probing mine. She'd washed her face until it was pink and shining. She was such a little beauty. How in hell had this miracle happened? How could it be?

'Come on. Let's eat,' I said.

'Spaghetti? Or *soup*?' she asked, then grinned.

I smiled at her.

I got it. She'd made a little joke.

'Very cute,' I told her. 'You're funny.'

'Yeah,' she said. 'I'm cute as a button. So they say.'

They? Who the hell was 'They'?

I pointed. 'That way. Straight down the hall.'

CHAPTER FIFTY-EIGHT

The two of us entered the tiny dining area just as Kit was bringing a full pitcher of sun tea to the table. He started, fumbled, but nimbly caught the pitcher as it was headed toward the floor. *Good hands.*

He recovered his cool admirably. The G-man. He carefully set the pitcher of tea down. He wiped his wet palms on the back of his jeans.

'Hi, guys,' he said. 'I see we've cleared up our little differences.'

'Maybe,' the girl said. 'We'll see.'

I saw Kit's jaw actually drop. It fell a good four inches. 'Oh. Well, that's nice to hear.'

It was amazing that the wild creature of just hours ago, the one who'd tried to break his bones, the one who'd bitten him, was talking to him now. She was witty and funny, too. Where had she learned to talk, and how to act? Where had she come from?

'This is my friend Kit,' I said to the girl.

'Hello,' she said softly. 'You're the cook, right?'

Kit's jaw dropped again. He nodded his head. 'Yeah, that's me. The chief cook and bottle-washer around here.'

I pulled out a chair for her and the girl wriggled into it. 'Thank you,' she said. She was *polite*, too.

I went to the kitchen, as if this were the most natural thing in the world to do. Alone in there, I tried to stop myself from hyperventilating, tried to get a grip. I brought out the salad bowl, utensils, napkins. I brought a dinner plate for the girl. Placed everything on the table.

My arms, my legs, my hands, everything felt strangely disconnected and discombobulated. My hands were clammy. My body felt as if it were lost in space. I was suffering a little tunnel vision. Other than that, no problem.

I couldn't tear my eyes away from her as I attempted to toss the salad.

'Kit,' I said.

He looked at me. Didn't understand. 'Yes, Frannie?'

'The spaghetti,' I said. 'Some of us are starved.'

'Oh. Right.' He stumbled against a chair, righted it, and went back to the kitchen. He soon returned with the steaming bowl of pasta.

All the while the girl was watching our every move. I was still trying to look nonchalant and wondered if either of them could hear my heart racing, thumping like an old oil well. Did the girl really trust us at all? Would she suddenly bolt from the table? Try to escape from the cabin?

Kit spoke to her, and he still sounded unbelievably calm. 'May I take your plate?' he asked.

She nodded and he slid the plate out from in front of her. He heaped it with spaghetti and covered it with pomodoro sauce. Then he sat down next to me. He served me and finally himself.

The girl looked at him with her perfectly round, bright green eyes. She was waiting for something. *What was it?* We both hung on her every word. How could we not? What would she tell us next? What would she reveal?

'Go ahead,' Kit said. He smiled that dazzler of his. 'Eat, please.'

'Eat the soup,' she said in a straight deadpan.

Kit didn't get it, but the girl and I laughed again. She wasn't just bright, she had good social skills. Where did she get them? Where had she grown up? She had definitely been around adults before.

She folded her hands tightly on the table and closed her eyes. Her voice was barely louder than a whisper.

'Thank you, Lord, for this good food, this very good spaghetti. Amen,' she said.

Tears just leaped out of my eyes.

CHAPTER FIFTY-NINE

Max eased back and forth in the antique rocking chair on the porch, just like any ordinary little girl on a beautiful summer morning.

She was wearing Koss earphones, listening to Meredith Brooks sing a little rocker called 'Bitch.' She felt calm – *calmer*, anyway. She wanted to trust the two of them, but she was still afraid, paranoid, a little nutso.

Afraid of your own shadow, aren't you, Maximum?

The tall, blond man named Kit was inside the house, talking to someone on a telephone. She worried about who it was. He made really good spaghetti – the best she'd ever tasted – but that didn't mean she could trust him with what she knew, with her darkest, deepest secrets, with the whole truth and nothing but the truth about the School.

Frannie had gone for a walk. She said she'd be back in about ten minutes, maybe sooner. She promised that she was bringing back a surprise. We'd see about that. And what kind of surprise?

Max knew that not all surprises were good. Understatement of the year! Most of the surprises in her life sucked big time.

She wanted Frannie and Kit to help her, but she had to find out if they were really good people, if they were worthy of her trust. She definitely liked the fact that they seemed to trust her. That made it easier. Frannie told her that it was okay to go in and out of the house as she pleased. Frannie seemed real nice and easy to be around. And so did Kit, actually.

The outside door at the School was always locked, Max remembered. She felt a shiver knife through her body. Bad memories flooded her brain.

She and Matthew had called it the Flight School. Two pretty good reasons. Number one, because the two of them desperately wanted to fly the hell out of there. Number two, because they were forbidden to fly at the School. So – the Flight School. A protest!

She'd been absolutely forbidden to go outside at the School. Under pain of being put to sleep.

But here she was. Awake. Alive. Listening to 'Bitch.'

The one time the guards had left a door open, the only time she remembered them ever being sloppy – she and Matthew had bolted. Flew the coop, as Matthew said, hollered and whooped, actually.

Max tucked her knees up under her chin. She admired how her legs looked in the black stretch pants Frannie had given her. She also liked the big blue shirt Kit was letting her wear. *'FBI'* was printed on it.

She had a suspicious thought. *The blue shirt covered her wings so that she couldn't fly.*

But it was clean and smelled nice and she didn't want to fly, anyway. Not right now. She wanted to sit in the creaky old rocking chair and listen to rock and roll and eat chocolate chip cookies until they came out of her nose. *God – unlimited cookies. What an idea.*

The rock music played and she liked the rhythm. It kind of matched up with her heartbeat. That was the trick of it, wasn't it?

She was thinking that if Frannie's 'surprise' was good, maybe she'd tell her one of the secrets about the School.

Just one secret, though.

Maybe about Matthew.

Or maybe she'd tell about Adam? Or start with poor Eve? The terrible, terrible night the two of them were put to sleep.

Maybe Kit and Frannie could help her find Matthew.

Her hands clenched automatically. This was very scary territory. One thing had been drilled into her time and time again. She could get into terrible trouble if she ever talked.

People could die, starting with her, and then anyone she talked to.

CHAPTER SIXTY

Pip was pulling me through the woods as if he were the engine of a miniature runaway train. Cicadas shrilled, close up and far away. Everything felt like a dream, but it definitely wasn't one, was it?

'Hold on, fool,' I yelled ahead, but Pip completely ignored me.

I was carrying all kinds of junk on my back: clothes for Max, a little black bag, a 35 mm camera – and Pip was intent on being at the cabin – *now*.

The lead finally jerked out of my hands and he was gone, scampering on ahead, dragging rope and chain behind him, yapping his fool head off.

'Pip! You little snip!'

The girl never had a chance to hear him with those damned earphones on her head. I dropped my pack and ran, but it was too late. He was all over her. Dear God. Would she know Pip was just a small, overeager dog? That he was nothing to be afraid of?

Then I could hear her laughing and the small, playful dog's yipping, and it was just about the neatest sound in the world. It certainly would do for right now.

Kit came flying out through the front door just as I got to the bottom steps of the cabin. He looked concerned – until he correctly sized up the situation.

'Is this my surprise?' the girl asked. Meanwhile, the squirming hunk of dog was slobbering all over her.

'Pip, manners,' I said. 'Yep, he's the surprise.'

The girl said, 'We have dogs at the School. Bandit and Gomer.'

I glanced at Kit. We filed the tidbit away for later.

'This is Pip,' I said. 'He's a good little pup.'

The girl smiled. 'Hello, Pip,' she said.

She picked up a stick and Pip went nuts; backing up, wagging his snippet of a tail, and yapping like the little whirligig and madman that he is.

The girl looked thoughtful for a moment, then she spoke.

'I'm Max,' she said, telling us her name for the first time. Then she threw the stick. 'Go fetch, Pip.'

CHAPTER SIXTY-ONE

I needed to examine Max for injuries and possible malnutrition. I couldn't wait to start. The suspense, the drama, was overwhelming. Most doctors would kill for this opportunity, and perhaps someone had.

I stood outside the familiar and usually nonthreatening door to the spare room of my house and I took one of the deepest breaths of my entire breathing career. Kit and I had just been talking about bringing Max to the 'authorities,' the local police, or maybe even to the University of Colorado at Boulder.

'I *am* the police,' Kit had argued. He was definitely against the move. 'And for the moment, I'm not certain who else we can trust. I'm working on that, Frannie. Please give me another day or so to check out some things.'

His reaction wasn't very reassuring, but I had my own misgivings about the local authorities in Nederland, or even Boulder. I didn't feel they were quite up to this. I hadn't from the beginning.

So Max was behind Door Number One, waiting for me to give her a full physical exam. She had already told me it was no big deal to her – she was used to them.

Well, it was a big deal for me.

I left Kit on the front deck, making calls around the country. He had a couple of notebooks filled with information about the outlaw group of scientists who might have settled somewhere in the area. He'd already interviewed dozens of doctors who knew someone in the group. He told me the investigation was like trying to cross the country by way of a network of blind alleys. He sure wasn't wearing his million-dollar smile today. He admitted that he was frustrated and nervous about what would happen now. Neither of us really knew what it was that we were getting into. How could we?

I knocked gently on the door. I heard Max say, 'Come in.'

I opened the door and walked in, carrying my black medical bag, trying not to appear as nervous as I was.

Max put down *People* magazine, which she said she read every week, and since we'd discussed the physical exam beforehand, she started to take off her clothes without my having to ask. I kept wondering *who* had examined her before this?

What I saw now squeezed the breath out of my body. I felt exhilarated, but also more nervous than ever, and afraid. I felt as if I had suddenly been recruited onto the

National Bioethics Committee. This was definitely medical history. This was a miracle.

The young girl standing before me had no nipples, no vestige of breasts. The massive depth of her chest was incredible. The drape of her smock when I first saw her and the bulk of Kit's shirt had disguised a rib cage fully two times as deep as mine.

That was understandable, I was thinking, as I prepared to examine her. Max had to pack an awful lot of musculature into that chest in order to fly. Also, her flight muscles had to be anchored into something very solid. Perhaps a super-heavy breastbone, or a Y-shaped collarbone. How had this happened? Who had created her – and why? It made me dizzy and weak-kneed.

I moved closer. 'Stethoscope,' I said, and she nodded that it was okay with her.

Her shoulders were broad, and her pectoral muscles were anchored to an oversized breastbone called the pectoral crest. Absolutely extraordinary. As I pressed my stethoscope to her back, or 'sternal keel,' she took a deep breath and then released it.

She knew exactly what she was supposed to do. She was accustomed to physical exams. By whom? For what reason? What was the School all about?

'Is the stethoscope too cold?' I asked Max.

'No,' she said. 'Toasty warm.'

She spoke very well for a young girl. Her language could be colorful and descriptive. I'd heard her use both humor and irony. She was bright. Why? How? Who had taught her to speak? How to act? To be polite and considerate, as she certainly was.

'Would you take another deep breath,' I said. Max nodded. She did as she was asked. She was being very cooperative, and she was almost always polite. Max was a very sweet young girl.

I couldn't believe what I heard inside her chest. She didn't have the bellows-type action of mammal lungs. Hers were relatively small, and from what I could hear, attached to air sacs, both anterior and posterior. What lungs! I could write a book on her lungs alone. Man, oh man! I was having a little trouble breathing now myself.

I couldn't be sure, but it followed logically that her bones were hollow, that some air sacs intruded into her bones.

'Thanks, Max. That's great.'

'It's okay. I understand. I'm a freak.' She shrugged her shoulders.

'No, you're just special.'

I turned her to face me and placed my stethoscope over her heart. Jesus. It was at a resting rate of 64 beats a minute, but it was *booming*.

Max had the heart of an athlete, a great athlete. The organ was huge. I figured it weighed a couple of pounds. She had the heart of a good-sized horse.

A large, powerful heart could pump a lot of blood. The connecting chain of air sacs indicated a one-way flow of air. A big pump and a lot of air surface made for a very efficient means of exchanging carbon dioxide for oxygen. This was understandable to me. It made good sense. It would give her the endurance she needed to fly long distances and would also keep her cells saturated with oxygen at high altitudes, where the atmosphere was thin.

As if she'd read my mind, Max began to beat her wings.

CHAPTER SIXTY-TWO

'**Y**ou *have* done this before,' I said and smiled. I couldn't help myself. She was such a cool little girl. Relaxed, well-mannered, and funny.

'Millions of times,' Max said.

She lifted a foot off the ground and hovered there.

I stood on a footstool and pressed the stethoscope to her chest again and listened to her heart as it pounded far too fast for me to count. I stopped listening and looked at her. I marveled at Max. My mind was in the process of being completely blown away.

'I can get it up to two hundred beats a minute without straining,' she said. Then she winked. 'Pretty cool, huh?'

'Very cool,' I said. I placed my hands on her hips. 'Okay,' I whispered. 'That's enough of this for right now. Thank you.'

'You're very welcome.'

Max stopped beating her wings and dropped to the

floor. I measured her from head to toe. I was trying to regain my composure.

'Fifty-seven inches,' she piped up.

Right. She was exactly four foot nine. Her arms and legs were slightly disproportionate; the legs were longer. The ring and pinky fingers of both hands were partially fused, but it wasn't noticeable unless you looked closely. There was tiny webbing between her toes.

These adaptations allowed her to use her hands and feet as a kind of rudder mechanism in lieu of a tail. There was also some feathering down the back of her legs. That would help in flight, too. Provide more rudder.

Her neck was very flexible. Her reflexes were much, much better than mine – or anybody else's. Her distance and peripheral vision were acute. No, they were extraordinary. She was superior in almost every way – the best of humans, the best of birds.

As I'd already suspected, her feathered wings were perfectly jointed. Blindfolded, I'd have thought they belonged to a large bird that did some serious long-distance soaring; hawks, for instance, or birds that fish the ocean. *Was Max part human, part hawk? How, how, how had this happened?*

I put my tape measure to a wing tip and, without my asking, Max spanned her wings.

'One hundred and ten inches,' she said with pride. Her soft voice had a rustling sound, like wind blowing over dried cornstalks.

'Thanks,' I said. 'A little over nine feet of wingspan.' Biggest wings I'd ever seen on an eleven-year-old girl.

I asked Max to please lie down on the bed. I palpated her abdominal cavity, got a fix on her organs, which were in the expected places, but small.

Again, this was logical and understandable. Flight was only possible if the wings could lift the body. So, strong chest muscles, small organs, and, unless I was way off the mark, her bones would not only be lightweight and hollow but also very strong in order to cope with the considerable stress of flight.

A perfect design, I thought.

She had been designed, hadn't she?

'Are you going to give me a pelvic?' Max asked.

She'd been given pelvic exams? I was shocked, but I didn't allow my discomfort to show.

'No,' I said. 'I'm not.'

'Oh. Well, I can tell you, anyway,' she said, putting on her pants. She grinned. 'I'm *oviparous*.'

Oviparous, indeed. That explained why Max had no breasts. If reproduction were possible, she wouldn't be delivering live offspring. And she wouldn't be nursing them.

Her babies would hatch from eggs.

CHAPTER SIXTY-THREE

My thoughts at this point in the physical exam were flying fast and furious. I felt as if my head had actually taken off and gone into permanent orbit. I had been aching for the chance to find out who or what this magical creature was. Now that I had examined her, I could hardly absorb what I had learned. She was supergirl, wasn't she?

A perfect design.

But who was the designer? Or designers?

I needed an X-ray machine. I needed blood analysis equipment. I needed medical and zoological experts to help me interpret the data. I had more questions now than ever before.

'So tell me, where do you come from, Max?' I said, as I put my stethoscope back in my medical bag.

She gave me one of her mischievous smiles. 'A cabbage patch,' she said. 'I was left there by a stork.'

Then her green eyes narrowed. 'How come I have wings and you don't?' she asked.

'I don't know. That *is* the big question, though.'

Max looked hurt. Did she think I was lying to her? Withholding? From the sudden pained look on her face, I could see that she'd really wanted me to give her a good answer. 'They' had kept her in the dark about herself, hadn't they?

'I'm going to try to find out,' I said. 'Give me some time. This is all new and overwhelming to me. Please, trust me a little, Max.'

'I trust no one,' she snapped. I saw a spark of anger, bitterness, and a lot of hurt in her eyes.

Had she been living with medical researchers? Young people? Lab techies? I'd noticed that her language could be very colloquial, and *young*. I kept testing her with figures of speech.

'You think grown-ups are full of it, don't you?' I said.

Max shrugged. 'Whatever. I'm going to play with Pip, okay? May I? Is that allowed? Or do I have to stay inside – now that you have what you want from me.'

'No, Max. Go play.'

She bolted from the room. She was angry. Was it with me, or something I'd said? Whatever it was, she was starting to cry. Max was able to cry, and that was stunning to me. I imagined an eagle soaring over the land that man was so obviously wasting, and being able to *cry* about it. Or a mother robin *crying* over an injured chick she couldn't help.

I found Kit out on the deck where I'd left him earlier. When he saw me, he hung up his cell phone.

'What happened in there? She looked like she was crying.'

'Well, she didn't tell me where she lives,' I said softly. 'But what I learned from examining her completely knocks me out. Kit, she's medical history. *However* it happened.'

'Tell me,' he said. His eyes became intense, probing. *I am the police.*

'I don't know where to start exactly. I think she's a human being who was born to fly. Max is definitely human. She's got a human brain, emotions, but the rest of her is an amalgam of human and avian pieces and parts. The human parts seem to dominate. And this *School* she's talked about, whatever it is, has scientists attached to it.'

Kit looked grim. 'How do you know for sure?'

'She's accustomed to being examined. Max knows a lot of medical terms. I don't know how or why. She told me that she's oviparous. She's an egg layer.'

There was a silence between us, broken only by the sounds of Max and Pip playing across the yard.

'Are you saying she's actually some kind of cross between a human and a bird? Is that possible?' Kit muttered.

'No. I don't think it is. Except for one small and very convincing detail . . .'

Kit finished my sentence. 'We're looking at it,' he said. 'My God.'

We watched as Max scooped Pip up into her arms.

There was the sound of beating wings, and then she was airborne. She was flying above the treetops with Pip, who didn't seem to mind in the least.

CHAPTER SIXTY-FOUR

D iscretion was absolutely critical. Nothing could go wrong from this moment on. The serious mistakes of the past day were already being rectified. Damage control was being done.

The important 'visitors' had begun to arrive in the greater Denver area as inconspicuously as possible. Painstaking thought and planning had gone into every facet of their individual journeys, but especially into keeping their presence here a secret, not only from the world at large, but from their business associates, even from their families.

Each of them knew what was at stake. Each understood that this was a profound moment, and that they were privileged to be a part of it, even by their high standards of privilege. And each knew the tremendous personal risks if they were caught. There would be convincing denials, but ultimately, they would be left out to hang.

Two of the principals came as a married couple, which

was the simplest, and the best possible disguise. The largest group comprised four German males who claimed to be enthusiastic freshwater fishermen bound for fly-fishing along the Continental Divide.

Two travelers came from a major corporation in Tokyo. If anybody asked, they were here to see the Colorado Shakespeare Festival. They were staying at the Boulder Victoria Historic Inn, and taking roll after roll of photos like stereotypical tourists. Another man represented one of the largest and most important corporations in France. According to his story, he was there to visit the Chatauqua Music Fest and also the Niwot Ragtime Festival. The visitors had agreed to stay in small, surrounding towns, with names like Lafayette, Nederland, Louisville, Long-mont, Blackhawk.

The married couple, who were from London, camped out, 'roughed it' American-style, in a tent at Rocky Mountain National Park, about fifty miles to the northwest of Boulder. An important CEO from Bernardsville, New Jersey, stayed at the splendid and quite beautiful Gold Lake Mountain Resort.

Each visitor had been *assigned* to a specific Colorado town. They had been requested to dress and act like vacationers; to stay in smallish lodges and inns like the Black Dog Bed & Breakfast, the Hotel Boulderado, the Briar Rose. As important as all the visitors were in their own sphere of influence, they did exactly as they were told.

They could see the larger picture: the history of humans was about to change.

CHAPTER SIXTY-FIVE

There could be no evidence.

There could be no witnesses.

Harding Thomas led a dozen hunters walking 'the grid' from Rough Rider Road out toward the Peak-to-Peak highway. They had dogs now, hounds stoked on the scent of the winged girl. The paired men and dogs were spaced ten feet apart. They marked off parallel lines as they cut back and forth through the woods. They were mostly former army officers. They chose to believe this exercise was in the spirit of national defense, and maybe even America's survival.

When they had walked the full length of the grid they stepped out of it. Then they would mark the next section. They methodically searched grid after grid for any traces of the missing girl.

They didn't speak or joke around or even light up smokes today. The only sounds were their heavy boots trampling the underbrush, and the constant snuffling of the frantic overtrained hounds.

On the other side of the Peak-to-Peak were the impressive foothills of the Rockies. Two choppers were presently scouting up there. They were equipped with infrared equipment that could scan wide swaths of the landscape below. It reported back on a view screen every warm-blooded creature that it passed over. Deer, moose, bears, rabbits, birds, all creatures great and small.

The girl wouldn't get away now. There was zero chance; zero possibility. She couldn't hide from the infrared for much longer. Or from the hunters, the methodical trackers, the trained dogs.

But somehow, that's exactly what she was doing so far. The girl seemed to have disappeared into thin air.

They'd been out here for several hours. The sun was going down in a hurry. It didn't matter. The intense search would continue through the night if necessary. More help had already been called in – very worried and concerned doctors and researchers from the Denver and Boulder area. Men and women who worked at the School, and could be trusted with the truth.

They already had a cover story, and it was the best kind because it happened to be true – they were searching for a young girl who was lost in the woods.

Max was now a threat to everything.

CHAPTER SIXTY-SIX

I felt as if I desperately needed to come up for air. I simply couldn't breathe. Kit had suggested that I go about my normal business for a couple of hours, take a break, and I figured that was a good idea.

Gillian and I had agreed to get together again soon, anyway. We'd made plans the night Frank McDonough drowned in his pool. Gillian had even made me promise to come. The circumstances of Frank's death still upset me terribly. I just couldn't imagine Frank drowning.

One of the reasons I don't go to her house more often is that it's about an hour ride. On the trip there, I started to have some really bad thoughts. First, David had died; then it had been Frank; now, I started to worry about Gillian. There wasn't any logical reason for my fears, but I had this feeling she might be in danger.

As I drove, I had the unwelcome fantasy that I might arrive at her house and find police cars and EMS. The only saving grace was that I knew it wasn't likely. But then, neither was David's death. Or Frank's.

I put my mind in a more positive place. Mind over paranoia. Visiting with Gillian was always one of the highpoints in my week. After David's death, no one had been more supportive, more of a friend, not even my sister Carole. I could talk to Gillian for hours, even over the phone, but in person was always the best. Gillian had lost her husband about two years earlier. That was part of our bond – but it was so much more now.

By the time I got to her house in the hills, I was more hyper and anxious than I thought I'd be. One tricky thing: Kit had sworn me to secrecy about the girl. Although I felt he was right to keep Max a secret for now, it was going to be a challenge to see Gillian, and not talk, not tell her about the extraordinary girl. Not telling almost seemed like lying.

Actually, I wanted to see if I could get some information from her. Gillian is 'good people,' very down-to-earth, but she has a medical degree from U.C.L.A. *and* a Ph.D. in biology from Stanford. She's an encyclopedia, not just on science topics, but also economics, astronomy, the Denver Nuggets, Colorado Rockies, you name it, Gillian knows it.

She's also a terrific mom, and that's probably what I like best about her.

I could see her now. She was safe and sound. I could also see her little boy, Michael, splashing in the pool as I climbed out of my car. I felt better already.

Breathe. In with the good, out with the bad, I told myself, but it was easier said than done.

'Did you bring a bathing suit?' Gillian asked. She was

wearing a blue-and-black-striped Speedo, and she was in terrific shape for fifty-one. She runs five miles a day, and has for the past thirty years. When she was in her forties, she ran in the New York City Marathon.

'As a matter of fact, I did bring a suit,' I said, and stripped off my blouse and shorts to prove it. I had on a red-and-white-striped one-piece that I liked well enough.

Gillian whistled and clapped her hands. She's a terrific cheerleader. 'Look at you! Frannie, you look great.'

I rolled my head around loosely on my shoulders, and did my best Jimmy Stewart – heck, b'gum, b'gosh. 'Been hiking and stuff, ya know. Busy at the critter hospital. Guess I lost a few pounds somewhere.' B'golly.

'Listen to you. Something else is different,' Gillian said and laughed. She has a big, toothy smile that I find quite wonderful. 'Did you color your hair, Dr O'Neill? If you did it looks great. There's definitely something going on.'

There certainly is, Gil. I'm just sorry I can't tell you what it is.

A blond boy of four emerged from the pool, looking all slick and silly. He ran to his mom, interrupting our talk, but doing it so innocently it was charming and sweet. Michael was only two when his father had died of a coronary in his office at Boulder Community. He was growing up beautifully, anyway.

'What, Doodlebug?' she said. 'Say hello to Aunt Frannie.'

'Hi, Aunt Frannie!' Michael beamed. I bent down and

he kissed me. He is a beautiful little doodlebug.

'I'm playing *seal*,' Michael announced. 'My seal name is Black Nose. This,' he said, pointing to an inflatable raft, 'is Iceland. *Cool*, huh?'

'Iceland is very cool,' I said and grinned.

We watched as Michael dived from the low board and slipped perfectly into the water without a splash. 'He's so cute,' I told her.

Gillian looked at me again. She stared into my eyes and something *clicked*. I could see her mind working. 'You're in love,' she said, accusingly. 'Yes you are. I'm sure of it.'

'Nope. No way. Get out of here,' I said and made a face.

'You are, too. Now you tell me this insta— what, Michael? Okay, I'll time you. Don't *you* go anywhere,' she said to me. 'I'm on to your game.'

Gillian marched to the deep end of the pool. She really was in excellent shape. She held a watch out in front of her. 'On your mark, get set, go for it.'

Black Nose the Seal did another dive. He swam nearly half the length of the pool underwater, right under Iceland. He finally surfaced.

I was feeling a little giddy. God, did I have news. I wanted to shout out to my friend – *Want to hear about another great kid? An amazing little girl! I'll tell you about a girl who's sweet and funny – and who can skim the treetops without breathing hard.*

'So, Frannie, tell all. You'd better tell me what's going on with you,' Gillian said, as she returned to the deck chair beside me, ' 'cause I'm going to find out. You know I will. Talk to me. Confess.'

'Well,' I said, 'in that case, I'll spare myself. I *might* be a little in love.'

I told her all about Kit, at least what I *could* tell. I left out the part about our finding Max, of course. And I also didn't mention that he was with the FBI.

CHAPTER SIXTY-SEVEN

Kit was worried, even more uptight than he'd been, but he was definitely feeling sick to his stomach.

He had what he jokingly called 'FBI stomach,' a recognizable queasiness, a tenderness and weakness that belied the hardness of his gut. He'd been hanging out with little Max all day, playing it as cool as he possibly could. He had hoped she'd drop some information about where she had come from. She hadn't so far.

He had checked in with Peter Stricker's office and they hadn't come up with a whole hell of a lot about Dr Frank McDonough – other than that he had once worked with James Kim in California, which Kit knew already. Actually, he had called in just about every favor he could in Washington and Quantico, but nothing he found out was too helpful.

This wasn't good. He was in an extremely tough place

now. He ought to tell Stricker about Max, but something inside told him not to do it yet. Call it his sixth sense. Call it certifiable insanity. Or death wish for his career.

Whatever the name, it was an emotional component that the Bureau wasn't as high on as he was. He understood that a lot of people wouldn't have agreed with his thinking, but they hadn't observed how the Bureau had treated this case. They hadn't been there. They hadn't seen the disparaging look on Peter Stricker's face, or the cynicism in his voice.

After Frannie returned from her friend Gillian's house they ate another pasta dinner with Max. Frannie definitely seemed more relaxed. They took a moonlit walk in the woods later that night. Max knew the names for most of the trees they passed, the flowers, shrubs. She seemed to like to talk once she got started.

'Impressive,' Frannie told her. 'You know more about these woods than I do.'

'I read a lot,' Max said and shrugged. 'And I retain information.'

'Did you go to classes at the School?' Kit asked as they circled back toward the cabin. The moon was a large white plate looming over the dark treetops.

'What do you think?' Max answered with a question, then she scooted on ahead of them – walking, not flying.

'I've got an idea,' Kit offered when they got close to the cabin. 'Let's all go for a car ride, see the sights a little. What do you say, Max?'

'I love that idea!' Max said and seemed terrifically

excited. Her green eyes beamed. She jumped into the air – and stayed up. 'I've never been in a car before! Never in my whole life!'

CHAPTER SIXTY-EIGHT

The Jeep held the three of us in front. Since it was already past midnight, Kit figured we would be safe enough. On the way out of Bear Bluff there wasn't another car on the road. So far, so good. Max was positively radiant as she peered out through the windows.

A little more than an hour later, we entered the city of Denver, which at that time of night was pretty much shut down. I knew the glittering skyline very well. The Daniels and Fisher Tower, modeled after the Venetian campanile, pierced the darkened sky. So did the State Capitol, a Federal Revival-style building, with a gold-leafed dome. The beautiful Cathedral of the Immaculate Conception was framed up ahead. And clearly visible, even at night, was the looming and magnificent Front Range of the Rockies.

I think Kit was trying to get on Max's good side, and maybe it was working out. We were taking a small risk coming here late at night, we knew, but not too much of one.

I watched Max out of the corner of my eye. She kept shaking her head in utter amazement and awe. 'Look at the buildings, the lights, the *everything*. I never knew there were so many tall buildings in the whole wide world.'

Kit and I pointed out the McNichols Sports Arena, Larimer Square, the Mile-High Stadium. Max made Kit stop the Jeep so she could look at a red-brick school building covered with expressive, very colorful murals. *A school*. A nice, peaceful one.

She'd never been in a city, but she knew a lot about them. She'd learned about them reading books at the School. She was having the adventure of a lifetime. She was taking in a lot of new information, and retaining it.

I pointed out a unique building nicknamed 'the Cash Register,' a big silvery rectangle with a rounded top. Suddenly, Max clapped her hands over her ears. Her hearing was acute. The noise was certainly a lot louder than the Jeep's engine. It was coming over our heads, but it was already moving away.

'It's a helicopter,' Kit said in a soft, calming voice. 'It's nothing to be afraid of, Max. See the large letters painted on the sides?'

Max nodded. '9 News – KUSA,' she read.

'KUSA is a TV station here in town. There are a couple of people in the helicopter sending television pictures back to the station. They're *good guys*. They bring the rest of us news about the world, about the Denver area, anyway. Probably there was an accident tonight. Something happened for them to be out this late.'

'The helicopter looks like a big, really weird bird,' Max said. 'No wonder the good guys want to fly in it. I would. I'd like to race it, too. *Hey good guys – want to race? You'd lose!'*

Kit finally pulled the Jeep over to the curb so that Max could get a better look as the helicopter banked west and spun away from us. He seemed to like showing her things. I wondered if he was remembering better times with his own children. There was a gentleness, a softness in his eyes, that was touching to see.

'Sometimes they're called "whirlybirds," ' he said.

'Whirlybirds,' Max repeated. 'I knew that from the School. My teacher's name was Mrs Beattie. I loved her. I think they put her to sleep,' she whispered sadly.

Without asking, she threw open the front door.

'Max,' I shouted. 'Max! Max!'

Too late, though. She had wriggled free. She ran a few yards down a dark city sidewalk, then took off. I could hear her wings flapping. Kit and I jumped out of the Jeep and watched her ascend higher and higher. I was afraid for a lot of reasons. Denver can have pretty wicked winds, even in the summer. Plus, somebody might see her.

'Max!' I called out again. Damn, damn, damn. She was already too far away.

Kit cupped his hands around his mouth and shouted with me. She *must* have heard us; her hearing was acute. She acted like she didn't hear a thing.

We watched her fly almost straight up the side of a tall,

sleek, thirty- or forty-story building. It was pretty amazing, I must admit. I wondered if she could see her own reflection in the dark glass, and what it felt like to fly around up there.

The news helicopter was out of view by the time Max began to circle the skyscraper. She was peering into offices. She soared toward another office building whose windows were lit to spell out the words 'GO ROCKIES!'

She could probably see the entire city of Denver laid out beneath her. Cherry Creek forked off from the Platte River. The Elitch Gardens Amusement Park was off in the distance.

I hoped that no one saw her, and if they did, that they couldn't believe their eyes. That's what happened to me the first time.

She did a couple of acrobatic loops. Then Max flew back down toward Kit and me. She *dived*, pulled out of it beautifully, and landed right next to the Jeep.

'This is so great!' she said, and she was smiling, laughing out loud. 'Thank you, thank you both. I dreamed about doing that since I was a little girl.'

We climbed back in the Jeep.

Max wrapped her soft, feathery arms around me and she hugged me all the way home.

CHAPTER SIXTY-NINE

In her warm, snuggly bed at the cabin, Max was replaying the glorious night in Denver. She was having good thoughts for a change, especially about Frannie and Kit. They were so nice to her. They were like the mother and father she'd never had.

Suddenly, Max stiffened. She tilted her head to one side. *They were coming.* She heard them, felt them in every part of her body.

All of her senses told her it was so. They were sneaking up on the cabin right now. She wasn't paranoid, wasn't making this up. She wanted to scream a warning for Frannie and Kit, but she held it inside.

Don't let the attackers know that you know.

She angled herself out of the bed and went to the closest window. She peeked outside. It was a moonlit night. She heard the crackling of the underbrush. One of the men appeared, came sneaking out of the woods.

She knew who he was – one of the meanest guards. The

Security people from the School were here. They had found her. And they were here for Frannie and Kit, too.

Suddenly, Max was eighty pounds of flapping wings, fueled with fear and fury. She flew out of the small bedroom! *She flew inside the house.*

She whipped back toward the rear bedrooms. Frannie and Kit were asleep in two of the rooms. Their senses weren't nearly as sharp as hers. But then again, neither were the Security creeps' senses.

Forbidden! Forbidden! She wasn't supposed to fly! But who gives a damn what the guards say! They don't run things out here in the real world. She ran her own life now.

Pip came out of nowhere, starting up a high-pitched barking frenzy. Pip *knew*, too. He sensed the danger, the men close by in the woods. What a good dog!

The barking woke Kit. He blew out of the back room with his gun in hand. He saw Max flying down the hall, coming straight at him. 'Jesus, Max!'

'They're coming, Kit! They're real close. Lots of them. They're here for us!'

'Who's coming, Max?'

'Not now! *Please.* Let's go. Let's go. They'll kill us. They'll kill all of us!'

Frannie had come out of the other bedroom. She was in the hallway with a look of pure astonishment on her face.

'Please! *Trust* me!' Max pleaded with both of them, and it was at that moment she realized how much they already meant to her.

'Get dressed, Frannie.' Kit nodded his head. 'Back door. The Jeep. I'll drive. Don't look back. Just run like hell.' He was shouting as he put on his clothes.

Kit grabbed Max's hand. They were running full blast. Frannie went ahead of them and threw open the back door! Man, woman, child, and dog spilled out of the house into the pitch blackness of the night. None of them looked back.

The Jeep started like a lucky charm. As it screeched out of the rear parking area, shots slammed into metal. Glass exploded. The rear window had been shot out. The Jeep bounced high over the deeply rutted dirt road. Kit drove through the gunfire as if he'd done it before.

They fled.

Frannie and Kit had trusted her, Max kept thinking, and that changed everything.

CHAPTER SEVENTY

There is nothing more exhilarating than to be shot at without result. I don't remember who said that first, but whoever it was, they were definitely right.

The insane tornado of the night's events had whipped us into persons we hardly knew, or even recognized. Coming off near death at my house, we looked like hell and felt worse. The idea of someone trying to kill us was so monstrous that it was difficult for me to make it concrete and real in my mind. *What had just happened couldn't have happened – and yet it did. Someone had shot at Kit's Jeep, at us. Someone had tried to kill Max, Kit, and myself.* I'd never had a terrifying thought like that before.

We were huddled in a cruddy, awful Motel Six somewhere off Interstate 70. I think we were in the town of Idaho Springs, which has its fair share of crummy motels. The door was locked and chained, but how safe were we? Not very. Cheap, lime-green curtains covered the plate-glass window. The room lights were out, but I could see

Max and Kit by the flickering light of the television set.

Max was eerily detached from what had happened, or so it seemed. She was up to her chin in bedcovers and Kit had pulled a chair right up to the bed.

I knew that he liked Max a lot, but they were locked in a struggle now. Kit believed we'd die if Max didn't talk to us about where she came from, and Max thought she'd die if she did.

His voice was cold. I had never heard him speak in that tone before. I guess he was being an FBI agent now. Professional, intense, very focused on what he felt had to be done.

'I really need some answers, Max. I'm telling you, you have to start trusting somebody soon. I mean, like right now. I'm talking to you, Max.'

'I know who you're talking to. I just don't like your tone,' she answered back.

Max's fragile composure broke suddenly. She leaped off the bed, ran to the bathroom, and locked herself in.

'Leave me alone! You sound just like them. *Trust me.*' She mimicked Kit. 'Why should I trust anybody? I'm not like you, Kit! Haven't you noticed?'

'Please, she's just a little girl, Kit,' I said, my own voice pinched thin by stress, fear, and the unhinged craziness of the past hour.

He shook his head – once. 'No. She's not *just* a little girl. Unfortunately, she's more than that. People are apparently dying because of her. We almost died back there, Frannie. We have to find the School where she was being kept, at least I do.'

That made me angry. 'Don't be like that, Kit. I have to find the so-called School, too. In case you haven't noticed, I'm involved up to my eyeballs.'

Every time I looked at Max I wanted to hug her, but Kit was right. She was no more *just* a little girl than this was *just* a road trip. The truth is, we had no idea exactly what Max was, or what her being here meant. Only Max knew, and she wasn't talking.

Kit turned and tripped over a tin trash can full of junk-food wrappers from McDonald's. He picked up the can and fired it hard against the wall. He kicked it a few times for good measure.

Reflexively, I threw my arm over my eyes as the noise reverberated. My dad used to lose his temper sometimes, back at our farm in Wisconsin. He'd throw things around, but never anything valuable; and he never hit anyone in our family, not even a spanking. Maybe that's why I wasn't really afraid of Kit's mild, almost humorous tantrum.

'Something wrong?' I asked when the noise stopped.

If I thought I'd get a smile out of him, or that I'd shift his mood, I was mistaken.

'I didn't mean to scare her,' Kit said, his voice catching. 'I really like her, Frannie. She's a great kid. It's just that – we could all die.'

'I know. She knows, too. She'll be okay.' Max had a hair-trigger flight response. I knew that people who'd been battered acted like that. What had been done to this little girl? Who had hurt her, and how? We needed to know more about the School. Where it was. How it had worked. What was going on there. Who the people were.

Kit walked to the bathroom door and knocked softly. 'Max, I'm sorry if I sounded mad,' he said. His voice was gentle, concerned. 'I *was* mad. I'm worried about your safety, and I don't know what to do without your help.' I guess that was one way of saying, *people are trying to kill us*.

Max was quiet behind the bathroom door. Not a peep from her. Sometimes, she *was* a little girl.

Kit appealed to me in a whispered voice. 'Please, get her out of there. Will you at least try? C'mon, Frannie, help me.'

CHAPTER SEVENTY-ONE

I slowly walked to the bathroom. I didn't know what I was going to say, didn't have a clue. I knew I wouldn't lie to her. I stood outside the locked door for a moment, composing my thoughts. When I opened my mouth to speak, the words came spontaneously and from the heart.

'Max, I promise that nobody is going to make you do anything you don't want to do. I know that. You know that. We'll figure out the best thing *together*. Don't you think that's the fair way? You have any other idea?'

There was a long pause. Total silence behind the bathroom door. Max could be incredibly wilful and stubborn sometimes. She was almost a teenager. I was seeing that already. Then the knob of the door slowly turned.

Max didn't look at either of us as she came out of the bathroom. 'I'm sorry. I just got scared,' she whispered as she climbed back into bed. She was being a little sweetheart under this incredible pressure.

Pip jumped on the bed and she folded herself around him. I sat down behind her and lightly preened her feathers. A bird will do this smoothing feathers, realigning microscopic hooks along the edges so that they form a seamless unit. I was thinking about how to break this impasse without upsetting her again.

'It's okay, Max,' I whispered.

'No it isn't, Frannie. You don't know.'

Tell us your secrets, Max. We trusted you. Now you trust us a little.

After a while I asked, 'What are the people like at the School? Just tell a little bit. Are they scientists? Doctors? Are they teachers?'

'Sort of,' she said. 'They taught me to read slides. Mostly science, but I could read what I liked on my own time. They put me to work. Most of them are scientists. They're doctors.'

Kit was pacing back and forth in the room, staring at the floor. When he heard the word 'slides,' he stopped moving. 'What do you mean, "slides"? What kind of slides, Max?'

'That you look at with a microscope. In the labs. I was allowed to work there. I was supposed to match alleles.'

The incredible tension kept building inside me. Chaos and confusion reigned in my mind. Alleles were alternative forms of a gene. What Max had said about the School so far was unbelievably scary and wrong.

'The doctors are working with chromosomes?' I asked. 'Why are they doing that? Do you know?'

'Of course I do. To improve the stock,' she said, and shrugged her shoulders.

'What kind of stock?' Kit asked. This had evolved into a question and answer session. I felt like a police officer.

Max's face went pale-white. 'I could get people in trouble if I talk,' she said. 'I've been warned. Talking is absolutely forbidden,' she murmured.

Max covered her eyes and sobbed hard. I stopped braiding her hair and gathered her into my arms. 'Please trust us, Max. You have to trust somebody. You know that you do, honey.'

I rocked the child, the beautiful little bird-girl. I felt as if I were back at the Inn-Patient, taking care of sick and injured animals. That's where I wanted to be.

Max spoke softly into the side of my neck. I could barely hear the words, but I *did*.

'Take me home,' she whispered.

BOOK 4

THE FLIGHT SCHOOL

CHAPTER SEVENTY-TWO

Take me home.

It had obviously been hard for Max to say the words. It sounded so innocent coming out of her mouth, but I knew it wasn't. We couldn't get out of the Motel Six fast enough.

We zoomed down the Interstate at eighty miles an hour and then some, hoping a highway patrolman wouldn't stop us for speeding.

We were going to the School, weren't we?

I was in the back with Max. She was clearly scared, so I held her tightly. I could feel her heart beating against my arm way too fast. Poor Max. Just a little girl. Caught up in something much larger than any of us could comprehend.

I stroked her as I talked, hoping it would soothe and calm the eleven-year-old. I told Max I'd grown up on a dairy farm in northern Wisconsin and asked her if she'd ever seen a real cow.

'We don't have any cows at the School,' she said. 'I've

seen lots of them on TV, though.'

I told her about our small herd of Holsteins, with their gooey tongues and liquid eyes. I even remembered their names and personalities. Max couldn't disguise her curiosity as I described Blossom Dearie and Nellie Foot-Foot and Please Louise and our spotted bull, Kool Kat.

I told her how my sister, Carole Anne, and I got up at five in the morning to help my dad; and how we washed the cows in the summer and turned on the electric fan so they'd stay cool. But it was how we got milk from them that really fascinated her.

She hooted out loud as I described the joys of early morning milkings. I loved to hear her laugh. It was infectious and always made me smile. Max took such delight in the world she hadn't been able to experience until now. And besides, laughing kept our minds off everything else that was going on.

I made up a goofy story about chocolate cows giving chocolate milk. Kit tossed in a thought. 'Tell her about the peppermint cows,' he said and winked.

'You two are crazy,' Max told us. 'It's nice, though. I like it. I love being here with you.'

'We love being with you, too,' I said.

'Me three,' Kit nodded agreement.

The Jeep sped through the early morning dark. I was thinking, pretending, *Hey, maybe it was just a road trip, after all* – when Max stiffened. She strained forward toward the front seat and the windshield.

Then she pointed to a narrow side road that slipped off behind a rocky outcropping. 'Turn here, Kit.'

'How do you know that?' I asked. I didn't doubt Max, but I was curious. I was pretty sure she'd never been on this road before. I lived near here, and I don't think I was ever on it.

She shrugged, then peered deeply into my eyes. She could be smiling, then suddenly turn very intense and serious. 'Can't you feel the dairy farm where you used to live?'

'It's far away,' I said. 'I'd need a map to find it.'

'I *feel* the School,' Max said. 'I know exactly where it is. I can see the way there in my mind.'

I understood what she was saying, and it hit me hard. I felt an uncomfortable lump in my throat. Like pigeons and house cats and migrating animals who can find their place of origin through either inertial navigation or God knows what, *Max could home!*

CHAPTER
SEVENTY-THREE

'**P**ull over,' she said before Kit made the actual turn.

Kit did as he had been asked. There was something in Max's voice that couldn't be ignored.

'Now, listen to me,' she said. 'You can't go any farther than this. If they catch you, I think they'll kill you. I'm serious.'

'This is definitely serious stuff,' Kit said to her. 'And that's exactly why we're going with you, little one. This is a serious gun,' he said and showed Max a handgun. It was a semiautomatic and it looked deadly.

'I have to come, Max. It's my job. It's the reason I came here to Colorado.'

'I can't leave either,' I told Max. 'I won't leave you and Kit. It's not going to happen.'

Max finally nodded. She didn't like it, but she could tell we weren't going away. For better or worse, we were in this together.

Kit pulled on the steering wheel and we turned off the main road, which wasn't exactly U.S. One. Now we were on something called Under Mountain Pass, a twisty service road that shot up into the foothills of the Rockies. The School was here someplace. Max seemed certain of it.

'Take a right,' Max said suddenly. 'Then you can let me out.'

'It's not going to happen, Max,' Kit insisted. 'We already went over that.'

'You're awfully stubborn, Kit.'

'Look who's talking.'

The road deteriorated and became an unmarked stream of dirt track that gave no clue as to where we were headed – neither by signage nor by buildings. It was appropriately desolate and eerie, though.

Every turn in the road was a driving challenge for Kit. Eyes glowed out at us. Deer and other forest critters wisely waited before sprinting to the other side. As we drove higher and higher into the mountains, Max finally began talking about where she had come from.

'The School moved a few times while I was growing up. I know it was in the state of Massachusetts, then out in California before we moved here. I went to classes every day, and it was okay at first. My teacher was Mrs Beattie. She was a doctor, too, but she said we didn't have to say "Doctor" before her name. She really loved Matthew and me, and we loved her. We're geniuses on the Stanford-Binet tests. We were told to take no credit for being smart, though, or being able to fly. We were made that way. We were just lab specimens, after all.'

I heard Max's breathing intensify. She was clutching my hand so hard it nearly went numb. Even though she had told us to turn back, I knew she hadn't totally meant it. She was too frightened to do this alone.

'Let me out,' she said, suddenly grabbing higher on my arm. 'I have to get out. I have to! Please, Kit? Right now! I promise not to fly away. I swear I won't.'

I reached over and pressed Kit's arm. He braked the car on the narrow shoulder of the road.

We were in the middle of nowhere – surrounded by nothing but tall fir trees and sharp outcroppings of rock, and the loud buzzing of cicadas.

I opened the Jeep's door, and Max scampered over me and out.

She was quick and athletic, and so strong for her age. Almost everything she did was amazing to observe. I prayed she wouldn't fly and leave us.

Max climbed up to the roof of the Jeep. We heard her footsteps pounding above us. Then a furious whooshing sound as she beat her wings.

'What's she doing?' we said, almost in unison.

Then she stepped off the Jeep and took to the air. Just like that.

'Oh, Jesus,' Kit whispered. He took the words right out of my mouth. 'Just look at her. Look at that. I hope we can keep up with her.'

'We have to. Move this thing.'

He revved the engine. Stepped on the gas. The Jeep lurched off the shoulder of the road and then found its center, climbed steeply up the mountain. We followed

Max's flight, at least we tried.

I stuck my head out of the side window like a kid. So did Pip. I couldn't take my eyes off her white and silver-blue wings as she flew before us. Cool air flowed past my face. I almost felt that I was flying, too. I was certainly having an out-of-body experience.

The Jeep bore into a long tunnel of darkness created by overhanging pines and towering fir trees. Max veered to the left, up another side road. This one was all dirt and deeply rutted.

We were following Max home. We were trusting her with our lives.

CHAPTER SEVENTY-FOUR

The School was close. She could taste it on her tongue – bitter and nasty as could be. She could feel it, like a deadly poison pumping through her bloodstream.

Max suddenly came swooping down to the ground. The Jeep screeched to a stop close behind her. Frannie and Kit scampered out in a hurry. Pip was running around in circles. Normally, he would have made her smile, giggle happily. Not now, though.

'What is it, honey?' Frannie called. She was always so concerned, and never bossy.

Max felt as if a rope were tied around her waist and she was being firmly, inexorably, reeled in. She could feel extreme tension in her neck and shoulders, right down into her chest plate. She was going home. She was voluntarily returning to the School. Then maybe all the secrets would be out – and she could be free.

And maybe not!

She decided to stay on the ground for a while. Walking

was probably safer. Frannie and Kit walked hurriedly right behind her.

She didn't look back, didn't have to. She could hear the struggling for breath in their lungs, the blood pumping through their hearts. She sensed their fear was growing. Finally, they would see the truth. See it for themselves. She prayed they were ready for this.

Suddenly, Max stopped!

She saw the physical boundary between her new freedom and her old life – the barbed-wire fence. The powerful sight chilled her, brought back a flood of terrifying memories. She could picture Uncle Thomas, the other creepy guards, and it made her retch. She almost lost it right then and there.

The School was close. She was almost there. It was as if the School were watching her approach, waiting for her, laughing because she'd come back.

The chain-link fence was ten feet high and topped with razor-sharp concertina wire. Behind it was everything she knew, loved, and hated with all of her heart. She had seen men parking trucks at the School. Maybe they were all gone by now.

A white metal sign read: *Absolutely No Admittance. This is a U.S. Government Installation. Trespassers Will Be Shot.*

She turned to Frannie and Kit. 'We're here.'

CHAPTER SEVENTY-FIVE

Max was staring back at us, her bright green eyes wide with fear.

'They're not kidding,' she said. 'Trespassers have been shot, believe me. You can still go back. I think you should.'

'We won't leave you,' Kit said.

Pip was barking and twirling in tight circles outside the fence. Suddenly two Dobermans came loping forward on the far side. They bared their teeth, barked and growled.

Kit pulled me away from the fence as spit and fury flew from the mouths of the Dobermans.

I felt the hackles rise on the back of my neck. And it wasn't just because of the dogs. Actually, the dogs didn't bother me so much.

Chain link and concertina wire and guard dogs in the middle of the woods were scary enough, but to see the words U.S. Government attached to 'Trespassers Will Be Shot' made me ill. Kit and I were close to being trespassers, and illegal trespassing was definitely on our minds.

'Is this the School?' I asked, but Max wasn't listening. She was busy with the Dobermans.

'Bandit, Gomer, it's me!' she called out crisply to the dogs.'Stop it. Stop it *now*! Heel, you two!'

Amazingly, the growling and barking trailed off and then stopped completely. Suspicious sniffs followed. Then happy woofing as the dogs seemed to recognize Max.

'Don't worry,' she said to us.'They're my friends. Their bark's much worse than their bite,' she grinned.

'Can we get over this fence anywhere?' I asked Kit.

He started to answer when Max interrupted.

'Frannie!' She was pulling at my arm. 'There's something wrong with Bandit and Gomer. Something is really wrong with the dogs! Please, come look at them.'

I moved closer but I didn't need to examine Bandit and Gomer to see what had happened to them. Their black coats were dull. Their rib cages were standing out sharply, the skin stretched taut over the bones.

'They're pretty hungry,' I said to Max.

It was an understatement. The dogs were suffering from malnutrition. Some cruel bastard was starving them.

Kit returned from a trip down the fence.'I couldn't find a break or access point in the wire,' he said.'Maybe around the other way.'

'I think I can fly you both over,' Max said. It was such an unexpected statement, I nearly laughed.

'I know I can do it. I'm stronger than I look,' she insisted. She was dead serious.

'No way,' Kit told her. He was right. There was no way an eighty-pound little girl could lift an adult twice her weight against the pull of gravity.

'Yes, I can.' Max was firm. 'You don't know what you're talking about. I know what I'm capable of.'

I listened to Max and reconsidered. I wasn't figuring in the stress factor. Stress produces adrenaline. And also, who knew what kind of strength Max actually did have?

'Let me try you first,' she said to me.

'I don't think it's a great idea, Max.'

She shrugged. 'Fine. Then I'll fly over by myself.'

I grabbed on to the chain link. I climbed a few feet and clung there. Then Max gripped me around my midsection with her strong legs. She was definitely powerful. God, this was the strangest thing.

Holding me from behind, Max's wings almost could have been mine. She flapped hard, then we took off. Suddenly we were suspended in the air. Then we started upward.

I could feel a breeze rushing around me. It was cold up in these hills, and getting chillier by the minute. For a moment I forgot everything, so focused was I on the sensation of being airborne in this unusual manner. For just the briefest instant I could imagine that I had wings myself.

We lifted. We hovered for a second or two. And then we flew. Not very far, but, dear God in heaven, I was definitely flying.

CHAPTER SEVENTY-SIX

Max set me down inside the fenced perimeter. I stared up at the grotesque and depressing rows of concertina wire. I gripped the fence, clawed the wire with my fingers, and waited for my heart to slow. I glanced around and Max was gone.

She was already back on the other side of the fence. She was straining to lift Kit. Her legs just barely encircled him. Her breathing was a stuttering *whoosh*, *whoosh*, *whoosh*. It didn't seem possible that she could get him airborne, but I hadn't believed she could lift me either.

I had no idea what she could tolerate, even for a few seconds. Her wings were displacing air, but she couldn't seem to budge Kit up and over.

'Max, please stop. He's too heavy for you,' I called to her. 'You'll hurt yourself.'

'No, he isn't too heavy. I'm superstrong. You have no idea how strong I am, Frannie. I was made that way.'

On my side of the fence, the two dogs were edging up

to me. Actually, they were a little too close for comfort. The female was cutting half circles in the dust, wheeling and dancing her anxiety. The male had small, runny eyes and was rooted to the ground about three feet away from me.

A warning rattled in his throat. His lips were peeled away from his gums, showing a pristine rack of teeth.

'Oh stop,' I told him. 'Get a life.' Dogs that showed their teeth and growled, I could handle.

My eyes darted back to Max and Kit, where they were still balanced on the perimeter fence. She finally pulled away, leaving him holding on to the wire, clinging there, still trying to climb over. Finally, he safely dropped back down to the ground.

'Nice try, sweetie,' I called to Max. But I could see she was upset. She didn't like to fail. Had 'They' made her that way, too?

She immediately flew back over the fence and joined me. She said 'stay' and 'good doggies' to the Dobermans. She was friendly but firm with them, and I wondered if that had anything to do with her recent escape.

Then Max was moving north away from the fence, picking up speed, heading somewhere.

I was almost jogging to keep up with her. The woods began to close around the narrow road. As each thick clump of trees was put behind us, another came and blocked my view.

A wall of firs opened onto a copse of birch that gave way to a grove of aspens shimmering like a curtain of glass beads. My heart was pounding, and it sounded louder to my ears than our footsteps. Without warning, the winding road opened into a sunlit clearing.

Before us sprawled a turn-of-the-century hunting lodge, or maybe a spa resort. There were countless windows cut into the stone face. White columns stood at the entrance. Rich verdigris on the aged roof spilled down and covered the building.

I looked at Max. Her pupils were the tiniest pinpoints. The irises were translucent gray disks fixed in a stare. I remembered that birds will often contract their pupils under duress.

'What is this?' I asked.

'It's the Central Colorado Induced Mutant Lab,' she said. 'The School of Genetic Research. I live here.'

CHAPTER
SEVENTY-SEVEN

There was no sound coming from the strange, eerie lodge, the place where Max had been kept, and God knows what else had happened to her.

There were no security guards, no parked cars or trucks. No immediate threat to us. Nothing that I could see, anyway.

'It's too quiet. Way too quiet,' Max said in a whisper. 'There should be guards somewhere. We should have been able to see them from the woods.'

'What does it mean, Max?'

'I don't know. It's never been like this before.'

Max and I skulked along the fringes of the clearing. We crossed quickly to one side of the building, then edged along the stone wall to an oak door halfway down the eastern side. There wasn't any shifting of shapes or shadows behind the many windows. No one seemed to be around.

My confidence was growing a little bit. I took a breath,

then I reached forward and groped the metal knob in my hand. The door opened easily. We entered the strange building and the heavy door swung shut behind us.

A dank, powerful smell of decay hit me. I knew what it was and I was repulsed.

'Something's dead,' Max said.

She was right. Something was dead for sure. Something was decomposing inside the building and the odor was acrid and strong. We covered our noses and mouths with our hands. We continued to walk away from the front door.

Max said, 'The fan must not be working.' She didn't seem overly upset by the smell – by death.

I scanned the room for security cameras. I was certain they were there, somewhere, but I couldn't find them. Was somebody watching us now?

I suspected that the small room we were standing in was used for decontamination. Bright yellow scrubs were piled in a large trash can near the door. Lab coats were hung from hooks. People worked here, didn't they? Scientists, if they could call themselves that. Doctors. Researchers. They were conducting illegal experiments of some kind.

There was an open metal closet filled with clean scrubs, and shelves lined with rubber-soled shoes stood next to a bank of lockers. The lockers were empty, cleaned out.

Jesus God, what had we come to? What kind of place was this?

Max pointed to an interior door leading from the room and beckoned to me to follow her. I had the thought that this building was like a Nazi extermination camp. They put people to sleep here. They experimented on human beings.

We followed a wide main corridor. Max's ballet slippers were quiet, but my shoes squeaked. A long fluorescent tube flickered above us in the ceiling. The beige-and-blue linoleum corridor unfurled in front of us and was crossed with transverse hallways.

We arrived in an open space, about fifty feet square. It was some kind of work place. Where were we now?

'Max? What's this?'

'It's just offices. For business stuff. No big deal. Pretty boring.'

'What kind of business?'

She shrugged. 'The boring kind. You know, *business*.'

Whatever old fixtures had once been in this part of the building were long gone. There was no wood paneling, no fireplace, no dentil moldings, just a warren of free-standing office-style cubes. Computers squatted on desk-tops of dull gray steel. A coffee pot on a file cabinet caught my eye. The pot was cracked, and a thick black gum coated the bottom.

I picked up a mug from a desk. *O.B.'s Coffee*, I read. The floating blue circle of mold told me the cup had been here at least a couple of days. Where is O.B.? Who is O.B.?

And what was dead and putrefying in the building? What had happened at this so-called School? What kind of business was conducted in this awful place?

I glanced at Max, but she was moving again. She was home sweet home. She obviously accepted all this horror and madness as normal. It was so quiet that even my normal breathing sounded loud. I held my breath and listened for a moment. I had a four-color expectation that as soon as my back was turned, someone would jump out of a closed room. But no one did.

Max pushed open another door. There was a soft, *clicking* sound. Were they photographing us? My heart was still pounding. I felt tired. Things were getting a little blurry. Where was Kit? Was he okay?

'This is where I work,' Max announced. 'It's usually full of doctors.'

CHAPTER SEVENTY-EIGHT

We entered a cavernous room that must have been sixty feet long and about half as wide. My eyes swept the workroom, quickly took everything in. It was a standard-issue laboratory, but a good one, with top-of-the-line, very expensive equipment. Who had funded this? Who was subsidizing this business?

There were a dozen fancy workstations. Slides were scattered everywhere on table and counter surfaces. Expensive microscopes were stacked on shelves.

I noted a scale/beam balance and several hydrometers. There were laser spectrographs, cell culture hoods, high-speed centrifuges. Obviously, no expense had been spared on the equipment.

A little pride crept into Max's voice. 'This is my station, Frannie. Come look. I was taught to make myself useful. So I did. I was a good worker.'

'I'll bet you were, sweetie.'

Max climbed up and sat proudly on a tall metal stool. Her workstation. She switched on an overhead fluorescent light. There was a small sign on the desk: TINKERBELL LIVES.

She showed me how she had used a glass pipette to transfer droplets of DNA cocktail from a tray of small wells onto plates of growing medium. 'We run out the chromosomes by cooking them in here,' she explained.

I didn't recognize the chrome-plated unit she pointed to, but it was a brand-new model. Before I could question her further, Max slid down from the stool.

'Let's go,' she said. 'There's a lot more to see.'

I followed her. 'I'm right behind you.'

'I know you are. I have a really good sense of hearing.'

'So I've noticed. Who's Tinkerbell?'

Max turned to me. She looked upset. 'Nobody, really. She's dead.'

Tinkerbell, I was thinking. Was that what they called Max here at the School? I suspected it was, and that she didn't like it. Tinkerbell was her lab name, wasn't it?

We passed through a smaller room filled with shiny steel cryogenic tanks. What in hell had they been freezing in there? Another, even smaller room, contained half-a-dozen blood diagnostic machines.

No worn-out university equipment for these folks. They were extremely well-funded. By whom? To do what?

'Mice,' said Max, pointing toward an enclosed room. 'This is the Mickey Mouse room. It's gross. Hold your nose, Frannie. I'm not kidding. You were warned.'

The smell of death seemed to be concentrated in here. I

tried to catch my breath; I *did* hold my breath, but even that didn't help much. I thought I was going to be sick. I held back a dry heave.

I peered into a windowed door and saw innumerable metal racks, each with a dozen shelves; each shelf was packed with dozens of plastic cages. As far as I could see there were cages, thousands of them filled with mice curled tightly in cedar-chip bedding.

The Mickey Mouse room was a rip-roaring horror show, the scariest thing I had ever seen in my life. Nothing even came close to this. There was high color in Max's face now. She seemed unaware of my presence. She was talking to herself, all sibilant phrasing, her speech lapsing into unintelligible phrases.

All I could make out was *'skitters'* and *'put to sleep.'*

We entered the Mouse room. I saw immediately that the mice weren't ordinary lab animals. Knobs of flesh protruded from unlikely junctures. Some of the mice had extra limbs and strange markings.

Mice are so genetically close to humans, it's a little scary. Eighty-five percent of their genes are identical to ours, which is why they make perfect lab animals. It's why you can give them human diseases: cancer, heart disease, muscular dystrophy – and from their reactions possibly learn how to cure these diseases in humans.

I love animals, and I'm also a doctor who's benefited from animal research. I can argue both sides of the animal-research issue passionately. But either way, I cannot abide cruelty. No matter what your reasons, you take responsibility for the animals.

I began pulling down the cages one at a time, shaking them. 'There's no food in these cages. All of these animals are dead. Son of a bitch,' I whispered.

'Put to sleep,' Max said. Tears welled up in her eyes.

It was something to see – this beautiful little girl crying over the fate of dead mice.

CHAPTER SEVENTY-NINE

Max hated it when she cried, hated to show weakness. She wouldn't let on to Frannie, but she was freaking out, creeping out real bad, scaring herself with her own thoughts, but the worst thing was the anger she felt. The rage inside of her. No one should be allowed to do these things.

Her senses were incredibly alive right now. Sight, hearing, smell, touch. She'd felt this way when she was running away from the School. She hadn't known how powerful her senses were until then.

Her nostrils differentiated the smells of burnt coffee, various chemicals, heated metal, and somewhere nearby – decaying flesh.

This was all wrong. It was so wrong. How could Harding Thomas and the other cretins do this? Was it because she had run away? Had she caused these deaths? Oh please, don't let it be that. Not because of me.

The second hand of the clock hanging above the

cryogenic tanks had stopped, and that made her think maybe time had died.

She kept moving. She entered the familiar Main Office Control, and was seized with quick, flashing memories. Memories of Uncle Thomas, his large hand protectively on her head. He liked to remind her that he was 'a scientist at heart.' He loved his little Tinkerbell, or so he always told her. She was such a smart girl. Precious little Tink.

Liar! she thought. *Murderer. Creep – lower than amoebae.*

She felt like curling up and having a good cry. Where was everyone, Uncle Thomas and the others? Were they hiding on her? Were they watching? They loved to watch, then spring out and catch you when you least expected it.

Her life here had been like a military school, or what she knew about them. Her days were always organized and controlled. She studied, worked, underwent tests, exercised or watched TV. She never received love, encouragement, satisfaction. She was one of their specimens, except she was smart enough to make herself useful. And to know somewhere inside her, that *she wasn't a specimen*.

Beyond the Main Office Control, the corridor branched two ways. Automatically, Max turned right. She knew the way, every inch of this place. She could find her way around it blindfolded.

Twenty paces became ten, became five. Ready for countdown.

And finally she came to the heavy metal door of the *Nursery*.

She heard something behind her and her breathing stopped. Her mind was racing like crazy. She definitely heard – footsteps. Running! Fast! More than one person was coming in a hurry.

She turned to Frannie, fear in her eyes. Prepared for the worst. Then she laughed. It was only Kit and Pip. What a relief. She could breathe again. She felt they should all be together for whatever was going to happen next.

'We got in farther down the fence,' Kit said between gasps.

Max didn't know what to think. Right now she didn't care. 'Kit, Frannie,' she said. 'Look here. This is important. Please. It's why I came back.'

Max opened the door to the Nursery, and she screamed.

CHAPTER EIGHTY

I jumped back.

What I saw inside the door made me want to scream, too, and strange as it may seem, to thank God at the same time.

There were four little ones lying in soiled blankets inside cages in the Nursery. The small children were alive and each one had wings.

'Peter, Ic, Wendy!' Max shrieked, as she ran to them. 'Oz!

'Oh poor Petey. Wendy!' she shrieked as she opened the cage that held two of the little ones. Peter and Wendy were entwined, hunched in the far corner, blinking against the sudden intrusion of light.

'Come to me,' Max called to them softly. 'Come to Max.' The sounds they made together were barely audible, but loving, a little like bird songs.

Max went to the next cage. She opened the doors. A little boy came crouching forward, then staggered out of the terrible cage. 'Ic!' she said. 'Icarus!

'I brought help,' she told him.

'Where's Matthew?' he asked.

'I don't know. Let's not talk about it now. How are you? You okay?'

'Cool as a ghoul,' said Ic. Finally, he smiled. Amazing.

The little ones fell over one another trying to reach Max. Once they found her, they clung to her. They whispered parched greetings, uttered sharp, high-pitched cries. And then in a burst of relief all the bird-children began to cry.

They cried as one.

As I helped Max free the children from their cages, I was overcome with the shakes. The children were so beautiful, so exquisite in every way. It was like finding priceless treasure in the least expected place. Each of them was a miracle.

I controlled my own nerves and astonishment long enough to evaluate the kids; they were malnourished and dehydrated, but that seemed to be all. It wasn't too bad, though it would have been soon. I hastened to the sink and got them some water. They had been locked in here to die like the mice. Four beautiful little kids, left to die in cages.

My eyes fell on a little boy who looked to be about seven. He had a stocky build, most of his bulk was in his upper body. His wings were feathered dark brown and pinfeathers of the same color covered his neck and shoulders, merging at the hairline with glossy chestnut-brown hair.

The boy's skin was damp, and his face was livid from crying. But his huge round eyes were bright and unafraid.

'I'm Ozymandias,' he said, with a belligerent thrust to his chin. 'Who the heck are you? Are you a scientist? A stinking doctor?'

'I'm Frannie,' I told him, 'and this is my friend, Kit. We came here with Max.'

'They're friends, Oz,' Max said. 'Hard as it might be to believe.'

'Hello, Oz. Ozymandias.' Kit offered his hand to the little boy who, after a slight hesitation, shook it.

Max pushed the little girl forward. She was a rosy-cheeked cherub of four or so, with black, bowl-cut hair and almond-shaped eyes. The girl was wearing a sleeveless smock like the one Max had worn the first time I saw her. She stretched out her wings toward me. They were white, tipped with blue. Beautiful.

Her wing feathers made a swishing sound, like a taffeta skirt swirling around a dancer's legs.

'Mama?' she said, in the most heartbreaking way.

'She calls all older women "Mama," ' Max explained. 'She never had one. None of us did.'

My heart leaped toward the little girl. Tears came to my eyes again. I would never be able to explain to anyone what I felt at this moment.

'She's Wendy. This is Frannie.' Max made polite, almost formal introductions.

Then Wendy spoke in a soft squeaky voice. 'You should see my twin!'

She pointed to her brother, Peter, who was a nearly perfect copy of his sister, another masterpiece.

An older boy, close to Max's age, hung back. His hair

was fine ash blond and it hung all around his face and down to his shoulders. His frame was lean, his bones fine and long.

It occurred to me that although these children had wings in common, their lineage was different. What could that mean? It meant something important, but I couldn't figure out what.

I reached out to the boy, but he hissed when I touched his arm. Of course the boy was afraid of me. How could he trust anyone? How could any of the children trust us?

Only with assurances from Max did this little boy named Icarus allow me to approach him.

'I would never hurt you,' I told him.

'Heard that one before,' he said. 'That's how they all talk. Liars!'

Icarus pushed his blond hair away from his face, and I saw then that his irises were an opaque bluish-gray. I looked at Max and she told me what I already knew.

'Icarus is blind,' she said.

'Yeah, I'm kind of a mistake,' said the boy. 'We all are.'

CHAPTER EIGHTY-ONE

K it had left Frannie and Max with the smaller children. There was so much that he needed to know about this place. He entered an executive office. Some kind of higher-up worked here. A bold sign in Helvetica type caught his eye: *Assume nothing. Question everything.*

'I'm already there,' he whispered under his breath.

Kit continued to be afraid for the children, and for Frannie. The fear was growing exponentially inside him. He felt that he'd been given responsibility for another family, to make sure they got through this safely. He took the responsibility seriously, and it scared him more than anything else could.

He surveyed the office. There were no photographs, no mementos on any of the table surfaces. Nothing personal was left out in plain sight.

Whose office was it? It had to be somebody important in the scheme of things. The room was about twenty feet square with a picture window opening out onto the lab. The floors were covered with plush, silver-gray carpet. The desk was old blond oak. There was a corkboard on the wall above it.

The papers on the corkboard mesmerized him. He stared at an amazing collection of pen-and-ink drawings of what looked to be theoretical improvements on human parts and organs. Whoever had done the drawings was a very good artist, he was thinking. He shuddered. A cold chill raced up his spine. *Whoever did these line drawings – wants to be God.*

He took down a manila envelope. Inside the packet were drawings of eyes of different shapes with cross-section illustrations, both lateral and transverse.

Da Vinci would have been proud of this artwork, Kit thought.

There was a complex sequence of drawings of a human leg. The leg was shown in various positions, some requiring a flexibility that seemed impossible to Kit. There was a tight line drawing of an arm, the fingers outstretched. Over the arm was a transparency upon which a new arm had been sketched.

A new arm? A better human arm? Is that what I'm looking at?

The new drawing showed longer muscles, and more streamlined digits. It certainly looked like an improvement on the current model. He hated to admit it, but it was actually quite thrilling.

It seemed as if some kind of extremely talented corporate body-part designer were sketching the new models for the coming season.

He was so immersed in studying the drawings that he almost missed the bunch of little keys hanging from a metal pushpin. They'd been right in front of him all the time. He grabbed them, and the corkboard almost came off the wall. The keys were labeled in small, meticulous print.

The first key was to the desk drawer. Kit pulled it so hard, it fell out of the desk, its contents spilling all over the floor.

He bent and rifled through the litter: paper clips and coins and stamps and pens – the usual universal desk debris. There was a Swiss Army knife amid the clutter. He pocketed it. It could come in handy.

The next key opened a long gray-metal cabinet beside the corkboard. Inside the dark recess were quart bottles, tightly sealed from the look of them.

He took down the first labeled AGE1 and held it up to the light.

Floating in dark fluid were a dozen embryos no larger than marbles.

Kit thought he might lose it. Right there in somebody's fancy office. He turned away and blew out hard. He finally calmed down a little. He looked back at the embryos.

Human, he thought. Little dead babies kept in a closet? God damn them!

He forced himself to study the embryonic heads, minuscule fingers and toes sloshing in the liquid. Silent and dead. His stomach was sloshing around pretty good, too.

Kit reached into the cabinet again and took out another

large jar. He held it carefully in both hands. This one was marked AGE2. It contained another embryo collection much the same as the first. AGE3 and AGE4 were identical to the first jars.

The entire cabinet was filled to capacity with jars of embryos so similar that he couldn't really differentiate between them.

He took up the third key and slipped it into the lock of a file cabinet standing to the left of the desk. The lock *clicked*. Kit slid open the top drawer.

Inside was an alphabetical arrangement of files: mundane interoffice memorandums, drafts of an untitled manuscript of some sort.

The middle drawer contained medical magazines dating back to the 80s and clippings from *Der Spiegel*, a German magazine, a clipping from *The Times*, of London.

In the back of the bottom drawer, he found notebooks filled with formulas and data in scientific techese. It was frustratingly incomprehensible, but looked important. He decided to take a few of the smaller notebooks with him.

As he leafed through the papers, Kit felt a cold prickling at his back. It was too quiet in here, too quiet in general. Why had the lab suddenly been deserted? Abandoned? Why had the bird-children been left behind?

The embryos in the bottles looked long dead. Some of the drawings were fly-specked. Each manuscript was annotated, so marked up and crossed off, it looked as if the author had started, stopped, started again, then finally given up.

And how did all of this link up with Max and the four

other children? The ones they'd found lying in their own waste, starving in the cages down the hall? The ones who were probably being put to sleep.

Kit heard a noise behind him and turned. It was only Frannie. He wanted to tell her everything, all at once.

'Come look at this amazing stuff. Tell me what you think.'

CHAPTER EIGHTY-TWO

'Their arrogance is absolutely astonishing. Like nothing I could begin to imagine,' I said angrily. My eyes were greedily taking in the elaborate line drawings on the walls.

Kit was emptying out a carton of documents onto the floor. He lifted up sheaves of paper to show me what he'd found.

'This box is filled with pictures and diagrams of wings. All kinds of wings. They were designing in here. Do you believe this?'

'More like redesigning,' I said, as I leafed through a fistful of the well-wrought line drawings. 'Whoever made these drawings is definitely playing God, Kit.'

'It's the group from Boston and Cambridge, the outlaws from M.I.T. They make their own rules. They always have. Anthony Peyser believes he's above the rest of us and above the law as well. Look at these.'

He showed Frannie a half-dozen *memos to staff*. At the

bottom of each page was a handwritten *A.P.* . . . Anthony Peyser.

I had been racking my brain trying to think if anyone I knew locally might be Dr Peyser. No one came to mind, and I had met most of the medical doctors and scientists in the area. David knew them all. Where could Peyser be hiding himself? Could this have been his office? Was he the mystery designer?

Kit sat in a desk chair in front of a computer. He was punching letters on the keyboard and a directory of contents had scrolled up.

'I've been calling up a few files at random. I haven't been asked for a password once. The front door is wide open. Why? The keys to the drawers are hanging on the bulletin board and . . . why?'

'Don't ask me. I don't get it either. Not yet.'

My eyes fell on a pile of the notebooks he'd spilled onto the floor. Whoever had made the notes had a brilliant way with a fine-line pen. The drawings were made with a high degree of medical accuracy, but there was art to them as well. Had Dr Anthony Peyser actually worked in this room? I suspected that he had. A.P. had been here.

I picked up a drawing from the pile before me. It showed a little boy, an infant, with a heart growing outside his chest cavity, a *huge* heart. I studied it carefully. It illustrated why tissue engineering was so problematic. No one knew how to reliably stop the cellular growth once the process had begun.

But even if that major problem had been solved, it was a hell of a leap from growing organs on lab animals to growing wings on a human child. And with Max it wasn't just that she had wings. Her entire cardiopulmonary system was avian, and that led me to conclude that she'd been created out of whole cloth.

My mind was churning at about a million miles an hour. I felt I could go stark-raving mad at the blink of an eye. The whole world was being turned upside-down. Someone had challenged everything we had learned to believe in and accept.

Assume nothing. Question everything. That's what this was about, wasn't it? To evolve life, as *man* chose to evolve it.

I was considering outrageous possibilities I hadn't dared to imagine before. One winged child could have been a biological accident, but now that I'd seen the other four, I had to accept that there had been a definite intent to create a new kind of being. And, by God or despite Him, someone had actually done it. Someone had succeeded at playing God here at the School.

What had they created?

CHAPTER EIGHTY-THREE

K it continued to work furiously at the desktop. Like many of the younger agents in the Bureau, he was good at it. He liked computers most of the time, and was comfortable around them. He brought up Netscape, then opened it. In the location field, he typed – *about:global*.

Up came all the sites the previous user of the desktop had visited in the last few months. Kit quickly scanned the list. He'd been doing similar detective work on the case before he left Boston.

He honed in on *www.ncbi.nbm.n.h.gov*. It was Genebank, the government-run repository for all known genetic sequences.

He looked for key words in red, indicating a previous user had clicked on them. There were several. He went to '*taxonomy*.' Under '*taxonomy browser*,' he clicked '*tree*.' Then he typed in '*aves*' in the search field.

Apodidae (swifts), Laridae (gulls), Columbidae (doves), and

Hirundinidae (swallows) had all been searched.

The plot thickened.

Kit closed the site and returned to the list *about:global*. Next, he went into the Cold Spring Harbor Laboratory site. He futzed around with a few entries, then tried *DSHL publications – Genome Research*.

He went into the September 1997 issue, where he became puzzled again. The previous user had called up a paper on *Double-Muscle Belgian Blue and Piedmontese Cattle*.

Cattle? He stopped typing and thought about the curious entry.

'Frannie. Come here for a second,' Kit said without looking away from the screen.

He showed her what he'd been doing, then the last article he found. 'What's all this stuff about cattle somebody from here was checking out? You understand it?'

'Some,' Frannie said. She read the rest of the article, then re-read key parts of it. She thought about what she had just absorbed. 'Son of a—' she finally said. 'I think I understand. I'll give you a wild theory, anyway.'

Kit nodded and listened.

'The article is about a mutated cow gene. Somebody produced double muscling in the chest of these cows. So here's a theory. Kit, I think this is how they could have made Max's chest muscles large enough to support wings and also carry her weight. This is part of how they made her.'

CHAPTER EIGHTY-FOUR

W e searched the computer files for a few more minutes, but found nothing else of interest. So Kit and I continued our tour of the School. The arrogance and amorality of the scientists working here affronted everything I believed in. I wanted to find one of 'Them' and strangle the person with my bare hands.

I looked at the foreboding metal sign on the locked door before us: 'Authorized Personnel Only.' So of course, Kit kicked it off its hinges. 'Authorization accepted,' he said.

We were instantly bombarded with alarms blaring in the room and out in the halls. We walked inside. The rank smell of human waste washed over us like a fetid cloud. The dark of the room was broken by neon-colored tracers flat-lining across unseen video monitors.

I found the light switch and flicked on the overhead lights.

I have been exposed to some really bad things in my

years of working with animals: abuse, neglect, occasional cruelty. But I'd never been confronted with anything as horrifying as this. Nothing even came close.

We were inside some kind of pediatric intensive-care ward. It was filled with shiny new life-support equipment, but also a dozen or so small cribs. All the equipment was new and expensive.

I shook my head slowly back and forth. This couldn't be real. I held back tears, but it was hard. I looked at Kit. He had turned pale.

Inside the cribs lay dead and dying children. Everywhere I looked, I saw failure of pulmonary, cardiac, and renal systems. The screeching electronic noise was meant to alert medical personnel to trouble, which was pretty much total. Empty IV bags, stalled ventilators and dialysis machines. Vomit and excrement coated the tiny patients.

I finally screamed. I couldn't stop screaming. Kit reached out and held me. I took long, steadying breaths, until I regained control of myself.

'We have to do something for them,' I whispered. 'We can't leave them to die like this. I can't do that.'

'I know, I know,' he whispered back. 'We'll do what we can, Frannie.'

The room was painted pale yellow, with a border of whimsical cartoon animals running along the top of the walls. The cartoons made it worse – much worse. A flannel board next to a refrigerator held crayoned pictures, and yellow-on-white happy faces were stuck up at random on the walls. The happy faces killed me. Just killed me. I steeled myself to peer down into the closest crib.

Inside, a naked female infant about several months old squirmed and waved her small, perfect hands in the air. The tiny baby had no face, no features at all.

A feeding tube was inserted into her small stomach, but the attached bag was empty. I put my hand gently on the top of her head. The green line of the heart rate monitor beat faster.

She was aware of me.

'Hello, baby,' I whispered. 'Hello, sweet little girl.'

I threw open the fridge, then the cabinet doors. I shoved aside bandages and tubes and syringes, but there was no food anywhere.

In mounting despair, I hurried to the next crib. The baby boy inside was already dead and decomposing. He had a head the size of a volleyball and the musculature of a child of four or five.

'You poor, poor thing.'

I pulled the plug from the monitor, ripped out the catheter in the little one's head. I covered his face with a blanket.

The third crib held another dead child, a year-old babe with a body shape as ordinary as any little kid on the block – except that his skin was separated in irregular tears. The skin hadn't grown at the same rate as the child.

The child's eyelids were inverted, and the sightless, bulging eyes stared up at me. I couldn't ever begin to imagine the pain he had endured before his death, possibly from sepsis. The fourth crib held year-old twins conjoined at the waist. One had died, and because they shared many organs, the other would be dead soon, too.

I gently put my hand on the living child's cool cheek and the eyes fluttered open.

'Hi, baby. Hi there.'

There was nothing I could do for the living twin, nothing anyone could do without medical supplies. I was sobbing now as I went from crib to crib.

A dialysis tube had once been hooked up, but was now dangling alongside the crib of a small being with simian features. The child was undernourished, dehydrated, comatose.

Everywhere I looked were deformed, impossible children. If I was right, the most incredible tragedy was that these children had been grown from ordinary human zygotes. They could have been perfectly normal, but they'd been mutated. Human experiments had been performed in this room again and again.

Kit was going from crib to crib, yanking out electrical cords and tubes. It was the only thing we could do.

Suddenly Max was in the lab beside us. I was afraid for her. I wanted to protect Max from this, but it was too late. Her eyes were sad, but knowing. 'They put the babies to sleep,' she whispered. 'They do it with the rejects, the losers. They do it all the time. Now you know.'

They! Whoever they were – I hated them fiercely. My fists were clenched tight at my side.

'We should get out of here right now,' Kit said. 'They have to come back at least one more time. They can't leave all this to be found.'

I looked at Kit. 'Or any witnesses.'

CHAPTER EIGHTY-FIVE

Max, the other children, Kit, and I hurried through the towering fir woods as if we were playing a bizarre game of tag or hide-and-seek. We were 'it.' 'They' would be after us soon. We were witnesses to horrible crimes that included murder.

Ironically, the mountains and woods looked so damn pretty. The light was softly dappled. Bluejays and phoebes twittered away. Leaves rustled and fluttered in a lightly pine-scented breeze. But it was as scary as an unexpected trip into Hades. We knew the horrible truth – at least a part of it.

The children were whistling, and I couldn't for the life of me understand why. Max seemed to be leading them and she was doing a good job so far.

I turned to Kit. 'Why are they whistling?'

He shook his head. 'No idea.'

Max screamed. 'They're coming! It's Security! Hunters!

Trust me on it. Run faster! Get away from here! Everybody run!'

I grabbed the closest child – Wendy – and I carried her down a narrow pathway that led deeper into the woods.

Kit took hold of Icarus, the little blind boy, who was frightened enough to go with him. Kit had his gun out, dark and scary, but also comforting.

'Wendy, *look*!' Peter called out to his sister.'Look *up*!' He was rooted to the ground, stunned by the sight of Max flying into the air.

No matter how many times I'd watched her fly, I was always struck dumb by the miraculous, indelible sight. I knew how Peter felt, but this was no time for gawking.

I yelled,'Pe-ter! Come here! Right this minute! Move it!'

Still clutching Wendy, I plucked him up, too. They clung to me. They weren't too heavy, but heavy enough.

I found temporary cover in the bushes. Gunfire crackled around us. A dark hole opened in the thick trunk of a nearby tree. I picked up the two small children again and stumbled and ran as fast as I could.

I looked back just in time to see Max drop out of a tree and land on one of the men doing the shooting. He was dressed in brown-and-green camouflage, like many hunters and survivalists in the area. Max fell on the man incredibly hard. From twelve to fifteen feet above, eighty pounds had the impact of a falling safe.

Bone cracked! I heard it. The writhing man screamed in extreme pain. I had no pity for him.

For a long moment, there was quiet again, but it was almost as scary as the noise and echoing gunshots. How many of them were chasing us? Where were they?

Then Kit dropped into a shooting crouch. A single shot burst from his semiautomatic. Another guard dropped, as if he were a felled tree. He held his shoulder.

I felt sick. I was a witness. All of us were.

The ground under my hiking boots suddenly bucked. It was a powerful explosion and it shivered every tree and shrub and the forest floor itself. We were almost knocked off our feet by the shock and concussion.

The air around us seemed to split open. The woods suddenly crackled with heat, then I smelled smoke and my heart sank.

Fire.

With a furious thundering, two deer streaked past us. Birds flew up in black clouds. The woods were suddenly alive with frightened animals, and even more frightened humans.

'The School!' Max screamed. 'It's back at the School.'

'That was a bomb,' Kit yelled to me. 'They're getting rid of the evidence. They're burning the place down. Keep moving! Keep going! There's nothing we can do about it now.'

We gathered up the children, kept them moving. We slid and fell and scraped our way down the hillside into a small valley. Then we climbed painfully up the side of a facing hill. Then down the opposite side. We ran until we couldn't run anymore, and then we ran some more.

Five children, two adults – *seven witnesses*.

CHAPTER EIGHTY-SIX

We finally stopped to rest and took cover under a formation of primeval-looking boulders. We were exhausted, wide-eyed, open-mouthed, and stunned to silence. Our recent small victory was only a brief respite. We had outrun a couple of Security geeks, but so what?

Five minutes passed – ten minutes – no one came up behind us. Not yet, anyway.

Kit had climbed a high, branched tree to do some quick surveillance. He shimmied up and down expertly, and I was impressed with his agility. He was full of surprises.

'I couldn't see anyone following us,' he reported. 'But that doesn't mean much. They know we've got a long way down with the kids in tow.'

Max was at my side, urgently tapping my arm. 'I should teach them to fly,' she said. 'It will be easy for them, Frannie. I have to do it. They'll be safer from the guards. I was.'

Night would be coming soon, and I was anxious and

frightened for the children. I didn't see how we could all safely make the trip down in darkness. Before today, I'd always thought of the woods as a personal refuge. No more.

'It's getting dark pretty fast,' I said to Max. I didn't want to scare her, but I hoped she would get my point.

'It'll be okay for now,' she answered. 'There's a moon. Please trust me. I have instincts about these things. Also, we can see better in the dark than you can.'

I was so impressed with Max. It had only been a few days since she'd thrown herself screaming against our net. Now she had assumed responsibility for her small charges. I did trust her judgment, her instincts.

She felt it was time to push the little birds out of the nest. She was probably right about that. It would be a stunning thing to witness.

First flight!

CHAPTER EIGHTY-SEVEN

We clustered together on the shelflike summit of a rocky outcropping. The moon was brilliant overhead. It seemed ominous, like the chandelier at the opening of *Phantom of the Opera*. It was a beautiful night, though thoroughly spooky because of the dangerous circumstances we found ourselves in.

'This is how you do it,' Max told the others in a firm voice. 'It starts in your head. You send *your mind* up and out of your body. Then just let your wings do the work. It'll be great tonight. We'll fly right by the moon, like in *E.T.* You guys remember that scene in the movie?'

'Cool!' Icarus yelled. 'I'm E.T.! I'm the hero. I called it!'

The other kids rolled their eyes, but nobody argued with Icarus. I could see that the children were unusually generous and supportive of one another. They had team – or maybe it was flock – instincts.

I looked at the leaning tower of striated schist that stood about fifteen feet off the ground. It was just high enough for a practiced flyer to achieve lift, but it could also make for a pretty bad fall if the smaller children weren't up to it. I held my breath a little. I trusted Max, though.

'*Watch me!*' she said to the other kids. 'Let's forget how hungry we are. Do exactly what I do.'

First, she beat her wings in place. Then, when there was a good stiff breeze coming at us – she simply stepped off the high rock.

'Wow!' the other kids chorused. 'Way to go, Max! Whoooo! That's really great!'

For a moment, Max hovered effortlessly in the air. She turned her head down to make sure that all eyes were on her. They certainly were. Then she took off to another level.

She flew up toward the treetops, and it was just incredible. The hair on my neck stood on end. My legs were wobbly. But I wouldn't have missed this for anything.

Using good sense, or instincts, she kept it real simple. No aerobatics and no showing off. She made one graceful circular loop and then came back down to the others.

'I can do that,' Peter bragged and thrust out chin and chest. 'No problema. No big deal.'

'So can I, then,' Wendy said. 'I've been waiting to fly all my life.'

'I fly in my dreams, all day and all night,' Icarus told us. They were so sweet and good with one another. How could anyone even think of harming them?

'Better let me go first,' Oz said, pushing past the smaller twins.

'No, me!' Peter insisted, holding his ground.

'Come *here*, Peter,' Max said, firmly. 'I'm going to be right next to you the whole time, every second. Don't mess around, you little messers! Come *here*!'

'Oohh! She's *mad*,' Peter said, and he crossed his eyes.

'On the count of three, we'll jump together,' Max told them. 'Any objections? Well, keep them to yourselves.'

I stood directly behind the children. Actually, I wanted to say, 'Me next!' I wanted to fly, too. I was overwhelmed with a sense of the possible.

It was a full moon, and I could see so clearly. The children suddenly pushed off from the rock, all five of them. Together.

'Look at that,' Kit whispered. 'Uh-oh.' Kit gently squeezed my fingers.

I gasped. It was Peter! His first movements were understandably unsure. Then he simply plummeted! 'Hey . . . helppp!' he called out.

Max swooped beneath him.

She deftly grabbed his lower torso and the boy flapped his wings harder and harder. He was putting everything he had into it.

'Push the air *down*,' Max urged him. 'Push that darned old air out of the way.' She was teaching him what to do. 'Relax, Peter. Don't tighten up. You were made for this!'

With that Peter leveled off. Max had given him just enough confidence. He seemed to float, then the boy rose steadily. The others were doing fine. The sky was a kind of plum-blue and was a magnificent background for the air show.

'My God, Frannie,' Kit said beside me. 'No one has ever

seen anything like this. Not even those fricking scientists.'

'Will you look at them go!'

There were no mishaps. The children flew as if they'd been doing it together for years. Max appeared to be giving them simple instruction: how to bank and how to create drag. They had whistled in the woods, and they whistled now.

'Chhee-rup. Chhee-rup.'

At first I hadn't gotten it. Now I understood that the whistling was a way for Icarus *to see*.

'Chhee-rup.'

Together the children flew across a deep, scary ravine. They circled and formed a figure eight in the air. I couldn't catch my breath as I watched them perform.

Max called out, 'I'm right here, Ic.'

Icarus whistled, then he spoke. His voice echoed through the night air. 'I *feel* you. I feel you moving in the air!'

And although it was a little too dark to clearly see his face, I could swear that Icarus was grinning his little fool head off.

CHAPTER EIGHTY-EIGHT

I cupped my hands together and called out clearly and loudly to Max, 'Time to come down. Okay, Max? Right now.'

To my relief, she waggled her wings and gave crisp orders for her tiny squadron to land. One after the other they did land, small feet smacking the dirt floor, accompanied by squeals of laughter and the purest delight that only children seem able to feel and display.

Actually, I felt guilty about giving them orders, knowing how discipline had always been instilled into them. But it had to be done. We still weren't safe in these woods. Not even close. Men with guns would be coming soon, if they weren't already nearby.

I hugged them all and even Pip was delirious with happiness. But there was no time to savor the astonishing event.

The air was cooling down fast, as it does in the mountains at the end of the summer. Kit didn't want to make a fire and he was right, unfortunately. It would be a lot safer without one. But a whole lot colder.

We found a reasonably protected place in the lee of a couple of large boulders. We pitched away loose stones and twigs and cleared a flat place for sleeping.

We gathered piles of leaves and loose wood to use for warmth during the night. The kids wrapped their wings around and were insulated.

'We'll be in a better place tomorrow,' I told the children. 'Maybe at my house.' And maybe not.

'You promise?' said Oz.

I wanted to promise him pancakes with syrup and all the milk he could drink. I wanted to promise him a real bed without bars and a happy-ever-after life. But I had no idea what the next twenty minutes would bring.

'Go to sleep,' I told them. I put my hand on Oz's head. 'Sweet dreams, okay?'

Oz gave me a cynical little smirk, and I couldn't blame him. I'd made him a wish, not a promise. I stood over him as he joined the huddle of bird-kids. They were scratched and bruised and I didn't have so much as a bandage. I didn't even have a ragged blanket to throw over them.

I bit my lips to stop them from trembling when Max began the Lord's Prayer. The others joined in and added names to the list of those God was to bless. I didn't recognize any of the names – except for Mrs Beattie's – didn't know whether they were animal or human, living or dead. There was so much history about the children I didn't know yet.

Max said, 'And God bless Frannie and Kit, our good friends. And God bless little Pip, too, our four-legged friend.'

Who had taught the children to pray in the midst of that depravity? Was it Mrs Beattie's influence? Was it instinct? I wondered if God was listening to the prayers. These special children needed Him, were under His protection. It was a knotty philosophical problem, and better left to theologians.

Once the others were sleeping, Max came and sat with Kit and me. Kit asked her for the fiftieth time about the School. *Who*, he wanted to know, were the people who worked there? Max still referred to the people as *Them*. She was afraid about the School in general. She had been conditioned for years not to breathe a word.

Kit kept pushing her, coaxing her.

'They'll put us to sleep,' she finally said. 'They're not fooling around.'

'How do you know that, Max?' I asked. I was hoping, praying, that she'd tell me a hokey bogeyman story; some Dr Frankenstein version of 'Wait till your daddy gets home.'

'They kill the skitters in jars.' She looked straight at me when she said it. Her face was a mask of total seriousness and truth. She turned pale. 'And they have a kill jar for each of us.'

My breath caught hard. I knew about kill jars. They were containers filled with carbon monoxide. Kill jars were used to euthanatize lab mice after they'd served their purpose in research labs.

'But they wouldn't put children like you to sleep,' I said to her.

'Yes, they sure would put children like me to sleep,' Max said. Her eyes were small and hard. 'They always put the rejects to sleep.' Her voice was barely audible, as if she were talking to herself.

'Eve was put to sleep. And so was Adam . . . and I think, so was my brother, Matthew.'

CHAPTER EIGHTY-NINE

I sat braced up against one of the boulders and tried to
let some of the shell shock wear off. I don't swear too
much, but I was thinking *holy shit, holy shit, holy shit*.
What a mind-boggling day. I realized that my heart hadn't
stopped pounding for the past several hours. I felt raw,
used up, and incredibly tired. I knew I badly needed to
sleep.

And yet I couldn't get my eyes to shut. My eyelids
weren't functioning as they should. I was breaking down.

I was also heartsick and stunned by Max's earlier
pronouncement – children like her had regularly been put
to death.

They always put the rejects to sleep, she'd said. They did it
as standard operating procedure.

Adam was put to sleep. So was Eve.

But who were these children with the auspicious-
sounding names? Why had they been killed? What
caused them to be rejected?

Kit came and sat down beside me. He looked exhausted and worried and I couldn't blame him. 'I've got a confession to make,' he said in a hoarse whisper. 'I have to get this out in the open.'

I wasn't expecting that. Not right now. 'Confession about what?' I stared at him. My stomach had already dropped a couple of notches. I didn't need any 'confessions,' but there was no way he could take back his words.

'Will you stop reading my eyes?' he said.

'I'm not. Okay, I am. I'll try not to. Talk. What is it that you have to say to me?'

He sat cross-legged, facing me. He considered, weighed, then finally spoke.

'A few weeks ago, a geneticist was killed in his bedroom in San Francisco. So was his live-in girlfriend. It was brutal and bloody. It was made to look like a burglary gone wrong. It wasn't, though. This geneticist,' he went on, 'had helped to discover a "promoter gene." The promoter gene was probably used at the School.'

I knew that promoter genes enable genetic material to be transferred from one organism to another. The promoter acts kind of like a key, opening a DNA lock, but it's not an all-purpose skeleton key. Different promoter genes are required for each type of genetic alteration.

'Who told you?' I asked. 'And why couldn't you have told me a couple of days ago, Kit? What else are you holding back?'

'This has to come out my way,' Kit said.

I sighed. 'Okay, do it your way.'

'Hopefully, when I'm done, you'll understand.'

'Hopefully, I will.'

'The geneticist, a man named James Kim, had confided to a friend of his at M.I.T. that he and a select group of biologists were part of an underground lab network. They were doing illegal experiments, but highly profitable ones. He was working with a team whose hub was somewhere in the Boulder area. The leak of information cost him his life. And the life of the doctor at M.I.T.'

'Wait, Kit, are you saying you knew that human experiments were going on?' I asked. 'Did you know that before we arrived at the School? Please tell me the whole truth.'

Kit shook his head. 'No. I didn't know anything for sure. I came out here to find the underground research team – if they existed as a team, if they were here. I didn't know if I'd find them, or what I'd do if I did. I still don't. And I had no idea beforehand about the horrors we discovered at the School. Or about Max. Who could have imagined that? Who would have dreamed?'

I sat up straight against the uncomfortable backrest of rock. Suddenly, I wasn't as tired as I'd thought. 'Kit, will you tell me exactly what's going on? I feel like I'm going crazy. I *know* my life is in danger. I know these kids are in grave danger, too. Just tell me the truth. I deserve that, don't I?'

'I'm trying to, Frannie. It's not black-and-white, though. Some of it is unbelievably hard to get at.'

'Why? Because you were such a good liar at first?'

He sighed and slowly nodded his head. 'Yes, because of that. And because I don't normally lie. And I guess, because of why I felt I had to lie.'

I felt my throat backing up. I couldn't stop thinking about the terrifying crimes, the conscienceless murders, what I'd seen in that horrible pediatrics ward at the School. What was Kit trying to tell me now? What else did he know?

'Kit. Just. Talk,' I finally said.

He gave a deep sigh. 'Okay. I believe that David was part of this. That's why they killed him. Your husband was murdered by the people he worked with.'

'Oh God.' I realized that I was holding myself tightly with both arms. *I'm just holding on*, I thought. *Barely*. My head was reeling. Images from a year and a half ago were flashing through my brain. They seemed fresh and raw. David's death. I was staring at Kit in the chalky moonlight in disbelief. I was in shock, and probably denial. How could David have been involved in something this bad? How could he have lied to me so convincingly and for such a long time?

'What else?' I whispered. I sensed there was more. I could see it in Kit's eyes.

'For one thing,' he said, 'I'm not here officially. The FBI actually pulled me off this case. And – my real name isn't Kit Harrison.'

CHAPTER NINETY

I felt so betrayed and hurt. I wanted to run away from *whomever*, but I was too tired. Maybe I was in shock. I was also afraid . . . of Kit Harrison.

I could barely speak, but I managed a few words. 'Please, leave me alone.'

'My name is—'

I waved him away. 'I don't care. It isn't important.'

His temper flared suddenly. 'I *am* from Boston. I worked in D.C. for a while, too. I was a senior agent with the FBI for twelve years. I was nearly fired off the job because I wouldn't back off this damn investigation. I'm not supposed to be here. They think I'm on vacation in Nantucket. I'm trying to do the right thing here, Frannie.'

I looked at him, stared hard into those deceptive blue eyes. 'Nantucket was where your wife and children were going when the plane crashed?'

He nodded. His face was flushed. His eyes were red-rimmed. 'Frannie, I'm sorry about everything. I'm sorry about your husband David. I'm not usually a liar. Actually, I never lie. I didn't have a choice. I'm obsessed with this case, I'll admit that. I've been tracking it for the past couple of years.'

'Are you sure about David?' I whispered.

'Yes, I'm sure. I talked to another doctor at M.I.T. She knew about the outlaw group. She gave me your husband's name, and she swore that David was murdered. David's name came up in association with Dr Kim in San Francisco. I'm sorry to have to tell you.'

I stared up at the dark, brooding sky. A false bottom had dropped out of my stomach. I needed to change the subject. 'What do you think happened to the men who were chasing us?'

Kit, or whoever he was, shook his head. 'Maybe the fire and the explosion at the School distracted them. They know they'll catch us before we get down the mountain with five children in tow.'

'Maybe one of us should go ahead,' I said.

He shook his head. His eyes were so intense now. 'Frannie, tell me your thoughts about the labs at the School. Your bottom line, best guess, whatever you think is going on there. What struck you back there? I think it's important.'

I tried to think straight, to concentrate, but it wasn't very easy. 'Honestly – shock at first. Then, sorrow. A sense that my soul had been invaded. Obviously, they were experimenting on humans, among other terrible things.'

'What other things?'

An idea had hit me very hard at the School. It was so horrifying I had wanted it to disappear. I still couldn't shake it off.

'No matter how these so-called scientists manipulated and combined genes, the children must have come from human stock. They weren't cooked up in lab beakers. A little of this, a dash of that. They got their hair, eyes, skin color, some of their intellectual capacity from their parents. Max, Oz, Peter, Wendy, Ic, they all have human mothers and fathers. I'm sure of it.'

His eyes were incredibly intense, probing, holding on to mine. 'Please go on, Frannie. I have to hear this, anything you suspect at this point. I'm trying to put together a lot of pieces.'

'There is no such thing as a test-tube baby. Not yet, anyway. There's simply no way to grow a child in anything other than the real thing. Even biologically engineered mouse embryos have to be implanted into living female mice until they're developed. Max and the other children were nurtured in the wombs of women. They have *human mothers*.'

My eyes were finally closing. I couldn't keep them open a minute longer. Unfortunately, the nightmarish thoughts kept coming in waves. Who were the women who had cooperated with the experiments? How had the genetically manipulated embryos been obtained? Where were the birth mothers?

'What's your real name?' I finally whispered. I had to know.

'My name is Tom,' I heard. 'I'm Tom Brennan, Frannie.

I'm sorry about that. I'm sorry about David.'

I nodded my head. I was close to tears, but I stubbornly held them off. An image of David flashed before my eyes.

'Me too,' I said.

CHAPTER NINETY-ONE

I t was half past nine and Kit/Tom was thoughtful and brooding as he walked lookout on the perimeter of the hideaway. At least he was operating decently as an agent. So far, he'd been able to protect everyone – but for how much longer?

He was worried about so many things right now, but he felt particularly bad about what happened earlier with Frannie. He hated that he'd let her down.

Pop. Something hit him on the head and he jumped back. He looked up, expecting trouble.

He found it, too. Max was bouncing on a sturdy tree limb above. She had dropped a pine cone on him.

'Funny girl. What's up? Besides you?' he called to her.

She smiled down.

'I want to show you something.' She pointed toward a distant hill that was outlined in glowing red. 'The fire's still burning.'

Kit needed to see for himself. He braced his foot on the

trunk. He reached for a low limb, pulled himself up to a crotch in the tree. He continued to climb quickly and expertly until he arrived at the crook where Max was sitting.

'That's the hard way up here,' Max said and made a face.

'I can't fly, Max. I'm not supposed to reveal that I'm Superman. Not yet.'

'Oh, okay. Your secret's safe with me. Hardee-har.' She had mimicked Matthew's crazy laugh and she regretted it instantly. Max scootched over to make room for Kit in the bough of the tree.

'I'll keep watch up here for now,' he said. 'Why don't you go down and get some sleep? Please get some rest.'

'I can't sleep,' she said. 'Anyway, I'm used to it, staying up. I was always afraid of being "put to sleep." I have nightmares about it all the time. So I don't sleep too much.'

'We'll be all right for a while,' he told her.

Max frowned. 'Bull.'

Kit smiled. 'A little bit, I guess. What's going on in there?' he asked, tapping the young girl's head.

'Too much for my own good, especially now. I hated the putrid School, but it *was* my putrid home.'

He nodded, understood a little bit. 'There are lots better places out here in the world. Honest. Wait and see.'

Max threw a deep sigh. 'I like Frannie a whole lot. I even like you – sometimes. Like now,' she teased.

'Are you going to breed with Frannie?' Max suddenly asked.

Kit started to laugh. He couldn't help it, and hoped it didn't hurt her feelings.

'Are you going to?' Max insisted. 'Your secret's safe with me, Kit. I'll pinkie-swear on it.'

'Frannie's not even talking to me,' he told Max, letting her into his confidence.

'How come?'

'Because,' he said, slowly, 'I didn't tell her some secrets I didn't feel I could tell anyone.'

Max nodded her head. 'Oh, I see. Like the secrets *I* wasn't supposed to tell anyone? But you insisted I should tell you?'

'Yeah. I guess so. Point taken.' She was so damn quick.

Max nodded with satisfaction. She licked her finger and made a mark, *a score*, in front of his face.

'Anyone ever tell you how smart you are?'

Max smiled, clearly pleased. She had such a beautiful, radiant face. 'Wendy and Peter are smarter. I only tested one forty-nine on the Stanford-Binet. They're in the high genius range. Adam and Eve were off the planet. But it didn't save them. I always wonder why. Don't you?'

'I wonder about a lot of things, Max. That's why I ask so many dumb questions. Do you know why they were put to sleep?'

Max shook her head. 'I remember the night it happened, though. There must have been an error, a flaw. They were rejected. Something was wrong with them.'

Kit listened and shook his head. 'Something is wrong with all of us, sweet-stuff. Nobody's perfect. That's what makes us interesting.'

'I know. I understand that part. I really like *your* imperfections.'

She leaned up against him. He felt incredibly warm feelings toward her. It was nice, almost father-daughter. Together they stared into the red-rimmed horizon. The fire was out there. *Danger*. Suddenly, he was remembering Tommy and Mike. His own children. He didn't want to remember, not now.

'Seriously. I like you a lot,' Max said to him. 'You have kind eyes. I know you wouldn't hurt someone unless you had to. It's the way you are.'

'Thank you,' he said, and nuzzled her cheek. 'One of us should sleep for a while, though. You go ahead.'

'I'm wide-awake,' Max said. 'Besides, I can see and hear better than you. I'm our best chance.'

He smiled. 'You're probably right,' he said. He let his eyes slowly close and it felt so good. 'My real name is Tom,' he whispered.

'I'm Maximum. You'll see why.'

CHAPTER NINETY-TWO

I was running for my life inside a shadowy, feverish
dream – David was in it – when I felt Pip yanking hard
at my sleeve.

'Stop it, Pip. You're already outside. Go pee by yourself.
Be a good boy. G'wan.'

Scolding and shoving him away didn't stop him. He was
such a persistent little bugger, so I forced my eyes open.

I half expected David to be there beside me, but he
wasn't of course.

I sniffed the air. The smell was noxious and I started to
choke. As in my dream, the air was hot and black and
stifling. I didn't know if it was day or night, only that
I'd fallen asleep by moonlight and now the moon was
completely gone. I couldn't see a thing, not even the sky,
or the overhanging trees that had been there when I
dropped off to sleep.

It was like being stricken blind. I was in a blanket of
heavy, nearly black fog.

'Hello? Somebody?' I called out.

With sickening clarity, I understood how bad things really were. Smoke had completely obliterated the moon and sky, even the overhanging trees. Smoke was all around, choking me, blinding me, making it impossible to see more than a couple of feet in any direction. The woods were on fire.

Pip was barking, demanding that I follow him. I pushed myself up. Stumbled over stumps and rocks calling, 'Kit! Kit! Where are you? There's a fire!'

He finally answered. 'Here. Over here. The wind must have shifted.'

The fire was on us like *that*.

I still couldn't locate Kit. I couldn't see any of the kids either. My eyes stung and watered. My visibility was only about three or four feet. I felt trapped, claustrophobic, completely closed in.

I heard something. An elk. I was looking right into the huge animal's eyes – glazed and frozen. It was as lost and afraid as I was. Then it pounded past me.

I could hear the fire now. It was a soft roar, seductive, almost melodic. Slowly, I began to see again. The smoke wasn't as bad on slightly higher ground. The sky was turning red, brightened by the fire. Gazing north, I could see rows of withered, blackened trees on a distant hillside.

A nearby tree caught and burned with a loud *whoosh*. A huge limb crashed to the ground. Sparks flew high into the air, like big firecrackers exploding.

The fire had definitely turned with the wind. It must have been racing over the ground for the past few hours, gaining strength as it moved. Now the monster was big. Huge. They had gotten rid of all the evidence, hadn't They? The School was long gone in the terrifying blaze.

I called out again.

This time I heard retching coughs. The kids were nearby. But where were they?

'Max? Icarus, Oz? *Max?*'

I saw Kit first. 'I've got the twins,' he said, as he staggered out of the curtain of smoke. One twin was hoisted over each shoulder. He *was* strong.

Pip started to growl again. He bared his little teeth. His coat was already covered in soot and ash.

There was a shot. A flare of light. *A gunshot in the middle of all of this.* Where had it come from? What direction?

Another tree limb fell in a blaze of orange-and-gold sparks. Pip yelped.

'Let's go. Let's go,' Kit yelled.

We started to run for it.

CHAPTER NINETY-THREE

Wendy was wrapped tightly in my arms. We were managing to stay ahead of the raging, thundering fire so far. Most likely the rapidly shifting winds had pushed it away from us for the time being.

I was trying to get my bearings when I heard Max shout, 'Look. Look out. More guards!'

I could see two men were poking around in the valley below us.

I was stunned. To my absolute shock, I recognized them. I knew both men standing down there. They were from Boulder Community Hospital. Colleagues of David's.

The taller of the two was wearing a blue satin L.A. Dodgers baseball jacket, a cap, rimless glasses. He had salt-and-pepper hair and a full beard. The other man was shorter but weighed more, a Humpty-Dumpty in plaid shirtsleeves and baggy khakis.

The taller man was Dr Michael Vaughan. He was in Neurology. The man with the spare tire was Bobby something. He was head nurse in the Ob-Gyn unit. I'd seen him at a party once, entertaining people with photos of babies whose deliveries he'd assisted. *His* babies, he'd called them.

They were David's friends. We had socialized with them.

Tears welled up in my eyes, and it wasn't from the smoke. It was the sense of betrayal I felt. Maybe they were just volunteers looking for survivors of the fire. It would be a great thing if Dr Vaughan and Nurse Bobby were a couple of concerned citizens, wouldn't it? All we'd have to do was whistle to them and we'd be heading out of the wilderness toward antibiotics, clean sheets, and warm food.

But a strange, intuitive feeling stopped me from yelling, 'Hey, we're over here.'

Kit and the children were being very quiet, too.

Then Kit pointed to the left and I saw our salvation: a black Jeep. Our Jeep.

Unfortunately, Vaughan and the male nurse had discovered it, too. They were trying the doors.

Kit forced a clip into his gun. His face was grim, stretched tight. His concentration was total.

He kept his gun in shooting position. They finally walked away from the Jeep. They were looking for something – us? Their eyes kept scanning the surrounding woods. Thank God, they didn't see us. I threw a deep, audible sigh.

Something bright flashed in my peripheral vision. I jumped back. What now?

Kit was holding up the car keys.

'Whatever made you lock the car?'

Flashing a grin I hadn't seen in a while, he said, 'It's what city kids do.'

CHAPTER NINETY-FOUR

W e hoped against hope that no one was looking for Kit's Jeep. We hoped *They* didn't know who he was, or why he was out here in Colorado. Then we worried about the FBI's lack of involvement, and specifically why Kit had been taken off the investigation. We had our plates full with worry.

This was not good. None of it was. We piled into the Jeep and Kit drove fast, almost dangerously, down the narrow, twisty mountain road we'd come on. The kids loved it, urging him to go even faster.

As we rounded a sharp curve over a ravine, I saw a small group of men and women standing by one side of the road. Hikers? They looked harmless enough.

Then I recognized them and my heart nearly stopped. They were from the hospital in Boulder, too. Some of them were wearing headphones with tiny mikes near their mouths.

Three men and a woman – all of them doctors at

Boulder Community. Wearing headphones to go hiking? Damn. I didn't think so. I wasn't real big on conspiracy theories, but I had a lot of faith in what I saw with my own two eyes.

'Get down. Please get down!' I told the kids. 'Get down below the window.'

The suspicious doctors looked up at our speeding Jeep, but the children stayed down, and the docs from Hell didn't seem to notice anything wrong.

'They're from Boulder Community Hospital.' I told Kit the latest bad news. 'This is getting so damn creepy. I can't stand it. I *wish* I was being paranoid.'

He stepped up the speed, and the kids whooped and hollered again. Even under the circumstances, it was a joyride to them. They were absolutely fearless. Somehow, we made it to the bottom of the mountain in one piece, and as far as we knew, without being spotted.

I remembered that Oz, the twins, and Icarus had never been outside the School before this. It was all brand new to them. They were on overload, complete overstimulation, maybe even more than me.

'Welcome to Bear Bluff, Colorado,' I said. I looked back and tried to make a happy face. 'It's actually a pretty nice place to live.'

'It's even creepier than the School,' Max said in a deep, croaky voice. She laughed. 'Just kidding, Frannie and Kit. It is nice. *If you like to eat red meat.* You'll love it, guys. *Not!*'

'I'm really, really scared,' Wendy trilled. Her brown eyes were bulging, and she did look petrified now.

'So am I,' said Peter.

'Care Bear stare!' Max said to them. Obviously, it was something they shared, a lucky saying, a charm.

'Care Bear stare!' the others chorused. 'Care Bear stare! Care Bear stare!'

Unfortunately, Max was right about the creepy part.

Now, two Army Jeeps were approaching in the opposite direction. Army Jeeps? Was the Army part of this, too? How could that be? Who were *They*? Everybody but *Us*?

'Down in back,' I whispered and the kids ducked again. I ducked down as well.

We passed by the grunting and groaning U.S. Army Jeeps without incident.

'Kit, please tell me this can't get any worse,' I said as we got on the last stretch toward my place. I needed to stop at the Inn-Patient for medical supplies. I had to treat the lacerations and bruises from our flight down the mountain.

'If you recognize any more hospital personnel, old friends and acquaintances and such, be sure to let me know,' he said.

We curled around the last familiar bend approaching the Inn-Patient. Kit almost stopped – then he sped up. He stepped on the gas hard and the Jeep lurched forward. We barreled right past the Inn-Patient, past my home.

'Kit, *stop*. We have to stop!' I yelled. 'Kit, stop this Jeep! Now!' I repeated.

'Frannie, no! It's no good. We can't stop,' he said and kept speeding down the road. The rear of the Jeep was fishtailing badly.

I knew Kit was right, but I couldn't believe what I saw.

I thought my heart was finally going to break.

They had burned down my house, my hospital, my everything. They had torched the Inn-Patient. All of my poor animals were inside.

BOOK 5

WHEN THE WIND BLOWS

CHAPTER NINETY-FIVE

W e streaked past the Inn-Patient at better than sixty miles an hour. I felt hollow and sick inside. I knew Kit was right to speed by my place without stopping, but that didn't make it any easier.

Max leaned in close from the backseat. 'Oh, Frannie, I'm so sorry. It's all my fault.'

'We're sorry, Frannie,' the other kids joined in.

In the back of the Jeep, little Pip was in a highly agitated state. Pip was barking and whining as we passed our old house, or what was left of it.

Damn Them. Damn Them to hell. Who had done this? Who was responsible? I wanted to do terrible things to them. I felt I had the right. I'd never felt anything close to this kind of anger and disgust.

'I know where we can go.' I finally managed to speak after we got a mile or so up the road where I used to live. 'I know where we'll be safe, for a little while at least. Until we can figure something out.'

I gave Kit directions to my sister Carole's. She lived in the town of Radcliff, which is about twenty miles south-west of Bear Bluff. We'd be okay there, for the rest of the day, anyway.

Carole had moved out to Colorado from Milwaukee, after she split with her husband, Charlie. She lived on a small working farm with her two daughters, Meredith and Brigid, and their dogs, two geese – Graham and Crackers – and a house-trained rabbit named Thumper. People can tell right away that we're sisters.

I would have gone to Carole's earlier, at least to talk to her, but she and the kids had been on a two-week camping trip to Gunnison National Forest. I wasn't even sure if they were back now, which might be even better.

But I spotted C-Bird working in her vegetable garden as we approached the house. She was nearly lost among the droopy-headed sunflowers. Bumblebees danced around her.

'Kit, would you stop here? Let me walk to the house. I have to sort of prepare Carole for this.'

'Doesn't she like kids?' Max cracked from the back.

'Yes, she does, and animals, too,' I said.

I climbed out of the Jeep and walked toward my sister. I wasn't sure I was doing the right thing now. I wasn't sure about anything anymore. In the last few hours I'd learned there were a lot of folks in the area whom I couldn't trust. I also had a better appreciation for what Kit had been going through with this case.

My sister, Carole, is five years older than I am and a great, great person in every way. Her husband, Charlie, a radiologist, was such a jerk to lose her and his kids. Carole summed it up. 'You snooze, you lose.'

'Instant family?' she said, looking toward the Jeep. She had on muddy gardening boots, plaid shorts, an old denim shirt, and a floppy straw hat. Sunblock was smeared unevenly on her forehead and cheeks. Behind her, a clothesline was heavy with towels and bathing suits from their trip.

'*Of course* you can bring them for a little unexpected visit, Frances. Who are they, though? Is that a *man* in the driver's seat?'

I nodded. 'His name is Kit – I mean it's Tom.'

Carole's eyebrows raised several inches.

'Uh-huh. He's Kit, Tom, whatever. And? The others?'

Man, oh man, oh man. The others?

'Carole, this is very strange. I'm your sister. You trust me, right?'

'Up to a point. You didn't get married to someone with a huge family, Frannie? Please tell me you didn't. Oh hell, I don't care if you did,' Carole said, pushing strands of loose hair away from her face. 'You *didn't*?'

I put my hand on her arm. No, that wasn't enough for me right now. I needed more. I hugged my sister tightly in the middle of her garden.

'Sweetie, are you all right? You're trembling,' she said against my cheek. 'You're trembling all over.'

'Someone is after us,' I whispered. 'I'm not kidding. I'm not making a joke. And – those children in the car? Carole, oh God, Carole. They uh, they uhm. Oh hell, they have wings and they can fly.'

CHAPTER NINETY-SIX

Supper at my sister's house is usually a spontaneous event, what with Thumper or possibly one of the geese, Graham or Crackers, encouraged to wander in and out of the dining room like an extra guest or two. Over the table is a quote that accurately captures the family's spirit: 'If the sky falls, one may hope to catch larks.'

The sky *was* falling.

I had to hand it to Carole, though, she was enormously cool under fire. So was Kit. And so were Meredith and Brigid, who are two of the nicest, kindest, smartest kids I've ever met.

'Is this your idea of payback for Frank the Swan?' Carole said, and we cracked up. So did Kit, though he had no way of knowing exactly what we were talking about. Before she had left for her camping trip, Carole had brought me an old, hopelessly injured swan for mending.

Over a home-cooked meal I told Carole as much as I

dared, and said that we would be out of her house as soon as we possibly could. It was also decided that Carole and the kids would return to Gunnison National Forest for another week of camping – just to be safe.

When dinner was finished, Kit and I had to leave for a while. It was Kit's idea. We were going to see Henrich Kroner, who had been David's boss at Boulder Community Hospital, and who was also high on Kit's list of suspects. Kroner had studied embryology under Dr Anthony Peyser in Boston.

Henrich had come to Colorado from M.I.T. He'd never been charged or indicted in Boston. He lived in Boulder with his current girlfriend, Jilly. I remembered that Jilly was a pediatric nurse, and worked at the hospital's in vitro fertilization clinic.

I couldn't help thinking of all the murdered babies at the School. All of the rejects. A pediatric nurse? It couldn't just be a coincidence.

We were afraid that Kit's Jeep might be easily recognized by now, so we borrowed Carole's Chevy 4×4. We were at Dr Kroner's before nine thirty. If he and Jilly were home, they'd be up. I remembered seeing Henrich at the McDonoughs' the night Frank had been murdered. Another coincidence? I doubted it.

The lights of the expensive and grossly oversized mountain 'cottage' were shining brightly. Henrich Kroner's triple-black Mercedes convertible was parked in the drive.

The two of us walked up a flagstone pathway. We stood outside the screen door and rang the front bell a couple of times.

Nobody came at first. I could see into the living room: pine furniture and brightly colored throw rugs. Audubon prints, Shaker doors, wide-board pine floors. No Henrich and Jilly, though. A little scary. Everything was new.

'Dr Kroner,' I finally called. 'It's Frannie O'Neill. Henrich Kroner. Jilly. Are you in there? Is anybody home?'

Total silence in the house. Only the loud shrilling of crickets and cicadas in the yard.

'Let's go round back,' Kit said. He started around the edge of the house. I took a deep breath and followed him. I didn't want to be alone. 'I'm two steps behind you, Kit.'

Kit stopped suddenly and I nearly walked into him. 'Oh, Christ,' he whispered. 'Stay there, Frannie. Stay back, please. It's bad.'

I could see Henrich and Jilly from where I stood. They were lying face up on a pair of bright yellow chaises longues. Blood was puddled around the chairs and seeping into cracks between the flagstones. Blood stained the chaises longues as well.

I could see that Jilly had been shot in the hollow of her throat. Henrich had been shot through the right eye.

My heart constricted and my mouth was very dry. I wanted to cover my eyes, but I didn't do it. I needed to see everything now, to describe it if I had to. If I was going to be a witness, I might as well be a good one.

Kit lightly touched my arm. 'You okay, Frannie?'

Not really. I had seen a lot of animals die, but it hadn't prepared me for the sight of a viciously murdered man and woman, especially people whom I'd known. 'I'm doing all right, I guess. Still on my feet, anyway,' I whispered.

'Two shots for each victim. Entry an inch or so apart,' Kit muttered.

'Kit, this just happened. Neither body is rigorous or discolored. We just missed the killers. Or, they just missed us.'

Neither Henrich Kroner nor Jilly had been friends of mine, but I'd known them. I didn't like Henrich, but David and I had come to a couple of parties at this house.

I had sat in one of these yellow lounge chairs. I wondered if Dr Anthony Peyser had ever been here? Could he be responsible for these deaths?

Bad thoughts were repeating in my brain. That happens under stress. I couldn't help remembering that I saw Kroner at Frank McDonough's the night Frank drowned. Or that Henrich Kroner had visited my house in Bear Bluff after David was killed. It was so awful, and none of it seemed coincidental.

'We have to go back to Carole's,' I said, grabbing Kit's arm. 'We have to get her and the kids out of there now.'

They were killing all the witnesses.

CHAPTER NINETY-SEVEN

K it was afraid, but he was trying not to show it for Frannie's sake. He pulled over at a 7-Eleven on Baseline Road in Boulder. The last twenty-four hours were testing everything he'd learned as an agent, and some things he hadn't. He did remember an old saying from his training at Quantico: *Fall seven times, stand up eight.*

'I'll be quick,' he said as he ripped open the 4×4's door. 'I'm going to try to talk to Peter Stricker at the FBI. I've got to make him believe me, which might not be so easy.'

'Okay,' Frannie said, 'but please hurry. I'm worried about Carole and the kids.'

Kit walked quickly toward the pay phone outside the brightly lit convenience store. He was still feeling alone in all of this. That's just the way it was. Realistically, there was only so much one agent could do. Why in hell had they shut him down? It made no sense and it was scary as hell.

He didn't want to call Peter Stricker. Not even now. It was like asking to be insulted and browbeaten and turned down again. It had been going on for more than a year. The same thing, over and over.

Even though it was past seven in Washington, he decided to try Stricker at his office first. He had Stricker's home phone number – they had been friends, right – but calling there was a last resort. Not a really good move.

Peter's secretary was still working at the office. She picked up after one ring.

'Cindy, this is Tom Brennan on the line. I have to talk to Peter. It's an emergency.'

'Mr Stricker is on the road,' the secretary said. 'I'll give him your message when he calls in.'

Kit yelled into the phone. 'Damn it, Cindy, people are dying. You beep Peter's number right now. I'll hold the line. I'm not going away this time. Tell him there have been more deaths, and it's his goddamn fault.'

It didn't take long for Cindy to reach Stricker, and Kit wondered if he'd been in the office all along. Probably, he had been.

He heard Stricker's familiar whisper. 'Tom, what is it?' He wished he could reach through the fiber-optic phone lines and strangle him.

'There's been another murder. *Two* murders. No, actually, Peter, there have been a lot more murders than that. Now let me talk, let me finish what I have to tell. Don't say a goddamn word.'

'Tom, where are you?'

'Not a fricking word!'

'I understand. Of course. Go on.'

'All right, well I'm *not* in Nantucket. I haven't been in Nantucket. I'm in Colorado, which is where I ought to be, which is where the Bureau should have sent me, where *you* should have sent me, Peter, if you'd listened to my warnings.'

'You've seen someone murdered. You said—'

'*Shut the hell up.* Yes, I just left the house of Dr Henrich Kroner. He's dead, and so is his girlfriend. That's our fault. No, it's *your* fault. Kroner used to work for Anthony Peyser.'

'All right, I hear you. Where are you now, Tom? Where exactly is Dr Kroner's house?'

'Forget about Henrich Kroner. Kroner is dead. I told you that. Peter, they've killed children. They destroyed embryos. They're experimenting on humans. I saw it myself. I saw the awful, horrible lab where they worked. I was *there*.'

'Tom, *where the hell are you*?' Peter Stricker finally raised his voice.

'I'm on a fucking phone in the middle of Hell, and in case you're interested, there are Seven-Elevens here! I want fifty agents now! Get everybody from Denver. Tell them to head to Bear Bluff, Colorado. Go to what used to be the Inn-Patient. It's an animal hospital. They can't miss it. Somebody burned it to the ground. I'll make contact with them – not the other way around. I'm running this now!'

Stricker sighed. 'All right, I hear you. We'll send people in.'

Kit hung up the pay phone and took a deep breath. That was pretty damn good. The cavalry was coming.

CHAPTER NINETY-EIGHT

I saw Kit get off the phone after a very animated conversation. He jogged back to the car, and he actually looked better. He had some of his color back. He told me that his old boss had finally listened. 'I don't know how much he believed, but he believed some of it. He's sending agents here.'

The feeling I had, the crazy imagery in my head, was that I had been thrust into a real-life scenario that roughly paralleled the one in *Invasion of the Body Snatchers*. I was beginning to think I could no longer trust anyone in Boulder or the surrounding towns.

We hurried back to Carole's house from Boulder. Carole saw the car lights and was waiting for us at the front door.

'Everything's cool here, Frannie,' she said. Obviously, she'd read the worried look on my face. 'The kids were really good. Nobody's been flying or anything.'

'Yeah, except for you, Meredith, and Brigid. You're flying

out of here right now. Another doctor from the hospital is dead. Henrich Kroner. Pack your things now.'

Carole and the girls were ready in fifteen minutes, which was a new land-speed record for them. I felt guilty about involving them, but I knew they would be, anyway. Whoever was after me could easily find out who my sister was, if they didn't already know, and where she lived. Camping in Gunnison National Forest was the safest place for Carole and her girls to be right now.

We hugged furiously hard and tried not to cry. Then everybody waved sad good-byes in front of the house. My sister and her girls drove off into the night. I prayed they would be safe, that all of us would be.

But I didn't really believe it. Too many bad things had happened, and we knew about most of them.

CHAPTER NINETY-NINE

Dr Anthony Peyser was slow climbing out of the slate-gray Mercedes sedan. His face showed the pain of the exertion. Peyser was in his late seventies, and genius or not, he hadn't been able to arrest the ravages of aging and a highly stressful life.

He walked slowly toward the men waiting for him in the small wooded clearing. He waved a greeting and looked to be a pleasant older chap.

'We haven't caught up with her yet.' Harding Thomas spoke before he did.

'So it would seem,' the doctor said and smiled thinly. 'Well, I'm not surprised. Under different circumstances, I might even be pleased with the results. She had avian instincts for survival and flight, and the clever intelligence of humans. She is superior to all of you, and she's proving it, isn't she? Of course she is. What a super girl.'

'We'll get her,' Thomas said.

Peyser nodded and pursed his thin lips. 'I have no doubt

of it. She's sought out help, and the humans will be her downfall. She's finally made a mistake.'

Harding Thomas nodded. As usual, the doctor was right.

'Bring her in alive if you possibly can. She's worth a small fortune,' Peyser said. 'But if that fails, bring her in dead. And that goes for anyone else who's seen her. The good that will ultimately come will justify everything. The most important days in history are almost here.'

CHAPTER ONE
HUNDRED

W e slept fitfully at Carole's house and we were all up before dawn. Kit needed to go to the Inn-Patient and we decided it was best if we all stayed together.

Help was supposedly on the way. FBI agents would meet us at the Inn-Patient. Kit had already checked around midnight, but they hadn't arrived yet.

We left Carole's before four and it was incredibly dark and eerie on the back roads. There were no streetlights out in Radcliff, or in Bear Bluff for that matter.

We were close to the Inn-Patient by four forty-five. We traveled up the familiar road, but Kit passed right by the place. He checked it out as we drove by.

'I don't see anybody. Maybe Stricker didn't believe me after all. That asshole.'

We turned around and drove back. Everything looked dark and deserted. The FBI wasn't there yet.

'Pull in, Kit. I have to look at my house.'

This had been my home and I couldn't just let it go. No one was there yet. Kit turned into the driveway.

I grabbed his flashlight. 'I'll be quick.'

I hurried out of the Jeep and climbed the front steps. My charbroiled front steps. I was oblivious to everything except that this was my house, my workplace, and my poor animals had been trapped inside, cruelly burned alive.

The building was still smoldering and the heavy, acrid smell of the fire was overpowering. My house was no more. I barely recognized it.

I got a surprise when I worked up the nerve to finally look inside. I moved the flashlight around and . . . the animals were gone. Someone had let them out before they started the fire. I was relieved and also thankful.

'Frannie.' Kit was suddenly there behind me. 'You okay?'

'I had to see it,' I whispered as my throat began to close up. I covered my nose with a handkerchief, but it didn't help much. A thick, dry taste like charcoal was on my tongue.

The fire had devoured everything. The furniture, rugs, and curtains were blackened rags and could never be salvaged. The walls and ceilings were blistered black.

Kit held me from behind. He knew the thing to do. I turned and looked into his eyes.

'Kit, maybe it's not the same people. Whoever burned my house let the animals loose. Those bastards at the School wouldn't have done that.'

'Maybe some of the doctors from Boulder started the

fire,' he offered, 'instead of the guards, the hunters.'

'Maybe those young Army guys, like the ones we saw yesterday.' I offered a paranoid thought of my own.

'Let's go outside,' he whispered softly. 'We'll wait there. There's nothing here anymore.'

'I know. Thanks for letting me see my house,' I whispered. I let him pull me out of the blackened shell of my house, away from my life for the past few years.

We made it out onto the porch. We stopped moving.

They were waiting for us. Not the FBI – the hunters, the guards from the School. Half a dozen of the home burners, the child murderers, were standing in my driveway. They had Max and the other kids.

CHAPTER ONE
HUNDRED-ONE

'Take your hands the hell off them!' Kit called down from the porch. 'They're just kids. They're children.'

I liked that, loved it, actually. They had rifles and handguns and here was Kit, barking orders. He was standing up to them.

The two guards holding Ozymandias and Max actually let them go, and even took a few steps back. They were dressed like local outdoor types – workboots, wrinkled and stained khakis, hunting vests. There was no way to identify who any of them were. Army? FBI? Mercenaries? I'd never seen any of these particular men at Boulder Community Hospital, anyway.

'Come down here off the porch!' The man who spoke was broad-shouldered, in his late forties or early fifties. His face was scarred and pitted, his eyes black marbles. I knew from Max's descriptions that he was Uncle Thomas.

'You've caused enough trouble already,' he called in a

booming voice. 'I *will shoot* you down off the porch.'

'*We've* caused enough trouble?' I snapped back. 'Give me a break.'

'You're a murderer!' Max screamed at the man, who clutched her hair with one hand. Her face was bright red and she was struggling in spite of his grasp on her. 'And you're an asshole, too. You're an even worse asshole than you are a murderer, *Uncle* Thomas!'

Thomas smiled, and he almost managed to look avuncular. 'Thank you, Tinkerbell.' He looked at us and pushed Max in front of him. 'You two, come down here. Come on, or I'll shoot one of the children right now.'

'He definitely will, Frannie. He's a coward and a bully. He's a useless, worthless pig.'

Kit and I slowly walked down the porch steps and joined the other captives. We had no choice. The guards had guns aimed at us. We'd hoped to find the FBI here, but we'd found these killers instead.

A couple of 4×4s were turning into the driveway behind our Jeep. Then a black RV pulled in.

'You know these people?' I asked Max.

'I know them,' she hissed. 'I wish I didn't. They're guards – *keepers*. They *keep* order at the School. They *keep* everybody in line. They *keep* you prisoner until they decide to put you to sleep. The head creepkeeper is Uncle Thomas.'

She snapped her head toward the burly man standing behind her. 'You're the worst of the worst. You betrayed us. You lie every time you open your mouth.'

'You're way out of line, Missy,' he warned. His face tightened. He raised his arm to strike her.

I threw myself at Uncle Thomas. I was in a rage. Thomas was momentarily caught off guard. Kit jumped into the fight. He hit one guy in the nose with an elbow. He knocked down a football-player-sized lug who had been threatening us with the butt of a rifle. Then a third guard put a revolver against the side of Kit's head.

Max broke loose. She raced a few yards toward the pine woods clustered on the far side of the house. Then she waved her wings and took off. She seemed to get stronger and smoother every time she flew.

'Don't shoot! Please don't shoot her!' I screamed at the top of my voice. I was yelling into Thomas's ear.

'Shoot her down,' he yelled. 'Don't hesitate. Bring her down.'

Two of the guards fired at Max as she lifted off. She didn't go straight up, though. Max shot like a dart back into the overhanging fir woods. She disappeared behind a copse of thick evergreen trees.

Several guards gave chase, but a few stayed with us and the other children.

'The rest of you – into the van! Now! Go on, or we'll shoot you right here.' Thomas gave the orders. Then he cuffed me on the side of the skull. My ears were ringing, and I almost went down. I hadn't expected to be hit.

'So shoot *me*!' Wendy stepped forward. Her chin and her little chest were thrust out boldly. 'Shoot me right in my face. Shoot me dead.'

'Shoot me, too,' Peter said. 'Pow, I'm dead! Who the heck cares? Go on and shoot another little kid.'

'I was thinking I'd start with him.' Thomas pointed his

weapon at Icarus. 'The blind boy. Ic!'

'Get in the van,' I said to the kids. 'Now! Right this second! Icarus first. Please.'

The kids looked at me, and I wanted to make it okay somehow. But it wasn't okay, and maybe it never would be for any of us again. Thomas kept his gun on us as we climbed into the van.

'Busted,' Icarus whispered from his seat beside Kit. 'We're all dead.'

CHAPTER ONE
HUNDRED-TWO

Kit, the children, and I were pushed and crowded inside the semidarkened van. I couldn't help thinking that it was like a hearse. Or remembering what Kit had said before: *They* want everything to disappear. There can't be any witnesses.

The hearse coughed once, then started up. It backed out of my driveway. The driver made a right turn, *away* from the village of Bear Bluff. Heading where?

'They're going to put us to sleep,' Oz said matter-of-factly. He bluntly stated my worst fears.

'Who did they put to sleep at the School?' Kit asked Oz. You could take the agent out of the FBI . . . he was still trying to collect information, to get at the truth.

'We're not supposed to talk about it,' Wendy warned. Her eyes were wide with fear.

'Lots of little skitters got killed,' Peter chirped back. He shrugged it off.

'What are skitters?' I asked Peter.

'Critters who live in the labs. Especially the new babies. They're called skitters. Or labbies,' Oz answered. 'Ask Max about it. She worked there. Oh yeah, Max isn't here to ask. Don't worry, she's smart. Max can take care of herself.'

I nodded at Oz. 'I know she can. What about Adam and Eve?' I asked. 'Who were they?'

'They were our dearest friends.' Peter volunteered more information with a sad little voice, and an even sadder look on his face. 'Same age as me, you know. Born in the same year. Nineteen hundred and ninety-four.'

'Put to sleep,' Oz said. He made a line across his throat and let his tongue hang out to the side. 'Best to forget them. Out of sight, out of mind. *One sleeps, the others weep.*'

'One sleeps, the others weep,' the kids repeated. 'One sleeps, the others weep.'

I was getting a clearer and even more terrifying picture of the School. The younger children were much more open about it than Max had been. They weren't as afraid to talk out of School.

'Jesus, Frannie,' Kit said, resting his hand on mine. 'These poor kids. You have any idea where they're taking us? Which direction we're headed?'

I shook my head and blew out air. 'Back into the mountains. West, I *think*. That's about all I can tell.'

Meanwhile, the kids' singsong played in my head. One sleeps, the others weep.

Or how about – they all sleep, nobody is left to weep.

CHAPTER ONE HUNDRED-THREE

The van struggled up a steep, nearly continuous grade for about half an hour. Then it jerked to a sudden stop. The engine shut down and I froze. We were here, wherever that was. Not the School – but where?

I could hear car doors slamming. Shoes and boots crunching gravel. The static of gruff male voices outside the van.

'Wherever we are, we're less than an hour from your place,' Kit whispered. We both sat very still in the rear of the van. There was nothing either of us could do now. It was killing me.

'You guys all okay?' I asked the kids. I tried to sound confident and somewhat in control. I found I was having powerful maternal feelings since I'd been around them.

'We're not anywhere near that shitty School again. I can feel we're not there,' Oz said with equal parts of boyish conviction and enthusiasm.

'We're someplace bad,' Ic said. 'It feels real bad. I can always tell.'

'Feels icky, right Ic?' Oz cracked. He made a face at his blind friend.

The van's door was unlocked and it swung open with a high-pitched *whirrr*. We blinked at the bright sunlight bursting in on us.

Men with guns were standing outside. They were staring in with faces like moonpies. The odds were hopelessly against us.

'You don't have to point those guns,' I said.

'We come in peace,' Ic said.

One of the men issued an order. 'Step out of the vehicle.' He sounded like a military person, and I wondered what army? 'This will be a lot easier if you follow instructions instead of trying to give them, ma'am. All of you – outside! Do it right now!'

'These are little kids. The guns scare them,' Kit said. 'Do you have any kids, mister? Any of you out there have kids?'

'Step the hell out of the vehicle, Agent Brennan. We know who you are. And yeah, I have two kids. Now shut up.'

I looked around at the kids again. Their faces were screwed up pretty tight, but they didn't show too much of their fear. Perhaps the terrifying atmosphere at the School had conditioned them to accept whatever might happen to them.

'Okay, we're coming. Out of the van, boys and girl,' I said. But as I climbed from the van, the words died on the tip of my tongue. If there had been any doubt about it, I had just entered the Twilight Zone. I felt as if I couldn't move another step.

I could see where we were. I didn't understand, and I didn't think I wanted to, but I knew exactly where I was now. *Oh God, I know this place.*

'Oh, Kit,' I muttered.

'What is it, Frannie?'

I shook my head back and forth in disbelief. I couldn't speak. We were at Gillian's place on the west side of Sugarloaf Mountain. We were at my friend's house, with the big, shimmery blue pool I'd been swimming in just a couple of days ago. I could see the Continental Divide off to the west, and Four Mile Canyon to the north.

The large, familiar parking area was filled with trucks, cars, and guards with guns. I also spotted half a dozen people I recognized from Boulder Community Hospital.

One of them caught my attention as I stood rooted to the ground. He was climbing out of a navy blue Land Rover. I noted a hospital sticker in the left corner of the windshield. David and I used to have stickers like that.

David had been one of Them, though, hadn't he? David had been a horrifying creep, too. Oh David, David, how could you?

'That's Dr John Brownhill.' I pointed him out to Kit. Brownhill wouldn't even look at me, wouldn't look our way.

'We've met. What's his specialty? Infanticide?' Kit asked.

'He's the head of the in vitro fertilization clinic at Boulder,' I muttered to myself. *The children had human mothers*, I couldn't help thinking again. Real birth mothers were involved, and that's why Dr Brownhill was here. It had to be the reason.

Then I saw Gillian Puris appear on her front porch. *My friend*. She looked so stern and unapproachable. I could have almost convinced myself that I didn't know her. Standing next to Gillian was her little boy. Michael was waving from the porch, and I thought he was waving at me.

He wasn't!

CHAPTER ONE
HUNDRED-FOUR

'It's Adam! Adam's okay! There he is on the front porch. Adam's alive!' Wendy and Peter crackled and shrieked in their high-pitched voices. They were incredibly animated and excited to see the boy – Gillian's son.

They knew him, and I could guess from where – the School! Michael had been at the School, too. *Michael was Adam, wasn't he?*

Suddenly, the little boy twisted back and forth and broke loose from Gillian. He was strong, too. He ran toward Peter and Wendy lickety-split. They continued to holler, 'Adam! Adam! Here we are.'

Gillian looked alarmed at first, but then just angry, infuriated in fact. 'Michael, stop!' she yelled, but the slim, blond boy continued to run like a streak toward his friends, his long-lost *compadres*, his School pals.

Michael was laughing and grinning, and he looked so innocent and free. I'd never seen him act like just a little boy. Then he and Wendy and Peter began to hug and dance for joy in the driveway. They made nonverbal sounds that only they seemed to understand.

I looked away from them and back at Gillian. She was still watching the scene with such cold, unforgiving eyes. It was a look I'd never seen before, and I wasn't prepared for it now. Who was this person I thought I'd known? My stomach was falling. She'd only pretended to be my friend, hadn't she? She was watching me after David's death.

'He's *Adam*! He's our friend!' Icarus shrieked in my ear. In his excitement, he flew a few feet off the ground. The amazing little boy hovered. 'Adam's alive! Isn't it great? Isn't it the best thing yet?'

Suddenly, Icarus was struck. One of the guards had punched him on the side of the head. *Punched* the little boy with a closed fist. Poor Ic fell to the ground and lay in a pathetic heap. He wasn't moving.

The blow was more than Kit could stand. He swung out at the attacker, connected solidly with jawbone. Cursing, two other guards began to strike at Kit. Then they held him at gunpoint, but Kit wouldn't calm down. He screamed at them. The kids were yelling too.

I was already down on my hands and knees, checking out poor Icarus. I worried about damage to his head, but his sightless eyes were open. He was shaking it off and seemed alert.

'Big bully,' he finally taunted the guard. Spat out his fury. Showed what a tough little trooper he was. 'Not much of a punch, though.'

'Attaboy, Ic,' I told him. 'But cool it a little.'

'Flying is forbidden!' the guard screamed at the children, but especially at Icarus. The man's face was red, even the thick veins on his thick neck stuck out. 'You know the rules. Flying is forbidden. You've been told a thousand times.'

Ic snarled at the menacing guard. 'Not anymore. The rules have changed.' He wasn't giving any ground.

I held Icarus close to me, trying to protect the boy from further harm. My maternal feelings were still coming on strong.

Gillian was in the driveway now. She was walking briskly toward me. 'This wasn't supposed to happen. None of it,' she said. 'I'm sorry, Frannie.'

'Right. Just bad timing,' I snapped, and realized I was just as furious as she looked. 'Too bad for David, and for Frank McDonough. Just bad timing.'

I wanted to scream at Gillian, and at the horrible monster called Uncle Thomas, but I forced myself to keep calm, not to show my anger, my rage. It was too dangerous now. Guards with guns were standing around everywhere. They seemed to be looking for an excuse to let loose.

'Hi, Aunt Frannie!' I heard from down close to the ground.

Michael innocently grabbed me around the legs and hugged me tightly. He was a beautiful little boy. I'd always loved him and raved about him, but now, honestly, he scared me a little. Everything did. Gillian scared me most of all. My so-called friend was an unrepentant monster.

Nothing was as it appeared to be; everything was part of this ongoing nightmare.

Michael was Adam.

Adam was God-only-knew-what.

Gillian wasn't my friend, after all. We had talked and laughed and cried together. All the time she was a horrible enemy, the worst of Them. Maybe she'd even thought about killing me?

I bent low to Michael and kissed the side of his face. 'So you and Peter and Wendy are friends?' I said.

'We're *best* friends,' he gushed.

Gillian interrupted us in a loud, stern voice. I'd never seen this side of her. 'I want you to go straight to your room until I tell you to come out. Go ahead, Michael. Now!'

The little boy stared up at his mother. At his biological mother? I wondered. He seemed confused and hurt, and I couldn't blame him one bit.

'Mommy,' he asked in total innocence, 'are you going to put them to sleep? Please don't do it. They're my friends. They'll be good!'

Then the little boy began to sob uncontrollably. He was frightened and the tears were real and touching. Gillian seemed to soften a bit. I saw the tiniest hint of the person I'd known. Then she pointed back toward the house.

'I said, go to your room, now go. Mister, go!' she shouted. 'That's an order.'

I looked in that direction, and sucked a sharp intake of air. 'Oh Gillian, no,' I said.

On the porch was another small child. A girl. She

looked nearly identical to Michael. She was Eve, wasn't she? I remembered the dying children at the School. The failed experiments. The 'rejects.' And now this.

The nightmare just wouldn't stop; it was coming in nauseating wave upon wave. I recognized a man standing in the doorway behind Eve. He was Dr Carl Puris, Gillian's husband! But he couldn't be! *Carl Puris had died of heart failure two summers before.*

Kit spoke up at my side. 'That's Anthony Peyser,' he said. 'Dr Peyser is alive and well in Colorado. I finally found the bastard.'

CHAPTER ONE
HUNDRED-FIVE

M aximum. Maximum. Just go for it. Go like the wind blows. Go even faster!

Max tried not to be too pitifully scared out of her mind as she extended her wings and power-dived between a pair of tall fir trees. She flew deeper and deeper into the heart of the woods, until she finally felt safe enough to hover and land.

Only then did she look behind to check her back.

No one was there.

She saw that she was all alone again. Actually, she didn't like that either. She hated it, in fact. Hated it. Something inside had warned her to get away, to escape, to fly as fast as she could.

She had to get help somehow, but Max didn't have a clue how to do it. Who could she go to – now that Frannie and Kit weren't around to give her their good advice? Had they ever told her something that might be helpful now? What lessons had she learned so far? Her brain was on fire with questions – but no answers.

She didn't know exactly how it worked at the School, but she was smart, and she *snooped*. She sensed that Adam was very special. She had thought he'd been put to sleep, but obviously that wasn't true. Adam was at that big house in the mountains. The house where Frannie's friend lived. Did that mean Frannie might be involved? Or Kit? Whom could she trust? How could she get help? How, how, how? Think, think, think, girl!

But nothing came to her. Her mind drew a big, fat blank. Finally, she decided to pray. 'Dear God in heaven, dear Father, please help me and my friends. We pray to You every single day, but nothing good ever seems to happen. I'm not complaining, but now is a good time to start. Okay?'

She knew about God and she liked the idea of Him pretty much. She had gone to church every Sunday morning for years – on the TV. Now she needed proof that there really was a God. Max needed her prayers answered just this once, and she felt she deserved it. All the children from the School deserved it. They always had.

And now she remembered something Uncle Thomas had said at the School. Like most things, he repeated it a lot, 'drummed it into her head.' He loved his own ideas and sayings, the big jerk. He'd said – 'The Lord helps those who help themselves.'

CHAPTER ONE
HUNDRED-SIX

W e were taken like pathetic, probably doomed prisoners to a place inside the large, sprawling mountainside house. I knew that the house had been built on what had originally been a mine site. It wasn't uncommon on Sugarloaf. Local kids had been playing in the shafts for years. The guards separated Kit and me from the four winged children. Wendy and Peter started to sob, but it didn't matter to the Security men, who seemed heartless and uncaring.

'It's okay, babies,' I told them.

'No it isn't. We know it isn't,' they wailed in unison.

They were probably right. Unfortunately, their instincts about danger, and maybe about some humans, were so true, so accurate.

Two levels of heavy concrete and metal basement had been constructed when the house was built. I had never been down here, and had no idea the basements existed. It was more deception, wasn't it. Nothing was as it seemed when it came to Gillian.

I took everything in; I was still being a witness. A bright red box on the wall was marked: *Safety Blanket*. Lab coats and safety goggles were hung on hooks everywhere. A stainless steel door was marked: *Safety Showers*. I doubted that the massive Defense Department shelters in New Mexico were anywhere near as complex or state-of-the-art. A great deal of money had been spent here.

We passed a lab and I could see inside. The new aesthetic of interior design. Burnished surfaces, not dull white walls. Brilliant lighting, not dingy fluorescents. A couple of scientists were working under a cell culture hood. Cells could be kept alive for long periods under the 'hood.'

I felt a sharp jab in the back. A guard was moving us along, moving me along.

Kit and I were taken to quarters near what one of our captors called the North Woods Labs. Oz, Icarus, and the twins were taken elsewhere. No one would tell us where.

'Are you going to put us to sleep?' I asked a black-bearded guard who stood at the door to our room. I was being bitterly sarcastic.

'I'm sure that's what the decision will be,' he said. He looked around at the others who had guns on Kit and me. 'If it was up to me, I'd fuck your brains out first. You don't have a lot up top, but your ass is cute.'

He laughed. So did the other brutish guards. Then the door banged shut on Kit and me.

'What the hell happened to Stricker?' Kit said and

slammed his hand against the wall. 'That was definitely Dr Peyser outside.'

'It was definitely Carl Puris, too. I went to his funeral in Boulder, Kit. God, my head hurts.'

'Peyser had a girlfriend named Susan Parkhill. She's another top biologist. I suspect Susan Parkhill is none other than your friend Gillian.'

I reached out and took Kit's hand. He had been alone in this awful mess for such a long time. He'd been working against incredible odds and strong forces. Only now did I understand what he'd been through.

There was a sharp rap on the door. It burst open almost immediately. One of the guards was there in the hallway.

'Gillian wants to see you,' he said. 'Just *you*, Dr O'Neill.'

CHAPTER ONE
HUNDRED-SEVEN

I was getting much better at cynically recognizing things for what they were, at seeing the dark side of life out here in Colorado, a place I had once considered Paradise Gained.

Gillian wasn't a friend.

She was my mortal enemy.

I knew exactly what was going to happen next.

This was to be an interrogation. It involved life or death.

Gillian wanted more information from me. I shouldn't give it to her.

'I do like you, Frannie.' Gillian began with one of her calculated, boldfaced lies. Who knows, maybe she even meant it? She was sitting on a high-backed black leather chair in the library-den upstairs. She stared deeply into my eyes.

I felt betrayed all over again. I wanted to scream at her, curse her out royally, but I held everything in. Well, almost everything.

'Was that before or after you had David murdered? And Frank McDonough,' I said.

A cold look swept into her dark brown eyes. Her face was flat and expressionless. It was as if I were meeting her for the first time. 'And I would do it again. In this case, the end totally justified the means. Da Vinci and Copernicus had to break laws to make their discoveries, Frannie. Think everything through before you judge too harshly. Please, join me.' She pointed to a chair facing hers at a long mahogany table.

I shook my head. I wasn't going to 'join' Gillian in anything. I was feeling sick in the pit of my stomach. 'Maybe this talk is good for your soul, but it doesn't do much for mine. Please take me back downstairs. I don't want to hear any more, *Susan*. Dr Susan Parkhill?'

She frowned and tapped her fingers impatiently. 'All right then, I need to hear things from you. Who have you spoken to? Make this easy for me, for yourself, and for those children you seem so fond of.'

'I haven't told anyone,' I said in the calmest tone I could manage. 'Now may I go back downstairs?'

Gillian's eyes bore into my skull. '*Who* did you tell? Anyone other than your sister Carole?'

It was like a sucker punch to my stomach. I couldn't speak.

'We haven't found Carole and her girls yet. We will, though. I don't need your help for that. Is there anyone else?'

I shook my head. God, how I hated her. There was a

moment of silence between us as she studied me. My old friend.

'You don't lie very well. That much I already know. So I suppose that I believe you, Frannie.'

The expression on her face changed; it actually softened. Gillian wanted to talk about herself. I recognized the self-satisfied look in her eyes.

'I'll tell you what happened,' she said. 'It's astonishing. You'll understand once you hear it. We turned all the expected research procedures over. Instead of inducing a minuscule amount of bird DNA into human zygotes, we induced a quite sizable amount of bird chromosome. We "melted" the chromosomes of several birds and of our human patients, by heating them until they separated into their component strands of DNA. This may sound exotic, but it is an accepted technique.'

'You don't have to talk down to me.'

She made a soft, *tutting* sound. 'My husband's breakthrough was to induce controlled genetic recombination between the strands. He actually directed what in Nature is a random process of swapping genes from strand to strand. He didn't actually expect the cells to divide so readily, but they did. We were stunned when the sonogram showed that Max was viable. She started everything. She was the first breakthrough, however imperfect.'

Sonogram. I was right then. The children had been implanted in women's uteruses . . . in uteruses of some kind, anyway.

Gillian continued. Her eyes were on my face, but she was staring right through me. 'We worked through Dr

Brownhill's in vitro fertilization clinics in Boulder and Denver. Couples trusted him, and he convinced them there was no precedent for his methods, which happened to be the truth. We'd harvest the woman's egg, fertilize it with the husband's sperm. Introduce a little DNA. Then we implanted the embryo into the woman's uterus.'

'You had the permission of these women and their husbands, of course?'

'The mothers aren't important,' Gillian said angrily. 'We studied birds at first, because birds live a very long time for their size.'

I nodded. I'd already figured that much out. The Wandering Albatross can live up to seventy years. Parrots live even longer. There are countless avian examples.

'The winged children were just the beginning . . . It was at that time we made the most important breakthrough. This is what changed everything. One of our worker bees discovered a promoter for a gene that soaks up free radicals. As you know, free radicals damage cells. Without cell damage, organisms do not, *cannot*, die of natural causes.'

Suddenly, I couldn't breathe. My body went cold. I could only listen to Gillian.

She smiled thinly. 'Michael looks like any other little kid, doesn't he?' she said. 'So does Eve. Actually, those darling children are worth any cost, any sacrifice. Michael's life expectancy is two hundred years. Maybe even more than that.'

I couldn't believe what I'd heard. Was that what all the costly research here and at the School was about? I think I may have gasped. My mouth certainly dropped open.

Michael's life expectancy is two hundred years.

Gillian nodded her head slowly. She had me. I understood what had been done. I finally *got* it.

'My son is the next step in the evolution of the human race.'

CHAPTER ONE HUNDRED-EIGHT

K it had probably been involved in a hundred inter-
rogations before, but he'd never been on the
wrong end of one.

'My name is Thomas,' the man sitting across from him
said. He was very much at ease, very sure of himself.

'I've heard a lot about you,' Kit said.

'I'll bet you have. I'll tell you my side, as long as we're
just talking here.'

'Sure, why not.'

'I was in the Air Force. I wanted more than anything to
be a pilot.'

'Nice to have dreams,' Kit said and nodded agreeably.
He was biding his time, trying to figure how to gain some
advantage.

'Sure it is. Unfortunately, my eyesight wasn't quite up to
Air Force specs. I don't even have to wear glasses, but I
couldn't be a pilot. I wound up teaching. Those who can't,
you know.'

'What level? Did you teach kids?' Kit asked.

'Oh, for a short time. But then I got an assistant professorship at the Air Force Academy. Taught biology there . . . to future pilots.'

'Very nice.'

'It was. Ironic, though. You know, you're good to talk to. A man's man.'

'Oh hell, I don't know about that. You're a good talker yourself. Seem like a nice guy.'

'Oh yeah. That helps now and then. Dr Peyser came to the Academy and recruited me.'

'Because of the background in biology?'

'Oh, hell no. His people are way out of my league as scientists. However, my science background did help me to understand his vision. That's how he works, you know. Looks for people with the capacity to understand, and to *believe*, then he offers them the opportunity of a lifetime.'

'Financially?'

'You bet, financially. But also in terms of satisfaction, knowing you're doing something important. So anyway, from what I understand you had the talent and other qualities to be an outstanding FBI agent yourself.'

'But I didn't believe in the vision, at least not the version of the vision that I heard.'

Thomas nodded. 'That's what I hear. So tell me, Kit, who have you told so far about the School? Simple question, requires a simple answer. Then we can both get out of here.'

'Nobody,' Kit said. 'I told nobody.'

Which was when Uncle Thomas went nuclear, and

when Kit finally understood how fear really worked at the School. And he also understood why the kids hated Thomas, because *he* sure did. He hated Thomas more with every vicious punch he took.

But Kit didn't talk, didn't confess, didn't tell.

Not a word.

CHAPTER ONE
HUNDRED-NINE

Max instantly recognized some of the hideous creeps from the School. They had been the keepers, the guards, the bullies. They were tramping all over the woods now, looking for her, trying to kill her if they could. Well, screw them.

She was hiding at the tippy-top of one of the thickest pine trees, but there was still danger up there. If she needed to fly in a hurry, it would be hard to take off from a wobbly branch in a tree. She knew she needed to get up some decent speed first. It was better if she could run first. She might have trapped herself here in the tree.

She desperately wanted to fly now, but a couple of helicopters were thundering above, crisscrossing over the dense patch of woods. She could hear their thudding roar, and occasionally saw one hovering above in the purplish-black night sky.

The helicopter door was wide open and she saw two

men with rifles inside. Everybody was looking for her. The awful creeps.

Kit had called the news helicopter they'd seen near Denver the 'good guys,' but Max was sure he didn't mean the ones fluttering through the woods now. The men up there wanted her dead. She could see their guns. They were hunters, and she already knew how horrible it was to be shot.

No, they sure weren't the 'good guys.' They were the worst scum of the earth. Such cowards. Such rotten, stinking bums.

She hadn't been this afraid since the beginning, since she was running away from the School with Matthew, before she had flown for the first time. She didn't like being out here all alone again.

She missed her brother, Matthew, and Oz, Ic, the twins. She missed Kit and Frannie, too. She had trusted them – with her life. When she thought about the two of them, she felt something she had never experienced before. The feeling made her heart beat faster. It made her choke up, as if she were going to cry. She absolutely, positively, refused to cry now.

Max's heart skipped a beat. A soldier was coming. Some kind of mean, nasty slug. He was down below her hideout.

He was wearing funny-looking goggles, and she thought she knew what they were. *Night glasses,* so he could see in the dark. *Like a vampire.*

She was so angry now. She wasn't going to die like this! No way was she going to cooperate with that lousy plan of theirs!

Max flapped her wings fast and real hard at the last possible second. The soldier or guard raised his head to look.

'Geronimo, asshole!' she yelled.

Max dropped from the tree. It was almost a free fall.

Fwap!

Fwap! Fwap! Fwap!

Fwapfwapfwapfwapfwap!

Max hit the man like a large, falling rock. His goggles flew off his face. The big, bad rifle spun away, too. He lay on the ground out cold.

Now that was dumb! What's that supposed to prove? she was thinking. *That you're just like him?*

But she knew the answer from somewhere deep inside. She could fight back!

She raised her arms into the air – raised her wings high, and she whispered real loud – 'Yesssss! I can fight Them!'

But then she heard the roaring thunder of approaching helicopters. She looked up. There was more than one. Now she wasn't so sure.

CHAPTER ONE HUNDRED-TEN

K it had cuts and lacerations and purplish bruises all over his face. His upper lip was split and leaking blood. His nose was bleeding, and probably broken at the bridge bone. He had been beaten up, really knocked around. He had been somebody's punching bag and they'd had quite a workout.

'What happened to you? What *happened*, Kit?'

'I didn't talk,' he was able to say. He tried to smile with his fat lip, and partly succeeded.

I sat down beside him on the bed. I wished I had a first-aid kit. I gently touched one of the bruises and he winced.

'I'm all right. I'm fine,' he said. 'I've taken a few punches before.'

He was pissed-off about the beating. He was like an animal that had been caged and mistreated. He was going to get even, somehow, and I loved his spirit. He never seemed to give up. He told me about his visit with Uncle

Thomas. Then I told him what I had learned upstairs with Gillian.

Kit slid his arm around me. He moaned as he did. I leaned my head against his shoulder and we were quiet for a couple of minutes.

'I'll never forget the first time I saw you,' Kit said against my cheek. I thought that he was smiling. I could hear it in his voice.

'When I was screaming at you to get off my property? To pack up and clear out? You said, "A deal is a deal." '

Kit nodded. 'I believe that. And also that a handshake's a handshake. You struck me as brave, wise, adventurous, obstreperous as hell. Not to mention extremely beautiful.'

'Right, I remember how glamorous I looked. I had blood and guts from a deer smeared all over my smock.'

'Yep. Blood on your blouse, fire in your eyes. God, you were a pretty sight. You *are* so pretty. I hope to hell we're going to get through this, Frannie. I don't exactly see how they can let us go, though. We're eyewitnesses to everything.'

'Our last day on earth,' I sighed, letting the words sink in a little, thinking about their meaning. 'How incredibly weird. What do you regret never having done? What would you do now if you could?'

'I'd like to fly with Max,' Kit said without hesitation. He sighed. 'I'd like to have said good-bye to Kim and my two little boys. It kills me that I didn't get the chance . . . I'd like to go on a camera safari to the Serengeti and Masai Mara. Maybe live for a couple of months in Tibet, in spite of the Brad Pitt movie. Go to Florence for a month or two.'

'Yeah, beam us to Florence, Scotty,' I said. I don't know why we were talking that way at such a bad time, oddly at peace, a little giddy. We were, though. Probably the thing I regretted most was that we wouldn't be with each other anymore. Kit and I were just beginning – and now we would suddenly end. It seemed unfair and wrong.

'I really couldn't bear to die unless I did this,' Kit whispered. Even though his lip must have hurt, he kissed me, very softly, on the lips. It was the sweetest thing. He kept surprising me like that.

I whispered, 'I wanted to do that, too, *really* wanted to. Right from the first time I saw you.'

'You sure had me fooled,' Kit whispered back. 'What else did you want to do?'

'Let me show you. Come here.'

We kissed again, tenderly but urgently. We pushed against each other's bodies. What else did I want to do? I wanted to undress him very slowly and luxuriously, and have him do the same to me. There wasn't enough time for us, and we knew it. It changed everything, changed every priority we might have had. Maybe it ordered our priorities correctly for the first time.

I gently touched his face. Kissed the cuts. I tasted the blood off his lip. I was learning all about him, memorizing, hoping to never forget anything about him. This was about the only thing we could do now, the only good thing that made sense. It was better than worrying, blaming ourselves for mistakes, banging on doors and screaming.

I reached and tugged at his wide leather belt. I was still

a little shy with him. Then, when I realized how foolish that was, I yanked hard on his belt. Everything between us had happened so fast, but at least it had happened. He was the sexiest, the best man I had ever known. I was so sure of it. Oh, I was sure.

The seconds passed slowly. I let them, wanted them to move slowly. There was nowhere for us to go, no better place to be. I felt a little dizzy, suddenly returning to intimacy like this. There was no guilt for me, though, not anymore.

Kit's face tilted toward mine. He held my chin tenderly with his fingers. He kissed my lips, then my cheeks, my nose, my eyes. His blue eyes never left mine.

I couldn't remember anyone ever kissing my eyes before. He kissed the hollow place in my throat. I loved that, loved the way he touched me. Maybe this shouldn't be happening now, but I couldn't stop, didn't want to.

It seemed so incredible that the two of us were together. My breathing was shallow, my breasts rapidly rising and falling. I wanted Kit so much. I ran my hands across his hard back, his shoulders, the insides of his muscular legs. He was aroused now, very hard, and I loved that he wanted me. I wanted him, too.

A fire had been rekindled inside me. It was spreading quickly. Kit entered and we began to rock slowly, then more quickly, much more quickly. I felt our bodies find a rhythm and it was so right, so good. I had the thought – that we were flying, and this was how it was supposed to be.

CHAPTER ONE HUNDRED-ELEVEN

Max had only dozed. It was all she dared to do. She had moved again, changed locations. She was hiding at the top of a small mountain thick with boulders and aspens. She had buried herself under damp leaves and brittle, old branches in a deep, narrow crevice.

After an hour or so, she raided a nearby summer house for food and water. Just for old times' sake. And because she was ravenously hungry and thirsty. Flying burned up tremendous amounts of energy.

She had gorged herself, eaten too fast. Now she was sick to her stomach. Her tummy was cramped and she felt nauseated, just plain awful. But it was time to go, anyway, time to rock-and-roll, time to live life to the fullest, and probably time to die.

That wasn't so great, but it was okay with her, Max was thinking. At least she'd been free for a while. She'd been able to fly and see a little corner of the world. Most people never got to do that. Not as she had.

The morning sun was coming up fast and she was so happy to view it one more time. She wanted to fly right into the glorious sunrise, to be one with the great orange-and-yellow ball of sun. She felt incredibly connected to the rest of the universe. Did that make sense – was she more connected than most people? She thought that she was. Maybe because she could fly.

God she felt stiff and achy all over. She needed to take a hot shower. Needed to have Frannie comb out her hair, preen her feathers. She wanted to be with her friends, and for once, have everyone else leave them alone.

Damn them all! She hated Uncle Thomas, the other guards, the strange men in the business suits, whoever they were. Hated them with all of her heart.

Max crept up onto a bluff that overlooked the upper part of the valley. She figured she was about two miles from the house. *Kittytoes*, she thought to herself. *Don't make any noise now. Don't blow it and get caught. You can't get caught now.*

Max lifted her head, peered out over the valley, and her heart nearly stopped. *Oh no!* She could see an army of men and women looking for her. She quickly ducked back down behind the rockface.

She raised her head again. Just a peek. She saw one of the helicopters, and it gave her an idea. She didn't know whether her idea was stupid or pretty cool or totally insane. She concentrated on the distant whirlybird, cleared her brain of everything else.

Yes, it was a pretty cool idea! Maybe because she didn't

have too many other choices. At least it was a plan. Something to get her through the next few minutes.

She stretched out her limbs and wicked pain punched through her body. She ignored it. She got herself as limber and loose as possible. She prepared herself mentally. God she still felt nauseated. The food she'd found must have been partly spoiled.

She warned herself: *Get up in the air fast. No fear. No hesitation. Stay inside the trees.*

Fly very, very fast.

No fear!

Stay low!

God save anybody who gets in my way!

Max stood up quickly, and started to run to beat the brass band. Her heart was beating fast and very hard. Too hard, in fact. It was threatening to break right out of her chest. She felt as if she might blow apart.

She saw no one as she lifted off the ground. Where were the searchers? She expected to be shot at. She winced at the thought, wanted to shut her eyes, but didn't.

Stay low, fly very fast.

Please don't let them shoot me down again. Just let me be okay for a few minutes. Let me fly for a minute more. Let me fly for ten more seconds.

Oh no! It was too late to slip in behind the trees. The guard was right there, so freaking close he could almost grab her.

He must have been sneaking up on her, silent and deadly as an Icarus fart. As he raised his rifle from hip level, Max dived like a bomber. She had no choice.

Try as she might, she couldn't knock him down. She was too achy and sore, too exhausted, and sick!

So she let it all go! Her insides, her sickness, her nausea. Gross times two!

Whatever she'd eaten at the summer house: cold beef stew, chocolate-chocolate chip ice cream, lots of milk that smelled a little sour, ham and provolone cheese and red pickle relish without any bread, whatever she'd found in the fridge – she returned the favor.

She threw up on the guard. All over his face and his dumb Colorado Rockies ball cap. His hands shot to his eyes. He probably didn't know what had hit him. He dropped his gun and let out a loud yell.

Max winged past him. She disappeared amid the maple and fir trees and thick brush. She was safe. She didn't get shot. She screamed *yessss, yessss*!

She was flying again, remembering how much she loved this.

Just let me fly for sixty more seconds, she made a wish.

Just let me fly one more time.

CHAPTER ONE
HUNDRED-TWELVE

I woke with my face inches from Kit's, and I liked being there, close to him like this. I was pressed against his body, holding him tightly. Strange, but it was the first morning in a long time that I hadn't come awake in the middle of a terrifying nightmare.

But of course, I really had.

He was awake. Kit was looking at me. His blue eyes were more dazzling than ever up close. How unexpectedly sensitive and sweet he had turned out to be. How easy to be with. *I'll bet you were a really, really good father.*

'Hi,' I whispered, and smiled, and felt warm and fuzzy for the first time in ages.

'Hi, back at you. I guess it wasn't a dream that we made wild and passionate love last night.'

Suddenly everything seemed so simple and right and the irony of it just killed me. Kit and I were falling in love, or maybe we had already fallen. Our situation couldn't have been any worse. Our chances of surviving were nonexistent. We were witnesses. We had seen the atrocities committed at the School.

There was a light tapping at the door. We looked at each other. Was this it? Had they come for us? Thomas and his band of goons.

Kit and I exchanged looks again. We heard a key slowly sliding into the lock, metal against metal. We climbed out of bed and hurried into some clothes.

The door opened, and I couldn't believe who it was.

'Hello, Aunt Frannie. It's me, Michael. I came to rescue you.'

CHAPTER ONE
HUNDRED-THIRTEEN

There was someone else there, too. A man in a blue summer suit stepped into the room right behind Michael. He had a semiautomatic in his hand and the gun was aimed at Kit. Inexplicably, he smiled.

'I came to rescue you, too,' he said. His voice was soft. Very quiet. It really made you pay attention.

'Who are you?' I asked. I'd never seen him before. I was pretty sure he wasn't from Boulder Community Hospital. I didn't think he was one of the guards either.

Kit spoke up. 'His name is Peter Stricker. He was my boss at the FBI, the regional head. Peter ordered me off this investigation, said it was going nowhere. He threatened to fire me when I wouldn't give up the case. And now, here he is. Hello, Peter. I see the case finally has your attention.'

Stricker was tall and well-muscled; he had slicked-back, light blond hair. He was a smug-looking yuppie, if ever there was one, with an easy, well-oiled smile.

'Who can you trust these days?' Stricker said in his whispery voice. 'Nobody, I guess. Not your closest friends. Not even some of your old buds at the FBI.'

'Does that mean there are still *some* people I can trust at the Bureau?' Kit asked.

'Oh sure. A few dinosaurs here and there. The Director happens to be one of them. Actually, only a couple of us are lucky enough to be involved in this. Plus a few very trusted stalwarts from the army. Everybody who found out about this wanted a piece of it. It's the American Way. You were right, though. This is big stuff. The biggest I've ever seen.'

'Does this mean the U.S. government is involved?' I asked.

'No, let's not get carried away. No need for too many paranoid fantasies or conspiracy theories. Certain people in the government are aware of what's going on here in Colorado, and before that in San Francisco and Boston. We're involved as private citizens only. There are only about fifty of us and we have a great deal at stake. There was a little insurrection among a few of the doctors, attacks of conscience, but we're past that now. We eliminated the problem.'

'You're greasing the way for progress, and being paid for your efforts?' Kit said. 'That *is* the American Way.'

'Very well paid. But don't forget, our work is important. I stopped you from interfering, didn't I? Did my part for the Cause. I happen to believe in it, by the way. I think Dr Peyser's work is critical for us all.'

'So, are you here to shoot us yourself?' I asked Stricker.

'Are you the one?' As I spoke I moved a step or two away from Kit. Put a little distance between us.

'That wasn't my plan when I came down here. Of course it could change at any moment. Don't do that, Dr O'Neill. Not a real good idea.'

I kept moving laterally. 'What isn't a good idea?'

'You never were a field agent,' Kit said. 'Never got your hands dirty, Peter. Stayed behind a desk all these years. That's why I wouldn't have promoted you to the regional job.'

'All right! Stop right there,' Stricker finally raised his voice and shifted the gun until it was pointed at my chest. 'I can do dirty work just fine, Tom. Watch me.'

Kit took a lightning-fast step-in and threw a hell of a punch at Stricker's jaw. It was a crushingly hard shot and the agent went down hard on one knee.

But he came bounding right back up. That surprised me. Stricker was stronger and a lot tougher than he looked.

Kit came back with a short, powerful uppercut. A haymaker, I guess you'd call it. He knocked the smug and satisfied look right off Stricker's face. I almost cheered.

Then he crunched another quick, hard shot into Stricker's stomach. Kit was tougher than he looked, too. A whole lot tougher, and Kit *looked* tough to begin with. I knew nothing about the Golden Gloves, and whatever time Kit had put into amateur boxing, but it was paying huge dividends now.

He fired a lightning-fast punch that landed right between Stricker's eyes, smashing his nose at the bridge.

The agent went down, and this time he didn't get up. He was out cold on the floor.

Kit reached down and took the handgun. He wasn't even out of breath. Clearly, he'd enjoyed the one-sided fistfight. Me too. 'Let's get out of here.'

Michael had been watching with rapt attention. 'That was real good,' he said. 'Wow. That was cool. You're a good fighter.'

'Thanks, Michael. Now show us where Oz and Icarus and the twins are,' I told him.

The next step in human evolution grinned, just like any other four-year-old would. He even took my hand.

'I know where they are, Aunt Frannie. I'll show you the way.'

CHAPTER ONE
HUNDRED-FOURTEEN

Michael was my hero. He led the way for us. We hurried down a short corridor that ended at a forbidding-looking metallic-gray door. I prayed the other children hadn't been hurt, or put to sleep.

'End of the road?' Kit muttered, as we came to the door. 'Where to now, Michael?'

'We can go this way. It's faster,' Michael said. 'Don't worry, I'm smart for my age.'

'You sure are. Here we go then,' said Kit. He shoved open the heavy-looking door, and we entered a large lab that took my breath away, shattered what was left of my senses.

Lab equipment was lying out everywhere. Graduated cylinders. Pasteur pipettes. Microcentrifuge tubes with a vortex mixer. Rockers – machines that shake test-tube racks because certain bacteria need to grow while being shaken. There were incubators the size of washing machines. I had no idea what they were here for, but they were scary. An autoclave was built into the wall to sterilize whatever needed it.

Three young women were lying on hospital beds on the far side of the room! It was obvious that each of the women was pregnant, probably past eight months. Close to term.

A tall, well-built male nurse saw us enter and hurried our way. He looked concerned, maybe angry, maybe both. 'Are you here for the inspection? The tour of our facilities? You know, you can't be down here unescorted,' he said.

Kit never said a word. He just hit him with an uppercut right that came looping from around his knees. The big thug didn't have a chance against Kit. He hit the floor with a heavy thud. His large head bounced off concrete, then rolled to one side.

Michael said, 'We should get out of here. Please?'

Michael was right, but I couldn't take my eyes off the pregnant women as we hurried through the room. They looked to be in their teens and early twenties. Good healthy specimens. What were they doing down here? What kind of babies were they carrying?

Silently, they watched us, and I finally saw the leather straps on their legs. The women were secured to their beds, tied down, bound. They couldn't get up and leave.

'We'll get help for them,' Kit whispered at my side. 'Let's go, Frannie.'

'We'll bring help. I promise,' I told the women. There was no way we could bring them with us now.

Michael was pulling me forward, toward another steel door in the rear. 'We'll come back for you,' I promised a pregnant woman who couldn't have been more than eighteen.

'I think I'm going into labor,' she said fearfully.

Human experiments.

CHAPTER ONE
HUNDRED-FIFTEEN

'**M**ost humans are like stones along the ground, useless to themselves and others, waiting for the next sixty seconds to reveal itself,' Gillian said in soft, confident tones. 'Fortunately, that depressing description doesn't fit any of us. Welcome to all of you. This small, very select group is incredibly important to mankind. We are ushering in a new era today. I promise you that, and I shall deliver on the promise.'

Gillian and Dr Anthony Peyser stared out at the audience from a long worktable positioned at the front of the conference room.

Dr Peyser spoke without rising from his chair. 'It's just eight o'clock in the morning, and everything is proceeding on schedule. Everything is going just about perfectly, I would have to say. Clearly, what we have assembled here are the shining stars of genetic engineering.

'As you can see, news of my departure from our planet

is a bit premature. As you can also see from my "tremble,"
I had a stroke. I'm healthy now. Actually, I've found a way
to add ten, maybe even a dozen years to my miserable life
span. More on that later in the proceedings. Believe me,
it's a mere footnote compared to what else we have in
store for you this morning.'

There were nods and faint smiles from the seventeen
men and women who had been invited to the inspections
and now . . . the most important auction of all time.

An auction.

Each of the seventeen represented a major biotech
company, or, in some cases, a country. One wealthy
individual had come prepared to finance a major new
corporation, based on the morning's results. These 'stars
of genetic engineering' seemed reluctant to look into each
other's eyes. They were there to bid competitively on the
most spectacular scientific discoveries in history and
appeared afraid or ashamed to reveal their common lust.
Truman Capote had once called J. Edgar Hoover and Roy
Cohn 'killer fruit.' If so, these were 'killer nerds.'

Dr Peyser continued to address the group. 'You've all
read the dossiers and previewed the lots. Each experiment, each miraculous child is unique and valuable
beyond measure. All the documents and data relating to
the "provenance of the lots" will be provided to the actual
buyers. We have established a reserve or minimum figure
at which we will sell each lot. This is also known as an
"upset price," probably because we will be upset if we
have to sell at it. Anyway – if there are no further
questions, we'll start the bidding process now.'

Gillian rose from her seat. She offered a polite smile, then placed a sheaf of papers before her on the table. She adjusted the wire-rimmed glasses that helped give her the look of a successful woman CEO. The world was changing, after all. Oh yes, the world was changing faster than any of these self-important executives could ever guess.

She finally announced, 'The auction is officially begun. From this moment, no one else will be allowed to enter the bidding. There will be no telephone bids, no sealed bids. The winner shall be indicated by the simple fall of the gavel.'

One of the competitors, a slope-shouldered, balding man in a dark pinstriped suit, leaned forward. He had a sharp, upturned nose and a pugnacious lower lip. He was from New Jersey, a wealthy suburb near AT&T headquarters. 'Can we take possession of the lots right away?' he asked. 'And the scientific papers?'

'Yes, of course you can. Do you wish to open the bidding, Dr Warner?'

'What about the increments?' came another voice, an impressive-looking man with a sandy-brown Dutch-boy haircut. 'What are the bid increments?'

'The bids, Dr Muller, shall be in multiples of one hundred million dollars,' Gillian announced.

There was a flurry of discussion, mild protests, fear that one competitor or another might have just gained some advantage.

'Gentlemen, ladies.' Gillian banged her gavel once. 'These proceedings will be civilized.'

The bidders settled down. They were well-mannered,

polite. Good citizens, one and all.

Gillian ran her eyes down the list of lots and back up to the spellbound audience again. The room remained silent, the competitors poised as if at an unseen starting gate. She paused briefly, as if she were considering something that she'd forgotten to tell them.

Actually, she was playing with their heads, toying with their overinflated egos. She thought that this must be how Prometheus felt right after he had stolen fire from the gods.

The atmosphere in the conference room was charged with tension, excitement, even fear. It was possible that man was about to leap forward, rather than crawl, as he always had in the past.

Gillian finally spoke again. 'The reserve is eight hundred million dollars cash on Item One, AGE 243, also known as "Peter." Peter is four years of age. He has very high intelligence. He's in excellent health. He can fly.

'Do I hear eight hundred million?'

A stentorian voice rose in the back, one of the German bidders. 'One billion dollars for AGE 243, little Peter, and his precious scientific papers.'

CHAPTER ONE HUNDRED-SIXTEEN

Matthew was alive, and he looked very well under the extreme circumstances he'd suffered during the past few days.

I had never seen Max's younger brother before, but there was no mistaking who the boy was. He had the same blond hair as Max, though he was broader around the chest and shoulders. He had white wings with silver and blue markings. This was definitely Max's brother, and he was impressive in his own way.

'I'm Matthew,' he said. His smile was a lot like Max's. We had entered another room, where the children were being held. The only way in was through the 'maternity ward.' The other doors were locked up tight.

'You must be Frannie and Kit. And look who else? Adam's back from the dead.'

Gillian's little boy shook his head sadly. 'They call me Michael now.'

'Yeah, well screw *Them*. Right, guys? Right, Adam?'

Oz, Icarus, and the twins were being kept in the smallish room. They loudly cheered and whooped. 'Screw *Them*!'

'We're moving out of here.' Kit interrupted the celebration. He had definitely taken charge. 'We have to go right now, kids.'

There was no argument from any of us. We followed little Michael scurrying down a couple of long underground tunnels. He seemed to know his way, and he certainly was smart as a whip. We climbed a narrow stairway leading to a heavy double door. I prayed this was a way out.

Kit pushed the door and it opened. A deafening alarm sounded over our heads. The good news – we were outside the house.

'Go! Go! Go!' I pushed and shouted behind the kids. 'Scatter. Get away from the house.'

'Keep going!' Kit urged. 'Don't stare. Don't look around. Go!'

'Going, going, gone!' Icarus called back.

'The great escape!' Oz yelled.

The kids thought this was a big adventure, and I guess that was a good thing. We were on the run again and headed toward the safety of the woods. But something was going on at the house.

We had to cross a large, graveled parking area. There were a dozen vehicles waiting in the lot. Town Cars, Range Rovers, Jeeps, minivans. Drivers were posted beside several of the cars. I'm sure they couldn't believe what they were seeing. Who could?

Five kids with wings! Two deranged-looking adult chaperones. Everybody running!

Suddenly, I saw others emerging from the house. I recognized some doctors from Boulder, but there were men and women I didn't know. They all wore business attire. They looked like businesspeople. What business did they have here?

They were leaving the house in an awful hurry. Alarms were sounding loudly everywhere. Someone on the porch saw us and pointed. Then they all looked our way.

Guards began to rush out from a couple of doors. They were heavily armed. They had already spotted us. I gauged that we were too far from the woods to get away.

'Fly!' I yelled at the kids. 'Fly away right now!'

And that's exactly what Oz, Ic, Peter and Wendy, and Matthew did. It was really something to see. The flock took off as if they'd been practicing together for years. Even Matthew fit right in.

'That's it – fly! Get away!' I kept shouting.

'Up and away!' Kit was at my side, calling to the kids, too. 'Get to the woods! Hurry!'

I saw Gillian and my heart froze. She was in a blue suit and she was running from the house. What kind of meeting had we interrupted? She screamed at the guards to shoot. *What are friends for?*

She was heading right toward me, shrieking her head off, when I suddenly took off and went straight for her. I zoned in on her. We were on a collision course.

That confused her for a couple of seconds. I could see it on her face. Maybe she wasn't so smart, after all.

'Fly away!' I kept yelling encouragement to the kids. 'Get out of here. Go, go. The woods!'

I looked at Gillian. She was still coming for me, even picking up speed.

Collision course.

All right, then. You'll be sorry, lady. You'll regret this.

I hit her head-on.

I tackled that awful bitch the same way I used to do with my brothers, about fifteen years ago when we played no-helmet, tackle football on the family farm in Wisconsin. I drove my shoulder into her pillow-soft stomach, no holding back. It was shades of Paul Hornung, Jimmy Taylor, Ray Nitschker and the world champion Green Bay Packers. I used to worship the Packers as a little kid, as a cheesehead up in Wisconsin.

Gillian groaned and actually said, 'Ooff!' It was an unbelievable, indescribable pleasure to give her some physical pain. I hoped I'd broken a few of her bones. I gave Gillian an extra kick while she was down, and I felt really good about that, too.

Then *ohmygoodGod*, I saw Max flying over the roof and chimney of the house.

CHAPTER ONE HUNDRED-SEVENTEEN

A balding, rugged-looking man named Eddy Friedfeld was piloting the KCNC Live News 4 chopper. He was in charge, and he was used to making fast, reasonably smart decisions. He usually could think over the hammering noise of the Bell Jet Ranger's blades.

Suddenly it wasn't possible for him to think in straight lines, though. Not now. Not anymore. His mind had been short-circuited.

He grabbed the cyclic, the central control that steered the chopper. He held on tight as he could. He glanced down at his primary instruments: air speed indicator, vertical velocity indicator, compass control, radio. All the controls looked okay. There was nothing wrong inside the cockpit.

He was doing about 105 m.p.h. Everything normal, right?

Wrong! Wrong! Wrong! There was nothing even close

to normal about what was happening to him this morning.

He had spotted the girl at about a hundred and fifty yards off the chopper's right side. He almost had a coronary, almost lost his cookies in the cockpit.

He blinked his eyes shut and open a few times. She was still there.

The little girl was flying!

It wasn't possible! But there she was!

She had the most beautiful white and silver-blue wings. It sure looked like she had wings!

And she sure as shit looked as if she were flying under her own power. As if she were the biggest, proudest hawk or American eagle he had ever seen.

'Randi?' he whispered into his mike.

His twenty-two-year-old camerawoman Randi Wittenauer's voice was in his headset: 'Are you seeing what I think I see? Please tell me I'm hallucinating, Eddy.'

'We're both hallucinating, pal. That must be the explanation. Has to be.'

The 'UFO,' whatever was out there, was at about five hundred feet now and closing on the helicopter fast.

Eddy Friedfeld was getting a prickle up and down his neck. His shoulders were tensed so tight they hurt. Like just before combat. Like Desert Storm. *Jesus! She was flying right at him.*

He touched the collective gently, slightly changed the angle of pitch. The thing he loved about flying helicopters was that it was a constant test of dexterity and sensory perception. That had never been any truer than right now.

He keyed the intercom. 'Randi, she's coming at us at three o'clock. I'm gonna rudder pedal around so you can get a better look.' Of course, he knew Randi was already shooting film. If this was real, she was getting it for the morning news.

So he slammed the cyclic hard right and the copter slid 30 degrees of bank. He slowed the Jet Ranger back around so he could see the UFO again himself. There she was. She was pulling ahead of him now. Jesus, she was a pretty little girl. With wings. Beautiful goddamn wings.

This had to be a prank. But what the hell? Who could pull this son of a bitch off?

'We're rolling tape! Lots of tape!' Randi let him know. 'I'm getting all of it, every amazing flap of her mind-blowing wings. Feeding it to home base. This should wake everybody up this morning! Wake Denver the hell up! Isn't she beautiful?'

Yes, she certainly was beautiful. She was a mindblower.

Friedfeld was literally afraid to blink his eyes. The little bird-girl with the golden yellow hair did a few pretty amazing turns and rolls.

She almost looked as if she were *writing* in the air. *Was she writing?* Was it some kind of message? What message, though?

He thumbed the toggle that patched him into production at the studio. 'Shadow Nine to studio. You getting this? Come back to me right now, Stephanie. Do you see this amazing shit? Or am I dead and on my way to heaven? Am I looking at an angel?'

He heard a voice in his earphones. 'What is this, Eddy?

Is this a joke? What the hell are these pictures you're sending us?' Stephanie Apt's voice crackled loudly in his headset. Steph was usually a realist, a cynical, no-nonsense newswoman. Friedfeld figured her mind was already blown to smithereens. Join the party. His mind certainly was gone.

'You're lookin' at exactly what I'm lookin' at,' he said. 'Get the state troopers and EMS, and anybody else you can think of ... We're maybe three miles north of the Hoover Road cutoff. I repeat – what you see is what we see. She's heading due north now. We're following her lead! She is definitely flying!

'I make her out to be eleven or twelve years of age. Looks like a regular Denver or Boulder or Pueblo grade-schooler – but with wings. And she *is* flying.

'On the soul of my dear deceased grandmother, this is really happening. The girl has beautiful white and silver-blue wings. Believe me. She's leading us somewhere, and frankly, I'd follow her anywhere. This is a News Four Special Report. And this is history. A girl is flying!'

CHAPTER ONE HUNDRED-EIGHTEEN

Max believed in the thinking-feeling place in her heart that she was about to crash and burn and die, that she *had* to die soon. Too bad, but it was her assigned fate in life. It was the way the universe wanted it. She had known it since the day she escaped. Matthew had probably known it, too.

The keepers couldn't allow her to live. She was a witness to everything they had done, all of the terrible murders and other crimes. She was Tinkerbell, 'Stinky Tinky.' Just another lab specimen. They were the stinky ones, though. She knew all of their dirty little secrets.

At least she had seen what the real world was like – some nasty, ugly things, but so much that was unbelievably beautiful, too. The outside world was way beyond her ability to imagine it at the School. It was a hundred times better than in books, or on TV, or even in the movies.

So here goes nothing! Or here goes everything! Same thing, right?

She was getting closer and closer to the big house, Gillian's place. She saw lots of people way down there, running around like tiny stick figures.

Max lowered her head and dived toward the men with guns. She realized she had no choice in the matter. This was her fate. They were trying to shoot at Oz and Icarus, who were flying away so beautifully and bravely. The other kids were flying to safety. God bless them.

Some of the guards were threatening Frannie near the main house. Frannie seemed to be doing okay by herself. She was kicking a little butt. So was Kit.

Then somebody shot Kit. He was hit. Kit fell to the ground and Max remembered how horrible it was to be struck by a bullet. She felt it, experienced Kit's pain. The wound was in his neck, and he wasn't moving, wasn't saying anything. Max felt as if she'd been shot again herself.

'Kit!' she screamed from the sky. 'Kit, get up. Please get up.'

She power-dived at one of the gunmen. Forty miles an hour – at least that. She hit him hard with the sweep of one wing. He went down and she was glad. Not glad that she'd hurt the man, but that she'd stopped him from hurting anyone else. She still couldn't conceive of hurting somebody without a good reason. It wasn't in her nature. She wasn't like Them, the keepers, maybe the whole human race.

Max was suddenly aware of more choppers following her, arriving from the east. More 'good guys.' There were three of them now approaching the house at high speeds.

They shuddered and thundered, whipping up the air terribly, rippling the leaves and branches of trees, and even the tall grass. At first there had only been one news helicopter, but then the others had seen the news and joined in pursuit. The helicopters she had brought, the 'good guys,' were filming everything. The names were brightly emblazoned on their sides. KCNC-News 4. KDVR-News 31 Fox. KMGH-News 7. KTVJ-News 20.

A 'bad guy' helicopter started to lift off from behind the house. *They have no right to get away*, Max thought to herself. *Those bums have no right to fly. No right.*

She leaned her body into an even steeper dive. Maybe too steep.

Suddenly, she was at three-quarters throttle, doing as much as sixty miles an hour. Too much, way too much speed. Scary. It was as if she were standing on her head.

She was dive-bombing straight for the windshield of the rising black helicopter. She couldn't let them get away, though.

They have no right to fly.

They mustn't escape.

And then she saw something coming fast at the rising helicopter from the opposite side, rising out of the fir trees. What a great surprise. The best thing she had ever seen.

'Matthew!' she screamed.

CHAPTER ONE HUNDRED-NINETEEN

Carole O'Neill and her two girls, Meredith and Brigid, were camping along a wide, bubbling stream in the Gunnison National Forest. They had brought along a small Sony TV. They had the set turned on, the volume as loud as it would go, but even that wasn't loud enough, and the picture was way too small.

'It's Max! And there's Aunt Frannie!' Brigid shrieked, as they watched the live news report inside their RV. 'Mom, *what* is going on? What's happening? Can you believe this?'

'Shhh. Shhh,' Carole spoke above the TV and her daughter. 'I want to hear this. Shhh, girls.'

Carole did a lightning-quick station check on the TV. The same startling, mind-blowing pictures were on every channel she reached. Something incredible was going on at Gillian Puris's house. What was it? Carole couldn't believe her own eyes. Of course, she hadn't been able to believe her eyes for the past twenty-four hours.

Max was doing a dangerous kamikaze dive at a helicopter. She was going to crash right into the chopper. Carole winced and she held her breath.

What was going on?

Frannie was punching Gillian Puris. Could that possibly be? Why would her sister hit Gillian?

Oh my God! It looked as if Kit had been shot. He was lying on the ground. He wasn't moving. Men with rifles were running everywhere.

Thousands and thousands of TVs in the populous greater Denver area were receiving the same live pictures with a voiceover description. Thousands more sets were switched on as word of the newscast traveled. Entire families gathered around their TVs. Late sleepers were hauled out of bed to come see. People surrounded TV sets at hotels, breakfast cafes, early-bird taverns, places of business.

Within a few minutes, the networks had patched in the live news feed from the Denver stations. Excited newscasters delivered the story in either high-pitched or very hushed tones.

The amazing, stunning pictures of the flying girl began to be transmitted around the world, to every continent, every country, big city, and small village. The striking image of the flying girl seemed spiritual to some. 'An angel,' 'awe-inspiring,' 'supernatural,' 'once-in-a-lifetime,' 'a miracle' were ways that people tried to describe what they saw and felt. The first sight of her was an indelible image, never to be forgotten. It struck the deepest chord in every man and woman, every child who saw it.

'The future has just arrived,' intoned one of the British news journalists, 'and we've got the pictures to prove it.'

CHAPTER ONE
HUNDRED-TWENTY

I saw everything as it developed from ground level. Kit was down and I was trying to comfort and aid him. He'd been shot below the clavicle and there was a great deal of blood on his neck and staining his shirt. He insisted that he wasn't hurt badly. I didn't believe him. I was shaking with fear.

'She brought the "good guys," ' he said in a low voice. 'She's a smart girl.'

She was also poetry in flight. I was so proud of Max, only I was also deeply disturbed and frightened for her. She was taking too many chances near the whirling helicopter blades – not to mention the guns. She was fearless.

The noise overhead was deafening and confusing. I could make out a bold scrawl of call letters on the sides of the helicopters.

The TV news was here – live. Max had brought the cavalry, hadn't she?

The TV choppers were filming all the surprised, guilty faces. Gillian and the rest of the bastards, including her husband. Maybe they wouldn't get away with this, after all. Their dirty secrets were being exposed. On TV. That's what I hoped, anyway.

Max suddenly banked sharply to the right. She wasn't just fearless; she was reckless. She dived toward the black Bell Jet Ranger helicopter that was rising from behind the main house. She was trying to hinder, or even stop the takeoff. She didn't want them to escape.

From out of the towering pines, Matthew joined her. Jesus, what a sight that was. Brother and sister finally reunited. They were getting their revenge, a little payback.

'Watch out!' I screamed. I stood up to yell. I waved my arms. 'Max, come down. Max, don't.'

There was no way she could hear me over the roaring, thundering noise that filled the sky. Max was definitely too close to the rising helicopter. She was doing it on purpose.

Too close. Too dangerous.

She appeared to collide with the helicopter in mid-air. It happened fast. I couldn't tell if she'd actually struck the copter, and if so, how much damage she'd done to herself.

I watched, and I was still yelling as she began to plummet. *Oh Max – don't fall. Please don't. Oh please, Max.*

The helicopter had jigged, tried to avoid her, but now it wobbled and spun. It was out of control, dropping rapidly from about five hundred feet. The chopper was definitely in trouble. The blades slowed and it began to shudder and shake. I could see men and women inside, looking out the windows, frightened, close to panic.

Matthew floated like a leaf above the failing chopper. He was watching close-up. Way too close, as if this were all some kind of game to him. As if he might be sucked down into the maelstrom.

I left Kit for the moment. I thought he'd be all right; I prayed that he would. I was racing toward Max when the ground shook, the result of a terrifying, fiery explosion.

The helicopter had crashed into treetops and limbs on its way down. A deafening metal-against-metal shriek pierced the air. The copter collided with the ground and burst into flames that shot high over the tops of the surrounding evergreens. Smoke, black as coal, billowed from the wreckage. Everyone on board must have died in that insane, terrifying instant.

I was a witness again. I didn't want to be. I desperately wanted my old life back.

I saw Max struggle out of a cloak of thick black smoke. Her wings and face were covered with soot and ash. She was still flying, but she looked exhausted. She was trying to fight off fatigue, but it weighted her down.

The other children were circling back from the shelter and safety of the woods. They whistled for Icarus and he managed to stay with them. They joined Max and she guided them down onto the rolling, Technicolor-green lawns beside the house.

No sooner had Max and the smaller kids landed, when she and Matthew began to race across the manicured patch of lawn. Their stamina was incredible. They took off again, shot straight up toward the shimmering morning sun.

I saw what they were up to, at least I thought I understood. They were following a grayish Mercedes sedan. It was moving at high speed along a dirt road, a back way to the main house. I had been on that poor excuse for a road a couple of times in the past.

I knew who was crammed inside the gray S600. I'd seen them climb in: Gillian, Dr Peyser, little Michael, a driver, and Harding Thomas. Except for Michael, it was the family from hell. Thomas was riding shotgun. They were getting away again.

A dusty Land Rover was idling a couple of yards from where I stood. I had no idea whose vehicle it was – but for now I decided it was mine. I borrowed the car.

I got in and chased after the speeding sedan. I didn't want to be a hero, didn't want any part of that. I just wanted to stop Max and Matthew somehow. I didn't want them to die.

CHAPTER ONE
HUNDRED TWENTY-ONE

I guess I was trying to follow the sage advice of Sophie Tucker: *keep breathing*. The Land Rover was built to handle most of the deep ruts and bumps in the dirt road. Almost fifty yards ahead I could see the Mercedes speeding ahead. The S600 was severely punishing its suspension. The driver was trying to go faster than he should on the mottled, makeshift road.

Max and Matthew were diving and swooping too close to the car. They were like angry gnats. Without a doubt, though, they were disturbing and irritating the driver.

Then Max did a power-dive. She struck the center strut on the roof of the Mercedes. A caroming hit that made a dent. She and Matthew were acting crazy, acting like children.

'Max, no!' I yelled out the side window. I stuck my head and shoulders out as far as I could. Wind whipped into my face, making me squint. I drove the Land Rover as best I could from the scary position.

I hit the horn hard with the heel of my hand. I sounded the alarm, the warning, over and over.

Max never looked back. Neither did Matthew. They must have heard my car horn. They must have known I was there. They just didn't care anymore.

I pressed down on the gas, had it to the floor. Trees rocketed past me on either side of the narrow, twisting road. I was going too fast, double the speed that would have been safe.

Max finally turned. She saw the Land Rover, with me hanging unceremoniously out the side window. I hadn't known how really connected I was to Max until that moment. All my maternal feelings had been building up, layering on, thickening around my heart. I couldn't bear it if she got hurt, if I lost her or Matthew or any of the children.

I saw what was about to happen, but Max couldn't. She was busy looking back at me.

'The car window. Max!' I was screaming at the top of my voice again. 'Look out! Max – turn around!'

She couldn't hear me. Couldn't, or wouldn't. She was smiling, laughing at the danger around her.

The side front window of the sedan was sliding down. Harding Thomas stuck his head out. Then I could see his hand. He had a gun outside the window. He was taking aim at Max or Matthew, who were both flying too close to the car.

Max finally saw Thomas. She and Matthew darted off toward the thick evergreens and pines on the side of the road. The daring kids whipped back through the trees at a tremendous, dangerous speed. They were laughing at Uncle Thomas, taunting and mocking him.

Thomas fired his gun, anyway. He blew a huge, furry branch off a tree. The S600 picked up more speed.

So did I. I was ready to do anything to stop them, to protect Max and Matthew if I could. They had suffered far too much from the monsters inside the car. Gillian, Dr Peyser, Thomas – they shouldn't escape again, shouldn't get away with this.

But they *were* getting away. The Mercedes was roaring down the mountainside and would soon be gone from sight.

CHAPTER ONE HUNDRED TWENTY-TWO

I shifted into fourth gear and the Land Rover obeyed, roared forward. The woods were still rushing by me, incredibly blurry and fast, extreme danger on either side. There was no room for even the smallest error.

I'd never driven at anything close to this speed. I realized I could easily spin out and crash. I could die in a split second and the thought terrified me. Still, I kept my foot pressed to the floor.

The slender, twisty road suddenly tilted up toward the sky again. It was a tricky, dangerous roller-coaster track, a wild-mouse ride. I'd thought it would take us down toward town, but it didn't happen that way.

Max and Matthew appeared again, flew into full view. Max went *right*, Matthew *left*. They seemed to have a plan this time.

They zigzagged directly behind the gray sedan, close on its tail. The car's brake lights were flashing repeatedly. The kids were flying too fast, though.

I saw Thomas twist around to get his gun sight on them again. He lunged even further out the open side window. Because of the slick turns of the road, Max and Matthew had no trouble keeping up with the slipping, sliding car. It was an amazing chase, stunning to watch.

The kids began shouting at Thomas again, teasing him, calling him 'murderer' and 'asshole.' Their taunting voices echoed back to me.

I slammed my palm into the horn again and again, but I finally stopped. It was useless. Max and Matthew were beyond listening to me or anyone else. I couldn't stand to watch what might happen.

But I couldn't look away either.

CHAPTER ONE HUNDRED TWENTY-THREE

M ax lowered her right wing, and she swooped at full speed toward the car. She didn't seem to care about Thomas and his gun.

She torpedoed herself straight at the Mercedes' windshield. She must have seen the driver's terrified eyes. Maybe even her own reflection as it rolled across the glass of the windshield.

She screamed, 'Murderers! Murderers!' at the top of her voice. I could hear her clearly from several car lengths behind.

The gray sedan went into a severe skid. Two of the wheels left the ground, the whole right side did. Then everything terrifying and bad seemed to happen at once, and much too fast.

Max had come close to hitting the windshield. She must have cut into the driver's vision. And now, both she and the car were spinning out of control.

The sedan tried to avoid colliding with her. Then Max

caromed off the spinning, sliding Mercedes.

She was thrown like a raggedy doll toward the woods.

I watched as she hurtled forward, then smashed into an oak tree. She hit the tree trunk unbelievably hard.

I was almost certain she died in that terrible instant of impact. My body shuddered.

Harding Thomas had turned to fire, his head thrust out the window again. He probably couldn't believe his eyes. He watched Max crash into the tree. But he didn't see a low tree hanging over the roadside until it was too late to duck back into the Mercedes.

Thomas's head was horribly wedged, then flattened between the metal of the car and the unyielding wood of the tree trunk. I could hear the savage crushing sound, the crisp snap of bone. I saw the terrified sneer on his mouth wiped away. Blood spattered and spurted everywhere. Flesh and bone was pulverized. I witnessed the instant of the terrible man's painful death.

I braked hard and the Land Rover went into a long skid. The car spun a full three hundred and sixty degrees.

The Mercedes sedan was fully out of control, the driver apparently unable to maneuver. Harding Thomas's head and shoulders hung lifelessly out the side window. The car struck the trunk of a tall oak. It bounced off. Ricocheted sharply to the right. The wheels rose up, then touched down again.

The powerful car plowed over large and small bushes. Then it rattled and bumped down a steep incline. The rocky ravine seemed to rise up to meet it.

I saw Gillian's face pressed against a side window, her

mouth open in a scream. I could also see the face of Dr Anthony Peyser trapped inside. His eyes were fixed wide and I thought he might be dead already.

The Mercedes rolled. It toppled again and again, picking up speed. The driver's head came crashing through the windshield. The sides of the car crumpled toward the center. The roof caved in. The windshield blew in a torrent of glass.

Finally the sedan crashed into moss-covered boulders that lay seventy or eighty yards below the road. *They must all be dead*, I thought to myself.

I pulled myself out of the Land Rover. My vision tunneled. Everything was chaos inside my head. My legs were weak, but I struggled forward toward Max. I was afraid that I was too late.

She lay in a twisted heap at the base of the tree she'd struck. There was a huge gash in her chest. At least one wing looked broken.

'Max! Max!' Matthew was yelling, shrilling loudly as he flew toward her. He made a pitiful, wailing sound that was more like a young bird's than a boy's.

'Max, oh, Max!' I found that I was screaming, too.

CHAPTER ONE HUNDRED TWENTY-FOUR

N early two hours had passed, but it seemed like only minutes. I was shaken, but it didn't matter. I needed to perform at the top range of my capabilities, or maybe even beyond that.

Everything was a blur of urgent, rushing bodies inside Boulder Community Hospital. Kit was being operated on just two rooms away. I was with Max in the largest operating theater. She was conscious, moaning softly, but at least she was alive.

She had sustained severe damage to her chest and to both wings. There were deep cuts and lacerations, broken bones, possibly a collapsed lung. She'd lost a lot of blood, and that was a serious problem in her case. It was also a unique problem. Max's blood type was nonhuman, non-avian. It was something in between. Matthew was a match. The twins were a match, and Peter and Wendy had donated what they could spare.

I was wearing a light blue mask and scrubs, and for the

first time I was in a hospital operating room as a doctor. I was the only real bird authority near Boulder Community. I'd done scores of operations on injured birds that none of the surgeons here knew the first thing about. I was *it*, and I guess I wouldn't have had it any other way. I didn't want anyone else to work on Max.

Her pulse was thready. Not a good sign. A bad sign, in fact. I looked around the operating room at the solemn and frightened eyes looking back at me. None of them knew what to do here, what to make of me or any of this. They did know that Max was in an extremely critical condition.

I sucked it in, and took charge as best I could. 'Let's go to work,' I said to the hastily assembled emergency team.

I chose isofluorine gas as an anesthetic because it was safer for birds, and I had no idea how sodium pentathol would affect Max. Also, my long familiarity with isofluorine allowed me to calculate a safe dosage. One or two of the other doctors looked skeptical, but no one questioned me.

Following my instructions, the surgical team carefully wrapped Max's wings to her body before masking her; if she panicked in the twilight of unconsciousness and beat the wings, she could do irreparable damage.

The gas hissed and Max struggled, as I knew she would. She was definitely a fighter. But then she finally went down. There were tears in my eyes and an OR nurse wiped them away. Not the time, not the place for emotions. 'I'm right here, Max,' I whispered. 'Trust me. I'm here, sweetie.

'She's a friend,' I explained to the surgical nurse on my right. 'I'll be all right.'

'I'm sure you will be,' the nurse whispered. 'I'm right by your side.'

I shook off my emotions as best I could. I was in a hospital operating room as a doctor. I had a life to save – a human life – the life of someone I cared about. But I also knew that Max's chances weren't good.

The anesthesiologist nodded at me. We were ready. After making sure that Max was unconscious, I slowly unwrapped her myself. I examined the tears in her wings, and worse, the sucking wound in her breast. The sight of the dark, gaping hole was unnerving.

I couldn't afford sentimentality or any other distractions as I plucked feathers from around the dangerous chest wound. I scrubbed the area and flushed out metal, wood, shards of glass, and more feathers. I was fearful that her lung might be punctured.

Using my scalpel, I began to debride the area, ridding it of ruined skin and tissue. Then I cut.

I worked on the chest wound first. I was afraid of blood leaking into the pericardial cavity. All of us were. But the lung wasn't punctured. It hadn't collapsed. I did what I could, then moved on to other problem areas, other serious wounds.

'I'm right here, Max. I'm still here,' I whispered. 'Can you hear me? I know you can hear things better than most of us.'

The tendon that stretches from the humerus to the third wing finger of her left wing was badly lacerated, but not severed. I used a Bunnell-Mayer suture pattern for the tendons, and then closed my incision. I was pretty much working on instinct now.

Beside me a pediatric surgeon worked on a long, deep gash in Max's cheek, and then one under her clavicle. The surgeon, a woman, was good. For long periods of time, I almost forgot she was there.

Max was fighting so bravely. I knew she would.

'You're doing great, Max. Keep it up. You're the best, Maximum.'

I became aware of a nurse sponging my brow. It was something I could definitely have used at the Inn-Patient.

I heard snatches of the hushed conversations of the nurses and doctors around me, but I was concentrating on the complicated operation and didn't pay attention to what they were saying. I needed to figure out how all the unusual pieces fit together. This operation wasn't in any anatomy books – not at the University of Colorado, not at Berkeley, or Harvard, or Chicago. Not yet, anyway.

I used a PDS suture and performed an end-to-end penorrhaphy. I quickly decided on a simple interrupted pattern, a long row of little knots.

I glanced up at the stainless-steel wall clock. I was stunned that nearly three and a half hours had gone by like an instant. I realized my body was soaking wet.

I felt a hand on my shoulder and heard one of the doctors softly say, 'We've done what we can for her.'

CHAPTER ONE HUNDRED TWENTY-FIVE

W e couldn't lose Max. Not after what we'd been through – after what *she'd* been through.

I waited until she was getting amoxicillin and saline subcue, and then I placed figure-eight-shaped bandages on each of her wings. This would help protect her if she went ballistic when she came to. It was a small thing, but I had done everything else I could for her. I hoped it was enough.

I was close to tears, but I wouldn't allow them to come. Not here, not with the hospital nurses and doctors looking on. I shed my scrubs in the surgeon's locker room and quickly washed up. Then I found my way to the ICU.

Kit had been operated on by a second team of surgeons, the best doctors available. He was plugged into so much monitoring equipment that it was hard to tell where the man ended and the tubes began.

His chart had him down with a broken clavicle, two

broken ribs, punctured lung, and pleurisy. He was receiving a blood transfusion, and antibiotics, and all of his vitals were being monitored. His signs were all strong, the opposite of Max's.

I pulled an armchair up to his bedside and I collapsed into it. I sat there for a long time, trancelike, just looking at him. I finally let myself cry. Tears streamed down both cheeks and I couldn't make them stop once they had started.

I remembered the first time I ever saw him at the Inn-Patient, when there *was* an Inn-Patient. And then the magic moment when he sang so beautifully at Villa Vittoria. And our 'last night on earth' in Gillian's basement. So much had happened to us in such a very short time. We'd been through so much together.

I whispered, 'I love you, Kit, Tom, whoever you are. I love you so much.'

I must have dozed off after that. I don't know for how long. I felt Kit softly stroking my hair.

'Oh, Kit,' I said, when I saw he was conscious. I kissed him on the cheek as gently as I could, and he smiled brilliantly.

'How is she?' he asked.

'She's extremely critical. I don't know what will happen. There's no precedent for the operation we did.'

I stayed in Kit's room for what seemed a long time, several hours. I didn't have a home to go to, anyway.

Then I slipped upstairs to see about Max. She should be coming out of the anesthetic right about now.

I said a few prayers as I climbed the stairs from the third

floor to the fifth. I was lost in thought, wondering about God, and how the recent advances in medicine and science fit into the grand scheme, if there was a grand scheme, or any scheme at all. A phrase was running through my head – *all God's creatures.* I wondered what it meant now.

I was thinking: *Don't let Max die. She's a good little girl, and she's special. Please don't let her die. Are You listening, Lord?*

Max was still asleep when I entered her room. She looked so vulnerable and innocent. Seeing Max sick like this was like watching a falling star.

I sat beside her and began a vigil.

Don't let Max die.

Don't let this little girl die.

It was early morning, and I was still with Max when her eyelids finally fluttered open. She looked up at me and I felt that my heart could break.

'Hi, Max. Hi there, sweetheart.'

'Hi. Where am I?' she whispered.

'Somewhere safe. A hospital in Boulder. You're with me.'

'I heard you talking to me. During the operation, Frannie,' she said. Her voice was very low and I had to strain to hear her words.

I gently kissed her cheek, then her forehead, her other cheek.

Don't let this little girl die, I kept repeating in my head. I was shaking with fear.

She smiled softly. 'Did you miss me?' she whispered.

'We all missed you so much. Where were you, sweet-heart?'

'Oh. I was *really* flying.'

Max was quiet again, and I could hear that her breathing was strained. She let me hold her hand, but she didn't say anything else for several minutes. I stroked her damp forehead, her hair. I kissed her warm cheek again and again.

She whispered, 'It really is like flying. It's nice. I like it there, Frannie.'

And then Max lightly, lightly squeezed my hand.

She closed her eyes.

Max slept.

EPILOGUE

ANGELS

CHAPTER ONE
HUNDRED TWENTY-SIX

S ometimes late at night, I sit in the dark on an old-fashioned rope swing in the front yard. I push myself higher and higher, hoping I might take off and fly. I think about what's happened, and try to make sense of it. I know that plenty of others are trying to do the same.

I'll tell you what happened after the showdown at Gillian's house. Weeks after the trouble, Kit and I did what we thought we had to do, what we felt was right – we disappeared with the kids: Matthew, Oz, Ic, the twins, and Max.

I won't tell where our home is, but it's safe for right now. Even though it's temporary, it's a good place to live. The government just didn't know what to do with the winged children, or with Kit and me, and the things that we know. We didn't know what to do with the government. Whom to trust? Whom to fear?

A group of conscienceless scientists, at least a couple of

powerful people in Washington, and unscrupulous and greedy higher-ups at some important biotech companies, committed unthinkable crimes. They murdered people, including my husband, David. They experimented on humans.

Several of the outlaw group of scientists are dead. Gillian, or rather, Dr Susan Parkhill, is gone. So is her son, Michael, who had a life expectancy of two hundred years. He perished at four years of age. Dr Anthony Peyser also died in the car crash near the house in Colorado.

Paranoid theories abound, but the government *was* involved in some way, and nobody knows exactly how yet. Maybe we never will. There *were* soldiers in Bear Bluff. To this day, no one has explained why they were there. A handful of FBI agents were involved. Powerful companies were prepared to bid huge sums of money for the first forbidden fruits of the biotech revolution.

Eve survived. She is at a secret army base in North Carolina. No word about the girl has been released to the public. I guess maybe the public *doesn't* have the right to know.

There was a recent story in the *New York Times* about the offspring from the three young pregnant women at Gillian's house. According to the report, the infants were born without faces. They were purposely designed that way by Dr Peyser and his team. The experimental children were created for 'parts.'

Meanwhile, we're out here in the woods. We're far, far from the civilized world. I suppose it's like a witness protection program, only it's much better for the witnesses, much better for us, anyway.

The kids love it, and so do Kit and I. The fresh air, the sprawling blue skies, our favorite swimming hole, the natural beauty of the land, the freedom to be ourselves without any scrutiny. You can't beat it.

But then somebody found us.

CHAPTER ONE HUNDRED TWENTY-SEVEN

I t was a bright, sunny, hopeful Saturday afternoon when we arrived at the army base in North Carolina where the surviving 'experimental' children were being kept. The base was located on over 40,000 acres of woods, which were perfect for army training exercises, as well as hiding the children away from the press and others.

We got there at 1200 hours, and were due at the general's quarters by 1400. Everyone at the military post was extremely nice, the MPs, the general's adjutant – a lieutenant colonel named James Dwyer – the soldiers themselves.

The children were allowed to go to the affair in casual clothes, which they loved. I wore a beige cowl-neck sweater and blue jeans, while Kit had on khaki pants and a blue blazer. We were incredibly nervous and jumpy as the momentous hour approached, and so were the kids. This would be the biggest day in their lives.

At 1400, we pulled up in front of a large, plantation-style house on a tree-lined road. Up and down the neat, pretty street were magnolias and pines, as well as several large brick houses. The general's house was the most impressive, the handsomest, the obvious choice for the upcoming event.

'We're in the Army now,' Matthew sing-sung a little ditty as we climbed out of the military base's khaki-green van.

General Hefferon and his wife came out to meet us in the driveway. The Hefferons had warm, friendly smiles, but several of the MPs were holding M-16 rifles and that brought back bad memories.

'Flying is probably forbidden here,' Max turned and said to me. 'I don't feel so good about this place anymore. It's creeping me out.'

'Give it a chance,' I whispered to her. 'This is a good idea, Max.'

'People are already gawking,' she said.

'That's because you're so beautiful.'

Just then, the front door of the house opened wide. Several men and women walked out onto the porch single-file. They stood there looking stiff and uncomfortable, nervous and afraid. I couldn't help thinking that they mirrored our own body language.

'Let's go up to the house, children,' the general's wife suggested.

Each of the children was given a name tag and pinned it on. I helped Peter, who was being a little pill, and Kit assisted Icarus, who seemed the most nervous of all the kids.

'Let's go up to the porch,' I said. 'Be good now.'

The children started to walk across the manicured front lawn. They were quiet and subdued. They had never met their birth parents before.

As we got closer, I could see that the men and women assembled on the porch wore name tags, too. They stood in distinct pairs inside the larger group. They fidgeted and didn't know what to do with their hands. They were trying not to stare at the children.

'Here's your mom and dad,' I whispered to Peter and Wendy, who were trailing close behind my skirt. I almost started to cry, but I held the tears back somehow. I felt as if something were about to break inside of me.

'This is Peter, and this is Wendy,' I said.

'We're Joe and Anne,' the parents introduced themselves. The woman's lips were quivering. Then they broke down. Joe was a large, generous-looking man and he bent low and put out his arms, and choked on his own tears.

Wendy surprised me, and ran right to her dad. Then Peter did the same, flinging himself into his mother's arms. 'Mommy,' he cried.

Just about the same thing was happening with the other children and their birth mothers and fathers. The kids had been wary and even cynical as we traveled to the army base, but all that was behind them. The army, the people in Washington, had done a good job arranging the reunion.

Most everybody on the porch had tears spilling from their eyes, including General Hefferon and his wife, and even a few MPs.

Max and Matthew were wrapped in the arms of a handsome-looking couple in their late thirties. I knew their names, Art and Teresa Marshall, and that they were good people from Revere, Massachusetts.

Icarus was being hugged by a slight-looking woman who was down on her knees and had one of the brightest, biggest smiles I've ever seen.

Oz was in the arms of his birth mom. She was cooing softly in his ear. Oz was cooing back to her.

Something had finally gone right for the children. I stood there holding Kit, and tears streamed down both our cheeks. I was almost blind with tears, but I couldn't take my eyes off the children and their mothers and fathers.

'Let's fly for them,' Peter started to chirp in his unmistakable, high-pitched voice. 'C'mon, let's show everybody. Come with me, Wendy. Let's go, slowpoke. Let's fly as high as we can.'

'*Peter! Don't you dare!*' It was Max calling from across the porch. The crackling sound of her voice stopped Peter in his tracks. He rolled his eyes and then he grinned.

'We'll all fly. We'll do it together,' Max said then.

And that's what they did.

The children ran across the front lawn together and they took to the air like an amazing flock. They whistled so that Icarus could keep up. They rose up over the rooftops of the houses, the surrounding magnolias and towering southern pines.

They floated effortlessly in the cloudless baby-blue skies.

It was so unbelievable to be there, like nothing anyone had ever seen in the history of our world, certainly like nothing the mothers and fathers had experienced before.

Just to watch the beautiful children fly like birds.

Headline hopes that you have enjoyed reading WHEN THE WIND BLOWS. We now invite you to sample James Patterson's latest and eagerly awaited Alex Cross thriller, POP GOES THE WEASEL, soon to be published by Headline.

Prologue

Pop Goes the Weasel

Chapter I

Geoffrey Shafer, dashingly outfitted in a single-breasted blue blazer, white shirt, striped tie and narrow gray trousers from H. Huntsman & Sons, walked out of his town house at seven thirty in the morning and climbed into a black Jaguar XJ12.

He backed the Jag slowly out of the driveway, then stepped on the accelerator. The sleek sports car rocketed up to fifty before it reached the stop sign at Connecticut Avenue, in the posh Kalorama section of Washington, DC.

When Shafer reached the busy intersection, he didn't stop. He floored the accelerator, picking up more speed.

He was doing sixty-five and ached to crash the Jag into the stately fieldstone wall bordering the avenue. He aimed the Jag closer to the wall. He could see the head-on collision, visualize it, feel it all over.

At the last possible second, he tried to avoid the deadly crash. He spun the wheel hard to the left. The sports car fishtailed all the way across the avenue, tires screeching and burning, the smell of rubber thick in the air.

The Jag skidded to a stop, headed the wrong way on the street, the windshield issuing its glossy black stare at a barrage of early oncoming traffic.

Shafer stepped on the accelerator again, and headed forward *against* the oncoming traffic. Every car and truck began to honk loud, sustained blasts.

Shafer didn't even try to catch his breath or bearings. He sped along the avenue, gaining speed. He zoomed across Rock Creek Bridge, made a left, then another left into Rock Creek Parkway.

A tiny scream of pain escaped from his lips. It was involuntary, coming swiftly and unexpectedly. A moment of fear, weakness.

He floored the pedal again and the engine roared. He was doing seventy, then pressing to eighty. He zigged and zagged around slower-moving sedans, sport-utility vehicles, a soot-covered A&P delivery truck.

Only a few honked now. Other drivers on the parkway were terrified, scared out of their minds.

He exited the Rock Creek Parkway at fifty miles an hour, then he gunned it again.

P Street was even more crowded at that hour than the parkway had been. Washington was just waking up and setting off to work. He could still *see* that inviting stone wall on Connecticut. He shouldn't have stopped. He began searching for another rock-solid object, looking for something to hit very hard.

He was doing eighty miles an hour as he approached Dupont Circle. He shot forward like a ground rocket. Two lines of traffic were backed up at a red light. No way out of this one, he thought. Nowhere to go left or right.

He didn't want to rear-end a dozen cars! That was no way to end this – end his life – by smashing into a commonplace Chevy Caprice, a Honda Accord, a delivery truck.

He swerved violently to the left and veered into the lanes of traffic coming east, coming right at him. He could see the panicked, disbelieving faces behind the dusty, grime-smeared windshields. The horns started to blast, a high-pitched symphony of fear.

He ran the next light and just barely squeezed between an oncoming Jeep and a concrete-mixer truck.

He sped down M Street, then onto Pennsylvania Avenue, and headed toward Washington Circle. The George Washington University Medical Center was up ahead – a perfect ending?

The Metro patrol car appeared out of nowhere, its siren-bullhorn screaming in protest, its rotating beacon glittering, signaling for him to pull over. Shafer slowed down and pulled to the curb.

The cop hurried to Shafer's car, his hand on his holster. He looked frightened and unsure.

'Get out of the car, sir,' the cop said in a commanding voice. 'Get out of the car right now.'

Shafer suddenly felt calm and relaxed. There was no tension left in his body.

'All right. All right. I'm getting out. No problem.'

'You know how fast you were going?' the cop asked in an agitated voice, his face flushed a bright red. Shafer noticed that his hand was still on his gun.

Shafer pursed his lips, thought about his answer. 'Well – I'd say about thirty, Officer,' he finally said. 'Maybe a little over the speed limit.'

Then he took out an ID card and handed it over. 'But you can't do anything about it. I'm with the British Embassy. I have *diplomatic immunity*.'

Chapter II

That night, as he was driving home from work, Geoffrey Shafer started to feel that he was losing control again. He was beginning to frighten himself. His whole life had begun to revolve around a fantasy game he played called The Four Horsemen. In the game, he was the player called Death. The game was everything to him, the only part of his life with meaning.

He sped across town from the British Embassy, all the way to the Petworth district of Northwest. He knew he shouldn't be there, a white man in a spiffy Jaguar. He couldn't help himself, though, any more than he could that morning.

He stopped the car just before he got to Petworth. Shafer took out his laptop and typed a message to the other players, the Horsemen.

FRIENDS,
  DEATH IS ON THE LOOSE IN WASHINGTON.
THE GAME IS ON.

He started the Jag again and rode a few more blocks to Petworth. The usual outrageously provocative hookers were already parading up and down Varnum and Webster Streets. A song called 'Nice and Slow' was playing from a vibrating blue BMW. Ronnie McCall's sweet voice blended into the early evening.

The girls waved to him and showed their large, flat, pert, or flabby breasts. Several wore colorful bustiers with matching hot pants and shiny silver or red platform shoes with pointy heels.

He slowed to a stop beside a small black girl who looked to be around sixteen, and had an unusually pretty face and long slender legs, for such a petite body. She wore too much makeup for his taste. Still, she was hard to resist, so why should he?

'Nice car. Jaguar. I like it a lot,' she cooed, smiled, made a sexy little *o* with her lipsticked mouth. 'You're cute, too, mistah.'

He smiled back at her. 'Jump in, then. Let's go for a test ride. See if it's true love or just infatuation.' He glanced around the street quickly. None of the other girls were working this corner.

'I'm a hundred for full service, sweetie,' she said, as she wiggled her tight little butt inside the Jag. Her perfume smelled like eau de bubble gum and she seemed to have bathed in it.

'As I said, get into the car. A hundred dollars is petty cash for me.'

He knew he shouldn't be picking her up in the Jaguar,

but he took her for a joy ride anyway. He couldn't help himself now.

He brought the girl to a small wooded park in a part of Washington called Shaw. He parked in a thicket of fir trees that hid the car from sight. He looked at the prostitute and she was even smaller and younger than he had thought.

'How old are you?' he asked.

'How old you want me to be?' she said and smiled. 'Sweetheart, I need the money first. You know how it works.'

'Yes. But do you?' he asked.

He reached into his pocket, and pulled out a switchblade knife. He had it at her throat in an instant.

'Don't hurt me,' she whispered. 'Just be cool.'

'Get out of the car. Slowly. Don't you dare scream. *You* be cool.'

Shafer got out with her, staying close, the knife still pressed to the hollow of her throat.

'This is a fantasy game,' he explained. 'It's all just a game, darling. I play with three other men – in England, Jamaica and Thailand. Their names are Famine, War and Conqueror. My name is Death. You're a very lucky girl – I'm the best player of all.'

As if to prove it, he stabbed her for the first time.

The Lake House

This is for the *other* Max, Maxine Paetro, who has been involved with the bird children from the beginning. She knows and loves them as I do. And they love her back!

AUTHOR'S NOTE

It surprises some readers that *When The Wind Blows* (featuring Max and the gang) is my most successful novel around the world. Who knows why for sure, but I suspect it's because an awful lot of people, myself included, have a recurring fantasy in which they fly. They treasure it. On the other hand, there are plenty of folks who won't fantasize or play make-believe. They wouldn't have gotten to Never Never Land with Peter Pan. There is one other thing that might be interesting to those who read this book. When I researched it I interviewed dozens of scientists. All of them said that things *like* those that happen in *The Lake House* will happen *in our lifetimes*. In fact, a scientist in New England claims that he can put wings on humans right now. I'll bet he can.

So settle in, you believers, and even you Muggles.

Let yourself fly.

PROLOGUE

RESURRECTION

The Hospital; somewhere in Maryland

At around eleven in the evening, Dr Ethan Kane trudged down the gray-and-blue-painted corridor toward a private elevator. His mind was filled with images of death and suffering, but also progress, *great progress that would change the world.*

A young and quite homely scrub nurse rounded the corner of the passageway, and nodded her head deferentially as she approached him. She had a crush on Dr Kane, and she wasn't the only one.

'Doctor,' she said, 'you're still working.'

'Esther, *you* go home now. Please,' Ethan Kane said, pretending to be solicitous and caring, which couldn't be farther from the truth. He considered the nurse inferior in every way, including the fact that she was female.

He was also exhausted from a surgical marathon: five major operations in a day. The elevator car finally arrived, the doors slid open, and he stepped inside.

'Goodnight, Esther,' he said, and showed the nurse a

---

lot of very white teeth, but no genuine warmth, because there was none to show.

He straightened his tall body and wearily passed his hand over his longish blond hair, cleaned his wire-rimmed glasses on the tail of his lab coat, then rubbed his eyes before putting his glasses back on as he descended to the sub-basement level.

One more thing to check on . . . always one more thing for him to do.

He walked a half-dozen quick steps to a thick steel door and pushed it open with the palm of his hand.

He entered the dark and chilly atmosphere of a base-ment storage room. A pungent odor struck him.

There, lying on a double row of gurneys, were six naked bodies. Four men, two women, all in their late teens or early twenties. Each was brain-dead, each as good as gone, but each had served a worthy purpose, a higher one. The plastic bracelets on their wrists said *DONOR*.

'You're making the world a better place,' Kane whisp-ered as he passed the bodies. 'Take comfort in that.'

Dr Kane strode to the far end of the room and pushed open another steel door, an exact duplicate of the first. This time, rather than a chill blast, he was met by a searing wave of hot air, the deafening roar of fire, and the unmistakable smell of death.

All three of the incinerators were going tonight. Two of his night-time porters, their powerful working-man bodies glistening with grime and sweat, looked up as

Dr Kane entered the cinderblock chamber. The men nodded respectfully, but their eyes showed fear.

'Let's pick up the pace, gentlemen. This is taking too long,' Kane called out. 'Let's go, let's go! You're being paid well for this scut-work. Too well.'

He glanced at a young woman's naked corpse laid out on the cement floor. She was white-blonde, pretty in a music-video sort of way. The porters had probably been diddling with her. That was why they were behind schedule, wasn't it?

Gurneys were shoved haphazardly into one corner, like discarded shopping carts in a supermarket parking lot. Quite a spectacle. *Hellish* to be sure.

As he watched, one of the sweat-glazed minions worked a wooden paddle under a young male's body while the other swung open the heavy glass door of an oven. Together they pushed, shoved, slid the body into the fire as if it were a pizza.

The flames dampened for a moment, then as the porters locked down the door, the inferno flared again. The cremation chamber was also called a 'retort'. Each retort burned at 3,600 degrees, and it took just over fifteen minutes to reduce a human body to nothing but ashes.

To Dr Ethan Kane that meant one thing: no evidence of what was happening at the Hospital. Absolutely no evidence of Resurrection.

'Pick up the pace!' he yelled again. 'Burn these bodies!'
The donors.

PART ONE

CHILD CUSTODY

CHAPTER ONE

It was being called 'the mother of all custody trials', and that might explain why an extra fifty thousand people had poured into Denver on that warm day in early spring.

The case was also being billed as potentially more wrenching and explosive than Baby M, or Elian Gonzales, or O.J. Simpson's. I happened to think that this time *maybe* the media hype was fitting and appropriate, and even a tiny bit underplayed.

The fate of six extraordinary children was at stake.

Six children who had been created in a laboratory, and had made history, both scientific and philosophical.

Six adorable, good-hearted kids whom I loved as if they were my own.

Max, Matthew, Icarus, Ozymandias, Peter and Wendy.

The actual trial was scheduled to begin in an hour in the City and County building, a gleaming white neoclassical-looking courthouse. Designed to appear unmistakably judicial, it was crowned with a pointy pediment just like the one atop the US Supreme Court building. I could see it now.

Kit and I slumped down on the front seat of my dusty, trusty beat-up blue Suburban. It was parked down the block from the courthouse, where we could see and not be seen, at least so far.

I had chewed my nails down to the quick, and there was a pesky muscle twitching in Kit's cheek.

'I know, Frannie,' he'd said just a moment before. 'I'm twitching again.'

We were suing for custody of the children, and we knew that the full weight of the law was against us. We *weren't* married, *weren't* related to the kids, and their biological parents *were* basically good people. Not too terrific for us.

What we did have going for us was our unshakable love for these children, with whom we'd gone through several degrees of hell, and their love for us.

Now all we had to do was prove that living with us was in the best interests of the children, and that meant I was going to have to tell a story that sounded crazy, even to my closest friends, sometimes even to myself.

But every word was true, so help me God.

CHAPTER TWO

The amazing story had actually started six months ago in the tiny burg of Bear Bluff, Colorado, which is fifty or so miles northwest of Boulder on the 'Peak-to-Peak' highway.

I was driving home late one night when I happened to see a streaking white flash – then realized it was a young girl running fast through the woods not too far from my home.

But that was just part of what I saw. I'm a veterinarian, 'Dr Frannie', and my brain didn't want to accept what my eyes told me, so I stopped my car and got out.

The strange girl looked to be eleven or twelve, with long blonde hair and a loose-fitting white smock that was stained with blood and ripped. I remember gasping for breath and literally steadying myself against a tree. I had the clear and distinct thought that I couldn't be seeing what I was seeing.

But my eyes didn't lie. Along with a pair of foreshortened arms, *the girl had wings!*

That's correct – wings! About a nine-foot span. Below the wings, and attached somehow, were her arms. She was *double-limbed*. And the fit of her wings was absolutely perfect. Extraordinary from a scientific and aesthetic point of view. A mind-altering dose of reality.

She had also been hurt, which was how I eventually came to capture her, in a 'mist net', and sedate her, with the help of an FBI agent named Thomas Brennan, whom I knew better as 'Kit'. We brought her to the animal hospital I operate, the Inn-Patient, where I examined her. I found very large pectoral muscles anchored to an oversized breastbone; anterior and posterior air sacs; a heart as large as a horse's.

She had been 'engineered' that way. A *perfect* design, actually. Totally brilliant.

But why? And by whom?

Her name was Max, short for Maximum, and it was incredibly hard to win her trust at first. But in her own good time she told me things that made me sick to my stomach, and also angrier than I'd ever been. She told me about a place called the School, where she'd been kept captive since the day she was born.

Everything you're about to hear is already *happening*, by the way. It's going on in outlaw labs across the United States and other countries as well. In our lifetimes! If it's hard to take, all I can say is, buckle up the seatbelts on your easy chairs. This is what happened to Max and a few others like her.

Biologists, trying to break the barrier on human

longevity, had melded bird DNA with human zygotes. It *can* be done. They had created Max and several other children. A *flock*. Unfortunately, the scientists couldn't grow the babies in test tubes, so the genetically modified embryos had to be implanted in their mothers' wombs.

When the mothers were close to term, labor was induced. The poor mothers were then told that their premature children had died. The preemies were shipped to an underground lab called the School. The School was, by any definition, a maximum-security prison. The children were kept in cages and the rejects were 'put to sleep', a horrible euphemism for cold-blooded murder.

Like I said, *buckle up those seatbelts!*

Anyway, that was why Max had done what she'd been forbidden to do. She had escaped from the School.

Kit and I listened to what Max had to tell us, then we went with her to try and rescue the children still trapped at the lab called the School. Amazingly, we succeeded. We even got to live with the kids a few months at a magical place we all called the Lake House.

When the smoke cleared, *literally*, the six surviving children, including Max and her brother, were sent to live with their biological parents – people they'd never known a day in their lives.

That should have been fine, I guess, but this real-life fairy tale didn't have a happy ending.

The kids, who ranged from twelve years old down to

about four, phoned Kit and me constantly every single day. They told us they were horribly depressed, bored, scared, miserable, suicidal, and I knew why. As a vet, I understood what no one else seemed to.

The children had done a bird thing: *they had imprinted on Kit and me.*

We were the only parents they knew and could love.

CHAPTER THREE

Outside my battle-scarred Suburban, the crowd was flowing like lava down Bannock Street. I had read somewhere that Denver had the fittest population of any major city in America. I'd always loved it here – until now. I was about to force a joke when Kit said, 'Brace yourself, Frannie. The kids are here.'

He pointed to a black town car slowly parting the crowd and finally coming to a stop at a no-parking zone right outside the courthouse. The hairs on my neck stood even before the crowd started chanting her name. My heart was in my throat.

'Max! Max! Max! We want Max!' somebody screamed.

'The freak show has arrived!' yelled another voice.

Car doors flew open and somber-looking gray-suited bodyguards and lawyers scrambled out on to the sidewalk. Then a second car braked behind the first.

A bull-necked man in a tight-fitting black jacket opened the passenger-side door for a petite, blonde woman about my age. She opened the rear door of the sedan, then reached into the back seat.

Max emerged from the town car. There was a sudden hush over the crowd. Even I caught my breath. She was stunning in every way. An amazing girl with extraordinary intelligence and strength – and wings that spanned close to ten feet now. They were feathered in pure white, with glints of blue and silver shining through.

'God, she's beautiful,' I whispered. 'I miss her, Kit. I miss all of the babies. This just breaks my heart.'

I remembered how stunned I had been when I saw her for the first time, and the crowd was having the same reaction now.

'Max, Max, Max,' people started to chant.

Cameras flashed. 'Here, Max, look over here.' 'Max, here.' 'Max, smile!' 'Max, fly for us!'

Four people burst through the police line holding aloft a banner that read: *Only God can make a tree. That goes for children too.*

Other signs read: *Cell no! Say no to cloning!*

Another banner had birds stenciled on it and read: *Bake them in a pie.*

Then the news choppers came in, and it got really loud and unruly. Max swung her head around to take in the astonishing scene. My heart lurched.

We grabbed up our papers for court, and as Kit locked the car doors he said softly, 'She's looking for us, Frannie.'

'She's scared. I can see it in her eyes.'

Max has the ultra-keen senses of a raptor. She can hear a caterpillar wriggle from a hundred yards away. She can *see* the caterpillar from a half-mile overhead.

She called out now, her voice shrill with fear, 'Frannie. Kit. I *need* you. Ple-e-e-e-ase. Where are you guys?'

Her piercing cry was still hanging in the air as more cars pulled up to the courthouse.

Burly men with buzz cuts leaped out on to the street. Several cars began discharging the other kids. They were so hesitant, so young and vulnerable. They shied away from the cameras, hid their darling little faces.

'Spawn of the devil!' someone screeched. 'These children are demons!'

CHAPTER FOUR

Courtroom No. 19 was on the sixth floor. It was the largest room in the complex by far, and would have to be to hold so many inquiring minds. As Kit and I approached with our attorney, we were besieged by a throng of reporters. 'Put your head down,' our lawyer advised, 'and just keep walking.'

'Agent Brennan, look over here. Dr O'Neill. Hey, Frannie! What makes you think you're a competent mother?' one of the press vultures shouted. 'What makes either of you think you can be good parents to these children?'

Kit finally looked up at the reporter. 'Because we love the little creeps,' he said, and winked. 'And because they love us. Life's simple like that.'

A couple of armed guards swung open the double set of doors to the courtroom and we disappeared inside. If the brouhaha on the street had sounded like a hurricane in motion, the one inside had the intensity of swarming bees.

The room was paneled in golden oak, and the gallery at the rear was furnished with matching benches that held over two hundred spectators. Every available space was filled with family members, scientists, and members of the press with real clout and, hopefully, better manners than those of the terrible horde outside.

Our lawyers and those representing the biological parents had gathered in small groups around the bar area. The lawyers' tables were situated in the middle of the room. Up front was the judge's seat, and it was vacant.

Our lawyer, Jeff Kussof, had told us that Colorado courts almost always rule in the 'best interests of the child'. I was holding on to that statement as tightly as I clasped Kit's hand when the door from the judge's chambers opened.

What I saw next kind of took my breath away. I suspect that it did the same thing to everybody else in Courtroom No. 19.

Eyes front, wings folded, the six children filed into the room, wearing their custom-tailored suits, and starched little smocks. They were eye-poppers, for sure. Dazzlers.

First came the four-year-old twins, Peter and Wendy. They were dark-haired, of Chinese descent, their snowy wing feathers glinting with dark blue lights.

Max's little brother, Matthew, an unruly towhead of nine, came next.

He was followed by the two handsome older boys, Icarus and Ozymandias.

And bringing up the rear was the lovely firstborn herself.

Maximum.

The crowd, as they say on the sporting pages, went wild.

CHAPTER FIVE

A couple of paces behind the six children strode Judge James Randolph Dwyer, a large, fit man of seventy-three. He had a face like a crumpled paper bag, wispy white hair, and a no-nonsense set to his jaw.

There was a loud *whooshing* sound as everyone in the courtroom sat down.

While the bailiff called the court to order, and then read from the docket, I was keenly aware of the men and women across the aisle from us. They were the four sets of biological parents, and they had assembled a formidable legal team of attorneys, headed by Catherine Fitzgibbons, a former prosecutor known for her aggressive parry-and-thrust style and impressive winning record. I suppose it didn't hurt their case that she was married, and pregnant with her fourth child.

'Your Honor,' said Jeffrey Kussof, our lawyer, 'I am quite certain this case will stretch the heartstrings of all concerned. There are *no bad people* here.

'The real conflict is about what is in the best interests of the children. We will prove that their best interests clearly lie with Dr O'Neill and Mr Brennan.

'I'd like to quote Marianne O. Battani, Judge of Wayne County Circuit Court, Detroit. In 1986 she said of a test-tube-baby case, "We really have no definition of *mother* in our law books. Mother was believed to have been so basic that no definition was deemed necessary." Your Honor, all that has changed. Today, in our complex and sometimes confusing world, a child can have as many as three mothers. The one who conceived the child, the one who bore the child, and the one who raised it.

'Agent Brennan and Dr O'Neill have been surrogate parents under extreme fire. They actually put their lives on the line for these children. I'll repeat that – *they put their lives at risk.*

'They never thought of anything but the children's safety. Dr O'Neill lost her animal hospital and her home in the process. To take blows and bullets for others shows love as fierce as any natural maternity or paternity.

'That said, this case isn't about my clients or about the respondents. It's about the children and the Colorado law that mandates children be united with their family. There is a *new* kind of family here, a family that came together through terrible adversity. And this powerful, loving family, for the good of the children, must be kept together. To separate Kit, Frannie, Max, Ic, Oz, Matthew, Wendy and Peter would be an injustice to everyone involved. It would be exceedingly *cruel*.'

I wanted to hug Jeffrey Kussof, and he did look mildly pleased with himself as he sat down. 'It's a start,' he whispered.

But Catherine Fitzgibbons was already on her feet.

CHAPTER SIX

'I'm here today to represent the rights of six American citizens, Max, Matthew, Oz, Icarus, Wendy and Peter,' said Attorney Fitzgibbons, 'as well as their *true* parents.'

'Why am I always the last one?' Little Peter suddenly spoke up from his seat in the second row. Everybody in the room laughed at the unexpected interruption from the small boy.

'No offense meant,' Catherine Fitzgibbons said, but she had turned the brightest red. Her face seemed to float like a balloon above the tailored navy-blue field of her maternity dress. 'Okay then – Peter, et al, I'm here to represent all of you,' she said, and smiled benevolently.

'I sincerely doubt it,' Icarus, who has been blind since birth, piped up next. 'You don't know us. As *blind* as I am, even I can see that.'

Once again, the room was moved to laughter and small talk, only quieting after Judge Dwyer's repeated gavel-banging and threats to clear the room. The kids finally settled down somewhat. They were all quick with a quip, though, probably because each of the six had a genius IQ. They tested off the charts – Stanford-Binet, WPPSI-R, WISC III, the Beery tests, Act III.

In her opening remarks, Fitzgibbons went on to laud Kit and me for what she called our 'heroic rescue' as a way of acknowledging our help in the past and putting it completely to rest. Then she began to make her critical points *against* us. Each was like a knife driven into my heart, and Kit's, and, I was quite certain, the children's.

'Your Honor, Dr O'Neill and Mr Brennan, for all their altruism on the part of these children, have *no legitimate claim* in this courtroom,' she pronounced. 'None.

'They are unmarried. They've only known each other and the children for a matter of months. Furthermore, and this hardly can be said strongly enough, the children's parents have done nothing whatsoever to forfeit their parental rights. To the contrary, we will show cause to irrevocably declare them the *lawful, legitimate,* and *exclusive* parents of their children once and for all.'

When Fitzgibbons had finished her opening remarks, Jeffrey Kussof stood up immediately and called Kit. I watched with pride, and love, as he took the stand.

Jeffrey cited Kit's law degree from NYU and his twelve years as an FBI agent. And he gently elicited the personal tragedy that was like a dark hole at the center of Kit's life. Four years ago, while he was working on a case, his wife and two small boys had left for a Nantucket vacation without Kit. Their small airplane went down and there were no survivors.

Kit testified calmly, yet passionately, and with a spark of humor and wit that defines his personality. I thought anyone seeing him for the first time would be entirely convinced not just that he was a brave man, but that he had been, and would be again, an unimpeachably good father.

Then, for two unrelenting hours, Catherine Fitzgibbons expertly filleted Kit's career – and just about every moment of his private life.

CHAPTER SEVEN

'Kit isn't your given name, is it?' she asked.

'No, actually it's Thomas. Thomas Brennan. Kit is a nickname. Frannie and the kids call me Kit. It's a long story.'

'Mr Brennan, you've been with the FBI for twelve years?'

'That's right.'

'Have you ever heard of Fox Mulder?'

Kit snorted and shook his head. He knew where this was going already. 'That's very cute.'

'Please instruct the witness to answer, Your Honor,' said Fitzgibbons.

'Mr Brennan, please respond to the question.'

'Fox Mulder is a fictitious character on a television series,' said Kit.

'Do you have an opinion of this fictitious character?'

'Yeah. He's a frickin' nutjob.'

The spectators laughed. So did I. And the children twittered with delight. They *adored* Kit.

'Have you any idea, Mr Brennan, why your colleagues at the FBI call you "Mulder"?' asked Fitzgibbons.

'Objection, Your Honor! Argumentative. Move to strike,' shouted Jeffrey Kussof.

Fitzgibbons bowed her head as if to show she was contrite. She wasn't, of course.

'I retract the question. Mr Brennan, do you consider yourself a workaholic?'

'Maybe. At times. I'm definitely committed to my work. I even like it sometimes.'

'And would you describe yourself as a stable person?'

'Yes, I certainly would.'

'But you've been medicated for depression.'

Fitzgibbons turned her back on Kit when she said this. It was good to see that even she could feel some shame.

'Yes. I was depressed, damned depressed when I lost my entire family,' Kit said, his voice rising sharply.

Catherine Fitzgibbons turned round to face him. She held her stomach in profile to Judge Dwyer.

'I see. So you *understand*, then, how the respondents must feel about losing *their* children?'

Kit didn't speak. Across from me, the twins sent up frightened, high-pitched screeches in protest at this attack on Kit.

'Agent Brennan, shall I repeat the question?'

'You heartless—' he said in a whisper.

'Permission to treat the witness as hostile, Your Honor,' said Fitzgibbons.

'Mr Brennan, please answer the question,' said the judge.

'Yes. Yes, I understand how it feels to lose a child,' Kit finally answered.

'And still you persist in this action? You say that *I'm* heartless? That will be all, Agent Brennan.'

CHAPTER EIGHT

I was feeling sick in the pit of my stomach when Jeffrey Kussof rose and spoke in a clear, confident voice.

'I call Dr Frances O'Neill.'

I immediately wondered *why* Jeffrey seemed so confident. Did he know something that I didn't? Why did he have more confidence in me than I had in myself?

As I stepped up to the witness seat, I think I had some idea of how it felt to be a four-hundred-pound lady in a wading pool. I looked out at the gallery and the gallery looked back at me. A little more than two hundred people staring right at me, waiting for me to convince them that I would be a great, no, a *flawless* mother for six unusual and very special children.

Well, that was what I planned to do.

Because I knew in my heart that I would be. Wasn't that worth something?

Jeffrey gave me a reassuring smile, then, under his direction, I cited my academic and professional credentials: the Westinghouse Science scholarship, my DVM from the Colorado State Teaching Hospital at Fort Collins, and all the rest of my laurels.

This prompted a little cheer and a round of whistles from the six kids, right under the noses of their seething parents. Even the twins were laughing. I chanced a quick look over at Kit, and he gave me a wink and one of his famous crooked smiles.

As the interview went on, for well over an hour, I began to feel a little more confident. I *knew* I would be a great mom; I *loved* these kids more than anyone else could. Because I was a veterinarian *and* a human being, I understood how complex they were. Jeffrey asked me to speak about my own recent tragedy – my husband had been murdered in a holdup two years before. And I talked about my successful one-woman animal practice on a squiggle of dirt road in Bear Bluff, a one-traffic-light town about fifty miles northwest of Boulder.

Jeffrey then went on to depict me as a woman with a heart as big as the Rockies, with an open door to every chipmunk and mule deer and pound puppy in Colorado. Okay, so I started to blush.

But most importantly, he told about my having operated on Max when she was near death. How I had saved her life when no one else could. That was a fact that no one could dispute, not even Ms Fitzgibbons.

Or so I hoped.

So I prayed.

A few moments later, Catherine Fitzgibbons came over to the stand and smiled as sweetly as if she were my own dear sister, Carole Anne. But she didn't waste much more of the court's time on niceties.

'Dr O'Neill, what is your annual salary?' she asked in her trademark huffy tone.

'I can't really say. It differs from year to year. Depends on whether I'm working on more chipmunks or horses in that particular year.'

'On average, more or less than thirty-five thousand a year?'

'Less,' I said, more emphatically than I'd meant to.

'And you expect to support six children—'

'I wouldn't do it alone! These kids need love more than money. They're depressed now.'

Catherine Fitzgibbons' eyebrows arched. 'You say the children are depressed. How do you know that? You aren't a psychologist, are you?'

'No, but—'

Fitzgibbons cut me off. 'You aren't any kind of a *people* doctor, are you, Dr O'Neill?'

'No. But these children are—' I started to say, but she rudely cut me off again. I was tempted to speak right over her next question, but I stopped myself. My mistake.

'You've never been a mother, have you, Dr O'Neill? Please answer yes or no.'

'No, but— No.'

I wanted to punch Fitzgibbons, I really did. She deserved it, too.

'You've been cohabiting with a man who is not your husband, is that correct?'

'I wouldn't say we're cohabiting.'

I definitely wanted to strangle her to death, then punch her lights out for good measure.

'Correction. Okay. Have it your way, then. You're having sex with a man not your husband?'

Jeffrey Kussof objected to the question, and he was sustained.

'Is this your idea of how to be a role model to underage children?' Fitzgibbons stayed on the attack.

Jeffrey was up in a flash. 'Objection, Your Honor. Calls for a conclusion on the part of the witness.'

'Sustained.'

'Dr O'Neill, if you were to have custody of the six young children, how would you manage to both work and care for them? Have you thought about that? Would you drive them to their various schools? Or would you just open the door and let them fly?'

'OBJECTION, Your Honor! Counsel is badgering the witness,' said my lawyer.

But Catherine Fitzgibbons gave him a curt, snide wave of dismissal. 'I have no further questions for this witness.'

She proudly waddled back to her seat.

CHAPTER NINE

J udge Dwyer gave us the most special gift that night, and I hoped it didn't come out of some combination of pity and guilt. He made a decision that the kids could spend part of the night with Kit and me. He kind of threw us a bone.

What a treat! Unforgettable.

The kids were brought to our hotel, the venerable old Brown Palace, by a phalanx of US Marshals. The first order of business was deciding on a place for dinner. Everyone was superstarved. The choices were room service, the Ship Tavern right there in the hotel, or the Little Italy in the Sixteenth Street Mall. Little Italy won in a landslide, six to two. Supposedly, they had great veggie pizza, the kids' all-time favorite food on the planet. Say no more.

We arrived at the Italian restaurant around eight thirty and the usual rules were in effect: no staring contests with other people; no food fights, especially under the circumstances; absolutely no flying inside Little Italy; no snide jokes about 'Uncle Frank' or 'little Joey', who were pictured all over the walls.

The kids were a dream to be with that night. Part of it was because they were on their best behavior, but part was because they were so smart, and they were growing up so fast. Max was twelve, but in human years she was probably twice that. She was even starting to look like a young woman in her midteens. And then there was Ozymandias, who was more handsome than Prince Harry on a good hair day.

This was the first time they had all been together to talk and 'vent' about their new parents.

Ozymandias started off by saying that his mom was a 'really good, really sweet person', but that she just didn't get the bird part of him, and kept suggesting that he would 'grow out of it'. He also revealed to us that his mother had engaged an agent and an entertainment lawyer because 'we don't want to be taken advantage of by Hollywood types, do we?'.

'I like her, you know,' he said, 'but she really isn't equipped to handle me. The press are always sniffing around the house, and she thinks it's okay. She likes the attention, I think. Not in a mean way. She's just human.'

All of the kids had horror stories about the press constantly being at their houses, at school, just about anywhere they went. The Chens had sold interviews with Peter and Wendy; the Marshalls would have, except that Max *forbade* it. She had also smashed up a camera during a particularly obnoxious interview.

'If goddamn ET shows up here tonight,' she warned, 'I'm going to take away their cameras, and film *them*.'

While we were waiting for various desserts to be served – gelato, sorbetto, chocolate zuccotto cake – Max took the floor. God, she was magnificent: looks, bearing, everything about her said *Hero. Follow me. I am the special one you've been waiting for*.

Imagine heightened mother-of-pearl and you would come pretty close to getting the color of her wings right. They had an iridescent sheen, flushed pink where the shafts emerged from her nearly translucent skin. They reminded me of the wings of ospreys or swans, but, of course, spanning ten feet, were much larger. The wings grew from behind her shoulders, but Max's arms seemed elegant and natural. Clearly, she represented the best of both species.

'Unaccustomed as I am to public speaking,' she said, and we all laughed. Actually, Max had been on just about every TV news and talk show going over the past few months. And of course, she was very good.

'Win, lose, or draw,' she continued, 'I just want Frannie and Kit to know how much we appreciate everything they've done for us, and I mean everything, from saving our pitiful butts, to getting shot at, and having Frances's wonderful house burned to the ground, and then coming here and offering to take all of us into their new home. My God, they're even willing to take in Icarus!'

'Sure, pick on the blind kid,' yelled Ic as he laughed

hysterically. He actually loved it that Max always took special care to include him.

'Frannie said in court today that we belong together, that we should never be separated, and I swear, that's the way it will be. It's the right thing to do, the only thing. Anyone with even half a brain has to see that. So we may be in trouble,' she said and winked, 'because our fate is now in the hands of this country's justice system.'

Then Max came around the table and gave Kit and me the biggest, warmest hug and kisses.

'We love you both,' she said. 'Mom and Dad.'

CHAPTER TEN

That night, a man who looked very much like Dr Ethan Kane walked through thick woods toward Frannie O'Neill's cabin in Bear Bluff. He'd flown into Denver that morning and actually watched a part of the trial. Dr Kane was extraordinarily interested in the bird-children, especially Maximum, who not only represented a forward step in evolution, but who might also know things *she shouldn't*.

Amazing to Dr Kane, the vet had left the door to her animal hospital unlocked. There was a note taped to it: handwritten instructions to someone named Jessie.

Ethan Kane proceeded inside the small house, preferring to use a flashlight rather than turning on the lamp in the foyer.

He found his way through a small office, then into some kind of operating suite, which seemed to double as a pharmacy.

The animals at the clinic already knew he was there. Dogs, cats, and Lord-knew-what-else began to bark, howl, hiss and chirp from the room in the back.

'*Shut up*, you *imbeciles*,' Kane said through gritted teeth. He hated pets, and even more, those who kept them. Did no one understand natural selection nowadays?

He made his way back to the office and started a search for Dr O'Neill's notes on Max. They had to be somewhere in the files – and they were. He located two manila folders thick with scribbly handwriting. *No computer nonsense for our Dr O'Neill, no sirreee!*

Dr Kane began to make mental notes from the examination findings . . .

Max is a human who has been 'improved' by genetic engineering, Dr O'Neill had written.

Injected with avian DNA as an embryo . . .

Examination specs:

Massive chest, fully three times deeper than that of a human . . . needs the extra musculature to support her wings.

Overlapping ribs and a protruding breastbone or 'keel' that runs the length of her ribcage.

No breasts or nipples . . . Max will not deliver live young.

Exceptionally long trachea or windpipe . . . thirty inches . . . folded accordion-style . . . fills with air during long flights.

Bones are hollow to keep her body light for flight.

Then Dr Kane heard a faint noise on the front porch. He too had exceptional hearing. Plus, he was paranoid.

Now who? he wondered.

'Frannie? . . . Are you in there, sweetie? . . . Fran? It's Jessie . . . I thought you—'

A very large woman was at the door that led into the

office – Jessie from the note on the door. She must have weighed two hundred fifty, and not even soaking wet.

She saw him.

'Hello, Jessie,' he said. 'I suppose there's no harm in telling you that I'm rifling through Dr O'Neill's notes on Max. And that it's vitally important for mankind. I'm sure you won't tell.'

Kane then pulled a handgun from his jacket pocket and shot the large woman twice. That was nothing. Not a problem. Getting rid of Jessie's body, making it disappear, now that took some real thought and effort.

But in the end – Jessie disappeared *as if she had never been.*

That was the genius of Dr Ethan Kane.

CHAPTER ELEVEN

The custody hearing began again at nine sharp the next morning. This was the big day, had to be. Catherine Fitzgibbons shot to her feet and called Oz's mother to the stand first thing. I thought I knew why, and it troubled me. The story that Anthea Taranto would tell now was sad and affecting. *It might even win the case for their side.*

Anthea was a pretty, graying woman of forty-nine. She wore a lavender silk skirt, white blouse, and a navy-blue blazer. She was recently widowed, her husband, Mike, having died of cancer the previous year. Ozymandias was her only child, and her only living relative.

Mrs Taranto spoke haltingly, but she told her story with heart-wrenching simplicity and tact. She and Mike had tried for years to have children. They had gone to a well-known, highly regarded *in vitro* fertilization clinic in Boulder. There had been false starts, but, finally, Anthea Taranto had conceived.

'I went in for a routine checkup at eight months,' she told the hushed room. 'I remember how happy Mike and I were that day. Dr Brownhill told us that it was all routine, then as he examined me, he became concerned. He told me that the fetus was in trouble and would have to be delivered right away. I had an emergency C-section on the spot. *I was told that my baby had died.* Can you imagine how I felt that day?'

Mrs Taranto touched her stomach unconsciously, and seemed to drift out of the courtroom and into her memory before she resumed her tragic and affecting story.

'When I found out my son was *alive*, not dead, it changed everything for me. Oz is the most important person in my life. He is my reason for living. I would do anything for him. Just give me a chance, Oz. Please let me be your mother, my angel.'

Then Anthea Taranto looked directly at Kit and me. She fired the next few breathtaking words at us.

'It doesn't matter that these children are different or that it is a challenge to parent them,' said Mrs Taranto. 'They are our children. No one should be allowed to take them from us again. Please don't take my baby away! I am Oz's mother. That has to mean something, even in this brave new world we're living in.'

There was a long pause. All eyes were on Anthea. Finally, Catherine Fitzgibbons said, 'I have nothing else for Mrs Taranto. Thank you so much.'

'I have no questions, Your Honor,' said our attorney.

In fact, Jeffrey had few questions for any of the biological parents who took the stand that morning. They were from different backgrounds, different socioeconomic groups, but all seemed like nice people. The issue was, *could these seven people raise such special children, and also keep them safe?*

I honestly didn't think so. Especially the *safe* part.

Jeffrey gently suggested to Max's father that he might be overly enjoying his fifteen minutes of fame. He got the Chens to admit that major advertisers were negotiating for Peter and Wendy to do product endorsements. He brought out that Oz had an agent in Hollywood. But even the lightest jabs made me squirm with embarrassment. Attacking the parents could only backfire. And it just wasn't fair.

But one thing about the parents did bother me. It bothered me a lot. None of them said, 'I want to do whatever is best for my child.' And none of them acknowledged the safety issue either.

The court recessed for lunch, which Kit and I both skipped. We went up on the roof and held hands and were unusually quiet for us. We also prayed for the kids, and for their parents. When the trial resumed, it was with a thunderbolt.

Jeffrey Kussof stood and turned toward the children. 'I call Max Marshall to the stand.'

CHAPTER TWELVE

When Max heard her name called, her heart started to pound *at flight rate*, close to one hundred and twenty beats a minute.

It was her turn on the spit. She'd seen what the lawyers could do to witnesses, and now she would be grilled. Almost every minute of her life had been classified as Top Secret. And she had been warned very explicitly:

You talk, you die.

It was that simple, that crystal clear.

She was supposed to tell the truth, the whole truth and nothing but the truth in this courtroom, right? But what if she did?

It would make everything worse than any of them could imagine. Max knew things that no little girl should be burdened with. And she knew the secrets had to remain that way.

You talk, you die.

The courtroom had gotten very quiet, and Max realized that every single person was gawking at her. She was in the dreaded spotlight, and she hated being there. Her *freak-meter* was sounding loud and clear.

'Max, *go*,' said her biological father, Art, who was a nice enough guy, though bossy sometimes. 'Go on now. You can do this, honey.'

'You'll be fine,' said her mother, Terry. 'Go ahead, Max. You're safe here. Just tell the truth.'

Yeah, right, Max couldn't help thinking. *Tell the truth, and die a horrible death*.

Such was her fear that when Max finally stood, she beat her wings and hovered a few inches off the ground.

The crowd whispered, '*Ohhhhhhhhhh*.'

Max grimaced and forced her wings to her sides. Then she made herself walk the twenty-five feet or so to the witness stand. *Just walk, Max. Be a normal twelve-year-old*.

She looked up and saw the two flags behind the bench: the American stars and stripes; and the Colorado state flag with its alternating blue and white stripes and the big red letter C with a yellow circle inside. Behind the judge was an inscription on the wall: 'In God We Trust'.

What did that mean right now? Could she really trust in God? Had God made her – or was it man?

A clerk offered Max the Bible and she placed a hand on it and swore to tell the truth. Her body was still shaking a little. This was so bad, almost unbearable.

You talk, you die. And so do the other five kids. And maybe Kit and Frannie, too.

'Don't be afraid,' said Judge Dwyer, as if he knew what she was thinking. 'We're all friends here.'

'Yes, that's right,' said Jeffrey Kussof. 'Just tell your story, Max. We want to hear it. Everyone does.'

Max nodded okay, though this wasn't okay at all. She flipped her long blonde hair back over her shoulders. She cleared her throat, then leaned in close to the microphone in front of her.

Damn, she didn't want to do this. What she wanted to do – was to fly away.

But instead, Max did the unspeakable.

She spoke.

CHAPTER THIRTEEN

'I know I'm just a young girl,' Max began in a whispery voice. 'I don't know a whole lot of things, because I haven't seen too much yet. But let me tell you some things I do know. All of this is the truth, so help me. I was there, you weren't.'

Max could see Kit and Frannie watching her from their seats up front. Frannie winked at her, and she could almost hear her say, '*Go, girl*,' which Frannie said all the time. It was their mantra, one of the countless small, silly things that connected them, and always would.

'People did obscene, really horrific things where we used to live – at the lab called the School,' Max finally said, her voice like aspen leaves quaking in the breeze. Just thinking about the School made her incredibly angry.

'Little babies were put to sleep there, which means they were *murdered*. I saw it happen. I saw dead bodies of kids just like me. *Look at me, please*. Look at Matthew, Ic, Oz, Peter and Wendy. Aren't we cute? Well, we were treated like lab rats. Usually, a lot worse than rats. There are *laws* to protect lab rats.'

Max twisted in her seat to Judge Dwyer. Maybe he could help her. She desperately wanted to fly out of here. Her wings rustled. It was the only sound that could be heard in the courtroom.

'We were put up for sale. People *still* want to buy us! To experiment on us horribly. To see how we work,' Max said. 'Visitors came to the School to check us out, to test us. We were just property to them. Their *creations*, right? We were going to be used in further experiments. That's why my brother Matthew and I escaped. Then we were hunted. I was *shot* down out of the sky by the same people who said that they loved me. If Frannie and Kit hadn't helped us, we'd all be dead now. I'm not exaggerating, am I, Frannie?'

'No, you're not, sweetie.' I spoke from my seat. 'You're just telling the truth.'

Matthew jumped up from his seat. He whooped, 'We made it, though, Max. We escaped. The bad guys were burned to crispy critters! So don't mess with us! Ever!'

It took several minutes for the crowd to quiet after that. When it did, Max said, 'Try to understand. We can't have rules like other kids. We can't be told what to eat for breakfast or how to say our prayers. We have to fly when we want to, especially at night. As you can see for yourselves, we're not exactly like the rest of you.'

The judge was listening to her. He was really listening, and he wasn't threatening or scaring her in any way. Max took solace in that. For the first time, she allowed herself to hope that people could do the right thing. It was a real long shot. But *maybe* it could happen.

'We look like little kids,' Max continued. 'But we've seen a lot of suffering and death.'

Her throat caught, then, and she had to stop. She willed herself not to cry, which was what she ached to do. 'We really, really love Kit and Frannie. I know they aren't our biological parents, but they are the best for us. We found that out when we all lived together at the Lake House. We lived there for a glorious four months. It was heaven. The Lake House is the only place where we've ever felt safe in our lives. The only place! We only feel safe when we're all together as a family. *We must be kept safe!* Please believe me, it's dangerous for us out in the world. It's so dangerous. You can't *believe* how dangerous. We have enemies out there! People want to use us, abuse us. Take us apart and put us back together again!'

When she looked around, Max saw that little Peter and Wendy were shivering, holding on to each other. Kit and Frannie had tears in their eyes. So did a lot of the spectators seated around the courtroom. Even the Marshalls. For a moment, anyway, they all believed her. They got it. Finally.

Slowly, spontaneously and one by one, the rows of spectators rose. They began to applaud Max. They called out her name, and then the names of the other kids.

'Thank you, Max,' said Judge Dwyer, as the courtroom quieted. 'Thank you for telling the truth, painful as it is. You may step down.'

Max got up and moved away from the witness chair. She had told a lot of the truth. But she hadn't told it all. She hadn't told *why* it was so dangerous for the six of them, and how she knew.

The judge was speaking again.

'The court is in recess. I want to see the parents, and Mr Brennan and Dr O'Neill and their attorney, and the children's advocate, Mrs Fitzgibbons. In my chambers. Now.'

CHAPTER FOURTEEN

M ax's mother came rushing over to her. 'Max, you must stay right here in the courtroom, okay? I mean it, young lady. It's the safest place for you and the other kids. I *do* understand safety. Your father and I have to go in with the judge. I think he's made his decision.'

Max felt a surge of resentment. She liked Terry Marshall well enough, but her biological mother didn't understand a fricking-fracking thing about her, or her safety, or the other kids. The other parents were nervously trying to quiet their children, too. She could hear the twins screeching, 'Leave us alone, please leave us alone . . . *Back off!'*

Max felt tension and fear mounting throughout her body and her head was throbbing. *You talk, you die.* She had to get away from all this, at least for a couple of minutes. She had to get out of this claustrophobic room. All the noise, the rude and pushy people. And worst of all, the press. Tamping their sneaky IFB earpieces in place. Twisting their network-logo-flagged microphones. Never

51

taking their nasty, beady eyes off her.

She needed space.

Even if it might be dangerous.

As soon as the Marshalls disappeared into the judge's chambers, Max practically flew through the open doors and veered sharply into a double-width hallway.

There was an elevator bank up ahead, shiny metal doors. Max looked back and saw Frannie and Kit holding back the crowd as best they could. She could hear Frannie saying, 'The kids just need to talk. They'll be fine. They're frightened and upset right now. Trust their instincts.' Then she heard the other kids coming, a rush of wings.

'Wait, Max! Wait up, for cripes' sakes,' yelled Oz. 'Max, let's stay together.'

Max listened to the grinding sound of an elevator as it climbed to the sixth floor. The elevator arrived, and the kids piled in.

Yes, trust our instincts.

'It's going up,' said Oz.

'Excellent,' Max said. 'I like *up* very, very much.'

The six of them whooped! They all liked *up*.

CHAPTER FIFTEEN

U*p! Up! Up!*
  The elevator doors opened again and the kids filed out into a wide, empty space. Max saw a metal door with bright red letters: *ROOF*. She used both hands and pried it open.

'Roof! Roof! Roof!' the other kids chanted. 'The roof is the place to be!'

'Let's just vamanos!' shouted Icarus. 'I'm talking *escape*. Let's go to the Lake House. *Please*, can we?'

'The Lake House! Go to the Lake House!' the kids chanted.

The afternoon sun beat down on the roof of the courthouse, but the breeze riffling Max's feathers offset the heat. The wind was coming from directly behind them. It was blowing from the north and that was perfect.

Just right.

For flight!

'Let's do it,' said Ozymandias, who stood poised on the roof like a handsome young prince. 'You know we should, don't you? They're going to screw us over. There's no such thing as justice in America. It's all a fairy tale.'

'C'mon, let's go,' said blind Ic. 'If I don't have you guys around, I can't fly at all.'

'Can we, please, Max, can we, please?' Wendy begged. 'We can, can't we?'

'*Fly, fly, fly,*' came the chant from the street below.

'We should fly the hell away from here and from all of them down there,' Oz said darkly. He was the eldest next to Max, the strongest, the alpha male. 'We should fly away and never come back. I mean it, Max. That's what my instincts tell me. You know I'm right about this. We won't survive in these separate little families.'

Max sighed and shook her head. 'I like the woods too, but I hate to tell you, Ozymandias, winter is coming.'

Matthew said, 'So, we'll steal blankets. We'll sock away SpaghettiOs and big red fart-your-brains-out beans.'

Max laughed at the image from her precocious younger brother. 'Sure, but you know, we also like *pillows* and *Timeports* and *vegetarian pizza* and the latest *videos.*'

Matthew looked crestfallen. She thought that he might actually start to cry.

'Hey, don't be sad,' said Max. 'Buck up, buckaroo. At least you'll be with me.'

'We're just *things* to them. Like toys from FAO Schwarz,' said Oz. 'They want to tell us what to do. They're total control freaks. They think they're superior to nature, to animals, plants, and birds.'

'Maybe,' Max said, 'but we wanted to live in the world

with other people. You know, we begged for it. We almost died for it. So maybe, just maybe, we should do what they say we should do. For a while anyway.'

'Well, guess what they say we should do,' said Oz. '*Listen* to the people, Max. What do you hear?'

The never-ending chant floated up to them from the street, where crowds were watching. 'Fly, fly, fly.'

Max cupped her hands in front of her mouth. 'Okay! Sure! Fine!' she shouted down from the eight-story-high rooftop. 'Okay!' she called out to the mass of people flooding the park, eddying around cars on the street below. 'But we're doing this because we *want to*. We're doing this *for us*. And we're not going to fly very far.'

Glee lit the children's faces, and they knew just what to do. They positioned themselves at ten-foot intervals around the curve of the roof. Hundreds of camera lenses were pointed upward. This was *the* picture the media had been waiting for.

And it only got better.

With a sudden flourish, the kids spread twelve magnificent wings and *thrssssssshhh!* their wingtips sailed up above their heads almost of their own accord. Sunlight glinted and sparks flickered off bright white-feathered wings.

At Max and Oz's signals, they bent their knees, pushed off hard, and launched themselves into the air. The people below sucked in their breath.

There was no hesitation. The kids flapped their powerful wings effortlessly in the heated air. They soared above the state capitol building, its golden dome glinting in the sunlight. Higher and higher, the six of them flew. *The flock.*

Max could see several of Denver's landmarks spread across the landscape: the public library, the art museum, the Pepsi Center, Six Flags Elitch Gardens amusement park. And, of course, the majestic front range of the Rocky Mountains off in the distance. The city, the entire state, was so gorgeous, and it had the most perfect skies anywhere.

They *chittered* as they flew so that blind Ic would know where they were. *'Cheee-rup. Chee-rup,'* Matthew screeched at the top of his voice. 'Let's go to the Lake House now! Let's go, let's go!'

Max reached forward with the tips of her fingers, then deflected the air with her wings. It was almost like rowing! She did it again and again. Found her rhythm. Nice.

Her magnificent body rose higher into the warm current. She felt her headache fall away. Suddenly, she was in another, better world.

'Stay with me, now,' she called to the others. 'Keep up. You too, Ic.'

'Don't pick on the blind kid,' he yelled back, his favorite joke, *their* favorite joke.

Max tipped her right wing and banked gracefully to the right. The others followed her lead. She tipped her left wing and banked left. This was effortless pleasure.

She kept her left shoulder down and completed a wide

and generous loop around the imposing, gray-granite capitol building with its golden dome. The kids were flying wing to wing at her sides.

She had to smile as she looked down. She even allowed herself to feel a little hopeful. The people on the streets were cheering and waving, motioning them to fly faster and higher.

Max knew what every one of them was thinking: *We want to fly. Oh God, we wish we could fly like you.*

CHAPTER SIXTEEN

But not everyone in the huge crowd wanted to fly like the six biological wonders.

Not everyone wanted the children to fly at all.

A gunman named Marco Vincenti was crouching beside piles of lumber on an unfinished floor of a building under construction not far from the City and County building in Denver. He didn't feel one way or the other about the flying kids, except for the fact that they were definitely little freakazoids. They were good-looking and all, even beautiful, but it just wasn't right, what they were, *whatever* the hell they were. Goddamn freaks of nature.

Still, they were fun to watch – until he got his orders to shoot them down.

Actually, he had no idea what the hell would happen next. Whatever it was, he was ready. If he had to take one of them out, it wouldn't be a problem.

He even figured he could take all six down if that was the job requirement. That wouldn't be a problem either. All hell would break loose after the murders, but he didn't give a crap about that. He had his back covered.

Slowly and smoothly he moved the sight of his rifle over the faces of the six of them. The Japanese-made sight was amazing, and he could see tiny imperfections – like a pimple or an ingrown hair – on the kids' individual faces.

He kept bringing the rifle sight back to the blonde female. She was the most impressive, the natural leader. Either she was, or the handsome boy they called Ozymandias. He was sleek and slender, but already had muscles like a laborer.

The rifleman wore a set of earphones, and he patiently waited for his orders to come. For all he knew, there were other snipers out there – *maybe one for each kid.*

Then he heard his name in the earphones. 'Marco, you there? Marco?'

'I'm here,' he said into the mike perched below his lip. *Where the hell else would I be?*

'Can you take out one of them now?'

'It's not a problem. Any of them. Which one do I hit? Your choice.'

'How about all of them?' the voice asked.

'Not a problem either. Just tell me when. *Now* would be a good time. Now is perfect. Not too much wind.'

There was silence for several seconds. Marco Vincenti's finger pressed lightly on the trigger. He was *so* ready.

'Put down the rifle,' said the voice. 'That's all we need for now. This was just a practice run. These children are incredibly valuable to science, and we hope there's another way to solve our problem. Please leave Denver as soon as possible. You're to go by car. You'll be paid for your time. As always, Marco, it's a pleasure to work with a professional. We'll be talking with you again.'

'I look forward to it,' said the contract killer.

And then his earphones went dead.

He held his sight on Max's left eye, then on her right one, and finally on a spot between the two about the size of a dime.

'Catch you next time, kid,' he whispered.

CHAPTER SEVENTEEN

I felt as if the whole world were about to end. *This was it, wasn't it?* My head was spinning, and it also hurt like hell. I couldn't even think about the *possibility* of losing the kids.

I took a seat in a brown leather wing chair in Judge Dwyer's spacious chambers. The wood paneling in the office was supposed to give off warmth and a feeling of security, but I didn't feel in the least bit secure, and the air-conditioning had made the room freezing cold.

Kit entered the crowded room, searched me out, and came over and took my hand. Finally Judge Dwyer arrived, followed by the court stenographer. The doors were shut with a bang.

'I've called you together,' Judge Dwyer immediately began, 'because I want to let you know my decision in advance. That way, you can tell the children privately.'

I almost couldn't breathe. I squeezed Kit's hand harder as I looked up at him, and he kissed my hair. I couldn't help thinking about what an absolutely terrific guy he was. I brought my attention back to the judge. He was talking about the experimental laboratory that the kids called the School.

'I read the reports on what happened at the School, that horrifying lab that defies description, and my mind nearly rejects the words . . . Had experiments been conducted on rabbits or chimpanzees, I could cite chapter and section finding criminality in the heinous way the victims were treated. But the crimes that have been committed against these children bear no resemblance to science and medicine as it has ever been practiced, even in the darkest ages of human understanding.'

There was a sob from across the room. It came from Anthea Taranto. She looked like she couldn't take any more. Others in the room burst into tears.

Judge Dwyer continued. 'I understand that the people who committed these acts are gone, jailed or dead. Over the past three days I have seen the tragic results of their unspeakable crimes. There are innocents involved. And I don't mean just the children. As Mr Kussof said in his opening statement, there are no bad people here. But my job is to concern myself with the children, and what is best for them.'

The judge took off his reading glasses and placed them on his desk. He gazed around his chambers.

'Here is my decision . . . The petitioners, Dr O'Neill and Mr Brennan, have taken on the task of demonstrating that the custody of these minors by their parents would be detrimental to their well-being. They state that the children will not be happy, or *safe*, with their biological parents. The children seem to believe this as well. That's important to this court. It carries weight with me. But Dr O'Neill and Mr Brennan have not sufficiently proved their case. Not today anyway. Accordingly, I must rule that the children stay with their parents.'

Suddenly, I felt incredibly empty and hollowed out, as if I had lost my own children. Hot tears were streaming down my cheeks. I held in a scream of despair.

'However,' Judge Dwyer continued, 'this is a temporary order. There is a contingency mandated by law that I hold another hearing at a later date. If, as Dr O'Neill posits, this "flock" fails to thrive, I will reverse this ruling. Dr O'Neill, Mr Brennan, please accept my regrets. I'm sorry. I know you love these children like your own.'

A clerk slipped quietly into the room and handed the judge a note. He put on his glasses, read the note, and then he did something unexpected – he smiled.

'Mr and Mrs Stern, Ms Taranto, Mr and Mrs Chen, Mr and Mrs Marshall, the children have returned from a spin around the Capitol building and are waiting for you in Courtroom Seven. You may take them home.'

PART TWO

FLYING LESSONS

CHAPTER EIGHTEEN

The Hospital; Fantasy Room B

Charlotte Donahue's ample body tensed as the stainless-steel earphones were tightly secured on her head. She felt as if she were in a spaceship. *This was getting weird already.*

The sounds of the busy operating room disappeared once the earphones were secure. Then Charlotte heard a voice *inside* her head!

'This is Dr Ethan Kane. Please don't fight the anesthesia, Charlotte. Are you comfortable? Anything you need? It's important that everything is perfect for you.'

Charlotte was feeling stranger and stranger by the second – but *good* strange. Her body was floating; her mind was still sharp. 'I think so. I think I like it.'

'Can you feel this?' the doctor asked as he inserted a long hypodermic needle into the twenty-three-year-old Cincinnati native's acne-scarred lower back.

'Nope. I don't feel anything,' Charlotte said.

Oh God, she wanted to laugh, though. Her long-standing fear of hospitals had evaporated completely, and her excitement was bubbling over. Something incredible was happening to her, something good, something exceptional.

Suddenly, Charlotte smelled a salty sea breeze. Was that possible? Where had it come from? *Isn't this the weirdest experience ever!* It certainly was.

Then she heard seagulls calling. Seagulls – she was sure of it.

And then she could *see* the SS *Nautica* looming above her, nine stories of pristine, shining white luxury. She looked down at herself in total amazement and befuddlement. Everything about her had changed. *When had this incredible makeover happened?* She was wearing a dress of thin red silk, and red slingbacks dusted with sparkling rhinestones. Her heels clacked pleasantly as she walked up the gangway toward the main deck of the *Nautica*. The decking was teakwood, and teak deckchairs were everywhere.

At the top of the gangway stood a blond-haired steward wearing a smart blue sailor's hat and crisply pressed blue uniform. He handed Charlotte a drink in a crystal glass and welcomed her aboard. 'Miss Donahue,' he said. 'A pleasure.' He even knew her name.

He winked at her, but Charlotte's thoughts were elsewhere. *The captain,* dressed all in white, peered down at her from the bridge. No doubt about it – he was actually watching her. Charlotte brazenly turned her face up to him, looked directly into his silver-blue eyes.

Ridiculous or not, she felt a wave of desire. Her skin was pleasantly warm – then Dr Kane spoke again.

Spoilsport!

'Can you still hear me, Charlotte?'

Somewhere on the deck a steel band had started to play a song she recognized as 'Mockingbird'. The band was halfway decent, too. Bob Marley-ish. Maybe a hint of Jimmy Cliff.

'Ms Donahue?'

'Go away, Dr Kane,' she said, and drank deeply from her champagne cocktail glass. 'I'm fine. I'm okay. This *is* perfect. Now let me have my fun in the sun.'

'What are you drinking?'

'It's pink,' she said. 'I think it's passion-fruit champagne. Delicious.'

The drink was sweet and pungent and made her feel a touch giddy. She didn't know where to look next, or what to do first. The bouncy rhythm of the steel drums called to her. The band had already found a nice groove. Oh yes, she wanted to dance! *With the captain!*

'Charlotte, go over to the railing and look down. You'll see me in the crowd. Wave to me, please,' said Dr Kane.

She wasn't sure why, but Charlotte did what she was told. She made her way to the railing and looked down at the cheering mob of well-wishers gathered on the pier. As she leaned against the rail, she could see lifeboats jutting out slightly from one of the decks below.

There he was! The very handsome, if somewhat cool and

restrained, Dr Kane. He was looking up at her.

'Goodbye,' she called out to her doctor. She lifted her hand and waved and started to laugh. She couldn't stop laughing. Streams of pink and baby-blue confetti streaked the air. Ropes fell heavily against the hull. The ship's bullhorn blew three deeply satisfying blasts.

'Bye-bye,' she called gaily.

The doctor spoke once more. 'Bon voyage, Charlotte. I'm sorry you have to die now. But you're helping someone . . . who is so much more important than yourself.'

CHAPTER NINETEEN

E than Kane stopped talking to silly ass Charlotte and went back to work on her.

The surgeon had nerves of steel, and hands that were even steadier. His instrument was a bovee, a scalpel that used heat rather than a blade. It burned blue at the tip and emanated a whispery sound as he made the first incision three millimeters deep, running laterally from one of Charlotte Donahue's shoulders all the way to the other.

The red bloodline turned black almost instantly and left a ghostly trail of smoke. The air filled with the unmistakable odor of burning flesh.

His next incision formed a T with the first, starting at the throat and ending at the pubic bone, a line so crisply defined it might have been drawn on the girl's milky skin with a fine-tip marking pen.

His third cut went deep into the subcutaneous layer, the thick yellow fat that rounded out Charlotte's voluptuous shape as a woman.

He then slid his hands inside her. Arteries were held with a guillotine clamp designed to press on one side, cut on the other. Dr Kane worked carefully to sever connective tissues and any adhesive attachments.

Within eighteen minutes, the woman's most precious organs floated freely inside the open cavity of her body. Bypass machines kept them shining and pink. Her heart still beat a strong sixty beats a minute.

Suddenly, there came an otherworldly hum from overhead. A stainless-steel mechanical device, looking like the jaws of an earthmoving apparatus, traveled over a metal track. A medical tech lowered 'the Scoop' by hand, then positioned it over the woman's body.

A slight, tinny, musical sound could be heard coming from Charlotte's earphones, an Island tune. *'Hot tea, rice, salt fish is nice and the rum is fine any time of year,'* Dr Kane sang along. He was being ironic.

'Okay, then,' he said, as he surveyed the work. 'I'm through in here. *C'est fini.'*

The anesthesiologist glanced at a monitor above Charlotte's head. Pictures aboard the SS *Nautica* flickered on the screen. 'Want to give the young lady a few more minutes to get laid? One last fling?'

'You're so sentimental,' Kane said, and frowned. 'No. My time is much more valuable than hers. Cut her off.'

The anesthesiologist shrugged, then ripped the cord from Charlotte's earphones and the music stopped.

'Thank you,' said Kane. 'I hate that reggae shit anyway.'

He flipped a switch, and the guillotine clamps made

their cuts. Blood immediately drained through large plastic tubes out of the body and into a huge stainless-steel canister. Charlotte Donahue's organs began to turn gray. The neon-colored tracers on the monitors went crazy.

Then they flat-lined, with the resultant high-pitched *bleeeeeeeeeeeeeeeep*.

'Okay, everyone,' Dr Kane said to the room at large. 'Let's shuck her.'

The open jaws of the Scoop closed. With a whine and a hum, the Scoop lifted the woman's internal system out of her body in one piece.

Charlotte Donahue had been shucked as clean as an oyster at DC Coast in nearby Washington, one of Dr Kane's favorite places to eat and drink. He might even grab the wife and go there tonight.

CHAPTER TWENTY

C olorado.
  Another day, another school, thought Max to herself. *But hopefully, this will be a good school. No, a great school! And a great beginning.*

The jarring ring of the bell marked the end of third period. She'd been listening to a talk on the diminishing populations of endangered species in Colorado: the black-tailed prairie dog, Hops Blue butterfly, peregrine falcon, osprey. It was her eleventh day of classes, and she was trying hard to do everything *imperfectly.* Smart, but not too smart; funny, but not too funny; humble, but not a smarmy kiss-ass.

She grabbed her very cool bicycle messenger bag from under her desk, stuffed her textbooks inside, and rose to join the bubbly throng flooding out of the classroom. The crowd included a dog. Her teacher, as usual, had brought his brown Labrador retriever to class. Kind of goofy, but kind of cool too.

Max never actually reached the doorway.

A scream coming from somewhere outside the building stopped her cold. She spun around. *Matthew! He was in trouble!* Max was sure it was her brother; his voice was impressed on her brain, hardwired into her nervous system.

None of the other kids heard it – but her sensitive hearing picked it right up. *Matthew!*

Max dropped her book bag, ran to the window, and looked two stories down into the dusty plain of the schoolyard. There he was! A pack of boys was chasing Matthew, a couple of them waving hockey sticks. And cans of something. *What the hell were they doing?*

She saw a flash of metal and a yellow mist fill the air. Then she got it. They were trying to paint Matthew's wings. It was the third time since they'd been at the school that a gang had gone after him.

'Hey,' she yelled. 'Hey, stop that! STOP IT NOW!'

She beat on the windowpane with her fists, but no one looked up. Of course not. *Their hearing sucked!* Max ran from the classroom, charged down the crowded flight of concrete fire stairs, and barreled out into the playground. She was careful not to fly at school. Not even now.

She could see the bully-boys at the far end of the playground. Oh so cool in their Aeropostale, American Eagle, and Abercrombie garb. Five boys, ninth-graders, had formed a semicircle near the chain-link fence. Nine-year-old Matthew was trapped in the middle of them. Their faces were twisted with hate and anger as they taunted him. Thank God the press wasn't around today or she and Matthew would be *Live at 5* again.

She could hear everything they said, but certain words stabbed into her heart. 'Freak show.' 'Carnival boy.' 'Maggot carrier.'

The biggest kid, a stocky, pear-shaped bully wearing baggy gangsta pants and an Avalanche sweatshirt, grabbed Matthew by the arms as another kid held up a can of spray paint. Red!

Max heard the harsh rattling of the metal ball inside the can, then the fizz of airborne Rustoleum.

'Stop that right now, you little brats!' she screamed.

The boys were momentarily startled and broke apart from their huddle. Matthew wrenched free from the biggest kid's grasp and immediately fell to the ground. His wing feathers and clothes were soaked with paint. He was forcing himself not to cry. Brave Matthew! What a damn good kid he was.

'Matty, I'm here,' Max said, gathering her brother to her, kissing the top of his head. That was all it took to break the bullies' ceasefire. Spray cans fizzed again.

'Who are you calling a brat, you freak bitch?' yelled the leader of the pack.

'Oh, I'm sorry, I was talking to *you.*' Max spat out venom. 'You're the one I want a piece of.'

The boy was probably fifteen and already weighed at least one-seventy. She knew him by reputation. His father had played pro football for the Denver Broncos, or something terribly impressive like that. He laughed at Max. 'Bring it on. Let's tussle.'

Max had promised the Marshalls never to hurt a kid at school. So had Matthew. She wanted to take this creepy punk apart, but she held back, which was really hard. Almost impossible.

Then she saw the bright red paint smeared on poor Matthew. It got her furious all over again. *Bring it on? This obnoxious jerk had no idea what he was asking for.*

'What's your name, punk?' she asked.

'You don't know who I am? Shit, girl, I'm Bryce Doulin. Everybody knows me.'

'*You* don't know who you're messing around with, bitch,' Max growled. 'You and your friends don't get it. But maybe you will in a minute.'

Doulin was a little fat, but muscular. He came at her, but Max grabbed him in a tight headlock. He pulled at her arm with both of his hands. 'Hey! Leggo!' he yelped.

Max's fingers were like steel pincers. They didn't budge. Doulin was gagging. His piggy eyes were bulging. She yanked the spray can out of his hand. Easily.

What they'd done to Matthew was a desecration. It was a hate crime. She knew that much. Now what should she do? Maybe paint Bryce Doulin from head to toe. Or mark him with the words *MAX'S BITCH.* And then what? She'd be the bully, wouldn't she?

She finally loosened her hold on Doulin's neck and shoved him away from her. He stumbled and fell over backwards on the lawn. The rest of the gang was looking on in disbelief. Bryce Doulin was on his ass, and a girl had done it.

Max crushed the spray can until it crumpled and *popped*. It was easy. She took her time and stared right into the eyes of every kid in the circle, but especially Doulin's.

'Matthew could have hurt you, too. He's almost as strong as I am,' she said. 'He chose not to because he's such a goddamn good kid. Don't ever mess with him again. *Ever*. Until the day you die and maggots eat your worthless guts.'

She helped Matthew to his feet and together they watched as the pack of older boys backed away, grumbling and cursing, but mostly scared out of their gourds. Max would remember the faces. She would remember every one of them for as long as she lived.

Why do they hate like that? Where does it come from? She was afraid she would never really understand humans.

But maybe that was a good thing.

CHAPTER TWENTY-ONE

On a Saturday morning about a week later, Max heard shouts, then a loud scream come from upstairs in the Marshall house. She turned to her brother, but he was lost in a game of *Grand Theft Auto* on his PlayStation II.

'We better go see,' Max finally said. 'C'mon, Matty. Put down the game. *Matthew*, now!'

'All right. I heard you the first time.'

Although they were forbidden to fly inside the house, they flew up to the second floor and then down the hall to the master bedroom.

They found Terry Marshall at the door to the room. She had on her cleaning outfit: a plaid kerchief, cut-off jeans, a T-shirt that had *Einstein Brothers Bagels* printed on it.

'It got in when I was airing out our bedroom,' she said. 'It will break everything I love in there. Can you help me, Max? I don't want to hurt it.'

Max took a peek inside the bedroom. 'It' was a female

mourning dove that apparently had flown in through an open window and was trapped.

A couple of the poor girl's feathers were stuck on the closed picture window that looked out on to a small pond. There was a smear of blood on the dove's beak.

'Poor baby, easy, baby,' Max whispered to the dove. 'It's okay, sweetie.'

'What can we do? Can't you talk to it?' Terry Marshall asked in a shaky voice. 'Get it out of here! Please.'

'*It's* petrified,' Max scolded, but then she went on, 'We'll take care of it, Moms.' Moms was what she usually called Terry, mostly out of respect, but sometimes just because it was the practical thing to do.

'We know how to do this. We'll talk to the dove,' Max said, then gently nudged Moms out of the room. 'Leave it to us,' she said. Then she closed the door.

Matthew immediately rolled his eyes at his big, usually smart sister. 'We'll talk to the dove? What are we gonna say to it? *Get a grip, dumb bird?*'

'I don't know, Matt. Something will come to me.'

'Should we rush it? I can be kinda gentle.'

'I don't think so, Matty. She'll freak. She's petrified to be in here.'

Max went and opened the French doors that led from the bedroom on to a small terrace.

The dove continued to fly against the picture window – the one way it *couldn't* get out of the room. It was so beautiful, warm brown in color, with pink feet and a pinkish cast to its breast feathers.

'Sit down with me, Matt,' said Max. 'Sit by the open door. Just *sit*, Matthew.'

Matt rolled his eyes again – his absolute favorite communication that meant something seemed particularly crazy to him – but he sat down. 'And now, we – what?' he asked.

'We talk to it,' said Max. 'It's called a mourning dove because of its call – *oooh-a-oo-whoo*.'

'Oooh-a-oo-whoo?' Matthew said, then snorted out a laugh.

'That's it, Matty. You've got it,' encouraged Max.

'Oooh-a-oo-whoo.'

'Oooh-a-oo-whoo.'

It took a couple of minutes, but the dove finally noticed the two of them. She didn't want them to know, but the female was checking them out. Also, she wasn't smacking herself against the picture window any more. Fluttering wildly, yes; but no more smacking her brains out against the glass.

'Oooh-a-oo-whoo,' Max and Matthew continued to whisper.

'Oooh-a-oo-whoo.'

'C'mon, sweetheart. You can do it,' Max coaxed.

'Oooh-a-oo-whoo.'

'This door is the way out. Come right through here.'

'Oooh-a-oo-whoo.'

'Oooh-a-oo-whoo.'

'It's so easy, dummy!' exclaimed a frustrated Matthew. 'Go. Out. The. Door.'

'Coo, Matty. She's a mother. She's worried about her young ones. Just be patient with her.'

'Oooh-a-oo-whoo.'

'Oooh-a-oo-whoo.'

'Oooh-a-oo-whoo.'

'Oooh-a-oo-whoo.'

Then very suddenly, and without so much as a thank you, the mourning dove darted out the terrace door to freedom. It flew at its absolute top speed across the mill pond, and disappeared into the thick grove of pines beyond.

When Terry Marshall finally came back to check, Max and Matthew were sitting on the bedroom floor, whispering 'oooh-a-oo-whoo' over and over.

'How strange,' their biological mother said. 'You two are really weird, you know that?'

Frannie told you, Max thought to herself.

CHAPTER TWENTY-TWO

After the custody trial had ended, I went home to jump-start my life again in the beautiful Colorado boonies.

Kit went back to Washington, DC.

I'm not sure that either of us knew why we were separating, but I think it had something to do with losing the kids, and needing to grieve. Kit said that his job was in Washington, at least for the time being, but he would be out to see me a lot, as often as he possibly could.

We phoned each other in the beginning, and sent e-mails, but there was not a single visit from him. I honestly believe we had sunk into depression. It wasn't admirable, but I suppose it was understandable, and human, but mostly cowardly and dumb on both our parts – if I may speak for Kit as well as for myself.

Life went on in Colorado, though there was one strange and very sad event – a good friend of mine simply disappeared. Jessie Horvath was there one day, and then she was gone. All traces of her, all two hundred and fifty pounds. Just gone.

It was about four on a Sunday afternoon and I was up to my wrists in blood and guts. My usual gig at the veterinary hospital.

I was in the room that doubled, tripled, actually, as the surgery suite, examining room, and pharmacy area. All around me were supplies ranging from cotton balls and tongue depressors to hundreds of plastic bottles filled with pills, all of them white. A single picture hung on the wall, a news photo of me at the head of the 'Cause for Paws' benefit hike in Boulder.

A tuna-fish sandwich lay half eaten on the sink ledge where I'd left it at noon when a cat-rescue lady brought in a carload of feral cats to be altered.

Thankfully, the end was in sight.

I was closing up my ninth and last patient, a big homeless tabby named Sophie, when I heard an ungodly racket out front.

It was an extremely loud police siren – *and the car was right outside my door*.

I hoped somebody in a 4x4 hadn't hit a deer or a horse. Clearly, it was some kind of emergency, though.

Damn. I didn't need this at all.

I knotted the last stitch in Sophie's incision, put her into a cage with a fluffy pink blanket, then hurried outside to greet whatever trouble the cops were bringing me.

'I'm coming,' I called ahead. 'I'm coming! Hold your water! Turn off that damn siren!'

CHAPTER TWENTY-THREE

The Inn-Patient, my small animal hospital, is a 2,000-square-foot glass-and-timber box that sits twenty feet off the highway near the intersection in Bear Bluff, a precious town, but one so tiny you could pass through it a couple of times without even noticing. The state troopers' barracks is only two miles up the road, and I've gotten to know most of the 'staties' from the hard-luck strays and hit-and-runs they've brought me over the years.

The cruiser's rotating beacon was still on when I stepped out into the parking area outside my front door. Suddenly I hoped this wasn't about my friend Jessie.

I saw Trooper James H. Blake get out of his car. A former fullback at Colorado State, he's a massive six-three with huge arms and torso. His strong arms carried a dun-colored sleeping bag, and it was soaked with blood.

Oh c'mon, James H, I said to myself.

I took another look at the cruiser, and saw a couple of plaid-shirted teenage boys in the back seat. A blond and a redhead; long shaggy hair; angry, pouty faces.

My sinking heart told me that whatever was in the sleeping bag had been hurt by these two boys. I've heard all the rationale, so don't bother to argue with me. *I hate hunting, and I always will.*

James Blake was obviously upset too. I could tell he was trying hard not to lose it. He's tried to date me a couple of times, and though I've declined, I do believe he's a nice, decent, stand-up guy. So why don't I date him? Because I'm a dumb bunny. Also, I'm holding out for Kit.

'Frannie, I hope you can do something,' James Blake said as he approached. Blood from the bundle in his arms was dripping on to the gravel underfoot.

I pushed open the glass doors for James, led him through reception, then past hospital Wards 1 and 2.

'Nothing on Jessie, I assume,' I said.

'Nothing,' answered James.

As we passed number 2, a looney-tunes black Lab who'd been dropped off to have his choppers cleaned started howling. That set off the basset hound with gastric torsion, and the stray shepherd-cross.

Also Pip, my own Jack Russell terrier who hangs out with the boarding dogs and can't say no to a good barkathon.

The clamor disturbed the animal in the sleeping bag, and it started a panicky stir.

'*Shut-UP, you guys!*' I hollered at the dogs.

I showed James into an exam room and shut the door

behind us. A stray dog was napping on a window seat, snug in a pile of pillows. I started to unwrap the folds of polyester-filled bag.

Dog, cat, raccoon, or whatever, this was going to be an awful mess. That much I knew already.

But I was totally unprepared to be staring into the glazed-over eyeballs of a *Gymnogyps Californianus* – a bird that, to my knowledge, hadn't been seen in Colorado in two hundred years.

'What the hell is it, Frannie?' he asked.

'It's a California condor,' I told him. 'I've never seen one in the flesh. That's because their flesh isn't supposed to be around here.'

And it was weird-looking flesh at that. My newest patient had a bald head about the size of a large mango, with a longish hooked beak partially cloaked in pink wattles. There was a patch of stiff black feathers on its forehead, and where its neck met its shoulders was a wild ruff of thin black feathers that continued down the whole of its body, making this poor creature look like a weary old man wearing half of a gorilla suit.

'He sure is pretty,' said Blake.

I laughed. 'Pretty rare anyway. There are only about a hundred and sixty of these left in the world, and of those, sixty are wild and the rest are in captive breeding facilities. Or so they say.'

It was the sad truth. Once ranging freely, by '87 all but a dozen of these birds had been poached, poisoned, and shot nearly out of existence. With dedication and hard work, they'd been brought back to their current number in captivity.

I could tell from the orange tag on its good wing that this bird was from the Vermilion Cliffs colony in northern Arizona, some three hundred miles away. That's actually a short hop for a condor. They can coast for hours without once batting their wings and can make speeds of fifty-five miles per hour.

Of course, this particular marvel might never fly again. The hunter's bullet had shattered its wing, maybe beyond repair.

As if it understood, the condor cracked its beak and *hissed* at me. 'Okay, buddy,' I crooned to the bird. 'Let's cross our fingers, James,' I told the trooper. 'It's lost a lot of blood. All I can do is my best. Might not be good enough.'

James H. Blake sighed. 'I'm going to take those two bad boys down to the barracks,' he said, 'and see what I can slap them with.'

'Go for it. I'm hoping fifteen to life.'

He smiled. 'You're such a softie. I'll check back with you, Frannie.'

'I *am* a softie,' I said. 'I'll be here.' But I'd already almost forgotten Trooper Blake.

I scrubbed my hands with antiseptic and went to work. Work was the only thing that had been saving me lately. It sure as heck beat rational thought.

CHAPTER TWENTY-FOUR

My fatigue had been replaced by an edgy kind of energy. And dread.

Operating on this rare bird was an awful responsibility, and I was going to have to do it unassisted. The dogs in Ward 2 were still in full throat, so I flipped on the radio and found a good music station. Good for my nerves, and good for the bird's nerves too. I recognized a cut from the latest Moby album. Good deal – I liked his stuff a lot.

I shone a light into the condor's eyes and hoped for a reflex. There was none. His condition was deteriorating by the minute.

'Come on, big boy. Don't give up on me. You've got a real big heart. Let's show it.'

I strapped a gas mask over the condor's beak, then cranked up the isofluorine mixture to five to knock him down fast.

The gas hissed through the tube. Only after the bird was out cold did I dare to entirely open the wraps and lay him out fully on the examination table.

I gently extended the shattered wing and, as I thought it would, it flapped open at a hideous and unnatural angle. I pushed the feathers away from the injured site and saw that the fractured bone had broken through the delicate, almost transparent skin. Worse, the wound was starting to turn green.

This big boy was a mess, all right.

I hoped I could keep him alive. But I also worried that if he lived, but couldn't fly, he'd be doomed to life in a cage.

Macy Gray was singing as I rummaged around in the cabinet over the sink for materials I would need. I liked Macy a lot too. The problem with pinning broken bird bones is that they're hollow and metal pins can't hold them together. I'd done a lot of work on hurt birds and had come up with my own MASH-unit-type surgical procedure, and frankly, it worked beautifully most of the time.

I stretched out the wing bones, then began to tease a small number 5 endo-tracheal tube into the break. It takes laserlike focus and a steady hand to do this just right. I held my breath and carefully threaded the tube through the broken bone, then back up to the proximal point of the fracture, where it held securely, and I could breathe again.

There's not much soft tissue in a bird's wing, but I cut away the damaged flesh, flushed out the wound with antiseptic solution, then closed the skin with a simple interrupted pattern of stitches.

I was satisfied. The surgery was pretty clean.

Bravo, dottore!

I folded the condor's wing and stabilized the fracture by securing the wing up against its body with a figure-eight, splintlike wrapping that works like a Chinese finger trap. If the bird tried to flap its wing, the bandage would only tighten more firmly.

Then I carried the thirty-pound condor into the storage room that my part-time assistant, Janna, and I use for medical supplies. There was no bow-wow chorus back here, but there *was* a large cage in the corner – a perfect Motel 8 for this fellow, who had certainly been hatched and raised in captivity.

I put the condor gently inside, covered the cage with a blanket, and turned off the light.

'Goodnight, big guy. Sleep well, you prince of Colorado.'

Finally, I went back into the operating room to clean up.

For the two hours that I'd been working on the condor, I'd been fighting off a feeling that I couldn't identify. Now that the surgery was done, I was overtaken by exhaustion, and also sadness. It was the kids. Working on the condor had reminded me how much I missed each and every one of them.

I pictured their faces.

Counted their fingers and toes.

I threw the dead tuna-on-eight-grain into the trash, and stuffed the bloodied sleeping bag in after it. I swabbed down the stainless-steel table, washed out the sink, and went to bed.

CHAPTER TWENTY-FIVE

'Frannie, if you're there, *pick up*,' said a whispery voice. 'C'mon, c'mon.'

I had been falling asleep, but suddenly I was awake. I reached out – and for at least the fourth time that month knocked over an ashtray from the original Hotel Boulderado, circa 1909. *Somebody was trying to tell me to stop smoking.*

Max? I thought to myself.

'Max, oh Max,' I said, grabbing up the phone. It was her voice on the answering machine. 'I was just thinking about you. Must be telepathy, kiddo. This is great. How *are* you?'

'Okay, I guess,' she said, but that *I guess* pierced my heart.

'What's wrong, sweetheart? Talk to me. I don't care if it's late. What's going on?'

'Oh, nothing,' she said in a false tone. Max can be such a twelve-year-old sometimes.

'Well, I guess you're not going to talk about yourself

tonight, huh? How's Matthew?'

'Aw, Frannie,' Max said. 'It's real hard for him being so different than other kids.'

'Tell me all about it,' I said.

I managed to get my old flannel robe on without disconnecting the phone as Max told me about crimes of hate in Pine Bush, Colorado. Every day at school there was at least one incident of serious taunting, or much worse.

I struggled to find the right words to tell Max, even as the accusatory voice of Catherine Fitzgibbons echoed in my mind: '*You've never been a mother, have you, Dr O'Neill?*'

'Kids can be kind of mean sometimes, Max,' I told her. 'I really think you handled everything right. You know human kids aren't the only ones who try to hurt each other. Sometimes, in a nest of birds, the oldest chicks try to push the newly hatched ones out so that they can have more food. It happens.'

'Yeah, I suppose,' Max said, but sounded unconvinced. It was hard to forget she has an IQ in the 180s. Plus a photographic mind.

'So, anyway. Moving on to cheerier things,' Max started to say, then changed the subject, maybe a little too quickly. She told me about a cute, 'sensitive' boy named Mickey whom she liked at school, 'and he seems to like me, wings and all,' she added. Then she asked about the goings-on at the new and improved Inn-Patient. I told her all about the condor I'd just operated on.

'Wow, I'd love to see that patched-up bird,' she said.

Some of her old spark was coming back. 'I miss you, Frannie. All of us do. Matthew sends major hugs and kisses. So does Ozymandias. And Ic.'

'I miss all of you too, honey,' I said gently.

I was careful not to make things harder for her by adding my own strong longing to hers. I expected her to sigh and agree as she always does, but I heard something different. Max's voice suddenly choked up. 'I gotta go.'

'Max, what is it? What's going on? There's something else, isn't there?'

'I can't talk about it. *Can't,*' she said. 'But it hurts so much to keep it a secret. It's bad, Frannie. Sorry, sorry, I've gotta go.'

'What are you talking about, Max? You're rambling. Slow down, honey.'

There was dead silence on her end of the line. So I asked again. I begged her, cajoled, reassured her. 'C'mon, Max. You're scared. I can hear it in your voice.'

'I *can't* tell you,' she said. 'It's dangerous, and hopeless. Frannie, it's worse than the School. The people there are worse, what they do is worse. Seriously. I even think somebody's watching Matthew and me. I know they are. I saw them twice. Gotta go! Gotta! I love you.'

Then Max hung up on me.

CHAPTER TWENTY-SIX

Max tried real hard not to think about the troubles ahead; about whoever was spying on her and Matthew. Even though she'd seen them again – *three* times now. She put her mind elsewhere – into small-town life.

As clever and smart as she was about some things, Max found herself in a tricky situation a few days later. She was kind of on a date, and it was with one of the real 'cuties' in her school – a tall, blond, athletic hunk named Mickey Bosco. She'd basically been anti-hunk – until Mickey asked her out.

She and the hunk didn't talk much as they climbed the steep, rocky hill that rose along the west side of Schoolhouse Road. As she pushed her way through the overgrown scrub brush, though, she suspected this might be a bad idea.

She was going to show Mickey what it was like to fly. She'd promised him.

'We need to climb that rocky outcropping over

there.' She sounded confident, but there was this Darth Vader warning voice in her head that wouldn't shut up. The voice said: *This is really stupid, Max. Smartest girl in the classroom; dumbest girl out on the street.*

'You're kind of quiet, Max,' Mickey said as he rock-climbed. 'You usually like this?'

'I'm just trying not to lose my balance. You might try the same.'

'Oh sure,' said Mickey. 'It's no problem. I was just checking on you. Making sure you're okay.'

'I'm fine. I am. Thanks for asking.'

Max's Reeboks grabbed on to the grain of the next rock. Mickey was right behind her. *So close.* Far below them was a noisy, fast-flowing highway. And across the highway, a vast stretch of open pastureland that looked promising. And much safer.

Finally, they were at the top. 'Ready?' Max asked. 'We don't have to do this if you don't want.'

'Are you kidding? I'm totally psyched. This is gonna be the best adventure ever! Talk about *extreme sports*.'

Max groaned as she bent at the waist, placing both hands on her knees. 'Climb on. Don't worry, I'm strong.'

Mickey Bosco climbed on to her back, hooking his legs around her waist. He wrapped his arms around her chest, under her wings. And he *was* kind of heavy.

'This isn't so bad,' he said, 'for me. You sure you're okay?'

'A one, and a two, and a three,' Max counted off. 'I'm just *ducky*.'

Then she pushed off the rock and they were airborne.

'Holy shiiiittt!' Mickey yelled. 'Awesome! Do the Dew! This is out-rageous! We're flying! I'm really flying.'

Max didn't think the adventure was quite so terrific. Actually, it went kind of wrong from the first second. Instead of gaining altitude, she dropped several feet toward the crowded lanes of speeding traffic. Mickey was a lot of extra weight to carry – even for her.

So Max beat her wings frantically. And suddenly she was scared! She'd only been aloft for a short time, and her lungs ached some. Her wing muscles burned like an engine about to catch on fire. *Not good*.

From the sound of Mickey's insane chortling, Max could tell that he had no clue how bad it actually was, and how scared he ought to be right now. She reached forward into the heavy air and pulled at it with her powerful wings. She finally caught a mild updraft and her body lifted.

'Having fun?' she managed to say a couple of seconds later.

'This is the bomb!' Mickey shouted into her ear. '*You* are the bomb, baby. The best ever!'

Max guessed that was a good thing, and she finally smiled. Maybe this could work out after all. She beat her wings again. She wouldn't feel totally safe until they had crossed the highway and were cruising over the pastureland.

Then she felt something shocking and totally unexpected. Mickey Bosco was moving his hands over her
chest, exploring.

He was feeling her up!

CHAPTER TWENTY-SEVEN

'Stop it!' Max yelled. 'Right now! Take your hands off me!' She twisted her neck to look into the blond boy's eyes. He kept right on rubbing her chest.

'*You don't have boobs.*' He shrieked with laughter. 'You're flat.'

Max felt her emotions collide. A while ago she'd kind of liked Mickey Bosco. Now she was sick with shame, and more embarrassed than she'd ever been in her life. She hated him for being so crude and rude and totally thoughtless.

'I don't need breasts,' she tried to explain.

'Well I do,' Mickey Bosco said, and laughed again. He sounded as if he were playing machoman in a locker room filled with his pals, and Max knew that this story would wind up there.

Her eyes had started to tear up and she couldn't see real well. Her heart felt incredibly heavy. She saw that there was a farm pond looming ahead. Canadian geese flew up from the water's edge in a honking flurry.

'I asked you to stop,' she pleaded. 'Please?'

'What am I hurting?' the boy said, roaring with laughter. 'Nothing to hurt, right?'

'Just somebody's feelings,' she muttered. *'Oh, screw you!'*

Then Max swooped down toward the acre or so of muddy water. When she was just about at the center of the pond, she closed her wings and made a tight, spiraling *dive*.

'I call this little stunt "the bullet",' she turned and said to Mickey Bosco. 'Isn't it *the bomb*? Do the Dew, right!'

She felt his grasp loosen, his hands and legs slide down her back. *'He-e-e-e-e-y-y-y-y,'* he shouted. 'Cut it out. Jesus Christ, Max. Slow down! I'm gonna fall.'

Max didn't answer. 'I call *this* "the roller coaster"!' she yelled again. 'Talk about extreme. Bon voyage, tricky Mickey!' She executed a sharp nose-*down*, then nose-*up* maneuver.

Mickey Bosco screeched as he lost his grip and began to slide off her body. Then he plunged at least fifty feet into the murky brown water. He made a satisfying splash, like the one she'd seen a couple of nights before in the movie *Shallow Hal* with one of her all-time favorites, Gwyneth Paltrow.

Max watched Bosco sink, then resurface with a sputter. She flew an unhurried circle to make sure that the stupid boy didn't drown. When he finally paddled his way to shore through pond scum and stinkweeds, he gave her the finger. Max blew him a kiss.

'To first love,' she called.

Her emotions were jangled, though, and she needed to figure out some things. To the north of the pond was a thicket of evergreens. She picked out the tallest lodgepole pine, dropped into the crown, and straddled a solid-looking branch.

She leaned her head against the rough bark of the tree. There were tears in her eyes and she hated that. She hated to be weak. How could she have let somebody like Mickey Bosco hurt her? Never again, she vowed. Not in this lifetime anyway.

Then she stopped and listened to the sounds around her: the constant *creak* of branches, the *rustle* of leaves, insects rubbing their wings. Her heartbeat began to slow to its resting rate: sixty beats a minute. Her breathing finally normalized.

Soon, the relevant issues became very clear in her mind.

She wanted to be accepted here in Pine Bush, Colorado, but she wasn't going to be.

She wanted to be able to trust people, but she couldn't. *No! Not even close!* She needed to accept that, to live with it.

The only ones she could count on were the bird-kids from the original School. And Frannie and Kit. Seven people in the whole world, and she couldn't even tell *them* the secret thing that scared her most. She had been warned not to.

You talk, you die.

No, she couldn't tell anyone about the horrible things that were happening at a place called the Hospital.

She would never, ever tell.

Not a word.

Besides, who would believe her?

CHAPTER TWENTY-EIGHT

It was getting dark and really nasty-looking to the west and south. Black rain clouds were gathering as Max finally flew back to the Marshalls' ranch house on Ames Road in Pine Bush. She was only a block away when she saw an old black Honda in the driveway and a tall, thin woman talking to her mother.

What was this all about?

She didn't recognize the visitor at first.

Then it clicked.

Denver!

Max recalled the visitor's face, even remembered the name of the woman who'd been at the custody trial. Linda Schein. A reporter with the *Denver Post*.

Why has she come here? What does she want in Pine Bush? Oh God, why can't they just leave us alone!

I won't do any more freak-show stories. I just won't! Forget about it!

Max pushed back on the air, effectively putting on the brakes. She dropped down to the front lawn, and saw the reporter's eyes go wide. She was probably pissed she hadn't brought along a cameraman.

Then Linda Schein smiled as she did when talking into a TV camera. 'Hi, Max. Nice of you to drop in,' she quipped.

'I live here,' Max said dryly. 'What do you want?'

Terry Marshall stood in the doorway under the light. 'Max, this is an important reporter from Denver. She drove all the way out here to see you.'

'Linda Schein,' the woman said, holding out her hand. She was around Frannie's age, sort of attractive, but too made-up for Max's taste. Max tried not to judge her because of her lipstick and mascara, though.

'I remember you, Ms Schein. I *think* you're the forty-seventh reporter to come to the house. Something like that. *Rocky Mountain News*? No, you're with the *Denver Post*, right?'

'Not now. I'm writing a book. I know I should have called first, but I just took a chance that you'd have a few moments to talk. I'm really sorry, Maximum. Your mother said it would be okay. If you agreed.'

My mother said? Max shook her head, but then she surrendered. 'C'mon inside, Ms Schein. Or would you rather we do the interview in a tree? Somebody asked me to do that once. Really creative, huh? But the best was the TV personality who wanted to jump out of a plane and interview me in the air. I said *OK* – if he didn't wear a parachute.'

Max walked inside the house and let the writer follow

if she wanted to. Her bedroom was painted a creamy white with a floral border under the moldings. She had a tangerine-colored iMac desktop computer with a flying goose screensaver, a canopied bed, several shelves holding books and fossilized rocks and other found treasures. The Marshalls had tried to make it nice here for her. Score one for Moms and Pops.

Max sat on the edge of her bed and watched as the woman writer perused the wall hangings. She commented politely on Max's funky star map of Hollywood and her *40 Days and 40 Nights* movie poster, but it didn't take long for her to get to the real point of her visit. Which was—

'I'm interested in child abuse. I was abused,' Linda Schein said as she settled into the chair beside the desk. Max wasn't sure whether to believe her. She already knew that some reporters would lie about anything, even in their news stories. 'After I listened to you and the other children at the custody trial, I got interested in institutional abuse. I especially wanted to know more about the School. Please tell me what happened there, Max. It's important – for both of us. I think you know it is.'

'That's in the past,' Max answered softly. 'The School is gone. The people who worked there are dead or in jail.'

The writer's eyes narrowed, focused. Max could tell she was a smart one. Wily. 'I don't think so,' said Linda Schein. 'And I don't think you do either. They're not *all* in jail. I'm not wrong, am I?'

'What do you mean?' Max asked. She couldn't keep an edge of concern out of her voice. She stared hard at the writer, the intruder.

'I *know* things, Max. I do. I have a contact in Washington with access to sealed government documents. I did some digging myself and found a memo from a Dr Brownhill mixed in with a sealed Grand Jury indictment. It was pretty terrifying. It detailed an ongoing project, an offshoot of the School. I know it exists. I know about something called the Resurrection Project. What is Resurrection, Max? Is there a place they call "the Hospital"? There is, isn't there? You have to tell me.'

'You really have to go,' Max said abruptly. 'You're way off base. This is too crazy. Why can't you reporters just leave us alone?'

She stood quickly and flung open the bedroom door for the reporter. Then she had an attack of conscience. She felt compelled to add something. 'Don't dig into this subject, Ms Schein. Please believe me. If you talk about it, you could die. I'm not exaggerating. *You talk, you die.* You're way off base, but you could get hurt anyway.'

The reporter found herself being led out into the hallway. But she wouldn't go away. Not that easily. 'Max, you can't leave it like this. I can see you're frightened. I guess I understand that. Give me a few more minutes. Talk to me, please. What is the Resurrection Project? Where is it?'

Max shook her head. 'I don't have anything to tell you. You're looking in the wrong places.' But then she had to add again, 'If you talk, you could die. Please remember those words, Ms Schein. Now go back to Denver. Drive safely.'

Panting with fear and close to tears, Max shut her door and leaned up hard against it. When she heard the writer's car finally drive away, she collapsed on to her bed, fully dressed. Wired, and coming apart, all at the same time.

She'd done it now – talked to a writer. An investigative journalist.

She would be found out. Then all the children would be in terrible danger.

You talk, you die.

Especially if you talk about Resurrection.

CHAPTER TWENTY-NINE

You talk, you die, you talk, you die, talk, die, talk, die.

It was two in the fricking-fracking morning and Max had been twisting and thrashing in bed for hours. Her head ached from the pressure of too many thoughts, and she couldn't stand it any more.

She made a call with her cell phone.

Her best friend in the world answered, and they talked for less than a minute. Just in case somebody might be listening.

Then Max threw off her blankets and dressed for a cold night flight. She had to meet her friend. *Right now.*

It didn't matter that night flights were against the rules set down by Terry and Art Marshall. Their absurd, tight-assed rules didn't matter to her. Not any more. Not ever, really. Most parents made up rules to keep *themselves* comfortable, right?

She had to see Ozymandias. Somebody knew about *Resurrection*. A reporter knew, and they weren't exactly known for keeping their big fat mouths shut.

Max crept down the back stairs and through the silent house. She went straight to the mudroom.

There, she took her silver vest down from a hook. Zipped it over her shirt and jeans.

She knotted the laces of her sneakers together and slung them around her neck. She tucked her CD player into one pocket, cell phone in another.

Then she left the Marshall house quietly, carefully, through the back door.

It was two twenty in the morning.

Time to rock and roll.

You talk, you die.

CHAPTER THIRTY

The moon was hidden behind thick clouds as Max ran barefoot down the entire length of the backyard. *Dewy, dewy, cold, cold.*

Max thought: I wish we were all back at the Lake House. I wish it was the way it used to be. Veggie pizzas and cookouts, long, long talks with Kit and Frannie, overnight hikes and fly-aways. But then Max stopped herself. The Lake House was in the past; ancient history; it was over. This was now. *You talk, you die.*

She pointed her arms forward and stretched out her beautiful wings. As the wings swung out, the joints opened automatically, and her flight feathers spread. *Bernoulli's principle in action, Jackson.*

As air flowed across the tops of her wings, Max rose as if she were being sucked right into the sky. Once aloft, she beat her wings until she was high above the treetops – and then she soared!

God, I love to fly. I was born for this, she thought.

Who wouldn't love a night flight?

Maybe George W. Bush? Nah, he'd like it a lot!

Max headed southeast over Pine Bush, rising like a jet through the moisture-laden clouds that dispersed as she cleared the town. The clouds didn't feel like much of anything as she passed through them – froth from the top of a latte? Spider webs? – but they were mysterious, ethereal, and she felt her face bead with water drops. The moon was so bright, and the stars were sharp white holes punched out of the fabric of a deep black sky.

And it was so *quiet* up here – so unearthly quiet and peaceful. If she wasn't so nervous and worried, and *scared half to death*, this would be perfect.

Max found the North Star by following the line connecting the two pointers in the Big Dipper. Then she adjusted her flight path so that she would travel along the eastern edge of the Roosevelt National Forest – toward the town of Fort Collins, about thirty miles away.

Oz lived near Fort Collins, and he actually liked the city a lot. God, she couldn't wait to see him. To talk to Ozymandias. To lean on his shoulder.

You talk, you die.

Max had her wings fully extended, catching the updrafts off the ridges, and glided for as long as ten minutes without beating her wings a single time. Fantastic! She knew bone deep that this miracle of flight was worth all she'd suffered for it.

She tried to put aside any fears and worries and surrendered herself to the pleasure of flying. Below her were thousands of acres of rolling hills against an awesome backdrop of snowy mountain peaks that rose up and pierced the clouds. Moonlight made the tiers of spruce and pine trees below her look like fantastical castles with silver spires. Oh hell, the poetry in her head didn't do it justice, not even close.

Max had been flying for about an hour when she picked out the metallic sheen of the Cache la Poudre River seven thousand feet below.

She flicked on her CD player and sang along with Nelly Furtado as she followed the river's course.

The cool night air buffeted her body all the way down to her tippy-toes. She could fly just fine with shoes, but bare feet gave her more rudder control. Felt better on the tootsies, too.

The Cache la Poudre ran parallel to a big four-laner, Route 287. Max followed the twisting ribbon of highway and flew above the subdued lights of Fort Collins, and from there about five miles east to her destination, the tiny town of Warren, Colorado.

Ozymandias was down there. The strongest of the six children, maybe even the future leader. Absolutely her best buddy in the world. Her secret hero.

She closed her wings a few degrees and descended to about a hundred feet. Then she skimmed the tree line until she could plainly see the Warren Raptor Center.

'Permission to land,' she whispered to nobody. Then, 'Permission granted.'

Max's night vision was superb, the moonlight as bright

to her as klieg lights would be to an ordinary person. The wildlife refuge was made up of a timbered administrative building with a little lawn in front and dirt paths leading from it.

At the edge of the sanctuary was a cluster of small screened-and-slatted pole barns that housed the raptors, the birds of prey.

Max dropped and braked on the cool, wet ground.

'Oz,' she called. 'Oz, you here? Of course you are. But where? Come out, come out wherever you are. C'mon, Oz. Oz?'

A barn owl called, *can-you-cook-for-meeee*. Max called back, 'I can cook for you.'

Then there was silence again.

'Oz? Don't play mind games with me. Not tonight. I'm scared. I'm really, really scared, Ozymandias. I *need* you, good buddy.'

'Max, I'm in the hawk house. Come on up here, you silly goose.'

CHAPTER THIRTY-ONE

I t was cozy and warm and, most important, safe in the low rafters of the hawk house.

Moonlight the color of butter slipped through the slatted roof, striping the faces of Max and Oz, who dangled their legs over the crossbeam and talked from their hearts.

'It's really good to see you,' Max whispered, and felt a lump in her throat.

'Good to be seen. But three in the morning? What's the matter? This better be good. And I'm sure it is, knowing you, Max.'

'We'll get to that. Maybe. I see that your friends are up late too. The hawks.'

The two red-tailed hawks that lived in the barn were perched nearby. The male, who was nearly blind, ruffled his feathers; and his mate, who had only one wing, moved closer to him. The hawks didn't mind their presence and Max found their sounds and smells comforting.

'*Cheeeeee,*' Oz called.

'*Cheeeeee,*' the male responded.

Max found herself smiling. Oz could be so gentle and sweet sometimes. Most of the time, actually.

She thought he had really changed since she had seen him last. He was small when they'd lived at the School. Now, although he was younger by a few months than Max, he was so much bigger. And stronger. The boyish twinkle was gone, the softness of his cheeks and jaw too. Jeez, Oz had grown into a real hunk. And she knew all about hunks, didn't she?

'Can I see your tattoo?' she asked.

'Yes. But then you have to tell me what scared you back at Bush League. You don't scare, Max.'

'Yeah, I do,' she said. 'So let me see your tat.'

Oz pulled up his black sweatshirt so that she could see the brown-and-red-and-yellow image of an American bald eagle depicted in full flight across his chest. The eagle held a shield in one talon and lightning bolts in the other. The motto, *Live Free or Die*, was etched underneath. It was magnificent.

'That is so damn cool,' said Max. 'Must've hurt like a bastard.'

Oz shrugged and said, '*This* one hurt.' He opened his palm and showed Max another tat. This one was an amateur job, clearly inked by Oz himself.

Max bent her head and read aloud: '*Ozymandias, King of Kings*. A little full of thyself, sire?' she asked.

'I mean it the way that poet Shelley meant it,' Oz said. 'Vanity means nothing, right. Even mighty Ozymandias,

Rameses II of Ancient Egypt, died and turned to dust. You ever wonder why I was given that name?'

'How can we understand anything they did at the fricking School?' Max said. 'Those nutjobs.'

'I still hate them so much. Can't stop hating,' Oz snapped. 'I wonder all the time what our lives would have been like if they hadn't messed with us. Sometimes I think we have more in common with these hawks than we have with people.'

'You're reading my mind,' Max said. 'Now *that's* scary. Brrrrr.'

'So what happened in lovely Bush League, I mean Pine Bush? Why did you want to see me?'

Max picked through a myriad of troubling thoughts before answering. This was going to be a *lit*-tle tricky. 'I took a boy on a flight,' she said. 'I know, *dumb*. The bastard felt me up. He really hurt my feelings, Oz. He rubbed up against me, and then he told me I was flat-chested. Like I didn't know already. Like I should care. Like I give two and a half shits. Which, obviously, I do.'

Oz shook his head and thought a few seconds before speaking. Very grown-up of him. 'I'm sorry that it happened, Max. But, honestly, I've been expecting something like this.'

Max couldn't believe what she'd heard. She searched Oz's face for an explanation. 'What are you talking about? *Honestly*, you've been *expecting* this?'

'That's what I said. Have you looked at yourself lately? You have any mirrors in that house?'

Max blinked her eyes rapidly. 'Sure,' she said. 'All the time. *And?*'

'You're beautiful, Max. You're gorgeous. You make Lara Croft *and* Angelina Jolie look like shit!'

Max felt a flush across her breastbone. The warm feeling shot through her veins and her stomach felt hollow, exactly the way it did when she did a barrel roll in the sky. Something a little weird was going on here. She wasn't ready for it. 'You need an eye exam, buddy.'

'One of us does,' said Oz. 'So what's really bothering you? Tell me true, Max.'

'You know already. Nothing. Everything. The kids at school can be unbelievably nasty, snide, cruel. You already know that. The press are even worse. They're clueless and they're everywhere we go. You know that, too.'

Oz grinned. 'Fox is filming us right now, Max. Sorry, I sold us out. I *needed* the cash. "Who Wants To Marry A Beautiful Girl With Wings?" '

Max stopped talking, and she looked around.

'Now *that* hurts my feelings. You thought, just for a nanosecond, that I might invite the sleazy press here.'

Max kissed Oz on the cheek. 'No, I didn't really. But yes, I am paranoid. I am very, very paranoid, Oz.'

You have no idea.

They sat there in the hawk house, neither of them saying a word for a moment or two. Usually that was okay, but right now it felt uncomfortable. She wanted to talk about Resurrection, the danger, but suddenly she couldn't get the words out. Maybe because she didn't want to drag Ozymandias into this mess.

'I have to go hunt,' Oz said finally. 'It's my nature.' He grinned.

'Now? I need to talk some more.'

'You can come with me. I'd like the company. But I *need* to hunt.'

Max had never hunted, and she didn't think she could. 'No, I'd better get going,' she said. 'It's almost morning.'

'Well, okay. I guess so. I wish you could stay. Safe home,' Oz said. 'I'm glad you came. I missed you.'

'Me too,' said Max.

'You're drop-dead gorgeous, Max. Live with it!'

'I'm a freak.'

'Gorgeous. You're a gorgeous freak. A beautiful creature.'

They hugged awkwardly. Then they hugged a second time, and Oz lightly kissed Max's cheek. Then they went their separate ways.

Max deeply regretted she hadn't talked about what was really bothering her, but she couldn't tell Oz about Resurrection yet. Why was that? Because she didn't want to put him in danger? Or was it that she didn't totally trust Oz in that area? He might get reckless. Try to be a hero. That was his nature, wasn't it? Oz *was* heroic, and heroes could get you hurt, or dead.

She flew home through a transcendent pink-and-baby-blue sunrise, but Max didn't much notice the sights.

Somebody knew about Resurrection. Somebody who really shouldn't. A snoopy reporter. A writer.

The horror-and-creep show was starting to warm up again, wasn't it?

Then Max felt the need to put her mind somewhere else, somewhere nice.

'*Oz thinks I'm beautiful,*' she whispered to the stars.

PART THREE

HOUSE CALLS

CHAPTER THIRTY-TWO

The Hospital

The place was jumping tonight. Doctors, nurses, dozens of gurneys on the move.

Seventeen-year-old James Lee nervously counted the passing fluorescent lighting panels in the dropped ceiling as the serious-faced, blue-gowned medical attendants rushed his gurney along the corridors of the Hospital. He was scared stiff, but also excited.

Dr Kane had already told him that he'd been selected to be a 'finalist'. 'Mr Lee, Mr Lee,' he'd said. 'You're a special young man. That's why we chose you. You have all the right stuff.'

'Do you have the tape I recorded?' Lee had asked. 'I need my tape for this.'

'We have it,' Dr Kane assured him. 'It's waiting for you in the OR. We wouldn't forget something like your tape. We're very buttoned-up here.'

'I've noticed that.'

James Lee clasped his fingers tightly together under the sheet so that his hands wouldn't shake. He licked his dry lips. He swayed against the sides of the gurney as it rounded a corner. Finally, the attendants arrived at the stainless-steel doors to the operating room. They opened with a loud *whoosh*. The gurney was wheeled forward, then parked parallel to an operating table.

'What, exactly, am I being operated on for?' James Lee asked.

'It's just a little exploratory operation, James. We're looking – *inside* you. Believe me, you won't feel a thing.'

The antiseptic smell was really strong in the operating theater, and the constant *pinging* sounds of medical equipment made everything a little too real. For a moment, James Lee's fear almost got the best of him. He had an impulse to say, 'Forget it. I've changed my mind.'

Then a deep voice directly above him said, 'On my count.'

He felt hands under him, two sets of strong male hands.

'One, two, three. Upsy-daisy, James.'

He was lifted easily on to the table and immediately covered with thin flannel sheets.

A nurse then swabbed the vein inside his left elbow with alcohol and pierced the skin with a needle. The IV drip began.

'You feeling okay, Mr Lee?'

It was Dr Kane, who always inspired supreme confidence in James. The doctor had a compact, muscular physique – even his hand felt hard and unyielding where he placed it on the young man's shoulder. The face looming above him was square and tanned beneath a blond brush cut. Intelligence radiated from the clear silver-blue eyes. Dr Kane was a real winner.

'I'm fine,' said James Lee as a nurse fitted a metal helmet over his shaved head. 'This really isn't going to hurt?'

'Not at all. Your tape is sensational, by the way. The best we've seen yet.'

CHAPTER THIRTY-THREE

James Lee couldn't believe what was happening inside his head. *Wow!* This was close to perfect. Just what he had imagined. Maybe even better! He clenched and unclenched his fists and prepared himself for his debut. This was the best!

He was on the stage of the world-famous Stardust Lounge in Las Vegas. In his mind anyway. But it felt as if he were really there.

And he was ready. Oh man, was he ready.

This was his tape! He'd been fantasizing about this exact scene for years! God, this was *exactly* what he'd had in mind.

Lee ran his small hands down the fitted bodice of his strapless white cocktail dress, and flounced the layered organza skirt. He pressed his freshly lipsticked lips together and touched his lacquered bouffant hairstyle. Everything was so right. So real.

Suddenly, a pin light in the ceiling came on and illuminated him with a small blue light. There was the rustling sound of people shifting in their seats and *ohs* of surprise coming from the audience. Hundreds of pairs of eyes were trained on him.

The opening notes from the orchestra rose from the pit and spilled on to the stage – followed by a dominant seventh chord that served as the transition from the intro to the main melody.

His tape was even better than he'd imagined. Fuller and richer.

James Lee heard the gasps and the moans of the audience as the stage lights blazed. Through the smoky haze, he could see friends and family who'd come to watch him perform. There was his mother smiling up at him from the front row. She'd always had faith in him. Man, he was about to prove himself to the one person who really loved him.

Lee slowly raised the mike to his mouth. Then, in a breathy Astrud Gilberto voice, he began a song made famous by the incomparable Brenda Lee.

'I'm sorry. So sorry . . . for treating you the way I did.'

Jesus, he sounded great too. The audience in the Stardust Lounge were eating him up. How could they not?

'Mr Lee? Jimmy?'

Someone was interrupting his performance. James Lee's head snapped around. It was a friendly, authoritative voice that seemed to speak *inside* his head!

'Ground control to James. Mr Lee, Mr Lee. Oh Mr Lee?'

Now he remembered. This was a medical procedure.

The stage show was all in his mind – just a distraction, but *what* a distraction. In some forgotten place, his naked body was lying on an operating table at the Hospital in Maryland.

'Yes,' James said. 'I hear you, Dr Kane. Now, *please* go away. You're ruining my performance.'

'Are you comfortable?'

'Yes, thank you. I'm in heaven,' he sighed.

'Not yet, but soon,' said Dr Ethan Kane. Then he whispered, 'Okay, shuck him.'

CHAPTER THIRTY-FOUR

D r Ethan Kane got to leave the Hospital early that
night; at least it was early for him. He decided to go
to his second home, which was out in the rolling, wooded
hills of Maryland, where he could have a little privacy.

Forty minutes later, as he climbed from his Mercedes at
the house, he heard the dogs start to bark and it brought
a rare and mischievous smile to his lips. 'Jesus, they're
well-trained animals. Keep out the riff-raff.'

He unlocked the front door of the large fieldstone
house and went inside. The dogs continued to bark.

A tall brunette woman wearing an apron over a
flowery blue dress emerged from the kitchen. She was
stunningly beautiful, and had the warmest, most open
smile this side of Ohio. 'Oh, you're home, Ethan. I'm so
happy. Your dinner will be ready at eight thirty. The
Washington Post and the *Wall Street Journal* are laid out
in the study, as is a Johnnie Black rocks. Go relax. You've
earned it.'

Ethan Kane never said a word to his wife, Juliette. He

didn't move to hug or kiss her. Instead, he pulled a compact black case from his pocket. It was similar to the locking device he used with the Mercedes, though considerably more complex.

Dr Kane pressed his forefinger to one of several buttons, and Juliette stopped talking immediately, stopped moving, shut down altogether. She just stood there frozen like a department store mannequin, in the center of the foyer.

'You're perfect, darling,' he muttered. 'The completely *evolved* woman. What would I do without you?'

Kane then pushed another button that turned off the barking of the dogs.

He walked to the study, where he read his favorite newspapers while he sipped his Scotch. Just past eight thirty he went into the kitchen and ate dinner: chicken marsala, fresh asparagus and broccoli rabe, risotto with morels, a sliver of apple crisp and cheddar cheese. All expertly prepared by Juliette.

Before he went upstairs, Dr Kane returned to the foyer and switched on the security alarms. He then turned Juliette back on.

'Hello, sweetheart,' she said and smiled demurely.

'Let's go up to bed, darling,' he whispered against her ear as she lightly stroked the front of his trousers. He put one hand on a pert, nicely rounded breast, the other between her legs. What waited there for him was the perfect *fit*. Kane knew that for certain. He'd measured.

'I need you, Ethan,' said Juliette – and there was that dazzling smile of hers again. 'You're such a wonderful lover.'

'*Carry* me up to bed, darling,' he whispered.

CHAPTER THIRTY-FIVE

Linda Schein's work desk faced a blank white wall without a single adornment. On purpose.

Her picture window afforded a stunning mountain view from her condo on Fourteenth Street near Market in Denver, but Linda couldn't handle the distraction when she was writing. And at the moment, she was drafting the story that would both make her career and make her rich.

As she typed on her laptop, Linda heard a creaky whine somewhere in the apartment. She ignored the sound.

She was in *the zone*, that rare and special creative state where time has no meaning and every word falls into place poetically and logically. The Resurrection Project story had incredible scope, scientific and ethical and religious implications. Potentially, it was more explosive than the original exposé of the School, and even the revelation of the bird-children themselves.

And it was *her* story.

No one else was even close to this. At least she hoped and prayed no one was. It was so ground-shaking she didn't mind having lied to Max about being abused as a child. Actually, her childhood in Ridgewood, New Jersey, had been splendid.

Linda imagined her story running serially in a major newspaper, ten or twelve installments of three thousand words or so spaced over a two-week period. She would pitch it to the *Washington Post*, the *New York Times*, *The Times* in London. Maybe *Time* and *Newsweek*, and *People*. Let them fight over her. Let them pay the big bucks. And then – *the Book*.

Linda drained her morning's fourth cup of coffee and blew a few pesky bangs off her forehead. She was polishing her lead, bracketing the letters TK where facts were still to come, and punching up the kicker.

She heard a squeak on the parquet floor in the foyer.

'Mrs Martinez?' She called out her housekeeper's name. 'Is that you? Hello there?'

Linda Schein felt a movement of air a fraction of a second before she felt something cold and hard at her temple. She took in a sharp breath.

Then she peeked, and almost wished she hadn't.

Gun.

'Be quiet, Linda. Do exactly as I say,' said a man's voice. Linda Schein soundlessly expelled the breath she'd inhaled a moment before. Her back muscles went slack.

She squelched the compulsion to cry out, or to struggle. She didn't turn her head any more than she had to see the *gun*. She hoped to God the intruder was wearing a mask because she didn't want to see his face. She suspected that her life depended on it.

'The only money here is in my purse,' she said. 'I'm not going to cause any trouble. I get the picture.'

'Well that's very good to hear. But I honestly don't know if I can believe you. My name is Dr Ethan Kane. You're writing a story about my life's work, so I thought we should talk. Hmmm? Shall we?'

Linda Schein felt total fear shoot through her body. He had *identified* himself. Oh God! Oh no!

Dr Ethan Kane.

The Resurrection Project.

'Am I supposed to know you?' she asked, pretending ignorance, trying to sidetrack him if she could.

'No, Linda. You're *not*. But you do. Now, let's talk.' He pressed the gun barrel harder against her temple. 'I want to hear everything.'

Linda Schein talked and talked until she realized she was repeating herself. 'That's fine,' Dr Kane finally said. 'I *believe* you, Linda. You *do* get the picture.'

There was a muffled explosion, then an intensely bright flash behind her eyes, and everything – her thoughts, her fantasies about fame, her fears of bodily violence – came to an end. The writer never knew that a nine-millimeter bullet had blown through her brain at about two thousand miles per hour.

'That didn't hurt, did it?' asked Dr Kane. 'Any more questions about my life's work? No? Well then, I guess we're through here. Excellent interview, Linda. Brief and right to the point. So rare with journalists today.'

CHAPTER THIRTY-SIX

M ax was up very late that night, getting absolutely nothing accomplished, futzing around in her room.

Anxious.

Uncomfortable.

Angry without reason.

Couldn't sit still.

Could not.

Sit.

Still.

She played her electric guitar, and she was getting pretty good. 'Watch out Sheryl Crow, Eric Clapton, B.B. King.'

Then she was 'down with' a Tony Hawk video game – skateboarding at its best.

Max went online, played a game of cribbage with a girl from San Diego. Her screen name was UPDRAFTGURL38.

She won at cribbage.

Of course.

She wrote in her journal, her *third* journal since she'd been at the Marshall house.

Current Likes	*And Dislikes*
Leather pants (all colors)	N'Sync
Buffy	*Chicken Soup for the Teenage Soul*
Mary Karr	*Bag of Bones*
'Firestarter'	Reality TV
'Under Rug Swept'	Sunday nights on CBS
Shania, Fiona, Sheryl	Reporters who lie their asses off
'The pellet with the poison's in the vessel with the pestle'	Righteous reporters who think they tell the truth, but lie
Watermelon lip gloss	The 'Mummy' movies
Josiah Bartlet	The way 'Moms' try too hard
The Flock	Bush League, Colorado
Especially Ozymandias!	Men's professional sports
Frannie and Kit!	The kids at school (most of them)

Max stopped writing her crazy, dumb, self-involved gibberish and cocked her head slightly. She heard a noise outside. Something just slightly out of sync with the other sounds of the night.

The wind?

Someone calling her name? Oz?

Come fly with me, Max.

Maybe it was time for another strictly forbidden night flight.

She picked up her cell phone, then put it down again.

She heard another noise outside.

Definitely not the wind. Something that really sucked.

Hunters!

CHAPTER THIRTY-SEVEN

Ethan Kane personally led the small team of three down the leaf-strewn slope of brambles and underbrush behind the house on Ames Road where the Marshalls lived. They all wore seamless black clothes and black ball caps; greasepaint smeared their faces. Even in moonlight, they seemed more like shadows than real men.

They had come for the two children, but the others in the house would probably have to die. They shouldn't take chances on detection. Not with Resurrection so close.

Ethan Kane held up his hand, a signal to the others to stop. 'Max and Matthew are very fast. They're also strong, and clever. Please don't underestimate them. In fact, don't think of them as children,' he said in an undertone.

Kane turned and studied the Marshall house. An unimpressive, slightly depressing ranch house. Dark at midnight. Not even a television glow at a single window.

This *might* be easier than he'd expected. They had no logical reason to have their guard up. Kane hadn't bothered to bring in professionals like Marco Vincenti. He felt he could trust his team tonight; he wasn't so sure about Mr Vincenti. He wanted the kids alive – for a while anyway.

He had his reasons. Extraordinarily good reasons that only he understood.

He signaled again, and the others fanned out around a jungle gym, then the brick patio and fireplace in the backyard. 'Just watch the house. I'll do the work inside,' he whispered.

Dr Ethan Kane walked directly to the mudroom door. He opened the lock with a twist and turn of a thin L-shaped pick.

Then he made his way silently through the mudroom to the kitchen, and to the stairs that led to the bedrooms.

He reached into a pocket in his jacket and took out a black case that held several syringes.

Silently, he climbed the stairs. The girl's room was on the right, the boy's on the left. Matthew and Max. The biological parents were in the master bedroom at the end of the hall. Terry and Art.

You talk, he said to himself, *you die. Or at least you get sold to the Chinese.*

Whatever the cost in human lives – Resurrection was worth it. And so were these amazing, amazing children – who could fly like eagles.

He gently pushed open the door to the girl's room. This

was it. The moment of truth. As he entered the room a flashlight beam *blinded him!*

'What the hell?' he muttered.

'You got that right, pal.'

Almost simultaneously, someone crashed into him, took the wind right out of Dr Kane's sails, nearly dislocated his shoulder.

My God, it was the girl! It was Maximum herself! Strong as a horse!

'Run, Matthew, run!' Max called out. 'They've come for us. I knew they would.'

But the two of them didn't run.

They flew!

Straight down the upstairs hallway and out an open window, like a pair of guided missiles.

'Don't shoot the little bastards.' Kane issued a fierce command. 'Catch them! Don't let them get away! Bring them back to me. Alive!'

CHAPTER THIRTY-EIGHT

'I'm really, *freezing* cold,' Matthew whispered to Max a few moments later. 'I'm fricking shivering. I'm mad as hell too. What was that about? Who were they? Who *are* they? What's happening to us, Max? Do I want to hear the answer to these questions?'

He and his sister were in their flannel PJs, huddled together in the top of a wobbly fir tree. They were maybe two hundred yards away from the Marshall house, fifty feet off the ground. Max figured they were pretty much invisible from the searching eyes below.

'Shhhh, Matty!' She was still panting from fear, still pretty much in shock herself.

The men were inside the house. The hunters. Were the Marshalls safe from them?

Or had they been put to sleep? Please, God, don't let that have happened. Please protect Art and Terry, Max prayed. *Please, oh please. I do love them.*

As she watched, a plain black panel van pulled up to the house. Her eyes followed the four men who crept from the shadows around the house. The tallest was holding his arm against his body and limping. *Good, she'd hurt his sorry ass. Good, good, good. Shame he could still walk.*

The men got into the vehicle, and it raced away. They were retreating.

'They were trying to kill us, weren't they, Max? To put us to sleep? Those worthless bastards. Those lousy, crummy shitheads.'

'I think so, Matty. I guess they were. OK, yeah, they were trying to kill us.'

She hugged Matthew so hard that he protested. 'Hey! That hurts. Jeez, Max. You know how strong you are. First you save me from the baddies. Then you almost kill me yourself.'

'Very funny. Glad you haven't lost your very strange sense of humor.'

Max gave him a big kiss and released her grip. Then she turned on her handheld and clicked to an Internet application. Oz was online.

Max sent him an instant message, one she hoped couldn't be captured or traced.

'SOS,' Max typed. 'Leave home NOW. Get Ic, NOW. As in NOW.'

'Meet at the Mine?' Ozymandias came right back to her.

'K,' Max affirmed. 'CU soon.'

Max and Matthew zipped back to the Marshall house to get their gear and check to see that everybody was all right. Amazingly, Art and Terry had slept through it all.

Then they did what Max had known they were going to do sooner or later – *they flew the coop.*

CHAPTER THIRTY-NINE

The old rutted roads that once led to the Mine near Prairie Divide had been totally consumed by the encroaching forest. Now it was only accessible from the air.

That worked.

Oz and Icarus ran out of the Mine entrance as Max and Matthew dropped out of the dark night sky. There was a flurry of excited but nervous greetings.

'I'm free, I'm free!' Icarus kept saying over and over. 'And a blind man shall lead them! I *am* that blind man!'

Max noticed that Ic had grown since she had last seen him. His white-blond hair was shoulder-length and he was almost as tall as she was. His sightless blue-gray eyes seemed to actually focus as he picked Matthew up and held him.

'Put me down, Icky!' her brother yelped. 'I'm not a fricking baby any more. I'm grown up!'

Breathlessly, Max told Oz and Ic about the men who'd broken into the Marshall house with murder or mayhem on their minds.

'I think one or more of them were doctors. It's a feeling I had,' said Max.

'It's starting all over again,' said Ic. 'We should go get the twins. The little ones aren't safe either. Damn, we should go get them now, this instant.'

'They're doing *cereal* commercials,' Matthew said. 'They're probably safe.'

Max raised her voice. 'They're *not* safe.'

There was no further dissent, so, with some agitated warbles and whistles, they took off one at a time, falling into formation at two hundred feet. They headed southeast toward the town of Fort Lupton, where Peter and Wendy lived with their biological parents, and were supposedly *safe*.

CHAPTER FORTY

The flight was so much different from the one Max had taken just two nights before. Everything had changed. She took no pleasure in the moonlight or the play of light and shadow on the forest below. As the eldest by a couple of months, she was the leader of the flock, and the others looked to her and to Oz for guidance. Max had already figured it might be hard to take the twins from their home. They were still babies really, hard to predict, hard to control.

But it had to be. There was no alternative.

Someone was coming for them.

They passed over the little town of Fort Lupton and soon neared the Chen farmhouse. It sat on a knoll a quarter of a mile up a driveway, at the end of a narrow dirt road. Their closest neighbor was more than half a mile away.

A perfect place for murder, Max thought. *Or capture. Or whatever the creeps in black are up to.*

She and the boys landed in a clump of pines that gave

them a clear view of the farmhouse.

A flagstone path, which bisected the front lawn, led up to a wraparound porch that was full of wicker furniture and shaped three sides of the house.

Oz pointed to the Garfield the Cat doll stuck to one of the upstairs windows. 'Wendy loves that dumb cat.'

'Okay,' said Max, nodding. 'That's their room. I'll go up. I don't want them to be frightened yet.'

Max flew to the porch roof, landing softly. Then she crept over to the twins' bedroom window.

It was unlocked. *Uh-oh.* She opened the casement window and began to climb inside.

Please don't let me be too late.

'Boo! Hey, Max,' said Peter. 'We saw you coming a mile away.'

'Heard ya too,' chorused Wendy.

If Max had worried that she would have to convince Peter and Wendy to join them, she was wrong. The four-year-olds grabbed her, hugged and kissed her, and trembled with happiness. There was a blowup of one of their cereal ads spanning the twin beds. *Disgusting*, Max thought. *Makes me want to start a war with Battle Creek.*

'Oh, wow, a night flight,' said Peter. 'Let's skedaddle.'

'A *flock* flight, we're going on a flock flight!' Wendy whooped.

There was a pounding on the wall. Then the muffled voice of Warren Chen. 'Knock it off, Peter and Wendy. You kids go to sleep right now! You know you have an important film shoot in the morning.'

'We're stars,' Peter whispered, and winked.

Max froze. She listened to her heart pounding. She waited until she was sure no footsteps could be heard outside the room. Then she helped Peter and Wendy dress and pack. Carefully, quietly, quickly.

Moments later, they were crouched on the porch roof. Shades of *Peter Pan*. Kind of cool, kind of crazy, kind of nuts.

Wendy whispered, 'Where are we going?'

'It's a secret,' Max whispered back.

They pushed off into the clear black night and followed Max's lead.

'*It's a secret!*' shouted little Peter and Wendy. '*It's a big secret*.'

CHAPTER FORTY-ONE

They were elated to be together again – the flock!
The tribe!

The family!

Just like it had been for a few precious months at the
Lake House.

They did fancy aerobatics high above the snow-dusted
woodland. Their innocent laughter floated clear and wide
for miles and miles around. They were a miracle to watch.
Better than any show the US Air Force had ever dreamed
up, or ever would.

Matthew, at the advanced age of nine, led the 'junior
squadron' in dive bombs and incredible triple-barrel
rolls. He took the twins on a chase over and around a
distressed pair of horned owls who were hunting. Oz
and Ic were also having the time of their lives. Because
he was blind, Ic needed Oz to help him 'see'. The kids
had developed a verbal code or flight language to guide
Icarus.

Chee-rup meant fly straight; *caw* was turn left; *cree* was the signal to turn right. A *talondrop* was a free-fall, feet first, and nothing in 'bird talk' satisfactorily replaced the fantastic power of the words 'climb' and 'dive'.

The kids combined some of the words together. *Caw-roll* meant roll to the left and *Chee-rup-te-rup-te-rup* meant to fly up and down like a roller coaster. When they were relaxed and gliding, Oz and Ic exchanged short whistles and tongue clacks and hoots, or sometimes they sang the lyrics to 'Bad to the Bone' and 'My Sharona'.

Max was filled with pride. They had survived the sick hellhole of the School, where they were forced to work in the labs, kept in cages, and lived under the constant fear of being put to sleep. Until last year, they had never ridden in a car or gone to a movie or a city, and they had never, never done what they were made to do.

They had never spread their wings to fly!

As she was having the brief happy thought, mischievous Matthew's enthusiasm overflowed. 'Snacks for the road,' he called out in a squeaky-high voice. 'Who's hungry as hound dogs?'

Matthew had spotted a 7-11 convenience store on the highway that ran through the town of Lyons. Blinding neon green and orange glowed up at them. He whistled to the twins, and they shot toward the inviting open doors like arrows toward a bull's eye.

All Max could do was yell, 'No! Guys! *No way!* Please, stop! Don't do this!'

She might just as well have saved her breath.

She watched helplessly as the kids buzzed the store shelves, spilling and knocking over jars and cans in their wake.

'Ring Dings!' Wendy shouted, grabbing a couple of packets of the chocolate cakes from the rack.

Peter hovered in front of the salty snack section before selecting a giant-sized package of Cheez Doodles corn puffs.

Matthew ripped off a box of Cracker Jack candied popcorn and some Tostitos tortilla chips. Finally they flew shrieking joyously out of the store, leaving the wide-eyed, grunged-out teenaged boy at the cash register bedazzled, and befuddled.

'Never again,' Max scolded when they'd gotten back into flight formation. 'What you did is stealing and that's wrong, wrong, wrong. That poor boy is going to have to clean up your mess.'

'We'll be good, Max,' Peter said, licking orange crumbs from his lips. 'Pinky swear. We'll be good *from now on.*'

Max wanted to smile, but she couldn't. She wasn't worried about the petty theft so much as she was about the fact that they'd been seen.

Now there was a witness only twenty or so miles from Bear Bluff.

And Frannie's house.

CHAPTER FORTY-TWO

I was having a pity party on the back porch of my place, with a nicely chilled bottle of Turning Leaf Chardonnay at my elbow, when I heard the phone ring. *Screw it*. I didn't pick up.

My medical emergency calls were being shunted over to my relief, Dr Monghil, in Clayton, the next town west. Right now I felt too low to inflict my blues on some innocent caller, whoever it might be.

I sat just soaking up the atmosphere: the crickets, the blinking stars and the all-you-can-drink vino, when the phone rang again, and now it really tweaked me.

World.

Leave me the hell alone.

Then I heard a police siren in the distance.

Now what?

I left my wine on the porch and went inside. I'd just about rewound the answering machine when I heard the infernal siren come to a stop. *This bud was for me*. I ran outside.

I saw a bright torchlight come shining through the woods. It was Trooper Brian McKenna. I called out, 'Hey, Mac.'

'Hey, Frannie. I *thought* you were here. Why didn't you answer your phone? You had me worried.'

'I punched out for the night,' I said. 'What's up?'

'The kids are missing,' said Mac, putting one heavily shod foot on the porch step and his meaty hand on the railing. Big Mac had tried to date me, too, and he was *married*. 'You know anything about that? I hope that you don't, Frannie.'

A shudder passed through me. '*Missing?* What do you mean? Who's missing?'

'All of them, Frannie. They're all gone, the six of them just vanished. Do you have them here, or have any knowledge of where they are? If you do, tell me, and that'll pretty much put an end to any kind of trouble for you.'

'I don't have them here, Mac,' I said. 'And I haven't heard a word from any of them.'

'Mind if I take a look inside?' the trooper asked.

'That hurts my feelings. But knock yourself out,' I said. 'Jeez, Mac.'

He gave me a sidelong glance that told me he disapproved of my attitude, or maybe I was slurring my words, I wasn't sure which. I definitely wasn't drunk, but I had made some progress in pain management. Still, I was stunned by the news! I talked to the kids a couple of times every week. Although I missed them terribly, I had lulled myself into thinking that they were safe, if not happy. That dull comfort had just evaporated.

I followed the serious young statie into my house and watched him poke around. When he was satisfied that I didn't have six young children under the bed or in the washer-dryer, he apologized for any rudeness and asked me to please stay in touch.

'If you hear from or see those kids, call me, Frannie. Beep me or you can talk to anyone at the barracks, okay? The parents are frantic.'

'I understand.' I actually did. I felt frantic myself.

The trooper touched the brim of his hat and went back down the wooded path toward the road.

The little buzz I'd been cultivating was completely gone. I had been lonely and self-pitying a few minutes ago. Now I was sick to my stomach and too scared for words.

There was only one person I could truly depend on for advice and solace right now.

And that would be Kit.

CHAPTER FORTY-THREE

I threw on every light in the kitchen, and I had no real idea why I did it. *Because I was scared?*

The tap was dripping, so I wrenched the knob to stop the relentless *pinging* in the stainless-steel sink. I slammed a couple of cabinet doors shut, then I perched on the edge of a stool.

I took a few deep breaths, then finally pressed buttons on the cordless phone.

I listened to the ringing sound in my ear.

It was half past midnight, so I wasn't surprised that I caught Kit at home sleeping. Happily for me, he recognized my voice and didn't hang up. I said as much.

'Why would I hang up on you, Frannie?'

Well, the last time I'd actually *seen* Kit had been after the custody trial in Denver. The way I remember it, he was trying to comfort me and I ran off in the Suburban without so much as a goodbye. Our phone conversation afterwards had been heartbreakingly short. *Let's take a break, yada-yada. We need to heal. If it's meant to be, it will be*. We'd both been too wounded to actually deal with each other. We hadn't spoken since I sent his things back by UPS.

'I just heard that the kids are missing, Kit. All of them! A state trooper was here and told me all six of them are gone.'

There was a pause and I knew that Kit was in shock, thinking of all the horrible possibilities just as I had done. Why would the kids run away together? Why now? Where would they go? But worst of all, had someone kidnapped them?

I was completely unprepared when Kit said, 'I know, Frannie. I couldn't tell you so I'm glad the local cops came by.'

'You *what*?' I actually yelled into the phone receiver. 'You *knew* about this?'

'I couldn't tell you. I wasn't allowed to call. I was forbidden under orders from the director.'

I just *hated* it when Kit went FBI on me.

'You jerk,' I said. 'You seriously thought it was better for me to hear this from a stranger? Oh, never mind,' I said.

Then I hung up on him.

CHAPTER FORTY-FOUR

I sat on the kitchen stool, holding a dead phone in my hand and fuming at Kit. I was really hot, *and* hurt. I stared at the Colorado State Wildlife calendar over my stove for a while. Pretty pictures, but they didn't help. I had to get out of the house or go crazy.

I took my denim Carhart jacket off the back of a chair and put it on. Then I whistled for Pip. 'You want to walk with me, little guy?' He couldn't believe his luck.

We set out on a trail that runs along the top of a ravine. Fortunately the moon was almost full, so we had plenty of light.

Pip ran up and down the gully snorting and chuffing. I could hear various four-footed beasts scurry deeper into the woods at the sounds of my footsteps on the forest floor.

Then I heard rustling in the trees overhead.

An image of a bobcat came full into my mind. I froze at the thought of a ninety-pound cat somewhere in the skinny branches right above my head. Not good. Very bad, actually.

There was more rustling up there. My knees went a little weak. Then a voice I recognized.

'Hey there, Frannie. How's life on the planet?'

First Max jumped down from the thick, overhanging branches. Then out came Matthew, Ic, Oz, and the twins. Everybody was hugging me at once. Wendy kept saying, 'Mama, Mama, it's you, Mama!' My heart was melting. Nothing I could do to stop it, not that I really wanted to.

The pack of us finally separated, and we scrambled, jogged and literally flew back to my cabin. We celebrated with hot chocolate and cookies, pineapple chunks for Wendy and Peter. I couldn't take my eyes off the little feathered wunderkinds.

I was so relieved to have them in my kitchen, each one alive and well. I mentally counted their fingers and toes. I kissed their sweet faces again and again. And I wondered, what was I going to do now?

After dessert, Max was still hungry. 'I've had a really long night,' she said, laughing. 'I could eat a rhino. But pasta with marinara will have to do.'

Max knew her way around my kitchen and insisted on doing the cooking. She took a large pot from the pegboard over the stove, filled it with water and put it on the burner. Ozymandias located a jar of red sauce in the pantry. Matthew started chopping parsley.

They were home again, home again. God, it was sweet. The best stuff on earth.

As Max and the crew cooked pasta, she told me why they had run away. With disturbing nonchalance, she described the armed men in black who'd broken into the Marshall house. She used a line from a recent movie poster: 'Same planet, different scum.'

I wasn't laughing. I was shocked, horrified, chilled to the bone. I asked Max point-blank if she knew *why* someone was after them.

She shrugged, then said, 'Because we're priceless works of art? Who knows? Let's leave it at that, Frannie.'

At about two a.m. Wendy and Peter and Matthew and Pip finally fell asleep on my bed. I put Max under a quilt on the sofa, threw blankets and pillows down on the floor for tough guy Oz. Ic tucked himself into the linen closet, which was where he felt most secure. I kissed everybody goodnight.

Once they were asleep, I knew I had to give some serious thought to the situation. Six extremely frightened kids were in my house, and they were on the run from someone who apparently wanted to harm, or possibly sell them. Who? And why, why, why?

Trooper McKenna had told me to call him, but I hadn't done it. Past experiences had taught me not to trust people just because they had badges or even positions with the government.

The FBI was involved.

If Kit couldn't tell me about the kids, could I tell him?

I fell asleep on that thought.

PART FOUR

YELLOW BRICK ROAD

CHAPTER FORTY-FIVE

The Hospital

Kristin Morgan was a senior medical technician who had one job only, but she figured that it made her an important, if small, part of medical history. In fact, her perspective on herself had given rise to her nickname, 'Cog'.

She was in charge of the Scoop, a streamlined titanium instrument with Porsche-like curves and sensitive calibrations, which, like an expensive car, needed constant fine-tuning. Cog was responsible for the Scoop's performance and maintenance, and it would be her neck if anything went wrong with this state-of-the-art technotool. And that was no joke at the Hospital.

A faint, rather sexy *hum* announced the Scoop's entrance into the operating theater and its movement along the grooved track in the ceiling.

Cog, anonymous in her cap, mask, and blue cotton

scrubs, followed below the Scoop as it made the first leg of its journey.

It finally came to rest above the naked body of Raoul Ramirez, an eighteen-year-old boy from Coral Gables, Florida.

Raoul's body had been split in a long H: the incisions cut from throat to groin and across the clavicles and the pelvis. Then the gaping cavity had been clamped wide open. The ribs were spread, and the organs, severed from the connective tissues, were laid bare.

Cog reached up and took hold of the Scoop's two lateral handles, which looked like the handlebars of a bicycle. She tried not to think about the person once known as Raoul Ramirez.

This was science, she told herself. It was important, necessary, and it was happening all around the world, but especially in China and Japan. It was essential that the United States keep up, and, ultimately, surpass other countries, wasn't it?

The Scoop was important, and so was Cog.

She guided the hydraulic Scoop's jaw to a precise position over the youth's torso. Checking by eye and correcting by judgment, she cranked open the Scoop's jaws, then lowered and fitted the titanium teeth under Raoul's internal organs. She adjusted the jaws so that the enclosed viscera wouldn't slip or break apart. Then she locked the machine's glittering maw and flicked a switch in the stem.

With a well-oiled hum, the Scoop grabbed hold of the

connected 'package' of organs and lifted them out. In medical lingo, Raoul's carcass was now a 'canoe'.

She threw another switch and followed the Scoop as it once again traveled along its track and through an opening to an adjacent room called 'the baths'.

To Cog, the baths resembled a photo-development lab. A long stainless-steel sink took up one wall, and in the center of the room was a gray metal table. On the table were three rectangular stainless-steel basins, ten inches deep, and filled with fluid.

The Scoop hummed along the track until it came to a shuddering stop over Basin 1.

Cog reached up and lowered the machine so that it was fully submerged. Satisfied with the procedure thus far, she opened the Scoop and inserted tubes into the severed ends of the two major arteries. She then opened the guillotine clamps in both the vena caval artery and the femoral artery.

Blood poured from the femoral artery and was conveyed into a waste canister, while a short-term oxygen source loaded with a plaque-cleaning enzyme flowed through the vena cava to the organs. When the heart and lungs and other organs were shining pink from the infusion of the oxygenated solution, she clamped off the arteries again. She closed the Scoop's hungry jaws.

The Scoop lifted the organ package and repositioned it over Basin 2. This container held a different enzymatic solution, a cloudy soup biologically tailored to seek and destroy fat nodules, blood, and any stray strands of connective tissues.

She let the package soak in the cleanser. In some cases she would manually strip fat from the liver and the heart.

But Raoul had been young and his organs were lean. He'd been a beautiful specimen, actually. A real hunk of chocolate.

Cog watched the Scoop rise out of Basin 2. This time she lowered it into Basin 3. As the 'canoe' soaked in a potent solution of saline infused with neural stem cells, ultrasound stimulated the nervous system with high-frequency sound waves. The stem cells, originally harvested from fetal tissue and then cloned, attached themselves to the severed nerve bundles, invigorating the nerve endings preparatory to reconnection.

Kristin Morgan breathed out a sigh of satisfaction. The process had gone well. After 'the package' was transferred to the blue room, she would carefully dismantle and disinfect the Scoop. There could be no danger of malfunction or infection in the next procedure, which was to take place not too long from now, actually.

Cog would soon forget about Raoul Ramirez, just as she'd forgotten about all the others before him.

Hundreds of donors.

All of them murdered in this very room.

CHAPTER FORTY-SIX

Dawn hadn't yet broken through the thick tree cover in the woods around Bear Bluff, Colorado. The air had a bracing crisp chill.

Dr Ethan Kane leaned against a tree trunk and cursed. He had to stop to massage the bruise on his right thigh where the little bastard girl had dared kick him. He had another deep bruise on his forearm. He was sure it had gone to the marrow.

The pain served as a lesson to remind him that he had underestimated the girl. She was a superior being, wasn't she? Well, now he knew.

He sucked on a brutally refreshing Altoids as he watched Frannie O'Neill's cabin through the best of the new German-made binoculars.

He was more than two hundred yards away, but he could clearly see the veterinarian. It was as if he were standing just outside the bitch's window.

He wondered if she got up this early every morning, or if maybe she'd had a premonition that this was the day she was going to die. *It was,* Dr Kane knew. *She was a dead woman; she just didn't know it.*

He could read the time on the stove clock: 4:22.

His own watch, a Breitling Aerospace #270, read the same. Dr O'Neill was careful about keeping the precise time. Probably careful about a lot of things.

All was quiet on the western front, he chuckled to himself. *Soon he could get back to his important work at the Hospital.*

His two-man teams were deep in the woods, positioned to watch the doors on the north and south sides of the cabin. Each member had a Motorola handheld radio, infrared goggles, a tool with assorted blades and cutters, and a GPS locator that could pinpoint just about any spot on planet Earth.

Dr Ethan Kane mentally reviewed his game plan. The team would *not break into* the cabin because it left too much room for confusion and failure. That much he'd learned. The children were frightfully strong, fast, and clever. They seemed to combine all the best characteristics of human and avian life.

Instead, they would stay in the woods. At the ready. This time there would be no painful mistakes.

When the children eventually left the house, the teams would simply grab them.

One bird-brat at a time.

CHAPTER FORTY-SEVEN

I think I slept for about a half-hour, but I really couldn't be sure. Maybe I was down for a whole hour. Suddenly, my eyes were wide open. And I knew there was trouble.

Nine-year-old Matthew was beside me, shaking my arm, staring at me in total horror.

'What is it, Matt?'

'There are some creepy sickos outside in the woods. Even Pip doesn't hear them. They're the ones who broke into our house in Pine Bush. Yes, *I'm sure*, Frannie. I can smell them. They smell of death. They're bad to the bone. Trust me on it.'

Terror flooded my body. If adrenaline were rocket fuel, I'd have been halfway to the moon. We were totally exposed, vulnerable! My cabin had a dozen or so windows, no curtains at all. I now knew that I had been stupid. Instead of a reunion with the kids last night, I should have called for help. *Or I should have run with them. We should have run!*

'Stay right here,' I whispered to Matthew. 'Stay here,

you superscout. Don't stand up or go anywhere near the windows.'

'Do I look that *dumb*?' Matthew retorted.

'Nope. So stay *down*.'

I sat on the floor and hurriedly dressed in yesterday's clothes. Then I heard Pip's toenails click on the hardwood floor. In a second, he located me, danced around on his hind legs.

'Hush,' I admonished him. 'You blew it, bub. Some watchdog you are.'

We crawled together to the kitchen. I went directly to the wall where the cordless phone was mounted.

I walked my fingers up the Sheetrock and patted around the cradle. Then I went into denial, unwilling to believe what my fingers were telling me.

The phone was missing!

The cradle was empty!

Where the hell was the phone? Where was the damned phone? What the hell? Were they in the house right now?

I held in a scream, but a tiny moan escaped from my mouth. Then I crawled along the floor, reached up and touched the countertop with my hand.

I found the sugar bowl, but knocked over the salt-shaker. *Damn it!*

Then my fingers closed on the cordless – right where I'd left it after talking with Kit. Talk about relief.

I pressed a button on the receiver.

There was no dial tone. Nothing at all.

Maybe the batteries were dead. It really didn't fucking

matter. I was up shit creek without a paddle. Six little kids were in the badly leaking boat with me. I was in the *panic room*, wasn't I? I wasn't Jodie Foster.

That was when I stood up in the kitchen.

And that was when I felt a hand on my leg and nearly screamed.

'Try this.' It was Max, pressing a cell phone into my hand.

I heaved a sigh of relief. The battery light was green – a full charge. 'Thanks,' I whispered.

Another shadow crept into the kitchen. Ozymandias the Brave. Looking as if he were ready to do war.

'They're moving on us, Frannie,' he reported. 'The cowards are coming closer to the house. We can fight them! We can win, too! Don't doubt it for a nanosecond.'

'Max, get all the kids together. You too, Oz. Get your coats. Take everyone and go down to the cellar quietly. And *crawl*. Don't fly. *Do not fly.*'

Hiding in the cellar was only a stopgap. If we stayed there, we'd be rounded up. And killed? I had another idea, though. It's been said that pressure makes diamonds. If so, my idea was a real gem.

And like all good gems, the price would be dear.

CHAPTER FORTY-EIGHT

I knew what I had to do, and I hated it more than drinking a quart of castor oil straight up and full to the brim. It made me unbelievably mad, and also inconsolably sad.

Maybe a little nuts, too.

This had to be one of the worst moments of my life, *and it hadn't even happened yet*.

I was also angry at Kit for not being here to help me. Maybe he could have come up with another, better plan. *Damn you, Kit*.

I crouched low behind the children as they filed down the stairs into the cellar. The twins were wild-eyed and hootering, distressed at being roused so suddenly from the comfort zone of sleep.

Max put her hands on each of their heads to silence them. 'Chill,' she whispered.

'I'll be right there!' I told her. 'Don't do anything crazy. I'll join you guys in a couple of minutes.'

I hoped it was a promise I could keep.

The brilliant early-morning sun was slanting through the windows. My hands were shaking some. Before sentiment could get its hooks into me, I did *the unspeakable*.

I took a really sharp carving knife to my sofa. I slashed the cushions until the frame was covered with feathers and goose down.

Next I piled the magazines from the coffee table on top of the ruined sofa. *Shit, shit, shit. This hurt. It really sucked.*

I looked around the living room, at the books and mementos of my marriage to Dr David Mekin: the model boat he'd constructed, signed and dated; our wedding photo on the mantel. I couldn't stop the flood of memories: nestbuilding, long evenings spent before the fire, lovemaking, and even fights that we worked through.

I pulled myself together and crawled to the hall closet. I swiftly stood and pulled down sheaves of my murdered husband David's old medical journals from the top shelf. I hadn't been allowed to throw them out while he was alive, and I hadn't wanted to throw them out after he died. David had been a medical researcher, and a good one. He had found out too much about the School a few years back, and the bastards had killed him. They did that sort of thing, and right now, someone appeared ready to pursue me and inflict mayhem. *Poor David,* I thought. *Poor kids. Poor me.*

Tears automatically welled in my eyes. I remembered seeing David's sheet-covered corpse on a stainless-steel slab. The horrible pain of his loss. After he was murdered, I'd moved out of the cabin we'd shared and into a spare room at the Inn-Patient. It was too painful to live with his artifacts and my memories. Then I discovered Max in the woods. After I'd gained her trust she took me and Kit to meet the other kids. When the bastards from the School found me, they burned down my animal hospital. Nothing remained but charred timbers. I was able to rebuild with insurance money. I'd re-established tenancy of my old cabin in the woods.

Well, it looked like it was time to move again – only this time I was pretty sure Nationwide wouldn't be picking up the tab.

A dozen Duraflame logs were stacked high next to the wood-burning stove. They would do just fine.

I tossed the flammable logs on to the mountain of magazines and feathers and added a kitchen stool for good measure.

I steeled myself to do what *had to be done*.

I touched a match to the pyre. The flame sputtered innocently enough, then caught with a flash.

I watched tendrils of smoke curl up toward the peak of the cathedral ceiling, and when the fire was burning well I took the cell phone from my pocket and made the call.

'*Please help me,*' I said, with genuine urgency. 'There's a house on fire in the woods behind the Inn-Patient animal hospital. Yes, right on Highway 34. Please hurry!'

I put on my jacket, grabbed and tucked a whimpering Pip under my arm. I was crying as I got ready to leave my burning house.

CHAPTER FORTY-NINE

I was also mad as hell, absolutely furious, bent on revenge *somehow, some way.* There was always a way.

I ran down the steep stair slats before second thoughts could slow me. It was totally dark in the cellar.

It took me several seconds to get my bearings.

I could hear scraping and dragging, and I went toward the sound. *Scraping, scraping, scraping.*

The kids were working, lifting and moving really heavy boxes and furniture. I mean incredibly heavy stuff.

With shock, I realized there was all sorts of old junk piled up in front of the cellar doors – our exit was blocked. And it only got worse. I looked back toward the stairs and saw smoke starting to seep under the door to the cellar. I hadn't expected the fire to get here so fast.

What a trap I'd set for us!

We would all die down here.

We'd be burned to death.

I had started the fire!

I waded into the fray and helped Oz, Max, and

Matthew move a bed frame and dozens of cartons of books away from the cellar door. We moved a couple of old dressers as well.

'Stronger than you look, lady,' Max said and smiled encouragement my way.

A bolt locked the door, but I was able to bang it off with a couple of blows from a sledgehammer.

Suddenly, an alarm went off upstairs! Then another!

Really loud! Screeching!

'It's just a fire, don't worry about it,' I told the kids. *I'm burning down my house.*

CHAPTER FIFTY

I listened to the piercing wail of the smoke detector with a mixture of sadness and satisfaction. When the timbered walls caught it would create a smokescreen outside, the diversion we needed. At least I hoped so. *But God, at what cost!*

The cellar doors were of the hatch type and the hinges were rusted from the weather. We put our shoulders and backs to them and pushed. The doors creaked open. I'd forgotten how incredibly strong Max and Oz were, especially Oz, who was really impressing me in all ways.

The hatch doors lie nearly flat to the ground on the east side of the house, about fifteen yards from a ravine. The ravine averages about ten feet deep, is lined with dramatic and striated rocks dripping with moss, and under normal conditions makes a nice little nature walk.

Now I saw the ravine as a long chute to safety. That was my prayer.

There had been *no way* we would escape – but now

there was. The fire, the smoke, all the distractions had worked so far. Now if we were just a little lucky . . .

Wendy was scared and crying. I couldn't blame her. I wanted to cry, too. I slowly stuck my head out of the hatch doors and looked around. I listened. No footsteps. No gunshots. I ducked back in and took Wendy in my arms and hugged her tightly.

'Mama!' she wheezed.

Damn it. See? I was their mother. The only mother they would ever have.

'It's okay, baby,' I whispered against Wendy's ear. 'We're going to get out of this. Somehow.'

Then, with Pip racing beside me, I sprinted to the lip of the ravine and slid down to the bottom on my butt. The children followed, Oz guiding Ic, Max shepherding Matthew and Peter.

I counted all the noses.

The kids were scared, but at least we were still together, and unharmed so far.

Now what to do, what to do?

Hot smoke clouded the cold morning air, and I thought I'd done as good a job as a girl could do under the circumstances. I'm no commando or Superwoman, *I'm a veterinarian!*

Before I could fall over from patting myself on the back, I heard a sharp pinging sound and rock fragments scattered.

There were bullets ringing out around us. *We'd been spotted again. Oh my good God, or bad God, or some kind of*

God, we were in such big trouble! Then we got a little break. Not much to cheer about, but it was something. The wind shifted. The smoke from the fire gave us some cover.

'Now *fly*! Keep low. Very low. Meet me at the car. Go! Run!'

I yelled to the children and for once they didn't question me; they actually obeyed. It was probably a quarter of a mile to the road where my car was parked at the Inn-Patient lot.

At least I hoped to hell the car was still there. I didn't have a plan B!

The kids flew away, as I clambered over rocks and logs and twisted bunches of fallen branches. I kept the smoke from the fire between myself and the armed men.

Just when the ravine became too shallow to hide me, I saw a large blue shape I had always loved.

Like a rock. The Suburban was there. And so were the kids, all of them. Thank God.

I leaped ahead and opened the doors for the children, and Pip, who all piled in without any extra urging from me.

'Where are we going?' Max and Oz both asked as I fired up the engine.

'Strap in, everyone. Put your seatbelts on,' I said by way of an answer.

I didn't have the heart to tell them that I was clueless and frightened.

I didn't have a plan.

CHAPTER FIFTY-ONE

In the course of the next three hundred miles or so, we drove through majestic plains and foothills, passing Pikes Peak and other scenic wonders that I would have marveled at any other time than this.

Once in a while one of the kids would wake up and I would stop for snacks and gas, but mostly they were good and stayed hidden in the car. All potty activity took place behind roadside bushes because that was the way it had to be. We weren't on vacation.

It was déjà vu all over again. We were on the run once more, and I wasn't the only one having sickening feelings as I recalled past events.

'It's just like old times, huh?' Max said, but her face showed sadness and irony rather than any hint of humor. 'I feel just like I did when Matthew and I escaped from that rotten, stinking, obscene School last year. Only back then we'd never seen the real world. Now we know.'

'I'd rather be on the run than with my bio mom,' said

Ozymandias. 'She called me Oliver. Didn't have a clue about avian life.'

'You got that right!' said Matthew. '*Oliver.*'

I'd been driving for about six hours when we passed an old volcanic cone near Walsenburg, east of the highway that was part of the old Santa Fe Trail. I was burning out from a high-test blend of fatigue and fear when we finally crossed Ratón Pass and the state line at noon.

That was when I spotted a sign for a motel called the Pines.

I pulled off the highway on to a smaller road just outside the town of Ratón, New Mexico, and checked in. I paid cash for one night in a bungalow, way off the road.

Then I backed the car right up to the door of number 8. I went inside and checked it out before I allowed the kids out of the Suburban.

It was a dank and cheesy place with no amenities, apart from a thirteen-inch RCA circa the mid-seventies. The carpet was dark gray, no doubt chosen for its dirt-hiding capacity. The two double beds were lumpy with blankets and covers that would never get the Good Housekeeping Seal of Approval, or mine either. The place was perfect for one of those Hollywood creepy-crawler movies.

The kids were hungry, and I told them I'd go shopping. But first, I wanted them to call their parents on the cell phone.

'The less said, the better,' I warned them. 'I'm worried about *their* safety, too. We have to keep it short and sweet. And please, be nice. They're scared too.'

We rehearsed our lines and put a thirty-second limit on the calls. One by one, they told their folks they were on a 'fly-away', that they were in no danger and would be home soon. When the kids were finished, I called Doc Monghil and told his answering machine – without explanation – that I needed him to watch over the Inn-Patient for a day or two, or maybe even three. *Or possibly for the rest of my life.*

Suddenly, I was more exhausted than I'd ever been. I was at the end of my own resources. I needed help myself.

My heart was pounding as I cleared switchboard security and also an executive assistant.

Then I heard a male voice say, 'Agent Brennan.'

'Kit,' I said, 'I'm in the middle of nowhere. Literally. I'm scared out of my mind. And I've got the kids, all six of them. I swear to God, someone's trying to kill us. I might be understating this situation a little.'

CHAPTER FIFTY-TWO

That night the kids and I sat around a cramped fourteen-by-sixteen-foot motel room and told each other ghost stories. Real ones! A baseball game was on the TV but nobody watched it. Mets and Rockies.

For the most part, the tales were about what the kids called their 'months in captivity without torture', or 'our bio-parent period', 'the abyss', 'nightmare in the suburbs', 'I know why the caged bird sings, too'. Basically, they sounded like most other kids growing up and being forced to obey rules for the first time. They hated it, and wanted to rebel; they wanted to do what they wanted to do, when they wanted to do it.

Of course, it was more complicated than that if you happened to be – gasp! – *different* from the other kids.

'We had to go into therapy,' Matthew confessed. 'Can you imagine *therapy* in Pine Bush, Colorado, with some Dr Phil-like guru who thought *he* knew what it had been like at the School for Max and me? Because he'd been tossed out of *two schools* himself as a kid.'

'Tell us about the *cereal* commercials.' Oz looked over at the twins, who were cuddled in my lap, and thought they were safe because they were little.

'No way.' Peter sat up straight and folded his arms across his chest. 'Up yours, Ozymandias. I mean, *Oliver*.'

'We *love* to fly,' said Wendy, 'and we also *love* to start our day with a balanced breakfast of Wingdingers. That's how the cereal commercial went.'

'That's *wrong*,' Peter interrupted. 'We love to start our day with a balanced breakfast *including* Wingdingers.'

'We're in test,' Wendy said proudly. 'Bridgeport, Connecticut and Columbus, Ohio.'

'Oohh,' said Matthew. 'I'm impressed. Or is it depressed?'

'C'mon, give me a break,' I finally edged in as referee. 'Anybody want to talk about the here and now? What we do next? Or should we start our careers in TV and cinema. Like Ic's appearance in *Touched By An Angel*?'

'Don't *anybody* go there,' Ic warned and put up his fists as if to box somebody's ears, even mine. 'Yeah, what *are* we going to do next? And who are the hunters?'

Suddenly everybody was looking at Max.

She threw up her hands. 'Not me, guys. I don't know who they are or what they want. I'm in the scary dark just like everyone else. Pinky swear.'

As I looked around the motel room at the others, I could tell that none of them really believed her, but they were afraid to challenge Max's leadership. Nobody took up the pinky swear invitation.

'Hey,' said Max and grinned. 'How 'bout those Mets?'

Nobody laughed.

CHAPTER FIFTY-THREE

The Hospital

Ethan Kane stood tall and very imperial-looking over a patient named Andrew Mellon McKay in the operating room. His mind was running fast on two tracks. On one, he prepared to do a miraculous arthoplasty for a $200,000 fee, and on the other he considered the disaster that had happened out in Colorado.

Max and the other bird-brats had disappeared off the radar screen. So had Dr Frannie O'Neill. And darling Max knew too much for her own, or anybody else's, good.

'We're just about ready, Dr Kane,' said one of the OR nurses.

'I'm aware of that,' Kane snapped.

She inserted a foley catheter into the patient's urethra to monitor hydration and kidney function. Dr Kane sighed and began.

He examined the draped knee joint on the operating table before he made an incision across the patella with his scalpel. He pulled back the skin and began separating the muscles and ligaments to expose the knee capsule, the tough gristle surrounding the joint.

Immediately he could see that the patella, or kneecap, had deteriorated beyond reasonable repair and it would be both quicker and better to remove it entirely. He had suspected as much.

Dr Kane selected a tool with a fine saw and a soft rasping sound. He sawed off the end of the patient's right femur and tibia, dropping the fragments and scrapings and the entire patella into a basin.

Then he chose a particularly fine-tooled drill, essentially a milling machine. It was three inches long and made of space-age metals and plastics. The holes it made were accurate to within a millimeter, perfectly calibrated to the dimensions of the pin ends of the artificial knee.

This perfect fit would make a difference of months in healing time. And when a patient was already eighty-three, months could matter.

Within seconds, the drilling was complete. He applied a medical glue to the pins before fitting them into the newly drilled holes. Satisfied with the perfect fit, Kane stepped back. Another doctor was waiting to attach the ligaments and muscles. He flexed his fingers absentmindedly, then moved to the other side of the table and the second draped knee.

'I've received unfortunate news,' Ethan Kane said to the team as they worked. 'The experiment named Maximum is still unaccounted for, still missing. So are the others.

They're running. We don't know where any of them are at this time.'

Kane thought about Max, her unquenchable curiosity and her fearlessness. And in that moment, he fumbled.

The scalpel spun at the ends of his fingers. The instrument dropped and clattered to the floor.

He stared at the knife lying on the brown-speckled linoleum, and his scalp prickled.

What the hell was going on?

This was unheard of.

Ethan Kane didn't make mistakes.

CHAPTER FIFTY-FOUR

Max's heart skipped as she watched through a narrow gap in the nearly closed grayish-blue curtains of the motel window. *What was this?*

A dusty black Jeep had backed into the parking slot in front of the cabin next to theirs. Who was here at Bungalow 8? Then Kit got out.

'*Oh God, hooray, hooray,*' Max whispered to herself. 'Now things get really interesting.'

She watched Kit stretch his long limbs, then shake himself like a big dog. He was dressed all in blue: blue denim shirt, blue jeans, and a navy-blue blazer that set off the shining gold of his hair. Max's heart lifted, and a sudden smile eclipsed her terrible, horse-spit mood.

'Frannie, he's here,' Max said in a whispery voice. 'It's Kit. The cavalry has arrived.'

Frannie's expression changed in a second from bone-tired and sad to bright and hopeful.

Max felt another surge of happiness – and it was *for Frannie.* Kit was here! And the question in her mind was, why had they been apart? How could two smart people be so dumb? They belonged together. Anybody could see that, and feel it too. Except, obviously, Kit and Frannie themselves.

Frannie pulled open the bungalow door and walked hurriedly to Kit's car. She was *so* cute sometimes. They reached out for each other, hesitant at first, then they hugged hard and swayed together.

Without completely knowing why, Max's eyes brimmed with tears. She got it then. *She loved the way they were with each other. She just loved it!*

The two grown-ups, 'Mom and Dad', finally let go of each other and started toward Bungalow 8. Kit was smiling.

Frannie entered first. 'Kids,' she said. 'Look who's here. Rumpelstiltskin!'

There was an explosion of excited laughter and yelling as the children flocked to hug Kit. He didn't have enough arms to hold them. From where she stood off to one side of the room, Max watched him greet each child in turn.

Then he sought her out.

'Hey, Maxie,' he said, walking over to her. 'How's my best girl in the world? Still playing hard to get, I see.'

'Why not? It always works,' said Max.

Kit was the only person who called her Maxie, and Max just loved that. He held out his arms to her and she wrapped herself around his waist and just held on. She was home. This *was* home – the eight of them together.

'I missed you, Kit,' she whispered. 'Corny but true.' For

the briefest moment, she had the feeling that everything just might turn out right.

But in her heart, Max didn't really believe in happy endings.

She knew too much about the way the big bad world really worked. She knew more than Kit and Frannie.

Max knew that she and the other kids would never be allowed to live. Sad but true.

It just wasn't in the cards.

A tragedy, that.

CHAPTER FIFTY-FIVE

This was so unexpectedly sweet. I was in Kit's arms again, both of us fully dressed – decent, maybe a little too decent – but definitely cozy.

We had kissed a couple of times and hugged, but too much water had flowed under the bridge since we'd last been together. Passionate embraces would have felt weird and inappropriate.

Or so I told myself.

Right now I had some control. Not much, I'll admit, but some. It's a scientific fact that when a woman makes love to a man a hormone called oxytocin is released in her brain which makes her bond to the guy like Krazy Glue. Accent on 'crazy'. If that wasn't enough, I still remembered how good it was to be with Kit. Like it says in the song, 'Nobody Does it Better'. Nope, if Kit and I made love I'd be handing him the keys to my heart, and I wasn't about to surrender mine in this creepy bungalow motel.

Not here, not now, not yet.

Nuh-uh. Not me.

Not that he'd asked!

It was such a good thing to be held again, after going so long without. Kit and I didn't talk at first, just breathed together quietly. Then out of pure nervousness, I suppose, I started to jabber about the situation at hand.

'I've got a lot to tell you,' I said.

'I'm here. I've got all night, Frances Jane,' he said. He always called me that when he was trying to calm me down. It was a little patronizing, but so what?

I told Kit how the kids had scared me silly by dropping out of the trees when I went for a walk in the woods. Then I told him why they had flown the coop. How I'd outsmarted the killers by setting fire to the only thing I owned in the world, my house. Kit looked at me fondly, a smile twitching at his lips as I described our steeplechase down the ravine, and when I caught him up on the four-hundred-mile dash to the Pines Motel, he laughed out loud.

'Jeez,' he said with a wide grin. 'You're actually better than Scully.'

'I am, aren't I?'

I loved it when Kit smiled like that. Hard not to! I grinned back at him and maybe I touched his long blond hair for a minute. I love his hair. *Don't lose control, Frannie. Just keep playing Scully.*

'The kids are maturing,' he said. 'Oz is a man and a half. He show you his tattoos?'

I nodded. 'Living out in the world has been good for them. Ic knows three languages already and he's making up a new one. Oz is our resident ornithologist. I think that his reading up on every kind of bird in the world is his version of *Roots*.'

'And Max? What's her story?'

'Um, she's still in charge, the mother-surrogate. Maybe she'll be a teacher some day. A professor.'

Kit was smiling at me, again. 'What I meant to say was, did Max tell you what's going on? I assume that she knows. Max always seems to know more than she lets on.'

I shook my head *no*. 'Max isn't talking. So, now *what?*'

Kit's face took on a serious mien. 'First things first,' he said. 'I think we need to set some priorities.'

'Like what?'

'Like we order out for three or four pizzas and all the fixings.'

I nodded. 'And then?'

'And then I'll have a private talk with Max.'

CHAPTER FIFTY-SIX

That was exactly what they did.

Veggie pizzas – then a heart-to-heart.

Max sat next to Kit on a low branch of a big old spruce tree in the nearby woods. The waistband of her jeans was pleasantly tight from the food she'd just packed away. She was treasuring the one-on-one with Kit.

She told him about living in Pine Bush, or 'Bush League', as Oz and Matthew called it, and how hard it was getting along with the 'regular folks'. She knew over fifty names the kids had made up and used behind her back. Max said she'd also been hurt by the lies told in several news stories. 'I just wanted to fit in, y'know,' she said. 'Is that too much to ask?' Kit seemed to understand. He almost always did.

'You've got a lot to deal with, kiddo,' he said. 'You're doing great. I'm really proud of you. So is Frannie.'

Max nodded. But she hadn't told Kit *half* of what was on her mind. She hadn't told him that she was on 24/7 red alert, listening and watching for anything out of place, or that she was certain she and the other kids were going to be abducted, maybe killed, and probably sooner rather than later.

Max had visualized their current location topographically. A quick flyover had given her a sense of the scale of the hillside and the height of the trees, as well as the wind speed and temperature in the forest microclimate. Actually, the area reminded her of the mountains around the Lake House. She and Kit had talked about that, too. Until Max finally said, 'Enough nostalgia, Kit. It's dumb.'

Now Max's ears registered a tightly woven symphony of traffic and forest sounds, and she could even hear Frannie running the shower in the bungalow.

She could have counted the whiskers sprouting in Kit's shaved face if she'd wanted to do it. No bug on a branch, no puff of pollen could escape her notice.

But Kit was there, and it made her feel a little more secure. Being with Kit was as close to feeling taken care of as Max had ever felt.

Dad. Dear old Dad. Except Kit wasn't so old. He sure didn't act old. He and Frannie were just about the coolest adults ever.

Max sighed and looked out on the totally gorgeous evening. The sun had just dropped below the horizon and the sky was red where it met the earth, fading upwards to a greenish-gold band, then a luminous cobalt-blue ceiling sprinkled with stars.

The other kids were playing, laughing and shouting in the woods behind the bungalow, and it was almost possible to believe the lie they'd all told their parents today.

It's just a fly-away, a harmless little run-away from home. No harm done. We'll be home soon. La-di-dah, la-di-dah.

'Maxie,' Kit said, 'we've got a real tough situation here. I think you know that.' Kit's expression had gone grave, and Max felt a pang. 'We're going to have to leave this motel soon. Then what?'

'You'll think of something,' Max said. 'You always do. Am I right?'

'Your confidence in Frannie and me is flattering. But it's not enough. I need to know what's really going on. Max? Who's after you? Why are they after you? Tell me what's going on, Maxie. I need your help.'

Max shook her head in the universal sign for *no way, absolutely no way.*

'Don't do that,' Kit said with an edge in his voice. 'Don't shut me out. I'm not Superman. I can't begin to protect you guys if you don't tell me *who* is after you, and what they want. You *know*, don't you, Maxie?'

'See, this's why Frannie hates it when you "go FBI" on her,' Max said, and shook her head from side to side again. Her ears and cheeks were hot from a rush of blood.

Then, before she could say anything worse, Max pushed off the branch, and with a loud rustle of wings she flew away from Kit and his probing questions.

She kept going up, up, up, until she was at least a half-mile high. Talk about the great escape! God, it was totally gorgeous up here!

Except for one terrible thing – flying away didn't change what was going on down below.

She knew things, horrible secrets, and they could all die because of that. It sounded crazy, but it was true. All eight of them could be murdered because of what she knew about the Hospital.

You know, don't you, Maxie?

Oh yeah, she sure did. She knew a lot more than she wanted to.

God, she felt so alone.

That was what she truly hated about Pine Bush – the loneliness.

She thought about the Lake House again – the one place where she hadn't been lonely, not for a single minute. The best place on earth. God, she'd loved it there. They all had. *Stop it, Max. Just let it go. The Lake House was too good to last. It's gone now.*

Then Max heard someone whistle and call her name. Was it possible? Yeah, it was.

'Hey, Max. *Ollie-ollie-oxen-freeeee.*'

It was Ozymandias.

CHAPTER FIFTY-SEVEN

It was Oz, and she was unbelievably happy to see him. He was flying, hovering actually, in the clouds above her – and then he dived right past her.

Max followed close behind. 'Watch your butt, bub,' she hollered. 'I'm on it!'

She spotted Oz bouncing on a tree limb down below, and since she could see every particle of movement, it seemed as if he were bouncing in slow motion.

She landed on the same slow-moving branch. 'Hey,' she said. 'I was just thinking about you.'

'Likewise, I'm sure.'

Ozymandias reached out his arm to steady Max, touching her at the sensitive place between her wings and shoulder blades.

A kind of electrical jolt went through her, an amazing shock of pleasure that made her a little dizzy. *Hey! What was that all about?*

She uttered an entirely involuntary whistle: 'Whooooooh.'

'You're flushed,' Oz said, concerned. 'You okay? Max?'

Max felt her face and her cheeks. They were warm. 'I had a fight with Kit,' she said. 'It's nothing. No biggie.'

'I heard.'

'We'll get over it,' she said. 'I can't stay mad at Kit for very long. Nobody can.'

'Come on, Max. Why are you keeping big bad secrets? From *everybody*.'

'Can we forget it right now?' Max said, and turned away from Oz. 'Just forget it.'

'Okay, okay.'

He plucked a spruce branchlet and stripped away the needles. He looked contemplative. Also, he looked incredibly beautiful, handsome, whatever. 'I'm glad to be away from home. I hated it there. My mother was always selling interviews and appearances. She played the saint, the martyr, but she wasn't.' He looked Max full in the eyes. 'I've been thinking about you a lot. Just about every day. Every minute.'

Max caught her breath. *So it wasn't just her thinking about Oz. Picturing him in her mind. Hearing his voice all the time.*

As they looked at each other, she felt the same dizzying feeling she'd had when she'd been with him at the raptor center. Oz's pupils dilated and contracted rapidly. His stare was superintense.

Max furtively grabbed the trunk of the tree and held on tight. *Oh boy. What now?*

'I'm feeling kind of crazy,' Oz told her. 'But I think I like it.'

'You *think* you do?'

'I *know* I like it. And I know I like you an awful lot, Max. I always have. Almost since we were babies.'

Max could barely contain the wild emotions she was feeling. She wanted to laugh out loud only she didn't think that would be the right thing to do.

But what was the right thing? What was she expected to do now? She was supposed to be so damn smart. Well, how did this work?

She wanted to touch Oz, to kiss him on his sweet mouth. And just about everywhere else.

She wanted to hold him so bad, and to be held.

If he felt it too, he would reach out for me. Max concentrated on that simple thought.

Do it, Ozymandias. Reach out and touch me. Do it now. Plee-ease.

Please kiss me, Oz. Then I'll know I'm not crazy. Or at least that we both are.

'I want to show you something,' Oz whispered. 'My secret.' He unzipped the hood he was wearing and lifted up his T-shirt.

'The eagle, I know. You showed me last time.'

'No, there's more to it than that. Look closely,' said Oz. 'Come closer, Max. Please. Don't be afraid to get close to me.'

Max did. She cozied up next to Ozymandias, feeling his warmth, smelling him, loving it. And there on the tattooed eagle's breast was a small red heart.

Inside it there were three inked letters in curling script: *MAX*.

Max gasped. 'Is that a tattoo? Like, it's permanent?'

'It's a little rough,' Oz said. 'But I did it myself. And you know, I was writing upside down.'

'Thank you. I love that you did that,' Max said softly. 'I mean – I *love* it.'

Max lifted her eyes to look at Oz. She searched the strong lines and planes of his face, the gentle slope of his nose, the curves of his mouth, the thin white scar across his right eyebrow, the curling lashes around his deep brown eyes. Frannie said that he looked eighteen. In bird-human years he might even be older than that.

She leaned over and kissed Oz on the cheek. Her lips lingered. The smell of his skin went straight to her brain and she was instantly overcome by feelings she couldn't begin to name.

Kiss me back, Oz. God, he is so handsome; he is gorgeous. A real-life prince.

Oz's face flushed with pleasure.

'Hey,' Max said then. 'Let's go for a fly, you and me. Let's go where no one's ever gone before.'

CHAPTER FIFTY-EIGHT

Without waiting for Oz's answer, Max assumed an athletic crouch and shoved off the branch, into the air.

'Whoo-eeee!' she yelled at the top of her voice. 'I say – whoo-eeee!'

She beat her wings rapidly, climbing fast and high, pointing her hands straight up, aiming for the moon. She was still feeling a little dizzy on account of Ozymandias being there with her.

Shake it off, girl, shake it off.

She turned her head when she heard a disturbance in the air. Then she smiled. Oz was right there again. She watched him. His flight pattern was beautiful, a work of art.

'Chee-rup-te-rup-te-rup,' she messaged, as she flew in a long, undulating upward flight path.

Oz followed, duplicating her movements exactly. She figured it had to be just about the most mindblowing game of follow-the-leader anyone had ever played. A couple of Air Force jets couldn't do it any better.

She peeled off, rolling to the left, again with Oz tailing only a few feet behind.

She couldn't lose him. *Kind of, well, sexy*, she thought. Whatever was going on, she liked it a lot.

Who wouldn't?

Then she dived straight toward the ground, pulling out of the dive just a hundred feet above the forest floor.

You still with me, Oz?

You keeping up? You on my tail?

When she saw that Oz, too, had pulled up right beside her, she shot him a smile, and winked outrageously; and did a 'talon drop' until they were a dozen feet above the treetops.

They were facing each other as they dropped. Max reached out for Oz and he did the same. Their hands touched briefly – *electrifying*.

They were doing an intricate dance and somehow both Max and Ozymandias seemed to know all the steps.

God, what does it mean? What is happening to us? Does Oz feel it, too? He must!

The moon was at its zenith, the light soft on his feathers, turning them platinum white. She had never seen anything more beautiful in her life. Nothing even came close.

'Chee,' Max said softly, tenderly, a sound just for Oz. The two of them beat their wings in unison, flying above the woodlands again.

This time, Oz fluttered just above her. Maybe a foot and

a half. No more than that. This was so great, so cool. Their movements were synchronized. Oz was so close that the air warmed her back. It was as if he had covered her with a cashmere blanket.

He called her name softly. 'Max, Max, sweet Max.'

Max called out his, the sound magical to her ears. 'Ozymandias.'

What is happening to us?

Why do I love it so much?

CHAPTER FIFTY-NINE

There was a picturesque clearing below them, like a deep bowl filled with moonlight. Max and Oz dropped toward the spot as if it had been placed there just for them.

Maybe it has been, Max thought. *Maybe God is watching out for us after all.*

Their feet touched down on thick layers of pine needles. Suddenly, their arms encircled each other. They were face to face. So close. Ozymandias kissed Max for the very first time. A *real* kiss. She had the notion that she had been dreaming about this kiss for a long while. Only it was even better, so much better and sweeter and sexier than she'd imagined it could ever be.

She felt a rush of heat flow through her body. As soon as the magical kiss had ended, she wanted to do it again. She couldn't stop kissing Ozymandias, couldn't get enough of his mouth. She'd never felt anything like it before, couldn't have imagined that it existed, whatever *it* was.

They clung fiercely together. Both of them were on fire; *their hearts and minds and bodies.* Then they lost their balance, fell head over wings over heels.

'Timber!' Oz called.

Laughing, they fell to the ground, which felt like a soft bed made with pine needles. *God must have taken care of this, too.*

The laughter stopped as suddenly as it had begun. Oz gently folded Max into his arms. She couldn't resist him. She didn't want to.

She blocked out the surrounding *buzz* and *whistle* and *whirr* of the forest. She was aware of their ragged breathing as they kissed again. A little voice in her head was saying, *This is so good. My God, I love this. It has to be right. I am so happy right now. I was never happy before. I didn't understand happiness.*

Oz touched her cheek, her lips, her neck, her shoulders, the small of her back. Everywhere he placed his hands was warmed under his touch.

Rapture, Max thought.

That is the right word. *This* is what it means.

Max began to unfasten her jeans with badly trembling fingers. God, she was shaking all over. Ozymandias pulled at his pants, his shoes, his shirt. Soon their clothes were in loose piles on the forest floor.

Max whispered, 'My prince. Oh my sweet prince. Ozymandias.'

He said, 'Princess.'

She smiled. 'No, just Mad Max.'

The feeling of their naked skin rubbing together was delicious, and Max's fear of the unknown spun out of her mind. It was replaced by incredible longing, need, love for someone other than herself. There was a brief moment when maybe she could have said no. But as she gazed into Oz's eyes and felt the intensity and honesty of his love for her, she returned the feelings. Then there was no turning back.

Rapture.

Max opened herself to Ozymandias. She trusted him completely. He fitted himself perfectly to her body. They rocked and they rolled and they waltzed. For a brief moment they fluttered their wings and rose a few feet above the forest floor. Oz sighed deeply and Max held him with her arms and legs, and, most important, her whole heart.

A warm feeling rippled through Max and left her tingling in its wake. She knew a truth had emerged from this, their first time. She thought, *We were meant to do this, Oz and I.*

We were made for this.

CHAPTER SIXTY

Max clung to Oz, and as their breathing slowed, she knew that her whole world had suddenly changed.

She'd been shy with Oz before, but that feeling was completely gone. It just was. Gone. She knew him now; she knew Oz as a natural being in the universe; she was one with him. And he knew her in a way that no one else had ever known her, and in a way that no one else ever would. She silently promised that to herself. Max felt a deep bonding with Oz. She was sure that Oz, her dearest friend, her lover, felt it too.

They were mated for life.

That was what birds did.

They lay together on the pine needles, shivering slightly as their skin began to cool.

Innocent.

Pure.

Yet more experienced.

And wiser.

They used their wings to cover each other, keeping

their damp chests pressed tightly together, their arms and legs and hips still entwined.

Max loved just lying there with him, listening to the subtle, very slow quieting of their heartbeats. She cooed in his ear, and blew softly on his pin feathers.

Then Oz spoke.

'Max?'

She lifted her eyes lovingly to his face.

'Hmmm? What is it, Ozymandias?'

'Did you hear that? A car stopped by the highway. Listen. I hear footsteps. Someone's coming fast. Someone's coming this way!'

CHAPTER SIXTY-ONE

'Just a SEC-ond,' I yelled to whoever was knocking like a crazy person on the bungalow door. I had a skimpy towel wrapped around my hair and another around my bod, so it took me a minute to dress before I could open up and stop the blasted racket.

It was Kit, and he had a disappointed look on his face.

'What happened with you and Max?' I asked. 'Are you all right? Is Max okay?'

'Sure,' he answered brusquely as he pushed past me and into the room. 'She's just fine. She's Max.'

'How'd it go? Really? The third degree.'

Kit pulled a face. 'Not well.'

'She stonewalled you, didn't she?'

'Yeah, well, she's awfully good at it,' Kit said. 'She's hiding something, Frannie. I'm sure of it. Something scares her, and that scares me.'

'Any ideas at all?'

Kit shook his head. 'Not a one. It's driving me crazy. What could she be hiding? Why hide it from us?'

I felt him watching me towel-dry my hair as I walked back and forth between the bathroom and the bedroom. I switched on the TV, got a fuzzy version of Oprah and Brad Pitt on her talk show. I stood in front of the set for a few seconds. Then I started stuffing empty pizza boxes into a tiny trash can.

'Why don't you sit, Frannie? You're twitching like a cat in a box,' Kit said finally.

'Yeah? I'm worried about the kids. I'm worried about you, me, everything. I'm worried about what Max won't tell us. She's hiding her secret because she thinks the information could hurt us. Has to be that.'

'Come sit over here. Please. I'll rub your back some. You look like you need it. Just a back rub.'

I looked into his big blues for one electrifying second and felt his gaze grabbing on to me like that tractor beam in *Star Trek*.

'Thanks, no,' I said. 'Thanks anyway. Really.'

Kit breathed an exaggerated and comical sigh. 'The two of you,' he said. 'You and Max are the most stubborn women I've ever known.'

I laughed because I didn't know how else to react. Well, actually I did. I wanted to go over to the bed. I wanted to lock the door, close the curtains, peel off every stitch I was wearing, and make love to Kit for the first time in months.

Okay, let me be honest here.

I was still very much in love with Kit, but what if he didn't feel that way? What if he just had, you know, an itch? Whoever said "Tis better to have loved—and lost than never to have loved at all' must've never loved and lost as hard as I'd done, because I didn't think I had the flexibility to withstand emotional whiplash again.

So back rubs were out until I got a better sense of Kit's true feelings. And yeah, I probably needed to hear those three little words.

Kit must have been reading my mind. He can do that sometimes. 'I know we've been apart,' he started to say. 'I got spooked. First I lost my family. Then the kids. Frannie, I still—'

Still? Still what? Say it!

But Kit was staring at something *behind* me. What? I slowly turned and saw that the front door had blown open. Max and Oz were peering at us, stricken and ashen-faced, looking as if they'd just survived a tornado.

'The woods are crawling with hunters,' Oz said.

CHAPTER SIXTY-TWO

This couldn't be happening again – but damn it, it was!

Kit didn't hesitate for more than a couple of seconds. He drew his scary automatic weapon, or semi-automatic, or whatever in hell it was, and bolted out of the bungalow at a gallop, moving on the ground as Oz and Max took to the air.

Kit didn't have their raw speed, but he was quick and agile on his feet. Pip and I were running behind him, trying to keep up, not doing such a great job of it to tell the truth.

There was a rough trail running through the woods and Kit stayed on it. Suddenly, he looked back and saw us coming.

'Goddamn it, Frannie,' he whispered loudly as he ducked behind a tree. 'Get down,' he hissed. 'Please get down. Now! I *mean* it, Frannie!'

I did as told. There was a lot of movement in the dark and overgrown woodland, so it took me a few seconds to understand that the rapid mothlike flapping at the bend in the trail was Matthew.

Jesus God! He was flying swooping circles over the four or five men dressed in black. He was swinging and kicking at their guns and their faces.

Matthew was attacking the gunmen! Dear God in heaven, he was nine years old! But he was so fast. And furious. And fearless, even if he had no right to be.

Then I noticed another small figure doing the same thing.

'Kit, look! Oh my God! Stop him!'

It was Peter! Four-year-old little Peter was imitating Matthew, fearlessly dive-bombing and attempting to create confusion with his hooting and hollering and kick-boxing.

The only problem was, Kit couldn't fire safely at the men in black. Peter was in the way.

There was no way to get off a clear shot.

It was frustrating, maddening, crazy. And I wasn't the one with the gun.

Just when I didn't think I could feel more helpless, Oz came out of nowhere and furiously threw himself into the action. He was like a missile, targeting one of the gunmen, who fired off a series of *rat-a-tats*, each deadly sound illustrated by an orange flameburst.

But the shooter *missed*. It almost seemed that he'd missed *on purpose*. What was going on here? Who were the hunters? What were their orders? Who was in control of them?

Oz knocked the gunman out cold with one swipe of his powerful wings. Talk about your winged avengers. I almost couldn't believe my eyes.

I was screaming at the kids to get away. So was Kit. Even Max was yelling. They might be super, but they weren't bulletproof.

Oz kick-boxed one of the shooters from behind. The bastard went down hard, and Oz gave him a good stomp to the head. I saw another gunman making a grab for a small dark shape as it fluttered past him.

Wendy! He had Wendy!

'Okay,' the gunman yelled out, and seemed really angry. 'Everyone back off. Drop the gun. Kick it toward me.'

The entire forest seemed frozen in time and space. I saw Kit's face as he weighed his limited options – drop the gun or shoot – when the silence was broken.

A shrill caw! Oz rose from the ground and slapped aside the shooter's gun. It was only a glancing blow, and the gunman turned fiercely against Oz. He backhanded him with his pistol.

The crack to Oz's head made a horrifying sound.

But Kit finally had a clear shot. He fired! The man was hit somewhere high in his chest. He staggered and fell down hard, holding his ribcage tightly with both arms, bleeding all over himself, probably dying before our eyes.

The other men were either down or in retreat. Wendy had managed to get away. She shouted in triumph. Then she darted into my arms, screeching, 'Mama, Mama! We won the war!'

CHAPTER SIXTY-THREE

I doubted it! I sincerely doubted it!

I was panting hard, nearly in shock, as I watched Kit holster his gun. Even though it had saved us, I still hated the weapon, despised what it could do, aware of its awful potential for deadly violence. And one other thing bothered me a lot. Why hadn't the gunmen fired right away? What had stopped them from shooting all of us? They certainly could have. *What was going on? Why weren't we all dead?*

'Okay, everyone,' Kit called out, still trying to catch his breath. 'Gather around so I can see you. Is anybody hurt?'

One by one, the children enveloped us. Oz got up from the ground and wiggled into the embrace. Kit kept talking them in. 'It's okay, everyone. It's okay for now.'

'Is anybody hurt? Yeah, *they* sure are,' Matthew finally piped up. 'We kicked some proper ass.'

'We were lucky,' Kit said.

'And we were good,' retorted Oz, and shook a fist over his head. 'I'm proud to go to war with you guys!'

'Yeah, right,' little Peter piped up. 'Bet your butt.'

I checked each of the kids for injuries. Oz had taken the worst of it. There was a darkening bruise on one side of his face.

Miraculously, bruises and scrapes were the only damage we'd sustained.

But Kit was right – we were lucky. Damned lucky! Or maybe it was more than just luck. *Of course it was more than luck.*

The battle we'd just been through had happened and ended quickly. It left me breathless. A five-minute assault, during which any one of us could have been killed! We hugged in pairs and then we hugged in a big pile. I was still breathless from all the excitement. Some of the kids started to whimper and shiver. Finally, reality was setting in.

I saw Kit walk Max away from the group and I followed them. Kit stooped down and took Max by the shoulders.

'This was too close, Maxie. I take responsibility. I should have kept everyone under lock and key until I could get us to safety. We have to get out of here. Now. But we have a problem, don't we? We still don't know what's going on.'

'They don't want us hurt. Not yet. They prefer capturing us,' she said. 'That's *obvious*, isn't it? What do they want? *What?*'

Max had scratches on her face and her eyes were as huge as saucers. I saw her shudder, and then make her decision.

She spoke softly, so faintly that Kit and I had to strain to hear.

'It's in Maryland,' she whispered. 'It's like another School, like the shit-awful place we were kept. Only I think it's even worse. They've taken this biotech madness even farther. They've gone to the limit this time. Maybe past the limit. Yeah, *way* past.'

'How do you know this, Max?' I asked. 'What is the limit?'

She shook her head, then stared at the ground. 'At the School they made me file and do other scut work on the computer. At first it was just to keep me out of their hair. But then they realized I did the job of three of their drones in less than half the time.

'So I filed their records and important communications. But I also *read*, and I remember it all. There's another experimental lab. In Maryland. Not too far from Washington, DC, where Kit lives. The doctor who runs it is supposed to be a genius, but personally, I think he's totally whacked. I know he is. He visited the School once, but I didn't get to see him. Not a good look anyway. They locked us away in our cages. I know that the doctors there were in awe of this guy, and whatever he was working on. They were also scared shitless of him. And *yes*, there are people in the government who *know* about the outlaw lab.'

Max looked into Kit's eyes, then into mine. She shook her head. 'You talk,' she said, 'you die. Looks like I die.'

CHAPTER SIXTY-FOUR

Max's confession changed everything.

That evening, around the golden hour, she and Ozymandias took the kids for a short flight with Frannie's permission. They were in tight formation, gorgeous to watch as they sailed toward the setting sun. She was thinking they were more like a squadron of jet fighters than a flock that night.

Icarus called out and Max turned to him. His sightless eyes were closed against the wind. 'Where are we going, guys? Tell all! What am I missing on the way?'

'Great sunset, Ic. Burnt orange against powder blue. Beautiful pine forests and mountains that seem to go on for ever,' Max called back. 'We're going up into the woods. Primeval forests. We're not coming back, little buddy. It's too dangerous for Frannie and Kit.'

'Oh, so we're the only ones who die?' Ic asked, his little voice thick with irony.

'Yeah. I'm afraid so, Icarus. This is our fight.'

He shrugged his small shoulders. 'I can live with that.'

It was Oz's plan, actually, and the first part was that the flock would have enough time to find safe shelter before darkness fell in the mountains. Oz had thought everything through. He was sure of it, and of himself. They would build temporary shelters high in trees, using branches and wild vines to weave sleeping baskets. The baskets could be lined with ferns and loose leaves.

Max approved. Basically. Actually, it sounded kind of comfy the way Oz described it, and everybody had confidence in him, especially since she did.

If they didn't want to be too ambitious at first, they could raid a nearby farm for food. Root vegetables and gourds, such as pumpkins and squash, were in season. Carrots, maybe peas, tomatoes, melons might also be available.

Plus, there would be sunflower seeds, which they all loved anyway. Oz explained that the delicious seeds were packed in flat discs at the center of every flower head.

'What if there are no farms?' Wendy asked. 'You ever think about that, guys?'

'No problem,' said Oz. 'There'll be plenty of nuts and seeds and roots. Pig nuts are pretty good. Burdock roots are sensational. And . . . turn over any log and you'll find fat white grubs. A great source of protein!'

Max looked around again. The kids made faces at the grub mention, but they seemed to be keeping their sense of adventure, and humor, as they flew into the mountains.

'Burdock roots and white grubs! Burdock roots and white grubs!' they chanted.

They were on their own.

Maybe back where they belonged.

It will be like the Lake House.

Well, almost, but never as good.

CHAPTER SIXTY-FIVE

O z and Max had decided they would share the watch. For the first night anyway.

They sat huddled together on a rocky ledge that was maybe fifty feet above the trees where the children slept. There was no way human hunters could sneak up on them, but Oz was especially nervous about mountain cats, which could be incredibly fast and vicious, tear you apart in about thirty seconds.

'Was this part of your studies in ornithology?' Max asked. 'How to survive in the wilderness? How to fight mountain lions?'

Oz smiled. 'Our instincts will kick in and keep us safe – the way it was for a while at the lake. It's the truth. Don't forget – burdock roots and white grubs.'

'You're so *sure* about things, Ozymandias. Be careful of too much pride. You could eat grubs?'

'I'm sure about some things. Grubs, *maybe*. I'm sure I want to be with you, y'know, even though you're a girl.'

'It's not just some kind of dumb infatuation? Are you sure about that?'

Oz laughed. 'I went through being infatuated with you when I was much younger, when we were both at the School. I used to go to sleep every night thinking about you. True tale. Every night.'

Max laughed. 'I had no idea.'

'Of course you didn't. You were too hung up on yourself. I was petrified around you. Whenever I had to talk to you I got the shimmy-shimmy-shakes.'

'Hold my hand,' Max said in a softer voice. 'Hug me for a little while, then I'll take first watch.'

Oz cuddled Max gently. 'Whenever I hold you, I never want to let go,' he said. 'I guess that could be dangerous tonight.'

'Oh, Oz, Oz, Oz,' Max sighed, then whispered against his cheek. She was starting to cry, and she almost never cried.

He felt her warm tears and pulled away sharply. 'What's the matter? Please don't cry. It's the one thing that could make me lose my nerve.'

She looked deeply into his beautiful, magnificent eyes. 'Oh, Oz, everything that could go wrong is going that way in a hurry. We're on our own with a little blind boy, two darling babies, and my kid brother, who's still pissed because of you and me. We had pine and pig nuts for supper. Humans are trying to capture or kill us and probably will. And you know what?'

Oz hugged her even harder. 'What, Max? Tell me what?'

'I have never been happier in my entire life. It's all because of you, tattoo-boy. I love you, Oz.'

'I love you, Max. Always have, always will. Now I'll take the first watch.'

Max grinned. 'I already knew that, sweet patooie. You're such a *guy*.'

CHAPTER SIXTY-SIX

This was not good!

Kit and I rode in the Suburban on a dirt road as far as it would take us, and fast. The damn trail just dead-ended into the mountain face. We were in the middle of nowhere. Smack dab.

Staring at a cold, hard rock face.

Not good at all.

'You could say that this is the end of the road,' Kit quipped from his place behind the steering wheel. 'Damn it. Damn Max.'

I immediately started to cry a little, and Kit slid over, put his arms around me, started kissing my tears away. I still liked being held by him, no use denying or fighting it any more.

'The kids'll be all right. For now anyway,' he said. 'I'm sure they just need to hash things through. Max was seriously programmed not to talk about anything she learned back at the School. She and Oz will do the right thing. They do act like grown-ups now.'

'They're all geniuses, Kit. Off the charts, remember? They know it, too.'

'So maybe they won't come back. But they'll be all right.'

'Don't say that.'

'Let's go back to the hacienda. Maybe the kids are already there waiting for us. Besides, we don't have any other choice.'

It took us a good half-hour to get to the Pines, in Ratón, New Mexico's finest. Neither Kit nor I saw signs of trouble. Nor did we see the kids.

We waited up for them – the kids. But there was also the awful possibility that more gunmen might show up. *Hunters*.

'I felt safer when the kids were around,' I said to Kit, who was putting another log on our fire. 'They could spot an intruder coming a long way off.'

Kit spread a wool blanket not too far from the fire. He *patted* the floor by his side.

'Woof! Woof!' I barked.

'That's not how I meant it. I'm just recommending a cozy spot by the fire here. Please, Frannie, *please*. See? I'm begging.'

I brought a couple of borderline-comfy pillows from the bed.

'That's all this is?' I asked Kit. 'Sit by the fire together? Warm our toes?'

'I didn't say that either.'

I finally lay down beside Kit and he took me in his

strong arms. 'I missed you every day, every hour, every minute, Frannie,' he whispered.

I rolled my eyes. 'That's a little thick.'

'You're tough,' Kit said and grinned. 'I missed you every day we were apart.'

'How about every day *and* most every hour?'

'That's about right. I did.'

'Me too. So, uhm, why did we stay apart?'

'Too much loss, too much awful pain, way too much chaos and confusion. My family dies, then we lose the kids in that courthouse fiasco in Denver. I thought you might bolt on me next, Frannie. I swear I did.'

'Kiss me,' I whispered. 'Shush up and kiss.'

He did. A whole lot of times. Tender, sweet, strong Kit kisses. Just like always. Kisses so true that I had to believe him about why he'd stayed away. Then Kit was touching me everywhere I wanted to be touched, which was every-where. God, how I loved his touch, too.

First he thoroughly explored my face; and I explored his. Then he covered my neck and shoulders with touches and kisses. He unbuttoned my flannel shirt and I returned the favor by unbuttoning his. He did my belt, my trousers; and I did his. Only when we were finally naked did I completely understand how much I had missed Kit, and maybe how much I loved him, which was with all my heart and soul, and, obviously, my body as well.

And for once he said exactly the right thing. 'I love you, Frannie. Simple as that. I really love you, Frances Jane. In fact, I adore you.'

And I whispered back, 'I love you, Thomas.'

Eventually, after a good long while, and some rather spectacular shenanigans, which I won't go into in a story that will be heard by old and young, we fell asleep on the blankets in front of the fire.

The first time I woke in the morning I was cold, and quickly stole my share of the covers. Maybe more than my share, but isn't that what love is all about?

I fell asleep again immediately. In the cocoon of Kit's arms. Safe and sound and blissful. Swaddled in blankets. Perfectly content.

The second time I woke, buttery sunlight was streaming through all the windows.

Something else was at the windows, too.

The kids! They had come back. My God, they were gawking at Kit and me.

'Get away from those windows, you little Peeping Toms,' Kit hollered at them.

'Nothing we haven't seen before,' said Icarus, blind poet that he is. 'You guys want some burdock roots?'

PART FIVE

THE HOSPITAL

CHAPTER SIXTY-SEVEN

The Hospital

Dr Ethan Kane was humming the Eagles' golden oldie 'Hotel California' and doing a lot of heavy thinking about Resurrection. It was almost here. His reverie was interrupted by an important phone call. It was long-distance from Los Angeles, and Kane had been expecting it for most of the day.

The California folk were attempting to play with his head, which was a very bad idea.

The voice on the other end was clipped and business-like, probably a transplanted New Yorker. 'Dr Kane, this is Anthony Depino calling.'

Dr Kane's tone of voice was the opposite of Depino's. It sounded jovial and unconcerned. 'Anthony, so good to hear from you. I'm afraid you caught me working late in my office. It's after nine. How are my friends the Stevensons?'

'They're *old*,' said the lawyer, and left it at that. Depino wasn't having any of the idle chitchat. Well, fine. He was one of the most powerful attorneys in Los Angeles, and had handled the Stevensons' private affairs for the last few years. Also, he seemed to believe that his shit didn't stink.

'Well, since they're not getting any younger, let's get down to business, Anthony,' said Ethan Kane.

'Splendid, Dr Kane. I might as well start by informing you that the figure you quoted for the procedures is totally unacceptable to us,' said the lawyer. 'The price for Resurrection is just too much, even for Roger Stevenson. You'll have to do better.'

'I understand perfectly,' said Ethan Kane. Then he hung up the phone on the snot-nosed lawyer.

He grinned, then scooped out a handful of M&Ms, candy-covered peanuts, one of his few serious vices. He put three different-colored candies in his mouth, and then the phone rang again.

'Some fucking negotiator,' Kane mumbled and smiled thinly.

He let it ring a few times before he picked up, put the receiver to his mouth, and bit down into the crunchy M&Ms. *Take that, Mr Depino from the City of the Angels, that second-rate dumping ground for second-raters.*

'Let me ask you a simple, but somewhat profound question.' Dr Kane spoke before being spoken to. 'What is one more day on earth worth to Roger Stevenson? Do you have a *final* number in mind? Does he? Have you actually consulted him on a number?'

'It's certainly not a hundred million dollars,' said Depino.

'Goodbye, sir. I have many others in line for the final spot in Resurrection.'

'Wait! Roger is just being cautious,' said the lawyer. 'So am I, on his behalf.'

'Mr Depino, I have other worthy candidates, but I happen to like Roger a great deal. And Roger was a great leader once, after all. The price is firm at one hundred million. To be perfectly honest, I could get *double* or *triple* that for the final spot in Resurrection. Now give me an answer. No more dilly-dallying. Is Roger Stevenson in or out?'

'We will pay your price,' said the lawyer.

'You won't regret it. Roger Stevenson will outlive you, Anthony. A hundred million is a pittance for this scientific miracle. We're going to make history. We're going to make the world a better place, and maybe even save it.'

CHAPTER SIXTY-EIGHT

The kids had decided, voted actually, to entrust their fates to us. I just hoped we were worthy of the task, and of their trust.

We certainly started out badly. We had made a small deal with the FBI. Kit hitched a ride for us to Washington, which just happens to be very close to Maryland. Exactly what we had to give back to the FBI wasn't clear yet. But I was sure they wanted *something*.

We all hung on to our armrests as the Beech King slammed down at Dulles International and bounced along the runway. The brakes squealed, the plane slewed to the left and then stopped a little hard, jerking us in our seatbelts.

We discovered that the wind was blowing fiercely as we disembarked and clung to the railing of the metal staircase that had been rolled up to the side of the plane.

Feathers ruffled, hair whipped across our faces, and dust scurried across the moonlit airfield.

First stop, Washington, DC.
Second stop, hell.

My arms prickled with goose bumps, and not just because of the chill wind. Three men in dark suits waited for us as Peter proceeded to get sick on the tarmac. Then they escorted us toward a freestanding aluminum utility shed that stood alongside the terminal building. I didn't like this. They had no right. But we'd made a deal.

The oldest of the three men, a lanky guy with a beakish nose, small dark eyes, and a receding hairline, introduced himself as Senior Agent Eric Breem. He nodded at the children and me, then swept Kit aside and engaged him in an intense conversation.

Man to man, of course. Very private. I was completely excluded from all this.

They were soon arguing about something, and Kit was clearly furious with Breem. I heard him exclaim, 'In a pig's ass you will. That's not gonna happen.'

Moments later we were assembled in the shed, and the door was shut and locked with a loud metallic clang. I guessed the place was used to detain illegal aliens or inspect contraband, because the furnishings were sparse: a long table and a stack of folding chairs leaned against one wall.

Now what?

A dark-haired, broad-shouldered agent with huge hands opened the metal chairs and the wary children sat down in a fidgety row – except for Max, who stood. 'Just a formality,' he said.

'Me no likee,' commented Peter, and his little joke seemed dead-on. None of us was very comfortable with this. The FBI can be really weird. They need a make-over. Trust me on this.

Another agent, blond and slight, wearing a bright yellow tie to enliven his charcoal-gray suit, addressed Kit. He introduced himself as Adam Warshaw. 'We'd like to question the children one at a time. It won't take very long. It's important. *Essential.*'

Kit shook his head. 'Sorry, that's not happening. It's past midnight and they've had a long day.'

'Okay, Brennan, it *is* going to happen. But we'll make it brief,' said Agent Warshaw. He turned his gaze toward Max, who was standing watchfully on the sidelines, as she tended to do.

'Max? You *are* Max?' Warshaw said. He had a pen and notepad in his hand.

Max stared at him, but didn't answer. She looked a little pale and shaky, but she stuck out her chin in a defiant gesture I thought of as 'Max's brave front'.

'Of course I'm Max,' she finally said. 'What of it?'

'Well, the way I understand it, some men broke into your parents' house with guns. Is that right?'

'Yes. Except for the parents' part. Frannie and Kit are our parents. We chose them as our parents. Write that down in your little notepad.'

'Max, do you have any idea why these men were trying to harm you and your brother? What did they want? What *do* they want?'

I read the distress on Max's face. 'No idea at all.'

'I'm sorry. I'm afraid I don't believe that,' said Warshaw.

Kit spoke up. 'Breem, this has to *stop*. You have no legal right to question these kids, so don't. I'll come into the office tomorrow. I'll tell you everything I know and everything the kids know. If that's not good enough, I'm instructing them not to speak to anyone without their parents and *attorneys* present at all times. Is that clear?' Kit looked over at me. 'Was that clear, Frannie?'

'I think that was amazingly clear, and also concise. Only a complete moron couldn't follow it. Right, Agents Breem and Warshaw?'

There was a tense silence as Kit faced off with Breem and Warshaw. Meanwhile, the wind rattled the aluminum walls, making a drumming sound like spoons beating on tin pie pans.

At last, Breem nodded. What else could he do? Then he showed some teeth. His idea of a smile, I guess. 'It has been a long day. Tomorrow morning, then, Brennan. Let's get you all someplace comfortable. We've made temporary arrangements in— '

'They're staying with me,' Kit said. 'We've taken good care of them before. We'll do it tonight. Let's go, kids, Frannie.'

Little Peter stood up tall and straight. 'Me likee,' he said. 'Let's get out of here.'

I grabbed on to Kit's arm and whispered, 'Your place?'

Kit's answer was chilling. 'If they wanted to kill us, we'd already be dead. Let's go, Frances Jane. Let's vamanos, kids.'

'Vamanos!' they chorused.

CHAPTER SIXTY-NINE

Two anonymous-looking black town cars sped down a wide-open avenue in our nation's capital late at night. I was so overtired that I distrusted everything, even my own feelings about staying in Kit's apartment. I wasn't so sure it was such a good place for us to go right now. On the other hand, I didn't have any better ideas, and I definitely distrusted the Federal Bureau of Investigation so far, especially Agents Breem and Warshaw.

There was a sudden, infectious burst of giggling in the back seat of the car I was riding in. I craned my head to see what had so amused the twins. *Oz had put his arm around Max!* What was this? Oz and Max?

I was still pondering the shiny new paradigm shift when the sedan pulled to a stop in front of Kit's apartment.

The apartment was in a residential neighborhood near Dupont Circle, a relatively short distance from the White House and also from several important monuments and federal buildings. Kit told us that the small apartment building had once been a single-family Victorian house.

When he opened the heavy old front door we thundered up four flights of stairs to the top floor. Kit's. A few of us *flew*.

'It's not much, but it's home,' Kit said as we stepped inside. His apartment was decorated with country furniture, Persian rugs, a piano, and crammed bookshelves. Very, very nice, actually. Homey. Kit-like.

'Watch your wings,' I hollered to the kids who were zooming around in a potentially destructive manner.

'Watch my *stuff*,' bellowed Kit. 'Have mercy. There are a lot of memories in here.'

Icarus found the piano and sat right down. He immediately launched into a spirited rendition of 'Fly Me to the Moon', both singing and playing. The kid was a born mimic and his linguistic skills were amazing. He sounded exactly like Frank Sinatra, down to the minutest detail of the song's phrasing.

My gaze snagged on some simple silver frames sitting on the piano top.

In one was a snapshot of a slender, pretty blonde woman with two handsome young boys who were spitting images of Kit.

I flashed on some others: Kit hugging his sons, teaching them to ride bikes, and playing ball. They told me how Kit had watched them as they grew. A wave of sadness washed over me and I felt a chill. Kit caught me looking at the grouping of photos.

'Beautiful,' I said. 'Your place is.'

'Thanks,' he murmured. 'It was a great time, Frannie, great time. But so is this.'

Then he walked me away from the piano, and toward the kitchen. I could tell he didn't want to talk about his family right now. I couldn't blame him.

The fridge was nearly full, and we were starving. Kit pulled bread and crackers out of a cabinet. Cheese and raw vegetables and cold cuts soon appeared on the oak dining table along with the remains of a roasted chicken. Pip was awarded the poultry, and the kids made short work of the rest. Kit poured me a glass of Pinot Grigio and I needed it. But after a few swallows, I found that I still couldn't relax. Reality was setting in:

I was homeless.

I'd seen a man in death throes a short while before. I'd narrowly missed getting shot at the same time.

I felt responsible for keeping six kids safe and sound, but I had no real idea how to do it.

Something truly horrifying might be taking place nearby in Maryland.

Nothing, and I mean *nothing*, was under my control at the moment.

Other than that, no problems.

I was so exhausted I think I could have slept standing up. So my jaw dropped when Ic announced, 'I've got energy to burn.'

'Me three,' shouted the twins.

'No, don't!' I shouted, too late. Oz had already opened a window and Ic had climbed out on to the ledge.

There was no stopping them now. With a few 'byes' and 'be back soons', the kids shot out of the windows. I managed to snag Wendy by the waistband of her jeans. She turned to me with a hurt look and a pitiful cry.

'Frannie, please. Everybody's going. It's a night flight! Pleeeeeeease? I have to. Like we used to at the lake! Pleeeeeeease?'

I cast a questioning look at Kit and he shrugged, so I turned the little girl loose. She spread her wings and darted up to join the others. She was so cute I couldn't stand it.

Kit came over and put his arm around me and we watched the children fly across the broad, beaming face of the moon. This was a sight that never failed to fill me with awe – until now.

'I feel the earth shifting under my feet,' I said. 'I don't feel safe anywhere. Not even here.'

'I was having the same thought,' he said. 'Unfortunately.'

'We're just paranoid, aren't we? We're paranoid, right?' Kit sighed.

'That was the wrong answer,' I said.

CHAPTER SEVENTY

The children were taking a night flight above Washington, DC. Icarus was singing 'Fly Me to the Moon' again. It was kind of close to perfect, actually. The kid could *croon*. 'Just don't call me Ole Blue Eyes!' he warned.

As always, Max thrilled to the powerful upward pull of the air on her wings as the winds gusted forcefully around her. It was like being on an amusement-park ride, and it was about a hundred times better. The other kids whooped with joy as the air lifted and dropped them. And lifted them yet again.

Max still had the best aerial dexterity, though Oz was faster and a bit stronger. She closed her wings a few degrees and used the wind as a chute or air flume to carry her in a long, breathtaking swoop.

But just when she was beginning to fully enjoy herself, she remembered.

People might be dying nearby in Maryland. No, people were definitely dying! In her opinion, modern science was spiraling out of control.

Everyone she cared about was in terrible danger.

'Mind a little company?' Oz asked. He glided to Max's right side. 'Or do you want to be alone?'

'I'd like some company.'

Max turned her face and smiled at the sight of him. She flew closer and touched his hurt cheek with her fingers. 'That's a very impressive bruise.'

'It's a war wound,' Oz said proudly. 'From the Battle of the Pines.'

'Sure is,' Max agreed. *And I'm afraid the war has just begun, Ozymandias. Only just begun.*

Oz did a somersault in the air, then looped back. He guided blind Icarus to Max's side as they crossed the moon-silvered Potomac River.

'Max, are you wearing *perfume*?' Ic asked. 'You are, aren't you? *Interesting.*'

'So you can follow me easier,' Max said, and laughed.

'What a city! Okay, listen up, everyone,' Oz called out so all could hear. 'Welcome to the nation's capital. I'm Ozymandias, and I'll be your tour guide tonight. On your right is the John F. Kennedy Center, and there, just below us, is the famous Iwo Jima statue. And that,' Oz said dramatically, 'is an American Airlines 747 coming straight at us. Let's get outta here before somebody calls in jet fighters to shoot us down!'

The kids screamed loudly with pleasure. Then their yells were drowned out by the incredible roar of the American jet passing overhead.

The flock, now in formation, flew almost directly over the Lincoln Memorial.

Oz continued his guided tour, pointing out the Vietnam Veterans Memorial and numerous traffic circles with avenues radiating out from them like spokes on a wheel. 'Isn't that the most amazing building?' Oz shouted as they flew over the Capitol.

'The dome-capped rotunda on the Capitol building is the biggest of its kind in America. *That's* Pennsylvania Avenue,' he said. 'Look straight down and you can see the White House where the President and his family live. And the Hoover building's down there somewhere close. The Federal Bureau of Investigation.

'C'mon, Ic. *Cawwww-roll!*' Oz shouted. He and Ic then barrel-rolled to the left, and the whole flock followed.

They flew very close to the ground, finally dipping their feathers in the reflecting pool, then, with a *chee-rupppp,* they rose and circled the amazing Capitol dome.

'Do you think the President knows what's happening out in the real world?' Oz asked as he came close to Max again. 'Like in Maryland? Like among us common folk? Like that people are trying to kill us?'

Her eyes shut, then opened slowly. 'I sincerely doubt it. Maybe we can tell him some time. Or *show* him. Now hold my hand, please. I need my hand held.'

Ozymandias did even better. He glided over Max, and then let her snuggle underneath. Magical! They flew like that all the way home to Kit's apartment.

CHAPTER SEVENTY-ONE

It was the crack of dawn, although in my current mood I preferred to think of it as the crack of doom. Kit and I had already started driving south on Route 1 toward the FBI's Critical Incident Response Group in Stafford, Virginia. It was something we had to do. Lives could be at stake, including ours and the kids.

We'd left the kids in Kit's apartment with a video game that had a play time of *700 hours*, I swear to God; a freezer full of frozen pizza; and strict orders not to fly under any circumstances.

We were headed straight for the nightmare that had haunted Max for so long, all of her life, actually. *You talk, you die*. Kit's apartment seemed to be the safest place for the kids. For the time being anyway.

I sucked on the sippin' lid of my coffee container, hopelessly trying to calm my nerves. Less than an hour after leaving DC, I caught sight of our destination.

There was no sign out front, no discernible address. Just two plain two-story red-brick office buildings connected by a concrete walkway.

'Looks innocent enough,' Kit said, 'but don't be fooled, Frances Jane. Not for a minute.'

'Don't worry, I'm not going to be taken in by any fast-talking FBI dudes,' I said, and winked at him. 'Been there, done that.'

The Critical Incident Response Group had been formed in 1994, post-Waco and Ruby Ridge. It had been housed at the FBI Academy at Quantico for five years, but it had recently been moved to a location about eight miles away. The unit's objective, Kit told me, was to 'provide emergency response to a variety of crises, including terrorist activities, hostage takings, and barricaded subject situations'.

Okay, that should cover just about everything. But then again, maybe not.

About three hundred people worked here, according to Kit, and the parking lot was mostly full when we pulled in. Kit parked and locked his Subaru Outback. Then we walked up a poured concrete path and through the glass doors to a vestibule that was empty except for a single elevator.

'Are they going to believe us? And are they going to help?' I finally asked Kit.

'I sincerely doubt it,' Kit said and frowned.

'I sincerely question why we're here. *Why are we here, Kit?*'

He ran his hand back over his blond hair. 'We're here because they might help us – inadvertently. They might know something important, and just not know that they know it. It happens more than you'd imagine inside the Bureau.'

'Oh. So we're here to interrogate them, not the other way around?'

Kit winked. 'That's the plan anyway. We'll soon find out. Besides, I promised I'd come.'

The door slid open and Kit and I took the elevator to the second-floor reception area. It was protected from the world by a thick pane of bulletproof glass. Kit presented his ID, and speaking into a grille in the bulletproof partition asked to see Special Agent Breem.

A female agent at the front desk smiled pleasantly and buzzed us in. 'Take a left and keep walking,' she said. 'Agent Breem is expecting you. We all are. We were hoping you'd bring the whiz-kids.'

CHAPTER SEVENTY-TWO

We followed the agent's instructions, our footsteps echoing eerily down the linoleum-tiled corridor. My anxiety level was rising pretty fast now. Visits with the FBI can do that to you, I guess. I'd had bad experiences with them before. Ironically, so had Kit. They're good people, mostly, but something got screwed up along the way. I guess that's what happens when Herbert Hoover is your daddy. Talk about the road to perdition.

There were pods of offices alongside both sides of the hallway, most of them brimming with agents, some in suits and ties, others in jeans and T-shirts. A surprisingly motley crew. Not as uptight as I'd imagined they would be.

At the end of the hall a slender, blond man in a blue suit was waiting for us. Agent Warshaw, from last night.

Prick. Jerk. Insensitive asshole. And yes, that was how I really felt about him.

'Dr O'Neill, Brennan. Come in. Please.'

'How could we refuse such an offer?' I said.

'What did I do to her?' Warshaw asked Kit, who merely shrugged.

First there was the de rigueur offer of coffee, that Kit and I turned down, followed by inane commentary about our drive down, the weather, and the Washington Redskins. Just to establish that we were all on the same side.

I wasn't buying it. We weren't. An old cartoon character called Pogo had once said, 'We have met the enemy and he is us.' That pretty much matched my feelings.

'Where's Breem?' Kit asked as Warshaw unfurled a cloth wall map of Maryland.

'He said he'll join us if he can,' Warshaw said, basically dismissing Kit's question. 'Now, suppose you tell me what you're looking for.'

'You already know what we're looking for. Help. Information. Max knows something that's pretty scary. It has to do with an unlawful experimental project,' Kit said. 'Illegal experiments may be going on somewhere in Maryland. Location *fuzzy*, name *unknown*. People, *unnamed*, are possibly being killed as we get ready to stick pins or whatever in your map. It's pretty much what happened at the School in Colorado.

'You *know* all this. *It's in the report I filed*. The problem is – nobody believes Max. Or me,' Kit said, the tension rising in his voice.

'You're here, aren't you?' said Warshaw. 'We're helping you.'

'Only because I have a little juice left in Washington.

Very little. Because nobody is really taking this very seriously.'

'All right, then, do I understand this much correctly?' Warshaw asked. 'Someone connected with so-called biotech experiments wants to shut Max up so bad, they're willing to kill all of the children to do it.'

'Something like that,' Kit said. 'Actually, I think they're trying to capture the kids. Murder might be a backup option. The children are valuable. I don't know why these people want them so badly. It's driving me crazy.'

'Come on,' Warshaw said derisively. '*Listen* to yourself. You have no real evidence, no documentation, nothing but the half-formed musings of a twelve-year-old who is probably under an awful lot of stress anyway.'

'I tend to agree with Warshaw,' said Agent Breem, just now entering the office. 'Why don't you tell us what you know, Agent Brennan. We need to hear it all firsthand. And Dr O'Neill, you feel free to contribute too.'

'Oh, thanks,' I said.

Kit could be as compelling as hell when he wanted to be. For the next hour, he filled Special Agent Breem in on *some* of Max's scary information. But only *some*. Seemed that Kit didn't completely trust Breem either.

Breem listened without questioning a single point. Then he tapped out several numbers on Warshaw's desk phone, relayed some information, paused, and said, 'Get back to me as soon as possible.'

No more than fifteen minutes had passed when a blonde woman appeared and handed an accordion file to

Breem. He looked carefully at the contents.

I read the label upside down. *Liberty General Hospital.* What is this?

Breem said, 'You do still have a few friends in the Hoover building. They want you to have assistance from us, so assistance is what you get. Liberty would seem to be a facility around here that *could* be the site the girl is referring to.

'Having said that, you can probably rule Liberty out. It's a first-class teaching hospital. Hell, Liberty is where the President and Vice President go for their checkups these days. It's the best hospital facility anywhere near DC. Better than Walter Reed.'

Kit nodded affirmatively as he flipped through the documents inside the file.

'Unlike some children her age, Max doesn't confabulate and she doesn't lie. She says there's an outlaw lab in Maryland. Wherever it is, they're conducting experiments. On humans.'

'*Maybe* there are illegal experiments being conducted somewhere, but I doubt it would be at Liberty,' said Breem.

I saw Kit tense, and a muscle in his cheek was doing the cha-cha. 'I understand,' he said. 'Thanks for the file anyway. We'll be going now.'

'I really don't like him,' I said when Kit and I were heading back to the car. 'I hate how he talked down to you. Same for Warshaw. Do you trust them?'

Kit looked right at me. 'At this point I trust you and the

kids. Nobody else. I figure that everybody else is trying to kill us.'

I stared at him. 'That sounds like something Max would say.'

'She did.'

CHAPTER SEVENTY-THREE

*E*verybody else is trying to kill us. What a concept.
Chilling, and possibly true.

It was late afternoon when we arrived back at Kit's
place in Washington. I was anxious, hyper, and flat-out
scared. So were the children. We spent the rest of the
day nervously peering out of Kit's windows, watching
office workers and tourists browse the toney galleries
and restaurants around Dupont Circle.

But as the saying goes, *It isn't paranoia if people really
are after you.*

When the offices and shops closed for the night and
the street darkened, we made our break.

One by one, the children slipped out of the bathroom
window that faced away from the street.

Six times, the flurry of their wingbeats echoed against
the brick and concrete of the back courtyard. I held
my breath and thanked God that there were no gunshots, no screams. I was beginning to think like Kit
about this whole scary nightmare. At this point I trusted

him and the kids, nobody else.

'I'm shaking some,' I finally admitted once the last of the kids was gone.

'Don't worry, it will probably get worse. *No*, we're okay. So far anyway.'

Kit and I waited half an hour before we left the building, then we walked to the corner of Massachusetts Avenue and caught a taxicab. I felt as if we were characters in a movie, a really scary one, the kind I don't go to.

We rode in silence as the cab took us south on Massachusetts Avenue for a couple of blocks, past several small embassies and the like. Then Kit hopped out at a red light and disappeared.

I stayed in the taxi as it turned right on to Sixteenth Street at Scott's Circle and continued on to P Street, where I got out. Real spy stuff.

The Subaru was still parked where we'd left it earlier. After a few minutes Kit came ambling up with the car keys.

He gave me a hug. 'You okay?'

'Hugs help. But *nope*.'

We took off to the west, looping and turning, passing right by his apartment again, then heading out toward the zoo. We collected the children from their hiding place behind a Safeway, four blocks northeast of Kalorama Park, and quickly loaded them into the car.

Mission accomplished. So far, so good.

'Buckle up,' Kit said. 'I mean it.'

He carried on with his expert driving maneuvers for

losing a tail – just in case there was one. This thrilled the kids no end, but scared me half to death. We zipped around cars at racetrack speed, backtracked, got off ramps and on to other ones. By the time we had finally eased off the main roads and checked into an idyllic and rustic motel called Alma's Valley Rest, in the backwoods of Maryland, we'd surely shaken anyone who might've been following us.

Or so I prayed.

Alma's was another funky, bungalow-type motel. We had our own four-hundred-square-foot cabin in the woods, and it was actually much nicer than our bungalow at the Pines. There were two double beds covered with matching powder-blue spreads, plus some folding cots, and a cable-powered TV.

To top it off there was a little brook out back shaded by the spreading branches of several elm trees. What more could a girl ask for?

I was even starting to like sleeping with all of us in one room. It was crowded, but very *nest-y,* and as sweet as a spoonful of molasses.

Then daybreak arrived and my storybook fantasy of Princess Frannie, her handsome Prince Kit, and six magical children burned off with the morning fog.

The *hunters* were out there somewhere. There was no doubt about it.

Somehow, we had to stop them, before they stopped us.

But *how?*

CHAPTER SEVENTY-FOUR

In the end, it was simple really – we had to hunt the hunters. We had to get them before they got us. There was no other way out of this.

Kit had managed to cast a spell over the FBI. Maybe he did have connections in the Hoover building. Anyway, *somebody* was instrumental in getting us an interview at the Hauer Institute inside Liberty General Hospital.

Half the kids were fast asleep and the others were watching the Cartoon Network while drinking milk and digging into a heaping pile of Krispy Kreme donuts when Kit and I left for Liberty Hospital, which we already knew was *beyond reproach*.

Once we were on the road Kit said, 'Man, this is one beautiful day,' and it *was* gorgeous, all golden yellows and soft blues.

October breezes puffed at the fluffy clouds, sounds of the sixties be-bopped from the radio, and Kit sang along with Bobby Darin's 'Dream Lover'.

Kit has a pretty good singing voice and was giving Walden Robert Cassotto a real run for his money. We were remembering how much we liked each other and forgetting for a little while that this wasn't the first day of summer vacation.

Unfortunately, we were headed straight into Max's nightmare. If not at Liberty Hospital, then somewhere else out here in rural Maryland.

I couldn't begin to imagine what these experiments might be like, but if they were anything like what I'd seen at the School in Colorado, maybe I didn't want to.

The very 'well-respected' Liberty General Hospital was in Carroll County, about thirty-three miles northwest of Baltimore, not far from the Liberty Reservoir. The hospital was so well hidden in a cleft between the gently rolling hills of Maryland that we overshot it at first.

On the second pass, I spotted the discreet bronze sign that directed us off the main road to a narrow lane, then to a wide gravel drive that wound through mature plantings and beautifully manicured grounds.

'It almost looks too good to be true,' I said to Kit. 'Maybe your pals at the Bureau are right for a change.'

'I don't have any pals at the Bureau. Not any more. They all think I'm Mulder, remember?'

The hospital appeared to be made up of two wings set at sixty-degree angles to each other, like the halves of an opened book standing on end. The three-story-high

buildings were made of white stone and had lots of wide
windows opening out to a magnificent view.

I had to admit, it looked totally benign.

So why did my hackles rise at the first sight of the place?

CHAPTER SEVENTY-FIVE

*A*nd why did my hackles stay up? Why did every instinct
tell me to run from this place as if I was at the gates of
eternal damnation? And why didn't I run?

Kit lightly touched the small of my back as we walked
through the automatic sliding doors that led to a large
open reception area. I needed to be touched right then, to
be reassured.

'I'm okay,' I turned and whispered. *Liar. Big fat liar.*

'I'm not,' he said. 'I get funny around places where they
might be doing experiments on humans.'

'*Not* at Liberty Hospital,' I said. 'The *President* and *Vice
President* come here for their checkups.'

'You think this is the place that Max found out about?
The Hospital? The Unholy of Holies?'

'For some totally crazy reason,' I said, 'I do. It's just a
feeling, Kit.'

'*Now* I'm scared,' he said.

Morning sunlight blazed across the terrazzo floor and
seemed to light the way to a circular granite information

desk. There, an extremely helpful and nice elderly man pointed us to a bank of elevators marked 'The Hauer Institute', where we would have our interview. He had our names and seemed genuinely impressed that we were there to see Dr Ethan Kane.

The elevator took us down to an underground level and opened on to a small, very tasty-looking reception room. It was thickly carpeted in deep blue and furnished with matching upholstered chairs.

There was a coffee table covered with crisp copies of daily newspapers foreign and domestic, and magazines. Coffee brewed on a nearby mahogany sideboard. Vivaldi's *Four Seasons* played from hidden speakers. Perfect, too perfect.

But the metallic smell of disinfectant broke the spell for me. We were still in a hospital. No doubt about it.

'You ever read *Coma* by Robin Cook?' Kit asked me. 'Gruesome stuff.'

'Stop it,' I said, but at least he'd made me smile.

'Listen, Kit, I know your FBI buddies set up this meeting, but why do you think the people here are willing to talk to us?'

Kit allowed himself a slight smile. 'Because if they refused, then we'd get *really* suspicious.'

'Too late. I'm already there.'

Kit presented his creds and a letter of introduction to the blue suit seated behind a small antique desk. The officious young man made a phone call to a Ms Analise Miller.

'Analise will be right out,' said the receptionist, and it was as good as done.

Ms Miller was a thin, prim woman in her late twenties. Her dark hair was tightly pulled back in a long ponytail. She was wearing a taupe pants suit that looked *très chic* and businesslike at the same time. Her smile was vivid, but in my opinion feigned, as if her light green eyes had failed to convey the message her mouth was sending.

She enthusiastically extended her slender hand. 'I've never met someone from the FBI before,' she said. I glanced over at Kit. Yeah, sure. Like this was such a big treat for her.

We were led to a different elevator bank. The elevator that responded to our call was vast, with doors on both sides. It had a composition-rubber floor and brushed-metal walls.

The car dropped like a shot to a floor that I suspected was at least twenty or thirty feet underground.

'Forty-four feet,' said Analise. I *believed* she could read minds.

The elevator door opened on to a gray, rubber-tiled corridor, where medical personnel in blue scrubs and white nurses' uniforms walked quickly in both directions.

'This is the research area at Liberty. The Hauer Institute is dedicated to carrying on the work of the famous team of Clara and Harold Hauer,' Ms Miller told us. 'They were killed in a tragic car accident outside Boston, as you probably know.'

I did know about the Hauers. 'Sad,' I said.

We paused in front of a glass-fronted room filled with floor-to-ceiling metal racks. Each held hundreds of cages resembling plastic shoeboxes.

The cages were alive with dark, rounded shapes. They were lab mice.

My hackles were hackling again.

'Our so-called fuzzy test tubes,' the PR lady said brightly. 'We do a huge amount of animal testing here – as you can well imagine.'

Her words triggered a flood of bad memories. Really bad ones.

I remembered a similar room at the School, that horrific place where Max and the other kids had *lived* for most of their young lives. There had actually been a 'Mouse Room' like the one I was staring at now, and also a 'Nursery' of horribly deformed children who had been left to die. I would never forget the first time I saw Peter and Oz and Ic and Wendy – the children were cowering in cages and covered with excrement.

I shook my head to banish the disturbing images. This *wasn't* the School, I reminded myself. The *President* came here for physicals.

Our escort didn't see these pictures in my mind, fortunately. Maybe Analise had some of her own. She led us briskly away from the fuzzy test tubes and down some corridors. We saw rooms filled with technicians sitting at computers. They were probably feeding DNA information into the center's database.

We took the elevator down another level and stepped

out. The third subterranean floor had laboratory after laboratory filled with shining, modern medical equipment and signs pointing to *Operating Rooms One Through Six*.

'The Hauers were pioneers in the field of stem-cell research,' proclaimed Ms Miller. 'As I'm sure you know, Dr O'Neill, stem cells are fresh primary, unassigned cells, harvested from fetuses or from bone marrow. When injected into the body, these cells have the ability to become whatever type of organ cells are required by the body. The cells seem to know where an injury has occurred, and they go to the site of the injury and repair it.'

'This is all terrific. Really helpful,' Kit said without a trace of cynicism; in fact, he was wearing his most winning smile. 'Now,' he said, 'take us to your leader.'

'Dr Ethan Kane is just around this corner,' said Analise. 'As usual, he's operating today. The man never stops, never seems to rest.'

CHAPTER SEVENTY-SIX

The killer named Marco Vincenti wasn't all that surprised when he got the call to go to Maryland and was told to get there pronto. He had sensed earlier that these particular employers were reluctant to hire too many outsiders, even when they desperately needed a specialist of his caliber, pun intended.

They had tried it the other way, though.

Catching the kids.

But they had failed.

So now it was time for other options. As he had prophesied on the rooftop of the building in Denver, *'Catch you next time, kid.'*

Vincenti's specialty: a long-distance sniper. Before he'd gone into business for himself, he'd been in the US Army. Nowadays the jobs were less frequent, but the pay was so much higher.

Marco had decided to drive from his house in Hempstead, Long Island, down to western Maryland, where the six freak-show kids were supposed to be hanging out. His job, specifically, was to kill only one of the kids – the older girl, Max. But there were other potential bonuses, and he planned to go home with as much money as he possibly could.

Marco listened to a 'Best of Mozart' tape all the way down from New York. The music didn't calm his nerves – he didn't need that – but he enjoyed the brilliance and, most of all, the precision of the compositions.

This job had a code name known only to him and to his secretive employer.

SKEET.

He liked that one.

Shooting targets that didn't, couldn't, shoot back.

CHAPTER SEVENTY-SEVEN

K it and I finally got to meet Dr Ethan Kane.
Analise Miller led us up to a man 'scrubbing' at a
wide metal sink outside one of the operating rooms. We
watched him take a towel from a nurse, who then helped
him out of his operating gown. Analise Miller reminded
him that the FBI had set up our visit. He smiled at the
woman, then nodded her away. Then he introduced
himself, offering up strong, soap-smelling handshakes
and twenty-twenty eye contact as Kit told him our
names.

Dr Kane was incredibly handsome, I'll give him that
much. He had a square, seamless face, thick salt-and-
blond hair, broad shoulders and a narrow waist. His eyes
were a luminous blue and his smile was as warm as a
Gerber baby's.

'Call me Ethan,' he said. 'I prefer that. It's very good to
meet you. What is this about again? The Federal Bureau
might be interested in using our hospital from time to
time? You don't know how much that pleases me. This

is a great research facility, perhaps the best in the United States. Have you got time to talk? I have a few minutes if you do.'

'That's very kind of you, Doctor,' Kit said in a gentle, mellifluous voice. I had never seen this very smooth, diplomatic side of him before. As we followed Dr Kane, Kit turned to me and whispered, 'Don't blow my nice-guy act. And don't laugh either.'

We knew from the PR document Analise Miller had given us that Dr Kane was the winner of the American Society of Transplant Surgeons' Pioneer Award and that he was doing 'breakthrough work with stem-cell therapies'. We followed him through a labyrinth of corridors to his office, an unimposing, very cozy space crowded with books that were stacked almost desk high on the floor. There were also pictures of Dr Kane with a few well-chosen political leaders, movie stars, and a financial wiz or three.

'Sorry about the *face*-dropping.' He waved dismissively at the photographs. 'It helps with our fund-raising. You can't imagine. Ours is the celebrity age, isn't it?'

There was also a large family portrait on the credenza. In the imposing picture, Dr Kane stood on the front steps of a gracious Greek Revival-style farmhouse. His arms were around a dark-haired woman, who had a Jackie Kennedy look about her, and two gorgeous children: a teenaged boy and girl; and a third child, a girl of about four, who was clowning at their feet.

'Sissy is our so-called change-of-life baby,' he told us,

pointing to the little one. 'And boy, did she change our lives. What a little pistol she is.' He smiled and put a bowl of M&Ms within our reach. 'I'm addicted.' He winked. 'There are worse things, I suppose.'

He cleared papers from two side chairs and asked us to make ourselves comfortable. He sat back in his desk chair, wadded up a piece of notepaper and tossed it through a miniature basketball hoop that hung just above a wastebasket. 'Two points,' he said, then rocked back in his chair, self-satisfied as an LA Lakers fan.

'To be honest, I'm awfully glad Washington takes an active interest in us,' Kane said. 'The more public awareness, the better. We need funds. Let me tell you about our pet project, which is incredible.

'Our singular mission is to extend human life, and to that end we're working on two tracks simultaneously,' he explained. Suddenly, he leaned forward, his chair making a springy squeak, and made a gesture with his hands, each pointing in opposite directions. He spoke of divergent paths.

'We're working with stem cells on one track – organ transplant on the other. As it should be, it's illegal to use human fetal material, so we're limited to clones of fetal cells taken prior to the ruling, and we're using stem cells from bone marrow. Of course, the work is slow going. But that's prudent, don't you agree? It's also the right thing to do.'

He tossed back a handful of M&Ms, and crunched them while we waited for him to continue. I could tell that he wasn't interested in our opinions, or interruptions.

'As for transplantation,' Dr Kane went on, 'the use of animal organs has been banned for good and bad reasons, so we're doing the best we can with available human organs. Human organs are in tremendous demand, and, historically, when we could get them, there was a really high rate of failure after transplantation.

'But we've had a couple of real breakthroughs in the last couple of years,' he said, a smile lighting his handsome face. 'We've learned that transplanting several organs in a system makes for better success than transplanting individual organs. So when we have a matching donor, we use the entire organ system.

'I want you to see this,' he said. He reached behind him and opened the doors of the credenza. He pulled out a chart and spread it open on the desk in front of us. We looked at the colored bars showing the number of multi-organ transplants and the success rate.

'We're up to eighty per cent success in the last six months. Can you imagine that? Five years ago, I wouldn't have believed it. Three years ago I wouldn't have!'

Dr Kane seemed completely caught up in the personal side of the work he was doing; he told us of a half-dozen case histories of young people who would have died but for organ transplantation, and of older people who'd been given a new lease on life.

I must admit, his confidence was bracing, his enthusiasm infectious.

THE LAKE HOUSE

'I can hardly sleep at night I'm so excited by some of this work,' he said. 'We're closer than ever to being able to keep people alive for a long, long time. I have hopes that soon the two tracks will merge. When that happens, we'll have so many choices. To either replace organs or use stem-cell technology to repair tissue. Or to use both methods simultaneously. I think we can bank on it, Frannie and Kit. We're all going to live to benefit from these most incredible advances. Isn't that glorious? Imagine it. In our lifetime. Now let me tell you about the rest of our hospital. I'll make it short but very sweet.'

Kit and I were a little dazzled as we left the facility. It was the opposite of what we'd seen and felt at the terrible School in Colorado. The evidence was compelling that this was an exceptional medical complex. The Hauer Institute was advanced, famous for good works, well run, possibly the best research center in America. Dr Ethan Kane was clearly brilliant, and he had a great reputation.

'I don't get it,' said Kit.

I did.

My hackles were still up.

273

CHAPTER SEVENTY-EIGHT

Dr Ethan Kane smiled as FBI Agent Brennan and Dr O'Neill finally left his office. What incredible fools they were. He knew exactly what they wanted here, and although he was disappointed that the Hospital was under suspicion, there wasn't much that he could do about it, was there? Besides, he was almost certain that those two imbeciles had believed his bullshit. He'd been so patient and ingratiating with them. Just thinking about the smarmy interview made him ill.

Ethan Kane left his office and boarded the private elevator down to the basement. He had an important meeting to attend.

He got out at B3 and hurried along a lengthy corridor to a conference room.

He would've loved to show Brennan and Dr O'Neill *this* on their guided tour of the Hospital. Blow their little minds.

Ethan Kane used a special pass-key to let himself into the conference room. Three men sat around a glass and metal table.

Even Dr Kane had to admit that they were extraordinary specimens, miracles, if you took the trouble to think about it.

Each of the three looked exactly like him.

They almost *were* him. But it was more like – they were the arms and legs, and he was the head. And, of course, the head ruled.

'Doctors Kane,' he addressed the three lookalikes, 'we have a lot of work to do, and not much time to do it. Resurrection is close, but there's something else on my mind right now. I want those children! I especially want the one called Maximum. I have seen the future, and Resurrection is only the beginning.'

CHAPTER SEVENTY-NINE

Ozymandias couldn't get the thought out of his head that he was happier than he'd ever been in his life. *By a lot! By miles and miles! By light years!*

Of course, he'd been mostly totally miserable before this. It was a weekday, and the woods were empty of human life but filled with other familiar and reassuring sounds. Brooks rippled musically over mossy rocks, and the air was filled with birdsong and squirrel chatter.

And best of all, he and Max were alone. The sweet, unbearably beautiful golden-haired girl was right beside him as they soared over the woodland, literally skimming the treetops with the tips of their wings.

As he glided on the soft, fresh-smelling air, Oz considered a profound thought: *how angry he'd been his entire life.*

Sad but true. And undeniable.

He'd raged and fought against his keepers at the School in Colorado, and ever since he'd been returned to his so-called biological mother, he'd been furious at the world. But in the last few days that hot red flame had almost completely gone out of him.

Max was the whole reason. He wanted her to feel as tremendous as he did, and thought he'd die if she didn't. He flashed her a conspiratorial look, then zoomed straight up into the air, disappearing into the blue as if he were a fighter jet trying to escape from a sneak missile attack.

Then he swooped down on Max, hugging her from behind. He kissed her on the nape of her neck as the two of them fell toward the earth.

This was glorious. Everybody should try it at least once. When it was almost too late to come out of the dive, Max said, 'Oz, let go! *Now!*'

He did! And they spread their beautiful wings wide, *beating, beating, beating* back against the air, stopping their fall in a move that would have brought a Cirque du Soleil crowd to its feet.

'You,' said Max laughing, 'could be dangerous!'

'But you like it, right? Right? You're not terribly tired of me already, are you?'

'No, Ozymandias, I love you to pieces. I've never felt like this before and I don't want it to end. We're, well, we're Romeo and Juliet.'

'Let's skip the suicide part if you don't mind.'

'I'm not the suicide type,' Max grinned.

She took long rowing strokes of air and pulled herself skyward in a ninety-degree trajectory. At the top of the climb, she folded her wings and swept down on Oz. She caressed his cheek with her fingers as she fell past him. God, she did love him.

'Catch me. If you can,' she called out.

'That's not a problem. Consider yourself as good as caught.'

'What a guy.'

The race was on.

Max shot over a gorgeous copse of ash trees, then dropped below their canopy, exhibiting a serpentine flight path between the trunks. Definitely a ten out of ten on the judges' scorecards.

Oz rushed right behind her, breathlessly beating his wings, which were a blur. They swooped past tree trunk after tree trunk, an incredible feat of daring and skill.

Then Max landed.

So did Oz.

They were wrapped in each other's arms even before their feet touched ground. Their trembling lips met. Their excited breathing seemed the loudest sound in the forest.

Oz raked back Max's golden hair with his fingers and gently held her head by the knot he made at the nape of her neck. He kissed her, and she sighed under him. Suddenly he became very hard and she laughed. '*What* a guy,' she whispered.

'And what a girl,' said Oz. 'What a *woman* you are, Max.'

'You really think so?' she whispered breathlessly.

'I know it.'

Their bodies rose and fell, rose and fell, under the dappled light cast by gently tossing branches of ash trees.

They were completely lost in each other. They were one with everything in the woods. There was something about their complicated genetic makeup that made this beyond compare. After quite a long time, they finally broke apart, the sweat shining on their perfect bodies.

Max was already thinking ahead to the next moments – when they would do it all over again. She didn't feel an ounce of guilt. She felt beautiful, pure. *We were made for this. It's so right.*

She and Oz lay together quietly for several breathless moments, gathering strength. Then Oz felt Max's fingers begin a slow dance, tracing the proud eagle on his chest, lingering as they brushed across his flat belly.

Oz took her hands, rolled over on to his stomach, and pinned her wings flat behind her. He looked deeply into her eyes. He lowered his face so that he could feel her sweet breath on his cheeks.

'You mean everything in the universe to me, Max,' he said. 'It will always be this way.'

'Even if we have to live on pig nuts someday?'

'Even if it comes to slugs.'

'I do love you,' she breathed. 'What we have is better than just human love. I don't think anyone has ever felt this way before. Isn't science wonderful? Occasionally, anyway.'

'Remember, they think we're a *mistake*.'

Max was still feeling lightheaded, so when she heard the sound of cracking branches it caught her off guard. She pushed away from Oz. Her whole body tensed.

She and Oz weren't alone.

Oz sprang to his feet, her warrior protector. He spread out his wings to their full ten feet across and assumed an eagle's crouch to shield her.

As he shifted on his haunches, a scream of rage exploded through the forest!

They both saw who it was – and it couldn't have been worse.

CHAPTER EIGHTY

I t was Matthew.
He was totally freaked out by what he had just seen in the woods. Max . . . and Ozymandias? They were doing the dirty deed. His sister was making whoopie with Oz. Gross. He was totally grossed-out.

'What the hell is going on?' he yelled at them. 'What are you two doing together? Stop it right now. Get away from her, Oz. I'm warning you. Jeez, Max. Oh man, oh man.'

It was dead quiet for a second, then Ozymandias spread his wings and shrieked. Matthew shivered and started to cry as Max quickly got dressed. He didn't turn around to look at his sister even when Max told him it was all right.

'I'm telling what you did,' he sobbed. 'I'm telling Frannie and Kit. I'm telling everybody.'

'Matty, come talk to me. Come here, you.'

'Matty, I wasn't hurting Max,' Oz said. He didn't look angry now. Maybe just embarrassed, and perhaps sensitive to Matthew's feelings. 'This is how it is with our kind. You'll see when you get a little older, buddy.'

He walked over to Matthew and took him by the shoulders, the better to see into his face. 'I love Max. I love you, too.'

But Matthew roughly pushed Oz away. 'Go fuck yourself, *buddy*. You too, Max. Oh, wait, it's too late for that! It already happened.'

Matthew ran blindly through the woods, and when he felt the air pull on his opened wings, he leaped upward and flew higher than he ever had before. Then Matthew screamed like a banshee into the heavens.

And Marco Vincenti had the little bird twerp right in his sights, in the crosshairs.

All he had to do was *pull*.

And down would come baby.

CHAPTER EIGHTY-ONE

K it and I had just turned into the parking spot at the ever dee-lightful Alma's Valley Rest when I heard one of the kids crying.

Which one? What was going on now?

I ran behind the cabin to the small clearing leading into the woods. Matthew came running toward me and blasted into my arms. *Matthew? He never cried.*

'Frannie!' he whined. 'Fran-neeee!'

'What is it? What happened, sweetie? What's the matter with you?' I asked as I hugged him tightly.

'They were naked in the woods! I swear to God, Frannie. I'm not making it up. I'm not.'

'Who, Matthew? What are you talking about?'

He turned and pointed. Max and Oz were walking out of the woods toward the motel. My heart sank. I think I might have gasped. I'm not exactly sure what I did. But I know that I felt what any other mother would have felt. Fear, disappointment, anger, *more* fear.

I kissed Matthew's face and then the top of his head.

'Matthew, please go to the car and help Kit with the presents we bought. Yeah, that's right, go on,' I said. 'Go.'

He stumbled off toward the car, and I turned back to Max and Oz with their rumpled clothes and leaf-bedecked hair.

'*What* is going on?' I asked. 'What happened in the woods? What is Matthew talking about?'

'Matty snuck up on us and I didn't know it was him. I got kind of fierce,' Oz said, trying to explain. 'I guess I scared him.'

'That's another matter,' I said, struggling to keep my own feelings very much under control. 'Part of this is that he snuck up, and part of it is what you were doing in the woods.'

I let silence rule for a second as I tried to figure out my role here. There was a voice in my head that belonged to a snooty lawyer lady who'd once said, '*You've never been a mother, have you, Dr O'Neill?*'

The uncomfortable silence dragged on, and Max and Oz weren't helping one bit. Their faces glowed, but they also looked strangely calm.

'Listen,' Max said reasonably. 'Please don't worry so much about us, Frannie. We know exactly what we're doing. This is natural. It's good. It's the right thing.'

'Oh, Max, Max, listen to yourself. What are you saying? How can you be so sure?'

'Because it's second nature for us,' Oz said, as if reading my thoughts. 'It just is. Besides, we don't exactly need your permission, Frannie.'

'Max, you are very young!' I said. 'And you too, Oz.'

'In *human* years, Frannie. But we're more than human,' Max said. 'We're special, remember? And we're also in love. Deeply, passionately, wonderfully in love.'

She combed her hair with her fingers and tied it up into a loose knot. 'Our bird genes make us mature for our age. In fact, I think we're probably about *your* age,' she added, her eyes twinkling irresistibly. 'You're old enough to mate, aren't you?'

She had me there.

CHAPTER EIGHTY-TWO

M ax sat *cooing* in a big, comfy blue armchair by the cabin's front window. She held Matthew in her lap and gently smoothed his silky blond hair. They had made up. Mostly anyway. As much as they were going to right now.

'I'm sorry, Matty, but don't hate me for ever,' she cooed affectionately. 'Okay? Coo. Coo. Please? Matty-poo? Coo, coo, coo.'

'Stop manipulating,' was all he said to her. 'Stop that stupid cooing.'

Kit and Frannie had gone to gas up the car and pick up food for dinner. Hopefully they'd be going back to DC soon. Max couldn't wait to leave this ratty motel and be as far from here as possible. Apparently, the awful experiments weren't being conducted at Liberty General Hospital. But they were happening *somewhere* near here. She was sure of that.

The hunters were near too. She sensed them in the air. She just *knew*.

'I will too hate you for ever, ' Matty said. 'You probably scarred me for life. Do you know that?'

That was when Pip started barking his little fool butt off.

Max parted the curtain and saw an SUV, a Dodge Durango, approaching the cabin. Her heart sank about a million and a half miles. Deep, deep, deeper into the abyss.

The Dodge stopped and three men climbed out and positioned themselves in front. The men were wearing ordinary clothes: jeans, khakis, dark shirts. They had guns, though. Big death-dealing weapons.

'Oh holy shii . . . iit,' Max groaned. 'Matthew, go in the bedroom. Right now.'

Matthew's eyes popped. 'Are *we* going to do it?'

'Just go! Right now! *Everybody!* In the bedroom.'

One of the men wore a black windbreaker over his shirt and a long-billed cap pulled down over his eyes. He was clean-cut and good-looking. He looked *right at Max* and spoke in a pleasant, singsong voice.

'Hey there, Maximum. I see you. My name is Ethan, and I need you to come outside with your friends. No one will be hurt if you do as I say. I know how valuable you are. Believe me, I know. I'm in awe of you children. I'm a fan.'

Max's senses prickled at the sound of his voice. She didn't know why, but she had the thought: *he's a doctor.* And he's a really bad person. The worst she'd ever met. Then she felt the little feathers on the back of her neck lift and a chill coursed through her body.

They were in terrible danger and there was only one exit – the front goddamn door. Right where they were standing with their guns.

The bathroom window was so small even Wendy wouldn't be able to squeeze through. Max shot to her feet and bolted the lock on the door.

'Our parents will be back any minute,' she called out.

'I don't think so,' Ethan said. 'Actually, they were spotted going to the market in Kit's car. That's how we found you this time. They're *still* at the market, Max. But a little earlier today they came to visit me at the Hospital. Wonder how that happened, hmmm? Do *you* know, Max?'

He leveled his gun at the window.

Then the son of a bitch fired!

A warning shot!

The plate-glass window tinkled, splintered, and scattered all over the floor. By instinct, the children dropped down low.

Oz screamed ferociously and puffed out his chest.

Pip let out a furious round of barking.

But it was all just fear.

They were trapped.

Like lab rats.

And the *rat fuckers* were right outside the front door.

CHAPTER EIGHTY-THREE

'Come out right now, children. Max! The rest of you! This is your last chance. I'm a busy man. You have no idea what trouble you're causing me. Come out right now or you all die!'

Oz, Max, Peter and Wendy, Icarus, Matthew, the six of them slowly filed out to the creaky wooden plank porch of the cabin.

Six kids.

Very, very special ones.

Priceless.

'We're not going to hurt you, Max,' said Ethan. 'Perish the thought. Not going to happen. *Unless* you run.'

She nodded. 'No. We're way too valuable to you, right? We're big money to you. A lot of people want a piece of us. What *else* do you want, you jerk?'

'Don't believe a word he says,' Oz whispered at her side. 'Look at his eyes. He's a total piece of shit. He's lying.'

'I know he's lying. Just be cool. We have to make the

best of a terrible situation, Oz.'

'Don't whisper, and don't do anything foolish.' Ethan spoke in the calmest, yet most authoritative voice.

Doctor? Scientist? A very bad dude. George Clooney's evil twin, Max thought. *And he wants us for some kind of collection, doesn't he? He's a collector, right? He's the one who runs the outlaw lab in Maryland. Has to be. He has the eyes of a stone-cold killer.*

'Oh, we won't do anything foolish,' said Oz. 'We aren't stupid.'

'No, you're anything but that,' said Ethan. 'You're all geniuses. I know that. I've seen your test scores.'

'Whatever I do, you do the opposite,' Oz whispered again. 'I love you, Max.'

Suddenly Max couldn't breathe. 'Oz, no.'

'I said no whispering and I mean it. Come down off the porch, children. Right now. That's an order. Do you hear me?'

'All right, all right.' Max spoke. 'We're doing exactly what you say.' *Dr Creep-Me-Out.*

'We won't do anything foolish,' Oz repeated. 'You know, like trust you for a second. *Go, Max!*' he screamed.

Oz took off like a bolt of lightning to the left. Max and the others veered right.

The woods on the right were closer. Oz was the one who would be exposed for the longest time, but he was the fastest, the strongest, the alpha male.

Dr Ethan Kane shook his head, cursed under his breath, then yelled, '*Pull!*'

Suddenly, gunfire erupted from at least two guns, maybe more. Max hadn't made it into the trees yet. She and the young ones were exposed.

So Oz made a decision and shot right over the gunmen's heads. He thought he saw goddamn Ethan smile. Then the doctor pointed to the south. *What?* Oz looked that way. *Oh shit.*

A rifleman in camouflage was perched on a hillside. He was perfectly still. His rifle had a long black scope. The barrel was aimed directly at Oz's eyes.

Pull!

CHAPTER EIGHTY-FOUR

He couldn't miss. He just had to decide which of the children to take out. *The little freaks were valuable. The head doctor wanted them alive, if possible, although no one had told Marco Vincenti why.* He knew the drill. If they couldn't be caught, one of them would be killed. Then another. And if necessary, all of them.

Like shooting skeet.

Marco Vincenti played a little mind-game with himself to make the slaughter easier. He thought of them as disgusting, godless freaks of nature.

Yeah, that helped a lot. And it was true, wasn't it?

Though in truth, they were stunningly beautiful, as striking as a Michelangelo sculpture. And the littlest ones were drop-dead cute. No—

Freaks!

Mutants!

Mistakes!

Monstrosities!

Just take 'em out. Do the world a favor.

He sighted on the girl – Max ... Maximum. He'd heard she was worth tens of millions and wondered who the hell would *buy* her. Europeans? The Japanese? Ragheads? What the hell would they do with her? Take her apart and put her back together again? *Why did Kane really want her? It was more than just the money, wasn't it?*

He moved his scope to the little ones, the smallest targets – Wendy and Peter.

Named after what? Characters in *Peter Pan*?

He thought he could easily do a one-two ... Max and her brother, Matthew?

Or Max and Oz? Obviously, they were the leaders of the flock.

That would probably produce the most disharmony and chaos, and get the others to give up.

He had watched them talk to Dr Kane on the porch ... and then the six of them *exploded* into the air. A little trickery. Okay. If that was the way they wanted to play it.

They split up. Beautiful timing. Perfect. He admired that. Then—

Bingo! The target was so obvious to Marco that it was a done deal.

The powerful-looking male was coming right at him. Had he spotted Marco and his rifle? Probably had. The kids' eyesight was supposed to be extraordinary, something else.

Freaks of nature, right! Come and get it, bird-boy.

Though Jesus God, this kid was flying right at him, looming incredibly large in his rifle sight. Coming on like a guided missile.

So dead on, it wasn't even funny.

Dead on the wing!

Marco's body was frozen still. So still, he could feel his own heartbeat, the pulse throbbing in his throat.

The aiming port of the rifle was floating on the bridge of the male's nose.

No, make that the right eye . . . make it *the center of the eyeball.*

His finger gently squeezed.

Something in Marco's peripheral vision was coming fast. From his left! How could that be?

Oh Jesus, no. Oh fuck! He'd made a mistake. Bad one.

The shot cracked loudly, and the noise almost seemed to follow the bullet's flight. Smoke rose gently above the rifle barrel.

And something went terribly wrong, so wrong.

One of the little freaks, the boy Peter, was coming at him.

He was barreling in from the side . . . a little bullet himself, a second guided missile.

No time to get out of the way.

Or even blink.

The boy hit Marco Vincenti at full speed with an outstretched arm. He clotheslined the sniper.

Something – a *rock* – was in his small hand.

Snap! It broke Marco's neck, just like that.
He was dead before he even hit the ground.
Zero ability to fly.

CHAPTER EIGHTY-FIVE

Max screamed, '*Noooooooooooooooooo.* Nooooo! Noooooo!'

She watched horror-stricken as Oz crashed through the trees, dropping toward the ground like a heavy rock in freefall.

There was only one thing for her to do. She had no other choice in the universe.

She had to go to him. Now! No matter what the risk to herself. Go! Now!

Her world narrowed to exclude everything but Ozymandias. She saw his dark form sprawled on the ground below her; his strong limbs splayed at crooked, at impossible angles, his wings obscenely twisted under him from the steep fall.

And yet his face seemed untouched, unhurt. Was it possible that he had survived? It had to be.

Oh, Ozymandias, I love you.

Her heart hammered almost to bursting as she dropped to the woodland floor. She ran and threw herself beside Oz. She waved her fingers in front of his unblinking eyes. She muttered his name over and over.

Max pushed a branch away from his chest and placed her face against his ribcage.

She heard no heartbeat, felt no rise and fall of his chest. Oh, Oz. Why?

'It's me, it's Max. Talk to me, Oz. Talk to me, damn you!'

She pinched his nose and cleared his air passage. She breathed into his mouth, her hair spilling softly around his face. She put pressure on his chest. She kept breathing air into him, mouth to mouth, again and again. She listened to his chest again.

Still no sound. So weird, so awful. Impossible. This couldn't have happened.

'Oz, *please breathe*,' she whispered, holding back tears with all of her strength. 'Remember what you said? Remember, Oz? We're together for ever.'

Max ripped open Oz's shirt, the buttons spinning into the dust and pine needles. That was when she saw the awful, ragged, absolutely obscene wound. It was an oozing hole, two fingers wide.

'Nooooooooo.'

The wound went through the heart of the eagle tattooed on Oz's chest, right where *Max* had been inscribed.

Oz can't be gone! This can't be happening.

He had been so alive just seconds ago. So strong, so beautiful. She could almost see him flying, his wings beating like an engine. She could still hear him calling out to her.

'No! No! No! I won't accept this!' she screamed, covering him with her body and wings. Peter and Matthew had gathered around her, their pitiful cries blending into undulating howls. The entire universe was a single howl now.

'Talk to me, Oz. Talk to me, talk to me. Please. I *know* you can hear me . . . Oz,' she whispered, 'at least say goodbye. At least that. Oh, Ozymandias, why?'

She never saw the shadows of the men, but she felt the heavy 'big bird' nets fall on top of her. Just as she'd thought – they wanted her alive, if possible. What a joke! Didn't they realize she was dead. *Inside*. Where it mattered.

Max's mind separated from her body. As if from a great distance, she felt someone lift her roughly and toss her over his shoulder. She writhed and struggled fiercely, screaming at the top of her voice, 'Put me down! I'll kill you. I swear I'll kill you!'

'I warned you,' said Ethan Kane, 'and now look what's happened. He was worth millions.'

An old image flickered into her mind. So strange. She'd seen a neighbor's tabby cat take a sparrow down from a feeder. The cat had trotted across the yard with the bird in its teeth and the bird was still, *but alive*.

Max felt like that now. Still fighting them with all her might, she began to keen.

She and Ozymandias were supposed to be for ever.

We were made for each other.
This couldn't be the end.
It just couldn't happen.
Could it?
Could it?

PART SIX

A BRAND NEW DAY

CHAPTER EIGHTY-SIX

Clouds hung heavily over the small private airfield to the south of the Hospital. The tarmac was empty except for a small flock of mourning doves pecking for bugs on the heat-retentive runway.

Dr Ethan Kane shot the right cuff of his black Burberry windbreaker and looked impatiently at his Baume and Mercier watch.

It was seven past three in the afternoon.

The plane was thirty-seven minutes late. Everything was ready. Damn it! Where were they?

He hated inefficiency. His precious time and energy were being wasted. It wasn't acceptable.

Ethan Kane wasn't alone at the airfield either. Six members of his medical team had been pulled from their jobs, still wearing their scrubs, and they waited restlessly for the flight to arrive. Kane clamped down on his rage at this *criminal* waste of time. It was inexcusable! Someone would pay.

He had pressing business at the Hospital, but leading

this welcoming committee was also critically important. Within hours, the resources of the Hauer Institute would be stretched as never before.

It was going to be a trial just to process the incoming shipment. Dr Kane was mentally running through a plan to 'warehouse the overage' when he was distracted by the low drone of an incoming aircraft.

'It's about goddamn time,' he snapped. 'Do you realize who you've kept waiting, you imbeciles?'

The sound grew louder, then an Embraer ERJ135 dropped from the cloud cover. Its gorgeous, streamlined shape seemed to magically materialize above the long, flat runway.

The landing was as slick as a cat's whisker. There was a discreet squeal of brakes, the rush of air against the flaps, and then the pristine white airplane rolled to a stop less than a hundred feet from the hangar.

Men in blue jumpsuits ran out from the maintenance shed and sprinted toward the plane. A staircase was wheeled up to the cabin door and Dr Kane's mood lifted.

Live from New York – his wonderful new shipment had finally arrived.

He watched intently as the passengers stepped one by one from the aircraft.

Thirty young men between the ages of seventeen and twenty-three. Each optimistic and brave, each disease-free. They filed down the staircase and on to the tarmac, looking like a professional sports team.

Dr Kane smiled as his eyes caressed the young faces.

They looked perfect, and only perfection would do.

He knew the specimens better than they knew themselves. He knew their blood types and hematocrits. He knew their heights and weights and bone lengths. He knew their ethnic and racial origins, their allergies and genetic predispositions. He also knew their names but not their faces, and he tried to guess which was *Charles, Tyrell, Bandy,* and *Sean.* Who was the prince in the tight black T-shirt? Was the massive young black in cords and green sweater Tyrell?

But it didn't really matter who was who, did it?

Only the parts mattered – not the whole. They would all be *shucked* soon.

Then his real work could begin.

Resurrection.

The time was here. Finally.

One of the most important moments in world history. And it was coming none too soon for the welfare of their pitiful civilization.

These thirty fine specimens were key to the special day which was so close now.

These thirty – and most of all, the thirty beneficiaries.

Dr Kane walked briskly toward the group with outstretched arms. 'Welcome,' he said, calling the group to attention. 'Welcome, welcome. What a great pleasure to see you . . . in the flesh. I can't tell you how happy this makes me.

'I'm Dr Ethan Kane, director of the Hauer Institute. My senior medical staff join me in welcoming all of you to

Maryland and to Liberty General Hospital.

'Think of it! You've been chosen to take an extraordinary journey with us. You'll be making medical history, making some very good money as well, and this will be the best experience you've ever had. I guarantee it!

'Young men, today is your lucky day. You are essential to the future of America! And the rest of the world for that matter.'

Resurrection was right on schedule.

The *donors* were marched inside.

The *beneficiaries* would all be here by nightfall.

CHAPTER EIGHTY-SEVEN

I wanted to be strong but I was getting pretty close to losing it, something I almost never did until lately. Well, until that night when I first met Max in the Colorado woods anyway.

Oh God, poor sweet Oz was already dead. What had we gotten into? Who else might die before this was over? How could we stop the madness? How could we turn it off?

I was in the front seat of Kit's car, speeding along Route 194 east toward the Liberty Hospital. A gathering storm was blowing in from the north. I shivered as seamless thunderheads dimmed the late-afternoon sun.

The children, the ones who were still alive, were being held at the Hospital, or somewhere nearby. Kit and I knew that much. Just enough to scare us half to death. To give us the willies.

'Maybe I should have taken the kids to the Lake House when we ran,' I said.

'Don't beat yourself up, Frannie. They would have found them no matter where you went. I'd rather take this fight to them. I don't see another way. I wish I did, but I don't.'

We had gotten a message just an hour ago: *Come and talk. Tell no one, or the children will die. Hurry!*

We have eyes and ears with the local police. And the FBI! We don't want to harm the children . . . But we will.

Pip lay curled up at my feet as Kit drove as fast as he could go on these narrow, twisting country roads. I thought of poor sweet Oz again and again. I could still hear him telling me that he loved Max, still see the incredible happiness in his face, especially in his eyes. And in hers. It was unthinkably cruel that he should die so young. None other than Emily Dickinson had written, *'Dying is a wild night and a new road.'* No, I didn't think so. Sorry, Miss Emily. *Dying usually sucks the big one. That is what you should have written. What you did write sounds cool, but it's bullshit.*

It was less than an hour's drive to the Hospital, but I had lost all sense of time, and even place. Whenever I looked over at Kit, I saw the terrible strain in his face. *Come and talk . . . We don't want to harm the children.*

I finally muttered Kit's name and he reached for me, held my hand tightly, almost too tightly.

A quarter of a mile later, I pointed to the discreet bronze sign, and Kit veered off the main road and on to the unlit narrow lane. Just seeing the name *Liberty General Hospital* again was unsettling and turned my stomach.

Soon the wide gravel drive appeared and Kit drove

slowly up it. Crushed stone cracked under our wheels.

We were about to loop around to the entranceway when a couple of bulky guys wearing hooded yellow rain slickers blocked our path.

'How thoughtful of them. A welcoming committee,' Kit said.

'Should we feel honored?' I said.

'Sure. I'll bet the goon squad is here just for us.'

'You haven't told anyone, Kit? Not even a few close friends at the Bureau?' I asked.

He didn't speak, didn't answer my question. Had he told someone in the FBI? Was that his plan?

One of the men in yellow pointed toward a service ramp, and we headed there in the misty gloom. The ramp terminated at the base of a concrete loading dock. God, this was eerie. I almost couldn't stand it.

Kit braked to a stop but left the car engine running.

'This is it. End of the line,' one of the yellow slickers said. How droll of him. Rubbing it in.

He opened Kit's door; the other bastard opened mine. 'Madam,' my bastard intoned deeply. 'This way, please. You're expected.'

From that point on, everything got a little fuzzy. Well, actually a lot fuzzy.

I remember Pip lifting his leg against the wall. '*Good boy,*' I whispered.

I remember being ordered to place my hands on the platform of the loading dock as the cold rain soaked right through my clothes.

I remember being felt up. Top and bottom. Wanting to punch somebody in the face, but holding back. I remember the sharp stab of a needle in my right bicep.

I remember the blur of faces as I swung my head around and saw the mirthless looks of our slickered captors.

I don't remember anything after that.

Until I woke up.

In a cage.

CHAPTER EIGHTY-EIGHT

Ozymandias came up close – so wonderfully close – and kissed Max on the mouth. His taste was always so clean and sweet and good. Then he whispered, 'Good-bye for now, my darling girl.'

'No! No!' Max started to scream. 'Please come back, Oz! Don't leave me again. *Ozymandias!*'

She burst out of the drugged sleep as if she were being pulled up from the depths of the ocean. She resisted consciousness, thinking instead of Oz, holding on to him. Pictures floated before her eyes; she heard his laughter. She imagined flying with him, soaring above the clouds, caressing him.

But that was all such fake bullshit. Ozymandias was dead. This was no fairy tale with a happy ending.

This was the world – as humans saw it, as they wished it to be. So sad, such a waste of potential, such a shame.

Max snapped open her eyes and took stock of her awful, hateful surroundings.

She was in a stuffy, foul-smelling, darkened, windowless

room at the Hospital. Prison! Worse than prison. Hell! No, this was worse than the fantasies man called hell.

There was a stainless-steel sink and some cabinets across from her, and a big white-faced clock. It read 4:36, but she honestly didn't know if it was morning or afternoon or even what day it was.

She was in a horrible, locked cage. She gauged the dimensions precisely: five feet long, three feet high, two feet deep. Just about right if you were a medium-sized dog.

There were other cages against the adjacent walls. She could make out two dispirited chimps, three beagles, a shelf full of caged rabbits and white rats.

She was a lab animal again.

Max's eyes continued to search the room until she located Peter and Wendy. My God! Their small forms were enclosed in cages too. How unbelievably sad. The twins were unconscious, but they seemed to be breathing.

Were they?

And where was Matthew?

Ic?

Frannie and Kit?

Max noted the shredded newspaper bedding on the floor of her cage. She'd also been given two chocolate-peanut power bars and a bottle of water. Thanks for nothing. She wasn't hungry or thirsty. She wanted to die. She couldn't stand captivity – not after being free.

The paper gown crackled as she shifted, seeking a

position that didn't hurt. But that was impossible, wasn't it?

She hurt everywhere.

The lab door opened, jolting her. Someone entered the semidarkness and closed the door. It was fricking Kane, the man she despised. The leader of the inhumans. She had been hearing about him since her days at the School – and now here he was, the monster of monsters.

'Hello, Max,' he said, walking up to her cage. 'I've got your latest test results back. Your intelligence is off the chart. That's fabulous. We can't even measure your IQ. Why, aren't we just full of surprises?'

'Why, aren't we just full of shit?' she barked at him.

'Now, now. You really knock my socks off. You're even funny.'

'Yeah, you're a scream too. They ought to get you to host *Saturday Night Live*. Are you letting us go? Of course you're not!'

'Well, no. I'm not. But I just wanted to tell you that you are one smart kid. It's too bad your internal systems are so, how shall I put this, unusual? But I do have a surprise for you.'

Max fricking *hated* surprises. They were always, always bad. She closed her eyes. Looked away.

'C'mon, Max, give me a nice smile. You're going to like this.'

She opened her eyes and turned them on her mortal enemy. 'What is it?'

'*Look*,' said Ethan Kane. He turned up the lights to

reveal the rear of the room. 'Your friends are here. Frannie, Kit, everybody. Except Ozymandias, of course.' Kane smiled again. What a scream he was, what a joker.

If she possibly could, if she ever got the chance, she would break his neck.

Break.

His.

Neck.

CHAPTER EIGHTY-NINE

Resurrection was beginning, and nothing would ever be the same again, and that was mostly because the fools of the world *just couldn't see it coming*. Science was about to change the ethics governing life and death. It would change the way the human race perceived life in virtually every country around the globe. The medical breakthroughs would hit like meteors crashing to earth, and it would have the same explosive impact as a meteor storm.

Patricia Stevenson held tightly to her husband's hand as their Lear jet approached the small, unimposing airport in the rolling hills of Maryland.

Patricia's clear gray eyes were full of compassion for her Roger, who kept fading in and out of sleep. His cancer was so far advanced that no one could, or would, perform any more surgeries; the cancer had metastasized from his colon into his lungs and spread to his liver.

Roger Stevenson, her hugely talented, wonderfully generous husband, had only days to live. If that. He needed to be here . . . because the world couldn't afford to lose him. Patricia genuinely believed that. And so, apparently, did the people at the Hospital.

When the captain announced that they would be landing momentarily, the eighty-year-old woman reached over and tightened her husband's seatbelt. She kissed him on the cheek, then adjusted the jade-green leather seat so that he would be in an upright position.

She smoothed his baby-blue cashmere lap throw. At this touch, his eyes opened, and he seemed a little disoriented.

'Patty? Is that you?'

'Yes, darling. I'm right here. I'll always be right here. We made it, Roger. We actually made it.'

She and Roger were both wearing the best clothing money could buy: cashmere and Harris tweed and three-thousand-dollar handmade shoes. The jet had cost seven million and it was their own, as were the houses in Dallas, Palm Beach, and Dah Bead. It had repeatedly been said that money couldn't buy happiness, but whoever said it was wrong. Money might not always bring happiness, but it certainly could.

Patricia stroked the mottled skin on Roger's hands and gazed fondly at his face. She knew every line and wrinkle, the part in his hair, the way his fingers quivered now, all of his appetites and aversions, and stories oft told. Patty had known Roger nearly her whole life. They had been lovers since their early twenties and married for fifty-seven years. Patty Jo Clark Stevenson, originally from Lake Forest,

Illinois, candy heiress, Vassar graduate, director of the Dallas Symphony Foundation, philanthropist, mother of five, grandmother of fourteen, felt the tug on her stomach as the airplane began its descent.

She glanced briefly at the runway below before closing her eyes. She prayed to God that this was the right thing to do – that this was His will. Of course it was! Roger was so important, not just to her but to the whole world. A brilliant engineer by training, he had gone on to found not one, but two, Fortune 500 companies; he'd been the president for one term; then a close adviser to two other presidents. Of course he had to live! He of all people.

The landing was soft, the Lear jet kissing the tarmac and swiftly rolling to a halt. The overly polite young captain came back to the passenger compartment and made certain that the Stevensons were all right. Then he personally escorted them off the plane.

As they walked very slowly down the steps, Patty saw the one man she trusted. Dr Ethan Kane was standing at the foot of the staircase. He had a wheelchair for Roger. He smiled brilliantly and she lifted her hand in greeting.

'Look, Roger. It's Ethan! Oh God, everything is going to be all right now.'

Stretched out on the airfield directly behind Dr Kane were several other private planes, twenty-three in all. Two more were just now landing. Yet another was waiting to land.

Everyone scheduled for Resurrection was here.

The chosen ones.

CHAPTER NINETY

They were in their fifties, sixties, seventies, and a few in their eighties.

All leaders of industry, science, and government from around the world. Powerbrokers, masters of the universe, legends in their own time.

All males, every one.

The chosen ones.

They wore expensive business suits, mostly in dark colors; all but a few disabled ones had proud, straight bearings as they deplaned. They were accustomed to being in command, in full control of the lives around them.

Ethan Kane watched the men come toward him, and even he was struck by the eeriness of the scene. Actually, the irony of it. That these *few men* should be saved.

He and his surgeons were the receiving line, and they greeted each powerful man with the required deference and respect. They were used to it, expected nothing less, even here, where they came like beggars to a king.

Dr Kane lightly took the hand of the current President of the United States, but then hurried him along, effectively dismissing the man.

Behind the President was someone much more important, more powerful, infinitely more worthy of salvation, the most pre-eminent scientist from Germany. A genius who was almost on a level with Kane himself.

And behind him, someone more important still – from mainland China.

Ethan Kane found it easy to make small talk with each one, and especially to smile at the thirty men. They had been *chosen* – and so had he.

They were the last best hope of the world.

CHAPTER NINETY-ONE

A loud groan, or possibly a snore, woke me from the deepest and probably creepiest sleep of my life.

It took me a few seconds to realize that I was the one making the godawful noise. The *good* news – I was still alive.

I was visually and aurally disoriented, hardly knew which way to look. Where was I? Then I heard Kit calling softly. He was alive too. We both were. At the Hospital.

But *why?* I wondered. Were we to be used as bargaining leverage? Was that it? It had to be. Kit and I were alive because we might be needed to influence the children in the next few hours. What part were they supposed to play in Resurrection? *Why were they so important?* The question was driving me crazy.

'Kit?' I mumbled. 'That really you? Or am I dreaming again?'

'Frannie,' he said. 'Frances Jane, it's me. In the flesh, such as it is. Misery sure loves company.'

I turned on to my side and I felt as if I were rolling

under water. *Oh God!* I saw Max first and I lazily waggled my fingers at her. Then I turned back to Kit, who was in a cage catercorner to mine.

'Where are we?' I asked.

'Liberty Hospital,' he whispered. 'We couldn't get a private room.'

Right. *In steel cages used for lab animals. Waiting for Resurrection, whatever that was.*

And I was also coming out of a morphine stupor.

'You okay?' Kit asked me. 'Within reason?'

'I don't know,' I said languidly. 'My head feels like it weighs a hundred pounds. You?'

'Nothing I couldn't remedy with one clear shot at Dr Ethan Kane. Something's going on out there. That's why they're not paying attention to us for the moment.'

Max called out to us from across the room. She was in a rage. 'I have to get out of here. I'm going to go break Dr Kane's neck. That's a promise I made to Ozymandias.'

'Calm down, Max,' I called to her. Then I rattled my bars for the hell of it.

We were in KennelPal cages, a brand I used myself, and I was quite familiar with this type of closure. To open it, you had to pinch two spring-loaded prongs together and that would cause a bolt to slide out of its sleeve. There was a heavy metal plate behind the latch, so it was impossible to squeeze the prongs from inside the cage. No one could do it. Thus the guards *outside* rather than in here with us. We were trapped.

I watched Max work quickly through all the possibilities mentally. She was frustrated, livid. But she wasn't giving up.

'Frannie, you ever read *The Adventures of Kavalier and Klay*? There was a character called "The Escapist",' she called from her cage.

'Max, what are you talking about?' I asked.

'Getting the hell out of here. *Trying*, anyway.'

I almost couldn't believe what I saw next. This was Max at her best.

I watched her spread the bars of her cage wide enough for her hand to go through. She had incredible strength. *Off the charts*. Sometimes I forgot about that.

She pinched the prongs together. The bolt instantly sprang loose from its metal sleeve and Max swung the door free.

'I'm a strong girl and my IQ is off the charts,' she said with a note of defiance that made my heart sing.

There were footsteps out in the hall and it sounded like people were coming our way. In a hurry.

'Let me take care of this,' said Max. 'It'll be a pleasure.' She started toward the steel-framed door.

'*Max*, come back here!' I yelled. 'Don't go out there.'

'Don't worry about me,' Max said.

Then she yanked open the door and disappeared outside.

There were three shots and my heart sank. Max screamed. Then nothing. Not a sound for several seconds.

The door to the outside finally flew open. Several

doctors rushed into the room where we were being held.

'What happened to Max?' I screamed. 'Where is she? Where is Max? Is she hurt?'

In answer, one of the doctors jabbed a needle into my arm. I saw another doctor stick Kit with a needle in his thigh.

And then the lights went out again, but not before I whispered or cried, 'Max, dear Max.'

CHAPTER NINETY-TWO

K it woke with an unbearable pressure at the back of his head, such a really bad feeling, like nothing he'd ever experienced before, or even thought possible. An old Doors song was playing over and over in his head, 'This is the End . . . the End, my friend.' He'd also been moved to another room in the Hospital. Frannie, the kids, Max, were nowhere to be seen.

Unreality.

Was.

Taking.

Over.

Very slowly, tentatively, he tried to look around. He needed to orient himself. He could almost *hear* his eyes move from side to side.

It took a few seconds for Kit to realize that he was lashed to a wheelchair and that all he could move was his head. Still, he could see the entire room from this position.

More than he wanted to see.

There were corpses all around. Young, naked, very dead. *Recently* dead. All males. Lying on gurneys parked casually at odd angles, like nobody cared, and obviously, they didn't.

These are murder victims, he thought. *This is a slaughter-house. I'm in a slaughterhouse.*

The bodies had been precisely and thoroughly carved up.

Why? And why all male victims? What in the name of God was Resurrection? Who was supposed to rise from the dead? Not these poor devils on the gurneys.

'Jesus God Almighty,' Kit whispered. 'Help us.'

The horrors just wouldn't stop coming and he had a terrible feeling that he was next on the chopping block.

Unreality.

Had.

Taken.

Over.

CHAPTER NINETY-THREE

God, it was so damn cold in here, Kit was thinking.

What was this place? A meat freezer? A hospital morgue? What?

Let it be some kind of high-tech medical morgue. Let the bodies be cadavers for legitimate research.

But the bodies were all too uniformly young. In their teens and early twenties. Just kids, really.

Am I next? To be disemboweled?

Kit's fear for the kids and Frannie finally overcame his terror for himself. Horrific guilt swamped him, but he couldn't even afford the luxury of despair. He had to get out of here. *But what a total crock that was!* How could he get away?

But how could he not try?

He had to find out what had happened to Max. Had she been murdered? And Frannie? Where were they? And why was he the only one in the meat locker?

He reared back against his tight restraints and the chair finally rocked back. Then it fell over!

Kit landed on his shoulder, and it hurt like hell. *Neat move, swiftie. You're so sharp sometimes.*

Just then, the door to the room creaked open. Dr Ethan Kane stepped inside. He seemed to be everywhere; totally hands-on.

'Hey, hey,' he said to Kit. 'Trying to escape? Hope springs eternal, doesn't it? Looks like you had a little accident here. No problem,' he said. 'We'll fix you right up.'

Then he kicked Kit hard in the ribs. *Jesus, that hurt! That really, really hurt! Who was this guy – Mengele?*

Kit wouldn't give up. Wanted to. But he wouldn't surrender. It wasn't his nature.

'Dr Kane. Now that I'm awake, let's talk. The kids will be missed. I'm going to be missed eventually.'

'Not as much as you'd think. I've taken care of all that. I'm sorry I can't stop and chat,' Kane said. 'I'm sure you have all sorts of fascinating questions and insights, but we're overbooked at the inn right now.'

'Listen to me!' Kit raged. He just couldn't *move*. Not an inch.

And Ethan Kane was walking away, not listening at all. Kit felt completely helpless; a bug caught in a spider's web. No way was Kane going to let them survive.

He watched the doctor walk to a wall of cabinets over a sink and remove a syringe and a small bottle. What was Dr Death doing now?

He screwed the needle on to the syringe, plunged the point into the rubber stopper at the top of the bottle, and retracted it.

He advanced on Kit again.

'Just tell me what you want,' Kit said. 'I'll tell you the truth. Everything I know.'

Ethan Kane laughed softly. 'This will pinch,' he said.

CHAPTER NINETY-FOUR

Everything was so unbelievably confusing. So chaotic. So hopeless.

I came out of my drugged stupor in Ethan Kane's office.

I was carefully, *artfully* positioned so that I was looking at about a two-gallon jug filled with a solution and dozens of dark floating objects.

I tried to focus my eyes.

What were those reddish gobs? Then I knew what the floating shapes were: *fetal hearts . . . The hearts of pre-born children!*

I whispered, 'My God, my God, why have You forsaken me? Why *now*?'

It got worse. I was bound to a wheelchair. And Dr Kane was working at his desk, calm as could be. 'I want to talk to you about the children,' he said without looking up from whatever he was writing. 'You can be of some help. I need to know everything I can about the work that was done on them at the School. I know you examined the children thoroughly.'

'*Where* are the kids? Where's Max?' I asked as soon as I could manage a few words.

'Oh, they're fine.' His eyes narrowed. 'And as for Max, don't worry, she'll never escape me. Fuck the kids though. I want to spend some quality time with *you*, Dr O'Neill. I have a feeling that you may understand my work more than you think you do. You were there at the School. And you certainly have useful information about the bird-children, don't you? You're a veterinarian. I'm not. You can help me with my work. If you so choose.'

'I wouldn't choose to help you if you were choking on a chicken bone,' I spat out.

Kane's face turned cold. 'Good one. For a trailer-park cretin like yourself. Now listen to me closely, Frannie. Don't say another word or I'll cut out your tongue.

'Don't you understand the value of improving and extending human life? You must! Last month, we "resurrected" a mathematical genius from London. The world desperately *needs* this man's brilliance. One can only imagine what his mind will produce in the coming decades! Do you comprehend what I'm saying? Maybe *a little*? Can you get past your own pitifully outmoded system of ethics?

'You may speak now. Frannie? You did tests on Maximum. Tell me exactly what you found. Strengths and weaknesses.'

'Absolutely not!' I shouted at him. 'What's going on here? What is Resurrection?'

Kane rose from behind his desk. 'What is Resurrection?

Where to start? OK, I'll let you in on a little secret. Our secret. I'm one of the first beneficiaries,' he said. 'New organs, and in my case, a new body and head!'

I felt as if the earth had come to a stop as I tried to absorb what I'd just heard. I looked at his smooth pink skin, his bright blue eyes, his full, thick head of hair.

He showed off his brilliant smile again. He *knew* that he'd just blown my mind.

'My name is Dr Harold Hauer. *The* Harold Hauer. I didn't die in a car accident outside Boston eleven years ago. I've been *resurrected*. I look pretty damn good for ninety-four, don't you think?'

CHAPTER NINETY-FIVE

Dr Harold Hauer was alive and he looked like he was in his mid-forties. I was still reeling with amazement and shock as Ethan Kane began to push my wheelchair out of his office. Fast! We were going somewhere.

'Ninety-four years old and my current life expectancy is unlimited. I'm smarter than I was, too. Wish I could say the same for you, Dr O'Neill. You obviously *won't* help me, so what good are you? To keep the kids in line? Maybe. So tell me the similarities and differences between Max and the birds she physically resembles. Where does her strength come from? Her intelligence?'

'I will not,' I said.

'Fine then. I can control the little bastards without you. So much for small minds like yours. My wife is smarter – and she's a *robot*.'

My wheelchair was pushed into an eggshell-white-painted ward full of sleeping patients. There must have been a dozen people in there, each with IV lines dripping from TPNs.

All of the patients wore metal helmets hooked up to monitors positioned over their heads. Each monitor showed a different film. The films seemed to be free-flowing dramas, romances, even nature documentaries.

'What are these movies?' I asked. 'What are they for?'

Kane/Hauer was standing at the foot of one bed, gazing up at a monitor, no longer paying attention to me.

'Oh, *this* is delightful,' he said of underwater cinematography of spectacular fish, the likes of which I'd never seen. He looked over at me. 'This is the Dream Room and what you're seeing is Simulated Reality – a kind of human-and-machine collaboration. See, there are electrodes in the helmet that stimulate areas of the patient's brain. We manipulate them, then the patient thinks or imagines or remembers, and the story that's created is more real to him than reality itself,' he said. 'You're looking at the patients' *dreams*.'

I didn't want to be, but I was dazzled. I turned from one monitor to another, taking in the vivid images: sailboats, passionate kisses, intercourse, ballet, abstract art, raw speed, a bordello, a palace.

Then something truly obscene caught my eye. My heart began to *thump* so hard it caused a pain in my chest.

I watched a small form in one of the beds, a girl of no more than four or five. A doe and its mother were nuzzling gently on her screen. *That was her dream, wasn't it?*

I strained to see the girl's face a little better. But I knew I'd seen it before. Photographs in his office.

'That's *Sissy*,' I said. 'It's your own daughter. My God, what have you done to her?'

There was an embarrassed chuckle from Dr Ghoul. 'Well, yes, it is the child I called Sissy. But she's not actually my daughter. This little girl has very special organs, and I'm keeping her here for a recipient in Germany.'

The monster saw my look of horror and disgust. 'Don't judge me, *you cow*. You're starting to really piss me off.'

The Q-and-A period was apparently over. Dr Kane/Hauer rolled my wheelchair down to the end of the nearest row of patients.

Another shock! Honestly, my heart couldn't take any more of this.

There, up to his armpits in crisp white sheets, was someone I hadn't been sure I would ever see again.

Kit.

A Simulated Reality helmet was strapped over his head. He had a soft, dreamy look on his face. A doctor was working on him, his back to the door.

On the screen a baseball game was in progress. It was Kit's beloved Yankee Stadium, and I was watching from the vantage point of home plate. A ball was coming in hard and fast . . .

'What are you doing to him?' I screamed.

'Giving him the time of his life,' said Kane/Hauer. 'And we've saved a bed for you, Frannie. Sweet dreams. Oh, and by the way, Frannie, watch this. Watch closely. *Oh, Doctor?*' he yelled across the room.

The physician working on Kit turned to us. I nearly fainted. I don't know why I didn't.

The doctor standing next to Kit was another Dr Ethan Kane. An exact fricking replica.

'Don't be alarmed.' The duplicate Kane spoke to me. 'I'm nobody. I'm just a clone.'

CHAPTER NINETY-SIX

I was lost in wild, dizzying thoughts about what was happening. The Hospital. Kane/Hauer. His robot-clone. Max. Was she alive? *And what was Resurrection? Who was being resurrected?*

Suddenly I heard the very loud buzzing of an electric gadget, followed by cold metal raking across my scalp.

Then something soft and loose was falling on my shoulders. I realized it was my own hair.

They'd cut off all my hair. I was bald.

An orderly slashed the duct tape holding me to the wheelchair with a box cutter and I was roughly transferred to a stainless-steel gurney. I punched out at him, but he merely laughed.

'Relax,' he said. 'This is the fun part. Fun for me anyway.' He jabbed me with another needle.

Boom! I was out like a light.

And the bastard had lied to me.

No Simulated Reality trip for me. No helmet, no comfy bed in the Dream Room. The needle went into my arm and that was it: *death, down and dirty*.

I rose up from the bed, or at least my 'spirit' or 'soul' or 'astral body' did.

I floated up to the corner of the room and hung there, face down, while the orderly drew the sheet over my face.

I'd been done in. Just like that.

I couldn't process my shock quickly enough. I had been alive seconds ago. Now I was dead. I hadn't said goodbye to anyone, hadn't truly prepared for this moment. *I'm only thirty-four*, I thought, and tears came into my eyes.

Before I could carry on like this any longer, I was drawn up through the ceiling. I felt as if there were a hand at the back of my neck, a cord in the middle of my back, attached to some winch high in the sky.

I passed upward through the floor above, just the way I'd seen it done in the movies about ghosts.

I was there, but not there.

No one saw me and nothing obstructed my passing as I materialized up through the reception area, where I'd been with Kit the day before. As I moved through the floors of the Hospital, I felt my anguish evaporate, replaced by a peacefulness I'd never experienced before.

I'm not overly religious, but I do believe in God. Something or someone was pulling me now, taking me away from my earthly life and concerns. I was conscious of a lack of control, and I felt relieved to float away from my responsibilities and grief.

I still loved Kit, Max and the kids, but I couldn't take

care of anyone any more. I realized that now.

My body cleared the top floor of the Hospital and I was surprised to see it was daytime. Last night's thunderstorm had drenched the landscape and moisture on the treetops sparkled like diamonds.

I kept moving effortlessly upward, and suddenly I could see the winding country roads Kit and I had driven along so recently. The hills looked gorgeous to me, like a rumpled calico quilt spread out below. I felt the sun gently warming my back, and it was supernaturally calming.

A flock of birds flew beneath me, and I could see the details of their feathers with astonishing clarity.

I stretched out my arms and saw the same denim shirt I'd been wearing for days – my torn nails – these were my hands, all right.

I rubbed my hand over my bald head and liked how that felt.

I tried to alter my course, but there was no jet propulsion with this astral body. I moved only in one direction and that was up.

As I rose I saw the whole of the Liberty Reservoir, and *there*, the city of Baltimore, its rivers leading to the Chesapeake Bay. I guessed I was at ten thousand feet and rising. The landscape was in miniature, the cars teeny, the houses and other buildings dotting the countryside with toylike precision.

I was bathed in soft mist, and it felt like a blessing.

I was cleansed.

Refreshed.

Redeemed.

The cloud cover seemed to last for a very long time, and when it cleared, I saw that I was high out over the Atlantic Ocean.

The water was aquamarine near the coastline, turning to dark navy blue, flecked with white, all of it astonishingly beautiful and real. I could see the eastern coast of the United States! *God bless America*.

The only sound was the brush of the wind on my ears.

I thought about my life and I could remember it all: a bake sale at a church, my first kiss in Dad's barn, the deer with a broken back that I'd put to sleep. I put my arms behind my head and looked into Kit's loving eyes. I saw Max running through the woods as I'd seen her the first time. The images came and went, each with newly minted crystal clarity. I could see all of the people I'd known and loved and feel their thoughts as well as mine. It was as if I were standing there with them, and in this way I got to say my goodbyes. But I soon tired of Frannie's life-retrospective and said goodbye to myself, to my life as a woman.

Earth was growing below me. Not like the satellite pictures we've all seen – this Earth filled the sky and was in sharp topographical focus. I could see the mountain ridges and the running rivers and the cities and the shifting seas. *Dear God, the magnificence of our planet defied description.*

As for me, the former Frances Jane O'Neill, I was a tiny

speck of human consciousness. I didn't know if I was falling out of the sky or going straight to heaven.

Either way was okay.

I knew I was going home.

CHAPTER NINETY-SEVEN

These had been the most intoxicating, heady days of his life, even more incredible than the time when he'd faked his own death – *and also murdered his first wife* – in an automobile crash outside Boston.

Resurrection was almost finished – at least the first stage, and hopefully the first of many to come.

Thirty 'new' beings had been created.

His creations.

And now they would go out and run the world properly for the next thirty to fifty years, or possibly even longer.

His world, in a manner of speaking.

The chosen ones – all males – had been recuperating for two days and every one of them was in good shape. Thank God, none had died during surgery. Of course, he could have brought them back to life. He was a miracle-maker.

They were ready to go back to their home cities now, and to do the specific jobs they had been chosen for. The world needed continuity and stabilization before third-world morons took the whole thing over, or possibly blew it up. These men, *all men*, were the best hope to maintain order and progress; they were the last hope.

Dr Kane/Hauer believed that. Several practical problems would have to be overcome eventually – like explaining how the thirty men were able to live so long – but the masses could be prepared for that, and all the scientific wonders of a brave new world. Those were small problems for small thinkers to worry about.

'God, I feel so good!' he exclaimed.

But something was missing, wasn't it?

Imagine that!

His day of days – and something was still missing. Well, he supposed that it went with the territory – being a perfectionist.

He took a handful of M&Ms into his mouth, and while good for what they were, the chocolate candies didn't do the trick.

He looked over at the couch in his office. The lovely Juliette sat there in an expensive blue pin-striped suit, creamy white blouse, heels. As always, his wife was stunningly perfect. She was at the Hospital to assist him in saying goodbye to some of the chosen. The more family-oriented ones liked that he had a loving wife. It made them comfortable.

He went over and turned on the lovely and talented Juliette.

'It's a glorious day for you, isn't it?' She spoke almost

immediately. 'You're amazing, darling. I adore you.'

'So *do* me,' he said in a thick whisper. 'Right here, right now.'

Looking incredibly proper in her pin-striped business suit, Juliette knelt before the doctor. She used her perfect white teeth to pull down his zipper.

'It would be an honor,' she said, and did the work she had been created for.

CHAPTER NINETY-EIGHT

A saying, a truism, played in Max's head: *fear is not the answer. Fear is not the answer.*

She woke up and realized she'd been knocked out cold for a while – maybe as much as half a day.

But then she knew it had to be longer than that. Maybe even a couple of days. Man! What had she missed? Her body seemed almost repaired from the gunshot wound suffered when she'd escaped.

Her left leg stung like crazy, but her anger had reduced the pain to something manageable. The bullet had caught her thigh. She'd wrapped a strip from her shirt around it to stop the bleeding.

She studied it now. The wound seemed okay.

This is nothing, she kept telling herself, compared to what happened to Ozymandias.

Get a move on, Max. Time is wasting. Go.

She had quite a struggle working her way through the air ducts, crawling on her elbows and knees. After a few minutes, she shimmied down a chute to the third floor, pushed out an air vent and dropped into a five-sided room.

The room was like an aquarium. *For people*.

It actually had glass walls, which looked like they were hurricane strength.

Behind the glass was a long, dimly lit room with rows of people who seemed to be . . . sleeping? Maybe thirty of them.

Max jumped as doors swung open on the far side of the dimly lit room. Her wings rustled. Then two female nurses entered, chatting in whispers.

The nurses calmly read the monitors at the sides of the beds, and checked several of the patients' vitals.

Who were these men on the beds? What had happened to them? If she'd been knocked out for a day or so in the air-conditioning chutes, how long had they been here? More important – where were the other kids? And Frannie, Kit?

One of the men began to stir. Max could hear clearly through a speaker in the ceiling.

'Thirsty,' he whispered in a raspy voice. 'Please. A little water?'

One of the nurses went right to him. She poured liquid into a cup, then tilted his head so that he could drink comfortably.

'There you are,' she said, 'Mr President.'

Oh.

My.

God.

With his head tilted like that, Max could see the man's face. It wasn't the current US president – it was the one two back.

She shook her head and almost started to gasp. He had to be close to eighty now, but he looked no older than fifty. How could that be?

None of the men in the room looked older than that.

Is this Resurrection? What is it?

Then more doctors and nurses began to enter the room. They were waking the patients.

Something was going on.

Something important.

Something very bad.

'Wake up, Prime Minister . . .'

'Wake up, Mr Chairman . . .'

'Wake up, Your Excellency . . .'

'It's a brand new day. You look fantastic. All of you do. Congratulations.'

CHAPTER NINETY-NINE

Get help get help get help get help get help.
   Get out get out get out get out.

It was an alarm going off in her head. Blood roared in her ears.

The important men in here are being given their wake-up calls. But what are they waking up to? Or are they resurrecting? Who are they?

Near the entrance to the room was a peculiar set of sliding doors that looked like doors to an elevator. Max rushed to them.

Panting with anxiety, she pressed the call button. *C'mon c'mon c'mon.* The doors finally slid open. No one was inside. *Score one for the good guys!*

Now what? Now where? Max ducked inside and rode the car up one story to the second floor. If she remembered correctly, the Animal Room was there. Hopefully, the other kids were too. Maybe Kit and Frannie.

She got off and saw no one in the hallway. Then she

heard voices, someone coming. She needed to get out of there.

Max spotted the Animal Room straight ahead. She raced to the door, pulled it open. She could have a heart attack any second now. That was exactly how she felt.

She heard someone inside the room! *Busted!*

'*Max!* You're back!' Wendy called out. Then there were more familiar voices calling her name, welcoming her and asking questions at the same time.

'Shhhh. Shhhh. Quiet down now. I said *quiet*! All hell is breaking loose outside. Something gigantic is going on. And it's bad.'

Max hurried to open the latches on the cages. She took a few seconds to hug them all: Peter, Matthew, Wendy and Ic. All except Ozymandias, of course.

'Where *were* you, Max?' Matthew wanted to know.

'In the air ducts. Getting better. I got shot. Enough questions for now.'

'What's going on outside?'

'*Stop* with the questions, Matty!'

The kids looked terrible – dirty, anxious, afraid – but especially poor Icarus who pushed her away as she tried to carry him out of his cage. 'Go away,' he hissed. 'Let me be, Max. Let me die here.'

'Ic, it's time to go, and you're *going*!'

'Leave me, please. I can't take it any more. Leave the blind boy. I can't go on like this.'

'We need you, Ic. Now shape up, little buddy. SHAPE UP *NOW*.' Max finally had to raise her voice.

Icarus looked startled, but then he grinned. '*That's* the Max I know and love.'

Damn right it was. She was in charge again. Without a map, without a weapon, without a real plan. And without Kit and Frannie. She had to hurry and find them.

'Matthew, you help out Ic. Peter and Wendy, stay with me,' she said. 'Stay close, you two.'

'I'm letting the lab animals out,' Matthew said. 'No arguments. I *have* to do it, Max. They're as scared as we are. They're our pals now.'

'Yeah! Release the skitters,' said Peter. 'Release the hounds!'

Max rolled her eyes, but she had to say yes. She couldn't bear to leave them in the cages either. 'Let'm out. The extra confusion might help.'

The two younger boys opened the chimp cages first, clowning and jabbering as if they had all the time in the world. Then Wendy let Pip out of his cage, and the beagles too.

Max opened the outside door and peered up and down the hallway. This was fricking crazy; it was the worst yet. Cold white fluorescent light illuminated every corner.

Soon the hallway filled with monkeys, rabbits, lab rats, and hounds. Maybe the chaos *would* be helpful! The hounds' vocal cords had been severed, but their harsh, breathy bays were still audible as, noses to the ground, they seemed to pursue some mystical quarry.

It was total chaos. What a mess. Insanity.

But that mess was probably the best chance they were going to get right now.

Max heard high-pitched female squeals as the rodents and monkeys arrived at the nurses' station. She stopped searching for Frannie and Kit for the moment and quickly herded the kids into the elevator. It was a tight squeeze and Pip seemed dead set against it, barking and yipping.

'Shape up, dog!' Max commanded, and the annoying barking stopped instantly.

There were half a dozen illuminated buttons on the panel. 'Damn this place. I *hate* everything about it.'

She pressed the button marked 'U' and the elevator started to ascend, thank God.

'Up is good,' said little Peter.

'Up is always good,' said Max.

CHAPTER ONE HUNDRED

U *must stand for 'unbelievably lucky'*, Max thought, but kept the notion to herself. She had other preoccupations right now. Frannie and Kit. The mystery men down in the recovery room. Getting out of this snake pit alive. At least getting up out of the basement where Dr Kane did all his nasty work.

She reminded herself: *fear is not the answer. Not ever!*

The elevator doors opened into a long underground tunnel, concrete on all four sides, an exit door at one end, lighting strips along the sides of the ceiling.

It was a damp, cold, fetid place, and Max didn't know where the tunnel went, but this was what she'd chosen. Or had it been chosen for her by fate?

It *could* be an escape route.

'Let's go!' she yelled. 'I said – move it or lose it, guys! Hustle your buns. *Now!*'

The kids and one small, yapping terrier ran toward the far doorway, the only direction that seemed to make any sense.

She had to get the kids out first, then she'd go look for Frannie and Kit, and tell them about what she'd seen – an ex-president and twenty or so of his closest friends in a *postoperative* state.

'Please stay together and keep up! Once we're outside and I give the order, you fly as fast as your wings will take you! Fly to safety. You hear me?'

'Yeah,' shouted Peter. 'We fly to safety!'

She heard the distinctive hum of the elevator moving downward, stop, but then the hum began again. It was coming back to their floor. *Shit. Who was inside the elevator?*

'Faster, faster,' she yelled as they hurried down the tunnel. 'Don't fly – yet!'

Max lunged for the EXIT door. *Please, open.*

The door swung out into the blinding daylight, and it seemed like so long since Max had seen the sun! A day? Two days? There was a gray galvanized metal building off to their right – an airplane hangar – and tarmac leading to a runway.

An awful lot of private planes were down there.

Max sought her bearings. That way was Washington, DC. Maybe they could get help there. Maybe, maybe not. Who were the good guys in this hopeless mess? And how could she know for sure? She *needed* Frannie and Kit. *Right now, right this instant. All right, you two guys, show your faces!*

But it didn't happen. No Frannie and Kit.

Her bewildering thoughts were interrupted by the

sputtering sound of an engine starting outside the airplane hangar. As she watched, a small cream-colored airplane with a red stripe along its side rolled forward, sending a flock of doves airborne.

The airplane stopped and two men in blue jumpsuits rolled a staircase up to the plane. A couple of the other small planes were being started up, too. A flurry of activity.

Off to the left, a tunnel door opened and two doctors came out, pushing a patient in a wheelchair. Then came bodyguards. Who was the patient?

Two more mysterious patients in wheelchairs were pushed out of another door. Then two more.

All in wheelchairs.

All males.

Was this what the wake-up call was all about? Time to go home? To do what?

One of the guards spotted Max. 'Hey!' he yelled. 'On the roof!' Then he was talking into his headset.

The doctors stared at her briefly, then one of them helped his important patient on to the staircase leading to his jet. The patient looked familiar. *Where had she seen him?* The guard drew his gun – and the bastard fired at her! At all of them!

'Get down!' Max ordered. *Goddamn them to hell. They shoot children, the cowardly bastards.*

Max peered over the edge and watched as the two doctors followed their patient into the plane. The door swung closed and the jet began to taxi.

Max was furious. At the guards, the doctors, the patients, Dr Ethan Kane, the whole goddamn shitty world that she and the other kids – *all kids*, actually – had been thrown into.

They would not get away with Resurrection, whatever it was.

They would not! Would not!

She couldn't let them get away. She wouldn't. Not even one stinking plane should get airborne.

'Get ready to fly out of here,' she told the kids. 'Those planes aren't going *up*! We own the sky.'

Then it hit her. She knew who the important patient was. Miguel Hijueras!

He was supposedly one of the richest men in the world. He owned communications companies all over Central and South America. He was supposed to be a real prick, too. An awful, awful bastard.

He was the patient.

One of them.

Who were all the rest – and what had been done to them in the operating rooms downstairs?

CHAPTER ONE HUNDRED
AND ONE

M ax realized she was beyond coherent rational thought at the present time. Her fury and outrage about the death of Oz, his *murder*, was making up for the lack of food; her anger filled her with a kind of heady bravery.

Or stupidity.

She stretched out her magnificent wings as far as they would go. Ten feet four inches. The wind passed over the leading edges and pulled her upward.

Max flew, and so did the others. They followed her – *anywhere*. No matter what side you were on, devil or angel, it was a beautiful, amazing thing to see.

'The flock!' Peter and Wendy howled.

'Pay attention!' Max yelled at them.

She beat her wings furiously and rose even as Mr Hijueras's private airplane still taxied on the ground. It had to travel along a runway before turning south and beginning its takeoff in the direction of Washington. What had happened to Hijueras at the Hospital? Why had all of these important men come here?

Some of the other private planes were being boarded now. *More famous patients?* For sure! What the hell had happened to them?

Max had a bit of a head start. The wind gusted suddenly, so when the airplane's nose lifted she was there ahead of it.

She whipped across, right in front of the cockpit. She saw a pair of totally surprised pilots. The small plane tipped back on to its left landing wheel, then quickly righted itself.

Get down! she signaled to the pilots. *Down!*

She heard yells behind her; the other kids were cheering her on, cheering for themselves as well.

Then they were in a tight formation of five, with Max in the lead.

Matthew was on her left; he assumed poor murdered Oz's position, calling out directions and commands to Ic. Wendy and Peter flew to her right. None of them were afraid – not any more.

They dropped down near the plane, swooping and crisscrossing in front of the cockpit. Now the pilot and co-pilot looked scared. Their eyes bulged.

Max signaled again for them to put the plane down.

'Get down, you bastards! Don't try to take this plane up!' she yelled into the wind.

Max looped over and back. She saw the pilot struggle to keep the plane's nose in the air. He was speaking into his radio. Then she heard spits of gunfire from behind.

'Look out! Look out! Break formation!' she screamed at the kids.

Down on the ground armed guards had burst out of the hangar and on to the small airfield. They were shooting at them! Rifles.

Her keen eyesight picked out a few of the bastards who'd been chasing them since Colorado. What kind of secrets were they guarding here? What horrors? *These rich bastards sure weren't here for their six-month physicals.*

'Keep the plane between us and the ground,' Max shouted. 'Follow me, guys. Keep it tight.'

The small plane was gathering speed and gaining altitude. Bursts of semi-automatic gunfire creased the air and then – something went wrong! Something even Max hadn't expected. Something unthinkable.

'Oh God, Max – look!' Matthew shrieked. 'They're hit! It's bad!'

'Who's hit?' Max moaned and turned to check the flock.

But it wasn't one of the kids. Bullets had pierced the right wing. Red and orange flames and black smoke spewed from the damaged plane. There was a loud *bang*, an explosion, and the engine was on fire. The cream-white plane seemed to hang in place for a sliver of a second. Then it started to plummet toward the tarmac.

'Oh, be careful. Be careful,' Max called out. 'Level off! Level off! Oh Jeez, don't crash.'

She saw the pilot talking frantically into his headset, but the plane was nosing down.

Too fast! Way too fast! Then it smashed down on the airstrip. The right wing ripped entirely from the slender body, the plane shrieking like a dying animal. It cartwheeled four times, rolling over and over, parts flying in all directions, then came to rest belly-up.

Suddenly it burst into flames! Black, oily smoke billowed from the mangled plane. A second bright explosion bloomed.

Max could feel the searing heat of the fire high up in the sky. Oh God, what had she done! Mr Hijueras and his doctors had to be dead, blown up or cooked.

She and the other children dropped closer to the ground and watched as a bright orange truck sped out from a maintenance shed.

Almost simultaneously, doors opened from the south wing of the Hospital. Personnel streamed toward the fallen aircraft from the other private planes.

Matthew saw him first and pointed. 'There! Max, over there!'

Dr Ethan Kane stood alone behind the crowd, staring at the catastrophe. He wore a black windbreaker over a white shirt. And a long-billed baseball hat with the words 'Pebble Beach' on the front – the same one he'd had on when he'd abducted them from Alma's Valley Rest.

It was the first time Max had seen the prideful doctor without his nasty smile of superiority. He was shaking his head in disbelief.

'I'm still gonna break your neck,' Max muttered. 'That's a promise, you murdering bastard.'

CHAPTER ONE HUNDRED AND TWO

Max exploded down toward the wretched excuse for a human being, much less a doctor, but even as she did, she couldn't help thinking about Oz. This was how he had died. *Reckless and ego-driven.*

She knew better. She'd already seen how this movie ended. *Badly. Horribly!*

So she waved off the other kids, and shouted, 'That's an order! Getoutofhere!' And they split away from her like the good kids they were. That wasn't the only reason. The fire in her voice scared them.

Max continued on alone. A dive-bomber focused on a target.

Kamikaze. Suicidal? Well, maybe. After all, she wanted to join Ozymandias more than anything.

Dr Kane saw her coming – and he waved her on. *Yes, c'mon, Max. Let's have a go at it. Let's end this right here.*

He was reckless and ego-driven too.

Apparently unafraid of the heat-seeking missile roaring down the runway at him.

I want to break his neck so badly, Max thought.

And she'd promised Oz.

But she pulled up hard and fast; she landed just a dozen yards or so from Ethan Kane. She was breathless. 'So what happened to your great goddamn Resurrection?' she panted. 'Is this it? Those pathetic men? What's so special about them?'

'They are indeed special!' Kane's voice was a low growl into the wind. 'They're what's needed to see us through this century. And now they'll live for most of it, and the world will be a better place. It might even survive. I've seen to that. I *did* it. But more to the point, Max, I know a secret about you. It's really juicy, want me to tell you?'

'I don't want *anything* from you!' Max looked at the old white men near their company-expense planes. The so-called *special* ones. Some were in wheelchairs, some lay on gurneys, recuperating, but most were up and walking. They glared at her as if they knew what she represented, the threat that she could be. 'Kill her now!' one of them shouted and shook his fist over his head. 'Get rid of her!'

Max looked at Ethan Kane and shook her head. '*They're* not the future,' she said. 'It would be too awful.'

She flapped her wings and flew straight at Ethan Kane again, screaming at the top of her voice, '*You killed Ozymandias!*'

Kane pulled out a gun, almost got it in shooting position, but he was an instant too late.

Max went for his head, his precious head, and hit it full

force with an outstretched wing. She clotheslined the creepy bastard. Blasted him with all her speed and strength.

He was still standing, and Max thought: *That's not right. That's definitely wrong!* She tried to figure out what had just happened. Couldn't.

And then Max saw something that seemed impossible. Kane's head hung down sideways on one shoulder, as if his neck were broken. It was so weird. He was *still talking*.

'You can't stop this – or me,' Kane told her. 'Do you understand? Do you get it, Maximum?'

She hit him again. *Maximum* force.

Finally, Kane crumpled to the ground. But he was still *talking*. 'You can't stop what's going to happen, you little freak. You can't stop the future.'

And with those words, Dr Kane fell over dead.

Max stared at the crumpled body in disbelief. 'Talk about *freaks*,' she muttered.

CHAPTER ONE HUNDRED AND THREE

A silent scream was inside me.

NO, no, no!

Turn the glorious stars back on. Turn them on! My God, the sun is so bright, so magnificent.

Suddenly, overhead lights just about blinded me. Two or three nurses were patting and shaking me all over. An oxygen mask was rudely slapped on my face.

Shit. I was still alive. I wasn't on the stairway to heaven after all.

I heard someone repeating my name, and when I turned my head I saw none other than Kit. He gently put his hand in mine. Squeezed.

I squeezed back. *Yep, he was real.*

I realized that his head of beautiful blond hair was shaved. *God, so was mine.*

'Waahhhhhhhhhh,' I said. 'Your hair.'

'I love you too, Baldie,' Kit whispered. 'Welcome back to the planet, Frannie.'

'Oh, it's good to be here.' Kind of, anyway. Except that

my Simulated Reality heaven had been such a trip.

We were in the Dream Room, the same ward I had seen through the glass wall. A day before? Whenever. There were still about a half-dozen patients in headgear, wired up to flickering overhead monitors and a lot of other expensive equipment: cardiac monitors, respirators, arterial lines.

But no Dr Ethan Kane, goddamn him to hell! No ninety-four-year-old Harold Hauer!

I heard a loud ruckus, a stampede of hurrying footsteps out in the hallway.

Then I saw the kids! I quickly counted noses. Max and Wendy and Ic and Matthew and little Peter swarmed around my bed, their faces pushed up against mine. They were *cooing*, and it had to be the sweetest sound in the world.

'Hello, Mama,' said Wendy, and I almost lost it right there.

Then I did lose it. Big time. I sobbed and sobbed and tried to hold all five of them at once and nearly succeeded. Then I took things a little slower. One darling face at a time.

Max was smudged with soot, and dried blood caked one leg of her blue jeans, but she had a luminous smile. She hugged me and I hugged her back. It was just about the best hugging ever.

'We made it,' I finally said.

'Not everybody,' Max said and shook her head. I knew she was talking about Ozymandias. 'But I did get Ethan

Kane. He's dead, Frannie. He won't hurt us again. I knocked his head off.'

I put my hand to Max's tangled hair, and as I did, I saw that I wore a plastic bracelet.

There was one very creepy word written on the plastic in fat black letters.

DONOR.

CHAPTER ONE HUNDRED AND FOUR

S omething very bad happened next.
Something unthinkable, and also scary as hell – or
scarier – as if there was anything unusual in that, as if I
ought to be surprised.

Nothing was written by the press about Resurrection, or
the powerful men who had obviously been involved. Not
one word in a major newspaper or magazine. It was as if
it had never happened. As if we hadn't seen what we'd
seen. As if we'd made it all up.

I'm not real big on conspiracy theories or paranoia – at
least I wasn't until I saw what was happening.

Not one word.

Some of you might say 'That's unbelievable!' All I can
say is – where have you been lately? And get your head
out of the sand. Truth is not at a premium these days.
Haven't you noticed?

Not one word.

Dr Ethan Kane/Harold Hauer believed he had changed
the world for the rest of the century – but no one in the

press seemed to notice or care, or maybe *believe* that monstrous things had happened.

Just as they had failed to notice the importance of biotechnology in the years leading up to the present. That biotechnology *is* our future. A done deal. Written in stone by *someone*, and not anyone I know, or you know.

Crazy things happened after I was set free, too. The men who we saw with our own eyes at the Hospital denied they were there, and seemed to have alibis, every one of them. What we had seen on the lower floor – gutted corpses, fetuses in bottles, incredible high-tech machinery – was all *gone* by the time law enforcement agencies went inside to look. The body of Ethan Kane/ Harold Hauer was gone too.

Or so they said.

So they said.

Finally, and maybe most disturbing of all, the body of Ozymandias had disappeared as well.

The only stories, *the only stories*, were the hoked-up ones in the sensationalist tabloids. Now what the hell did that say about the current state of the world? And besides, stories in the tabloids *guaranteed* that nobody would believe what had happened, what we had seen.

Another month passed and nothing too terribly, earth-shakingly insane, rambunctious, chaotic, or particularly dangerous happened. There was *still* no exposure about the Hospital or what had happened there. Kit and I went back to Denver. One more time – with feeling – we had decided to fight for custody of the children.

The five who had survived.

We had vowed to keep them safe.

And the children promised to do the same for us.

We solemnly promised – we made pinky swears – that we would get to the Lake House again, at least one more time.

CHAPTER ONE HUNDRED AND FIVE

It was only a hearing, but Judge Dwyer had promised us he would review his previous decision and our lawyer was holding him to his word. So were the children.

On a scale of one to ten, the local media hullabaloo was nudging a hundred, and Bannock Street was crowded beyond belief, certainly beyond capacity. Everyone wanted a piece of *this* story. To hell with Resurrection, and whatever else Ethan Kane had done at Liberty General Hospital. The public couldn't get enough of the bird-kids.

Of course, neither could Kit and I.

We hurriedly made our way to Courtroom No. 19. Kit wore a navy-blue jacket, white dress shirt, gray wool pants. He looked good – a hint of Tom Cruise cockiness, a dash of Harrison Ford slyness, something kind of neat like that.

I had on a forest-green sweater dress and high black boots, and hoped that I looked like an adult – a hint of J.C. Penney, a dash of Dillard's.

Kit and I had both grown a half-inch of brand-new hair, giving us a 'prisoner of war' look that our lawyer said couldn't hurt.

We exchanged falsely cheerful hellos with Jeffrey, our faithful legal pit bull, then we found two seats on the left side of the oak-paneled courtroom.

Our old antagonist and foe, Catherine Fitzgibbons, dressed in serious black, was going over her notes across the aisle. The bitch of the Rockies looked ready for us.

Soon the children would arrive. With their other families, their biological ones. Also expected was the mother of Ozymandias, who would testify against Kit and me.

This was the hearing's second day, actually. The first day had been intense, to say the least. Catherine Fitzgibbons, *speaking for the parents*, had ranted, stabbed the air, and laced her arguments with hurtful accusations aimed at Kit and me. She had her shining moment when she spun on her well-turned heel, pointed at us and shouted, 'Judge, if those two hadn't kidnapped Oz, he would be alive today!'

Jeffrey Kussof shot out of his seat. 'I object, Your Honor, on the grounds that opposing counsel is out of her mind! And she's also dead wrong. *Was she there?*'

'Sustained,' said the judge. 'And both of you cut it out!'

Meanwhile, I had looked over at the kids and saw tears streaming down Max's cheeks. I knew she couldn't take this arguing about Ozymandias much longer. It was so cruel, so heartless and wrong. But that was our legal system, wasn't it? Anything goes. The end of civility, manners, maybe even civilization.

Then Jeffrey Kussof delivered our argument with great fire and resolve, and, I thought, intelligence and wisdom. He told the judge that the parents were laboring under the erroneous notion that their kids were 'normal' when they clearly were not. The kids were unique and had unique needs, and the parents hadn't been able to fulfill those needs. Wasn't it true that armed men had attacked Max and Matthew Marshall in their own home? And what had Terry and Art been able to do? Nothing. They slept through it.

On that second morning, I glanced up at the large oak-framed schoolhouse clock on the southern wall of the courtroom. In about five minutes, the judge would speak, or so we'd been told. What would Judge Dwyer say? Could the ruling possibly go our way? I doubted it. But we had to take our shot.

The atmosphere was heating up and getting ready to boil over. Every time the doors opened, *more* people poured in.

Suddenly the kids, along with their lawyers and parents, filed into the room for the second day. As always, Max, Matthew, Ic, Peter and Wendy were magnificent to behold. They were also the best kids in the whole wide world and they deserved better than this public fiasco.

'Frannie! Kit! Hey, hey,' they called and waved to us. 'We *love* you guys. We miss you.'

'We love you too,' I called. 'Hugs and kisses!' Long live sentimentalism.

'Hello, Mama,' Wendy cooed. She *was* my baby; my sweetheart of sweethearts; my little girl.

I shot a grin and a thumbs-up as they climbed, jumped, and flew into their seats. Then a solemn hush fell over the court.

The bailiff took his place beside the bench and called the room to order: 'All rise.'

The judge entered from his chambers, and I swear he looked older than he had just *yesterday*. His wispy white hair was flying everywhere and his aged face seemed about ready to cave in.

'Hear ye, hear ye, the court is now in session, the Honorable Judge James Randolph Dwyer presiding.'

The judge dropped on to his chair. 'Please be seated,' he said. 'Please.'

The room became so still it was as if all the sound in the world had been turned off. It almost seemed a trick of nature. Judge Dwyer's voice was the only one that mattered. I could just about tell from the look on his face that he'd already made his decision. I prayed to whoever was listening that it was the right one for everyone involved.

'They can't take these kids away from us again,' I whispered against Kit's cheek. 'They can't, can they?'

Then Kit turned and looked me in the eye. His gaze was absolutely steely. 'We're going to be a family again. I promise you, Frances Jane.'

CHAPTER ONE HUNDRED AND SIX

There had been several times in the past few weeks when I'd involuntarily called up the images of my Simulated Reality dream. Apparently, new neural pathways had been burned into my brain by that incredible vision of the earth, and sometimes remembering the awe-inspiring perspective from outer space was the only way I could find a center of calm.

I called upon it now as Judge Dwyer cast his heavy gray eyes around his courtroom. He caught my eyes, and oh-my-God, *the great man smiled*.

'Ladies and gentlemen, and children,' the judge said in his deep, resonant voice. 'This has been the hardest case I've ever adjudicated and all of you know why.

'Aleksandr Solzhenitsyn once said, "One can build the Empire State Building, discipline the Prussian army, make a state hierarchy mightier than God, yet fail to overcome the unaccountable superiority of certain human beings." Some people think they can destroy and manipulate human life with criminal impunity. A while back, a group of scientists right here in Colorado apparently believed this. Now, I've been charged with deciding the fate of these delightful children.

'All of the parties, Agent Brennan and Dr O'Neill, the natural parents, and especially the children, have exhibited extraordinary and unparalleled courage.

'I want to reward this courage equitably, to make everyone happy. And that, of course, is impossible.'

There was a rolling rumble from the gallery as people turned to one another to mutter their predictions.

Judge Dwyer banged his gavel loudly, calling out, 'Order. Please.'

In the chastened silence that followed, he continued. 'The laws of the State of Colorado are clear. *The best interests of the children are paramount.* The law also usually falls on the side of the parents. The parents of these children may not be prepared for what the future holds for Max, Matthew, Icarus, Peter and Wendy – but is anyone? I honestly don't know the answer to that. In any event, the parents of these children have demonstrated parental excellence. I asked myself over and over, how could I deprive them or their children of familial bonds?'

I edged myself into Kit's shoulder and felt like I was going to cry. My heart was breaking. It seemed clear to me what Judge Dwyer would say next. I tried to prepare myself, but I just couldn't. Not again.

The judge continued. 'While I deliberated, I remembered something that Max had said to me at the time of the first hearing. She said, "I know you're a good guy, but you've made a mistake. You're only human, right. And that's the problem, Judge – *we're not.*" '

I had pulled my face out of the crook of Kit's shoulder. I had also inched up toward the edge of my seat.

Judge Dwyer stopped for a breath, but then he went on. 'Well, I *am* only human. Maybe no one but the five of you kids can truly understand that *you are a flock,* and that you need to be together. And that Frannie and Kit *are* Mama and Papa for you. I don't know if I completely understand it, Max . . . but that's what I believe.

'And so, that is the judgment of this court – the children will go with Frannie and Kit. You're a flock again. You're also a family. Be a great flock, and a great family. I'm pretty sure you will be.'

The courtroom erupted in noise, which was mostly applause, and then the kids were all over Kit and me.

'We're a flock and a family!' Peter yelled for all to hear. 'Victory lap!'

And then the amazing kids flew once, twice, three times around the room.

THE LAKE HOUSE

CHAPTER ONE HUNDRED AND SEVEN

And so, the seven of us finally went *home*. Isn't that something?

The Lake House was where we had gone with the kids after we helped them escape from the dreaded School. It was secluded, high on a picture-postcard mountainside, overlooking our own private lake. I won't tell you where it is exactly. It's safer that way. Leave it at this: the kids love it, and so do Kit and I. My mother used to always say that there are two important things you can give to your children – one is roots, and the other is wings. I agree with that wholeheartedly. That was my plan. *Roots and wings.*

Then one afternoon I was toasting marshmallows in the fireplace with Wendy as feathery flakes of snow drifted across the sky. Kit and the boys watched a couple of college football teams trash each other on the fifty-one-inch Sony. They were cheering for 'the Buffaloes', whoever the Buffaloes were. Probably the University of Colorado.

Out of the blue, a nagging thought crossed my mind.

Max had been in her room almost all day, ever since just past breakfast. I worried that maybe something was wrong.

Then I thought I knew what it was: *she was missing Ozymandias again. We all were, of course. He was such a great boy, so much potential. Every time I thought about Oz I choked up myself.*

Max's room was upstairs in the southeast corner, and it had a special view of the quarry, the lake and the woods.

I went up there on tippy-toes.

At the door, I thought I heard her moan. *What was going on in there? What now?*

Every one of us had had night terrors and waking nightmares, post-traumatic stress syndrome that just wouldn't quit. The most graphic scenes from the Hospital and the School were still with us. They always will be.

'Max? You okay in there?' I called out. 'Max, sweetie?'

She didn't answer. So I opened the bedroom door a crack and peeked inside. I relaxed as I saw Max in bed under a lot of fluffy covers. She stretched out a hand and beckoned.

'Frannie, come in. Please, Mama. I need to talk to you.'

'Okay. I'm right here.' I shut the door behind me.

I could see that Max was flushed. She was perspiring. Then, to my shock, I saw blood on her outstretched fingers!

'I need your help, Frannie. I really need you right now. Seriously.'

I clamped down on my fear as I walked across the creaking bedroom floor. I dragged a chair up to Max's bedside and sat beside her. 'I'm here.'

I put my hand on her forehead. She was extraordinarily warm. Her long hair was matted and damp.

The doctor in me began to take over.

'Honey? What's the matter with you? What are you feeling? How long have you had a fever? Talk to me.'

'I'm not exactly *sick*, Frannie. I've just been working real hard,' Max said.

I must have had a puzzled look on my face.

'*Labor*,' she said. 'Labor is hard work. I had some babies!'

I gasped when I finally understood. I think I almost fainted. 'Oh Max, why didn't you tell me? Oh Max, sweetheart. Oh Max, oh God, Max.'

She shrugged and then said, 'I wanted this to be private. But I'm really glad you're here, Frannie. Just us two girls.'

'Just the two of us,' I promised.

Now I stared at a miracle never before seen in this world, at least I didn't expect so. *My God!* Snuggled right up to Max's body, lying in the crook of her arm, were two magnificent human eggs. *Oh Max.*

The eggs were quite large, the shells ivory white, with a pearly pink sheen. They looked to be three or four pounds and the sight of them made me weak with tenderness.

I imagined Max's precious babies inside the eggs, their

arms and legs tucked in the fetal position. Two beautiful babies with wings.

'You're going to be a mother,' I whispered. 'This is so beautiful.' Then I started to choke up.

'They're mine with Ozymandias,' Max said, whispering too. 'I have to keep them warm. I don't know how I know that, but I do. Oh, I wish Oz was here to see this.'

I reached out and gently put my arms around Max, holding her, calling her name. I felt tears rolling down my cheeks.

Max's face was so joyful and radiant, so full of hope. 'Aren't they just the most beautiful things? Isn't life a miracle sometimes?' she said. 'OK, you can call the other kids now. And Kit. This is gonna blow all their minds, isn't it? I'm going to be a mother.'

CHAPTER ONE HUNDRED AND EIGHT

Over the next few weeks Max began to learn real honest-to-God PATIENCE for the first time in her life. She was going to be a mom, and she'd need it. It was so quiet in her part of the house that she sometimes thought she might be going a little mad. Going, going, *gone*.

Her mind was frayed from being alone too much, watching and nursing her eggs every minute, thinking about Oz constantly, missing him so much it hurt. Constantly and *for ever*.

But she had good reason to be extra watchful and careful. She was going to be a mother, and her children were going to be very special. Of course, Max knew, just about every mother felt that same way.

She was all cozied up in bed, re-reading *The Hobbit* by candlelight, when she heard a creak coming from the deck right outside her bedroom window.

Strange.

What was that?

Perhaps the low, steady whistle of the wind had frightened an animal. There were plenty of critters out there skittering here and there in the woods. If anything, her superior hearing was better than ever.

She touched the eggs with her fingertips, *one, two*.

Buckle my shoe.

Going, going, gone.

Max couldn't take her eyes off the two eggs. The babies were growing bigger day by day. They were also starting to move now. She could see their shapes pressed up against the shells. *That* got her every time. She was going to be a mom.

Max blew out the candle, lay very still, and *listened*. She heard the same funny creak again.

Probably nothing.

Probably . . .

It was like the sound of a branch or the wind pushing at the deck, but there were no overhanging branches out there, were there?

No, the creak was more like a damn footstep. Out on the deck.

A footstep she was imagining in her head? A bogey-man footstep? A fantasy footstep?

Max held her breath and listened closely again. *This was too dopey for words.*

Finally, she slipped out of bed. *Even dopier.*

She moved three paces to the window, waited, then parted the white eyelet curtains Frannie had made for her. She looked out on to the second-story deck.

Then Max jumped back.

She was staring into another pair of eyes!

Eyes she knew. And hated. A face she knew. And hated. *Yes, it's me.* The mouth formed words. *Hel-lo, Max. I've come for you.*

The window broke inward as a gloved fist smashed through it. Shattered glass rained around her. Then Dr Ethan Kane/Harold Hauer burst into the room, and she knew this just had to be a dream, like really *bad* simulated reality.

But it wasn't!

He was alive.

He was in her bedroom. He had come for her and the eggs.

CHAPTER ONE HUNDRED AND NINE

'**G**et out of here!' Max shrieked.

But Hauer grabbed her around the waist and threw her backward, toward the bed. He had a scalpel in his hand. And he was strong – much more so than normal men. He *wasn't* normal.

Of course he wasn't! He had made himself over; he was the first to experience Resurrection; he was the new Frankenstein.

Max twisted her body as she fell, to avoid the pillow nest she'd made for her babies. She just missed crushing the eggs.

When she lifted her head, there was a sharp blade pressing into her throat. Hauer's free hand covered her nose and mouth. He was suffocating her. Did he even know how strong he was?

'Why, hello, Max. So nice to see you again, dear girl. Yes, I'm alive. You killed a clone, Max, not me. Of course, you probably don't know that.'

Then he warned, 'Don't you dare move, you

fine-feathered freak. Don't even think of screaming for help because I'll kill *them,* too. In the blink of an eye. Fight me and I'll kill you. You'll die without seeing your babies. You're smart. You understand me. Don't you?'

Max nodded. Her lungs were aching. She needed air. Hauer finally took his hand from her mouth and she actually *growled,* a sound she'd never, ever made before.

'You're the freak. Godless creep. What do you want?'

'Well, I've come for a few of my papers, which Frances Jane apparently swiped. And the *eggs* of course. I've come for your eggs, Max.'

'You can't have them,' Max hissed. 'I'll die first.'

Hauer shrugged. 'It doesn't matter to me. You die, you live. Either way, I have your precious eggs. I *am* Harold Hauer. Not a clone. Do you know why I'm here, Max? Do you know why I kept you alive all this time? Want to know the secret? You're even bigger than Resurrection. Really and truly you are. These eggs are more important than anything I've ever done before. I've seen the future, Max, and it flies!'

Max couldn't speak at first. Finally, she understood why she'd been allowed to survive. *I've seen the future, and it flies!*

'You're a sick ghoul,' she said.

Then Max found herself making the terrible *growling* sound again. What was that noise anyway? Her way of protecting the eggs?

'You're incorrigible, hopeless. I should have done this at the Hospital. Die, you little twit.'

'I don't feel like it!' Max shouted. She kicked out and sent the doctor reeling against her dresser. Taken off guard, he dropped the knife.

He recovered quickly though. Bearlike, he shook himself off, cursed and felt around for the scalpel in the darkened room. Found it in a fold of the scatter rug.

'Dead or alive?' he asked as he showed Max the sharp blade. 'It's your choice.'

'I choose my babies,' said Max.

She spread her wings, making a wall of feathers and bone between Hauer and her eggs. 'Get out of here! Get out of here now,' she screamed. 'I'll kill you, Hauer! Kane! Whatever your name is, you creepy bastard! Get away from my babies!'

He rushed her, and Max sidestepped the attack. Barely. He was quick, too.

She reached out and grasped for something. *What?* She felt a brass candle holder. She swung it very hard, very fast, very accurately, too.

There was a solid crunch as the heavy object connected with Dr Hauer's skull. She'd hurt him! He moaned and fell against her, pulling at Max with the full weight of his body, dragging her toward the far wall.

'Let go! Don't *touch* me.'

'You little son of a bitch,' he groaned through gritted teeth. 'I'll show you something. I'll show you pain. Then *death.*'

Max heard yells and footsteps in the house. Frannie and Kit were coming. Running. The kids, too!

Hauer was so strong, though, obviously something else he'd engineered in his lab. He was relentlessly pushing her backward. Max lost her footing. She was going down.

She was falling right through the broken window behind her. No way to stop it. She reached out. *For something, anything!* Grabbed Dr Hauer with both hands. Held on to him as if her life depended on it.

'You're coming too!'

The bedroom was only on the second floor – that was the good news.

The bad part was that her window overlooked a steep cliff, a drop of another hundred and twenty feet into the woods, which was *so far* below.

Max and Dr Hauer crashed through the picture window, and fell several feet together – then she let him go. Just like that! Say goodbye to old rubbish! Max flapped her wings furiously, struggled, but then hovered as she watched the screeching doctor falling to the forest floor far below. He spiraled; he cartwheeled; he dived. It took a few seconds that seemed so much longer.

'Help me, Max!' he screamed. Maybe she would have if she could, but she couldn't dive and swoop up his falling body. Even if she'd wanted to.

She saw him hit a tree then carom to the ground with a sickening *thud*, then he lay very still. Crumpled, twisted, *still*. As she had hoped, as she'd solemnly promised Ozymandias – *she'd broken the bastard's neck*.

Dr Harold Hauer, ninety-four years old, was finally

dead. Good riddance to the human monster, the creep of creeps, the sick prick. The *real* deal, the *real* person, was dead as dogshit down there.

Max whispered, 'I've seen the future, too . . . and you're not in it.'

She finally had to look away. She caught a breath, and then flapped her wings and took off toward the bedroom window of the house.

Frannie and Kit were up there, with the other kids, and also her precious babies, her eggs.

Less than four weeks later they were born.

In the perfect, perfect spot.

At the Lake House.

A boy and a girl, just what she'd wanted.

The most special and beautiful babies in the whole world – tiny infants with gossamer wings like angels. Maybe they *were* angels.

Frances Jane and Ozymandias.

She couldn't wait to teach them to fly.